ON THE EDGE OF THE FORGOTTEN SEA

THE EARTHEN-CREST KINGDOMS
The Earth-Treader – Book 1
From the Mountains to the Valley - Epilogue

YOUNG ADULT STANDALONES
Endlewood
Unearth the Tides

COLLECTION OF SHORT STORIES
Aliferous

MIDDLE GRADE STANDALONE
The Wishing Seed

"*On the Edge of the Forgotten Sea* is the book version of a warm cup of tea. Steeped in the traditions of fairy tales past and woven with an Austen-esque romance, Zavalianos' lyrical prose dances across the page, beckoning its readers on a journey that will stir heart and soul into believing in magic again."

— CHELSEA BOBULSKI, author of *The Wood*, *Remember Me*, and the *All I Want for Christmas* Series

THE CHRONICLES OF CHAERA

ON THE EDGE OF THE FORGOTTEN SEA

ALISSA J. ZAVALIANOS

Scripture quotation taken from the English Standard Version of the Bible

Printed in the United States of America

Cover & Dust Jacket Design by A.C. Sanders
Case Laminate Design by Bethany Günthir
Maps by Alissa J. Zavalianos
Edited by Caitlin Miller
Proofreading by Micaiah Keough
Interior Artwork from Canva

ISBN 979-8-9881439-6-3 (paperback)
ISBN 979-8-9881439-5-6 (hardcover)
ISBN 979-8-9881439-7-0 (ebook)

To anyone who has ever felt lost, abandoned, or forgotten—
The Lord sees you and He is near.
He is sovereign over the hurt places.
And His plans are always better than our own.

And for Sarah & Jordan—
S. my very first and lifelong friend.
J. my kindred-heart in every way.

"The heart of man plans his way,
but the LORD establishes his steps."
~ Proverbs 16:9

"The Gray Inkwell"

Green for peace
Purple for might
Black for perfidy
Red for sight
Orange for wrath
Blue for doom
White for hope
Writ' Winderplume.

~ Anonymous, The Old Archives, Vol. 1

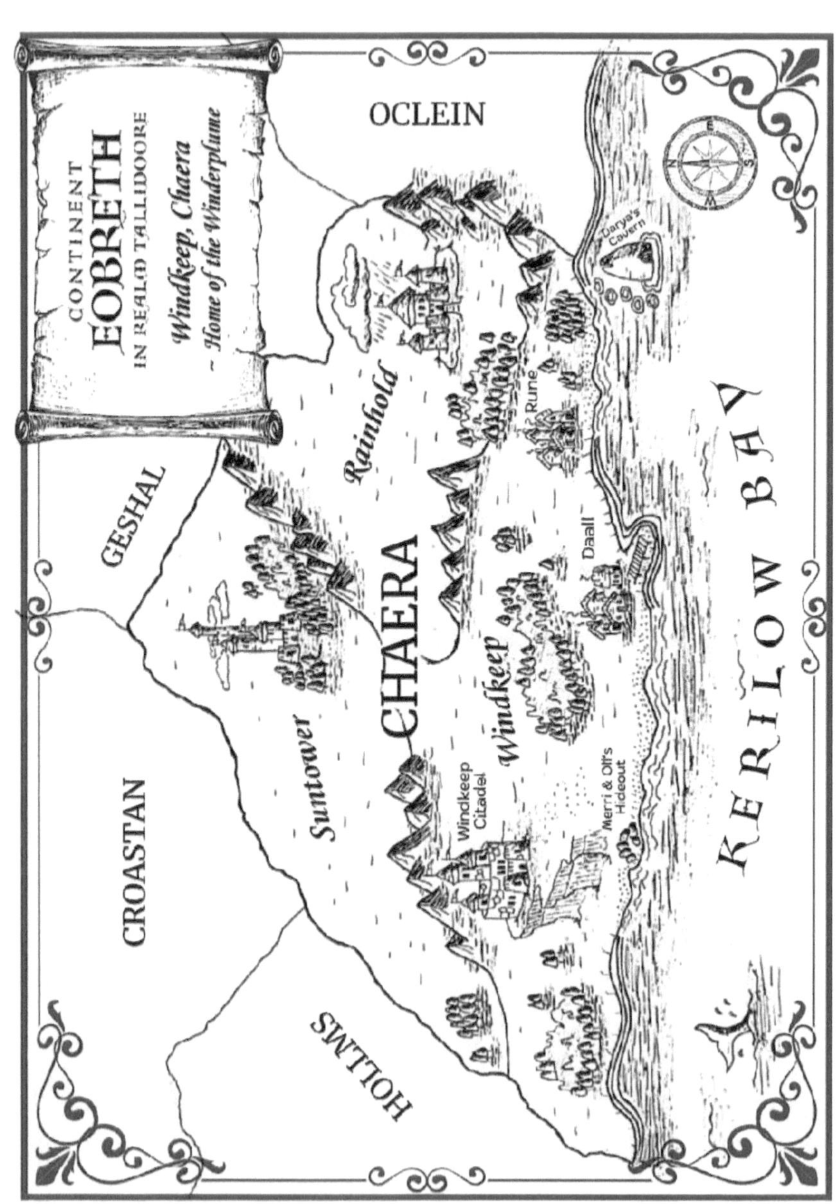

CONTINENT
EOBRETH
IN REALO TALLIDOORE
Windkeep, Chaera
~ Home of the Winderplume
OCLEIN
GESHAL
CROASTAN
HOLLIS
CHAERA
Rainhold
Suntower
Windkeep
Windkeep Citadel
Rune
Daall
Darya's Cavern
Merri & Ott's Hideout
KERILOW BAY

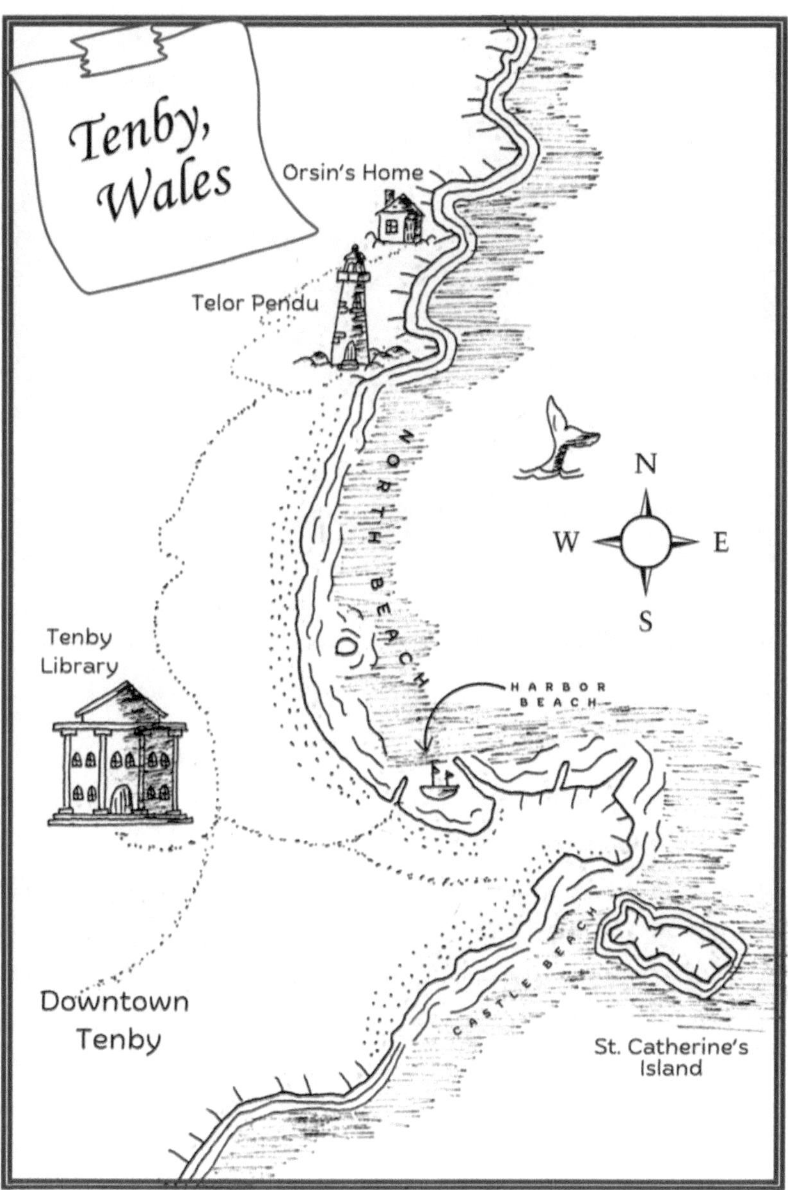

Tenby, Wales
Orsin's Home
Telor Pendu
NORTH BEACH
Tenby Library
HARBOR BEACH
N
W
E
S
Downtown Tenby
CASTLE BEACH
St. Catherine's Island

TABLE OF CONTENTS

PROLOGUE

Windkeep, Chaera
Maunt 1180

"Did you bring it?"

The young man stood in a dimly lit cavern on the outskirts of the kingdom, his boots barely grazing the edge of a rippling pool. He nodded his reply. "His hair, as you requested." He held out the light strand and watched as the woman, with a single snap, caused it to fly toward her. She was seated in a strange-looking chair in the middle of the water, gaze unwavering as she added it to the glass bottle in her hand. The fiber dissolved in the liquid, radiating purple before turning as clear as glass. The man's eyes grew round. The first time he'd searched for this place and the one rumored to reside within had taken him far too long, what with navigating the dark. But that had been nine months ago. It shocked him how easy it had been to find her again.

"Now it is complete," she said, her yellow tail poking out of the water. The man noted the fin wasn't as bright as it had been on his first visit.

He tugged at his collar. "Are you certain he won't remember?" The woman had given him her word that this would work. Still, he couldn't help but worry that promises weren't enough. Everything hinged on this going right.

"Not even those in Chaera, nor the lands beyond, will remember. Save for you and myself. He will be but a distant memory, an itch on the mind. Something too far away to recall," came the woman's reply.

"I just wonder…what if forgetting isn't enough?" *Maybe I've been going about this all wrong. I didn't have to make it this complicated. But this is the only way…the only way that leaves no traces back to me.*

"A shipwreck can take care of that." The woman flashed a wicked grin. "It is how I got rid of the other, or do you not recall?"

Oh, I recall it perfectly well. But is it sufficient?

She snapped her fingers again, and the bottle flew forward until it hovered inches before the man's face. "Take it."

Hesitant, he grasped the floating item. He stared at the contents, his mouth growing dry. "So I slip this into his drink…but what about the healing charm—"

"Will you cease your senseless inquiries?" Her tone fumed with frustration. "My spells are infinitely stronger than that *pure* dust. I work with the remnants. The scraps. Mark my words." Her eyes sparked fire. "With that hair, the enchantment has begun, but it needs years to grow in potency. It won't work on a mere baby. Only when he's older must the contents of that vial be consumed."

Confound these regulations. "H-how long then?" *Dare I hope?*

"The prophecy." The woman moved her hand toward the ceiling, and up shot a scroll from the water beneath her. She'd enchanted the paper when he'd handed it over on his last visit, promising to keep the contents hidden until the proper time to collect it. "That should tell you all you need to know."

The man choked back words and nodded at the incriminating ink. *Eighteen years. She had said this the last time, too. Was it foolhardy to think it would be different now that everything was in place?* He swallowed hard. *I can wait that long. I have no other choice.* Altering time was out of his control. He would simply have to pace himself.

He looked once more at the floating prophecy, the one thing he hadn't accounted for in his plans. "The keeper," he continued. "You said you took care of him. But the ink tells no lies." *This is why I fear it won't be enough.*

The woman smirked. "It has been less than two days. Give it time. These words will turn when they are ready."

The man nodded again, still unsure, but he'd questioned the woman plenty. No amount of visits would ease his conscience until this was all said and done. "So eighteen years, then I'll finally have my reward."

She cleared her throat. "Do not forget our agreement. For it is the reward you promised *me* which has granted you yours in the first place." Her voice was like ice, her gaze zeroing in on the bottle in his hands. "You will bring me the scraps of his *Winderplume* before the end of *Verd.* No later. This enchantment of yours has rendered a sizable portion of my stash dry." She clutched the vial hanging around her neck containing the meager remains of red dust as if to prove her point. "My daughter will wait eighteen years to claim her share of this bargain. She needs only to get her legs."

The man trembled. "Ye-yes. How could I forget?"

"You won't." The woman let the vial fall against her chest, her confidence sending a shiver down the man's spine. She stared at him until he squirmed. "These years will go by much faster than you think.

Until we meet again."

Bowing slightly, the man tightened his grip on the enchantment and fled. *Scraps of his Winderplume.* Scraps, indeed. That's all anyone would get after this was all said and done. The Winderplume had been in the wrong hands for far too long, and he was determined to fix that.

If all went as planned, he'd get his wish. He'd visit the woman at the appointed time, and then he'd run, never having to see her, or her *daughter*, as long as he lived.

The bargain be hanged.

PART 1

CURSED

1

THE PROPHECY

Olivander

Eighteen Years Later

Windkeep, Chaera

Maunt 1198

THE SUN STRETCHED ITS GOLDEN RAYS between the clouds, beginning its illumination of the world below. Light fell upon dewy grass in dappled beams and glistened off the shores of the nearby bay, warming the terrain and wishing away the last remnants of winter's snow. That very light filtered into the limestone of the citadel, through stained glass windows and any crack it could find.

Olivander sighed as he studied the world beyond the pane of glass, his hand clutching the small vial of lavender dust hanging from a corded rope around his neck. It wasn't his usual routine to wake at this hour, but with the citadel in chaos, he found himself needing a few moments of solitude. He longed for quieter days but knew they wouldn't improve. So if waking with the birds was his only option, he'd sacrifice the sleep.

Pushing away from the window, Olivander sucked in a breath before surveying his chambers. They were a mess; garments hung over the bed rail, tan breeches on the stone floor—splain among the rushes of days-old sandalwood—boots half-kicked beneath his dresser. He'd ransacked his room only to don a simple cream blouse and blue trousers. *Jasper will have something to say about this.* But Olivander had an appointment to keep, and it was one he looked forward to. Now if only he could make it outside without being seen.

Windkeep was coming alive with Winderplume charms cast left and right, especially these days: maids ran to the guest wings with freshly laundered sheets, washed to a sparkle in a vat of magicked water; Head Cook ordered about the confectioner, larderer, butler, and cellarer on how to serve dishes and maintain a proper kitchen all the while sprinkling charms in each of her meals; the falconer exercised vigorous training sessions with his hawks to provide the entertainment, a gust of Winderplume beneath their wings to fly longer and faster; the master of the wardrobe went over every detail time and time again for the ceremony (Olivander hated this one most of all), with dust-infused thread making the stitches gleam gold; the Captain of the Guard double-checked security measures and gave his soldiers glistening cordial to remain vigilant. Windkeep Citadel had never seen such activity since their beloved king passed nearly three years ago, his wife following shortly after.

And now their son—Olivander Soryn Daws, crown prince of Chaera's largest province of Windkeep—would assume the throne within a fortnight on his eighteenth birthday. It was then that Lord Aylward, serving as regent, would step down, finally allowing the prince to claim his birthright.

The citadel was busy preparing for such an occasion, but it was

Lord Aylward who, having made it his responsibility to ensure the safety of the kingdom, kept his eyes a little too vigilant when it came to the prince, much to Olivander's chagrin.

He was doing his best to avoid him and had just turned a corner when the very man himself spied Olivander and attempted to match his pace.

Bay's Depths. The prince bit his tongue.

"Your Highness," Lord Alyward said.

Olivander kept walking, boots thudding against the dark gray stone floors. *How long can I avoid this?*

"Your Highness, a word," Lord Alyward said again, undeterred. By now he'd caught up to him, following closely on his heels. "Everyone is gathering in the throne room. Your presence is required."

Olivander didn't know how much longer he could endure being told what he should wear, where to stand or how to walk, and the best angle for him to pose to capture his princely profile. Not to mention being ordered about in regard to where he should or should not be and what he should or should not say. "I'm sure this can wait."

Lord Alyward huffed. "Need I remind you of the prophecy? What is inked in red can no longer be ignored. We have been waiting long enough."

Not this again. Olivander suppressed the urge to roll his eyes. They were now in the midst of a long corridor lined with tapestries and potted plants, a set of stairs at the end of the hall leading to a secluded passage outdoors. *So close.*

"You would do well to cease this madness and listen."

Olivander groaned inwardly. He turned, and Lord Aylward nearly collided into his torso. The prince could have sworn he'd caught a whiff of brandy on the regent's breath with how close he stood. Brown eyes scowling, the man smoothed the front of his cotton garment and took a sturdy step backward. Though years older than the prince, he stood a head shorter, allowing Olivander the perfect view of his thinning pate of midnight-black hair.

"Aylward, must we revisit this now? I'm about to go play Hobsmatch with Gabe." Hobsmatch was a game Olivander and Gabeheart invented a few years ago, which involved using the broadside of an oar and the largest head of cabbage they could find. "You know he's even more impatient than I am." Which was why they'd scheduled a match so early. Even as the prince, Olivander couldn't say no to Cook's youngest son.

"But, Your Highness, we only have so much time."

"'Time has no master,'" Olivander said.

"Using your father's words on me will not change the fact that your life may very well be at stake."

Prince Olivander smiled and placed a hand on the regent's white-and-blue clad shoulder, the colors of the citadel. "That is why I have you around, Alyward. To keep my life very well at un-stake. Or alive, rather."

Lord Alyward's lips twitched. "I have little control over prophecies and their outcomes. But I *can* ensure your safety."

"Windkeep has had countless prophecies since its inception, most harmless and amounting to nothing. Why should we pay special attention to this one?"

"Because it involves you and this kingdom. You think I can serve as regent from beyond the grave?"

Olivander assessed the man before him. Lord Alyward wasn't *old*, per se, but without the prince marrying and producing an offspring, there would be no one else to claim the throne when he inevitably passed. The late king had no siblings, nor did Olivander. And the regent wasn't getting any younger.

But was this prophecy such a serious matter?

"Come, Your Highness. This is not a request. It is time to make preparations and warn the kingdom, especially before the guests arrive. Time waits for no one."

Olivander begrudgingly followed the regent through gilded halls, the weight of duty heavy upon his shoulders. His one consolation was that the sooner he listened to Lord Alyward, the sooner he could go back into hiding and pretend he wasn't some stray dog attached to a short leash.

Within a half hour, the entire staff was gathered in the throne room. If it wasn't almost the middle of *Maunt,* the large space would feel stuffy and cramped, but as it was, the salty breeze blowing in from Kerilow Bay kept the area cool. It ruffled the citadel-colored curtains framing the lancet widows and pulled at tunics and tapestries not nailed or weighed down. Refreshing.

Olivander stood beside Lord Alyward. The regent sat upon the king's throne fashioned of birchwood while his gaze scanned all those in attendance. The two of them were on the dais, and everyone else appeared small. Uncertain. Nervous.

"*Wylecuman,* Windkeep's residents," the regent began, using the *Old Chaeran* language hardly anyone spoke except for greetings, goodbyes, or random words in between. Nowadays, everyone spoke *Common Englasi,* a language developed centuries ago so the continents of *Tallidoore* could communicate with each other. "With the upcoming celebration and crowning of His Royal Highness, it is no pleasing matter that I gather you here with somber news."

Murmurs issued amongst the people, as if confirming their fears. Cook looked tense, and Gibbs, the falconer, eyed his hawk with suspicion. *Why bring the bird indoors? Surely, he could've returned it to the mews before coming here.*

Lord Alyward continued, "While some receive gifts and trinkets for their naming days, others are bestowed words. Most of you have heard of the prophecy at Prince Olivander's birth." Most in the room nodded. "But do you recall its contents?"

No one breathed a word. And why would they? It hadn't been talked about in years, hardly worth remembering.

The regent sighed and stood, motioning for Reve to meet him on the dais. The man had been one of the late king's advisors before he was appointed Keeper of Prophecies when Olivander was born. "I fear we have enjoyed these years too freely," Lord Alyward said. "Let us refresh your memory."

He nodded at the keeper, who, now standing beside him, recited the contents of the prophecy from memory. "Here lies as follows, the prophecy for His Royal Highness, Prince Olivander Soryn Daws, born in Maunt on the vernal equinox, the year of our Lord, Esias, 1180. Given as a gift on his naming day, nearly 222 turnings ago.

A prince of Chaera
In the province of Wind
The Keepers of Plume
And peace within.
Born of land
A maiden shall come
Branding fire
That rivals the sun.
This prince, beware,
Whose reign draws near,
She seeks to destroy
In his eighteenth year.
Stone by stone
Will Citadel bend
With Windkeep's fall
And the prince's end."

The keeper tipped his head to signal that he had finished. The room filled with a marked silence. The weight of it was stifling, and Olivander felt himself grow hot. Gooseflesh climbed his back, causing the hairs on the nape of his neck to tingle. Had the prophecy really said all of that? Lord Alyward had warned him, but it didn't seem as dreadful in the corridor on the way to playing a childhood game. If his life was in so much danger, why wait until *now* to do something about it, when it was only a fortnight away?

Finally, someone from the crowd spoke. "Balderdash!" It was Matilde, Head Cook, who threw her hands up in protest. "Are we to let our prince die while we stand idly by?"

Gilda, one of Cook's helpers, shook her head in turn.

"This maiden will have my boot!" the butler, Horace, chimed in.

"Galahad will have her eye," Gibbs said, raising the hand holding his hawk.

"How do we know who this maiden is?" Cook asked. "Are we to monitor the comings and goings of every female in the citadel? Our staff isn't big enough for the likes of—"

Lord Alyward raised his hand and cut her off. He squared his shoulders, commanding authority in that singular move. "Precisely." The barest inclination of his head. "Which is why I have come up with a plan."

Of course you did, Olivander thought.

The room held its breath as they awaited the regent's verdict.

Lord Alyward cleared his throat. "We shall send every maiden away from Chaera."

Bay's Depths. Olivander hadn't expected *that.*

Cook's eyes grew round.

Gilda's mouth fell open. "For how long, My Lord?"

"Until the year passes, once Prince Olivander finishes out his eighteenth year. That way, we can ensure his safety."

"What about a wife? Every king needs a wife!" Cook planted her hands on her hips. "I'm sure he's already set his sights on someone. Are you to send her away, too?"

Olivander's cheeks reddened. Though it wasn't rare for royalty to marry commoners in Chaera—his father had married his mother after all—that didn't mean there was anyone special. At least, she wouldn't have him *now*.

"Prince Olivander can marry whomever he wants when he turns nineteen. That is only twelve more turnings," Lord Alyward said. "Since he is not engaged at present, another year should not matter."

The prince appreciated the sentiment, but he'd appreciate it more if everyone stopped talking about him as if he wasn't in the same room.

"Begging your pardon, My Lord, but are we to send every female into exile? The citadel needs to be run," the butler stated. "What would we do without Cook?" Clearly, he was only thinking with his stomach.

Lord Alyward laughed. "I said *maiden*, Horace. Those between the ages of fifteen and twenty-three. No offense, Mrs. Lamson." This last part he addressed to Cook herself.

The older woman waved away his placation.

"This can't be the only solution." Gilda wrapped her arms around her middle as if in pain. "Is there not a better way?" She had a daughter who was too old to fall into Lord Alyward's age restrictions, yet if anyone in the citadel embodied motherly instincts for children that weren't her own, it was Gilda.

Olivander finally stepped forward. He had heard enough. He agreed with the protests; the regent's idea wasn't worth its salt. "Those numbers seem arbitrary. Plenty in that age range are young mothers, and you want to separate them from their children? Like Gilda said, there has to be another option. Why not post more guards? Utilize the

Winderplume?" He held up the vial around his neck. He knew Lord Alyward and most of the staff had their own even if they didn't wear them as visibly as he did. Plus, there was a whole swirling vessel of it a few stories above them; surely they could come together and figure out a better way. Though Olivander's life may be in danger, the idea of sending every young woman helter-skelter for an entire year was ludicrous. Did no one realize he could think and fend for himself? He was tall and broad of shoulder; a maiden would have quite the nerve to think she could undermine him that easily, nevermind an entire citadel.

"The guard is stretched thin as it is. As for the Winderplume, a charm of that magnitude would rid the whole vat dry. We don't even know if it is capable…" Lord Alyward droned on.

Olivander scanned the throne room, hardly listening. All he could hear was the blood rushing to his head. His palms sweating with the vial in his grip. *This is wrong. This is all wrong.* "What if it's a mistake?" he whispered. "What if this prophecy isn't even true?" His voice was louder now.

Gasps issued from the crowd. All heads swiveled to look at the prince.

"What is written in red cannot be ignored. *Everyone* knows that." Lord Alyward gritted his teeth.

Olivander faced the keeper. "Reve, you would know better than most if this is as serious as we fear."

The keeper opened his mouth to respond, but the regent's words came first.

"Surely, this is not necessary—"

But Olivander wasn't finished. "Why send all the maidens from Chaera when it's only Windkeep the prophecy addresses? Where's the merit in that? There must be a better way—"

"Enough!" Lord Alyward snapped. The room went deathly still.

"In six days hence, all maidens will be exported to foreign lands, with the promise of a safe return once the prince turns nineteen." Suppressed frustration filled his tone. "And any mothers will have the option to take their children with them or leave them behind. That is not my concern."

"But, Alyward—"

"This is my final decree as regent, and I am not changing my mind, Your Highness."

Olivander bit his tongue and watched Gilda's head slump forward. Why even try? He wasn't yet king; there was little sway in his command when it came to Lord Alyward. The prince knew the regent had Windkeep's best interests in mind, but it was moments like this where he keenly felt the insufficiency in his current role.

What's the purpose of being royalty if all my opinions mean nothing?

"How shall we proceed, My Lord?" a guard spoke up from the back of the room. "What of the other provinces?"

"Search out every eligible maiden of whom the prophecy could be referencing in Windkeep. Gather the carts and ready the carriages as we make for redistribution. Leave Suntower and Rainhold to me. We have six days."

2

A BARGAIN

Merri

Kerilow Bay, Chaera
Maunt 1198

IN A SECLUDED CAVE SOMEWHERE IN the murky shallows of Kerilow
Bay, darkness had a name. And Merri found herself seeking it. She'd
avoided three underwater rivers, dodged at least two blooms of box
jellyfish, and swum through a massive kelp field in order to get here,
nearly getting herself tangled in the process.

Though what currently lay before her in the shadows frightened
her ten-fold.

"Those most desperate have the most to risk," a slippery voice
issued from the gloom. "What are *you* willing to risk, young sea
maiden? For those on land and sea who come to me want *something*.

What brings you here?"

Merri's skin crawled with invisible sea gnats as she squinted toward the void. "L-love," she stammered. All was darkness above, but she didn't have to see to know a ledge and an exit to the outside world rested beyond the surface of the water, much like the tunnel she'd just entered. That was how the land-folk accessed the cave and made their bargains. It was only slightly less dark beneath the pool where Darya dwelt. A green, fiery glow flickered over the underwater cavern, radiating from whatever bubbled out of the cauldron in the center of the alcove. It was enough to illuminate the small space for what it was, save for where the voice crept. Weapons hung upon the walls like some armored shrine, potions and tinctures of all different hues lined various shelves, and the tide…it smelled otherworldly, with fog-like swirls raking across the sea floor.

This is worse than I'd imagined. Merri's hands shook, but she kept them firmly by her sides, barely grazing the scales of her luminescent tail.

"Bah!" the voice spat from the void. "They all want love. A useless affectation."

"It's not useless! And it's not an affec…affectation," Merri said before she thought better of it.

Laughter cackled in the underwater cavern, making the green flames dance amidst the tide. "This love—it makes you bold." The voice drew closer, the whites of the being's eyes now present, glowing like angler fish in the dark. "A fool with a spine."

A tremor ran down the maiden's aforementioned spine and prickled her skin like barnacles; it took everything in her power not to swim away. She'd come here for a reason, but her resolve was fading.

"Not many seek out my lair. Few have the wits to face me." The voice and eyes drew nearer still. "Even fewer return from whence they came."

Now Merri's stomach was in her throat. Maybe if she stated her purpose, she could get what she wanted and leave. Maybe she could be one of the few who safely returned. "I only ask for one thing."

"*Only?* It is no small matter to bargain with a sea witch."

Merri gulped. It was foolhardy to consult Darya's enchantments, never mind seeking out her cave. But she'd heard rumors of her abilities, and Merri was desperate enough to test them. She pushed aside the guilt that told her otherwise, that to trust Esias was enough.

Suddenly, something slimy slipped through the shadows and wound its way up Merri's fin, tightening its hold, constricting her ribcage. She could hardly breathe. *What is this?* Her vision swam, and she could barely make out something sickly green against the purple of her scales.

"Are you afraid, young sea maiden?" The sea witch cackled. "You should be."

I'm terrified. Merri's head pulsed, her heart palpitating like a jellyfish. She blinked, trying to focus her eyes, tracing the origin of the green monster wrapped around her torso. It ran the length of the ocean cave and disappeared into the void before her. Was this…?

She didn't have long to guess; emerging from the darkness itself was Darya, whose tail was the very thing suffocating her.

Merri had heard rumors that Darya was no ordinary sea maiden, that she'd bargained much to become who she was today, forsaking Esias entirely. And it was evidenced by her tail, the eel-like thing as sickly and unsettling as it was something to marvel at. *What has she done to become like this?*

The maiden squirmed as the sea witch drew nearer, her eyes no longer floating and now fitted inside the hallows of her face. All speech was forgotten in the presence of one so striking. Darya's skin was as white as a freshwater pearl—from what Merri could tell beneath the witch's shiny black top of shells and coral—and her irises were as turquoise as the tides surrounding the coral reefs. And her hair? As dark and luminous as a twilight sky devoid of stars. She was hauntingly beautiful, and that made her all the more intimidating. She was all things fair aside from her tail, which seemed to be the one reminder that she was not to be trifled with.

"I have had my eye on you, young one," Darya said, swimming nearer to the sea maiden. "Wondering when you'd come."

Merri blanched. *Darya was waiting for me?*

"Though I'm surprised you left your pet behind."

Merri frowned. "He's not my pet." She knew Darya was talking about Eldarwielle. At this point, all of Kerilow Bay had seen them together, but the white whale was his own beast, free to come and go as he desired.

Whales were traversers of the tides, endless wanderers, kings of the sea—and should be respected as such. It was only when Merri had freed the giant white humpback from a fisherman's line many years ago that a special kinship was born. Since then they hardly went anywhere without the other, which was why she made it a point to seek out Darya alone. Eldarwielle wouldn't have liked this.

"I see." Darya gave an amused smile.

"How…how did you know…I would come?" Merri struggled to draw breath, steering the conversation back to her purpose.

The sea witch chuckled. "Love is a foolhardy thing, but even I can see when it has someone in its grips. I know what it is you seek." She circled the maiden, assessing her with her prying gaze. "Or should I say…*whom.*"

Heat climbed Merri's cheeks at the implication. Was she really that easy to read?

"I have seen your gaze cast to the shoreline," Darya continued.

Unease wormed its way deeper into the maiden's middle. *How?* If the sea witch—who lived far away in a hidden chasm—noticed, then how much more had those closest to her? It was dangerous to swim too near to shore.

"Ah," she said knowingly. "You seem surprised. Most are by what I learn."

"Then why—" Merri fought for air. "Then why did you ask why I've come?"

Darya smirked. "I delight in watching people squirm." The maiden opened her mouth to speak, but the sea witch pressed on, circling again before coming to a stop beside a coral chair, gilded in gold and sea glass and as large as a throne. "Someone has captured your attention. A boy from Daall has your heart. You wish to go to him, but you are bound by the sea. Two separate lives. So close, and yet so far." Darya punctuated each of her words with distaste. "Am I correct?"

Merri stared at her in shock.

"Your silence is answer enough. What are you willing to risk to go to him?"

It was quiet in the darkness of the cave as the maiden watched Darya sit, waiting. What *was* she willing to risk? It was true; she'd fallen in love with a boy on the mainland—a fisherman—whose gray-eyed gaze was as beguiling as the lapping tides and whose nature was even more so.

"Pitar, be careful along those rocks."

"Luci, come look at this shell. It matches your eyes."

"Calla, do you remember Papa's yarn of the captain lost at sea?"

She recalled bits of conversations she'd overheard the boy, Iun, speak to his siblings whenever they visited the ocean.

And then there were other memories she held even more dear.

"Merri, such a pretty name for a pretty face."

"What's it like under there, beneath all those waves you call home?"

"Won't you sing for me, sea maiden?"

She replayed his words over and over again. But nothing struck Merri's heartstrings more than the one he said the most often.

"If only you were human."

She'd observed Iun for what felt like months, Eldarwielle faithfully awaiting in deeper water as she hid behind some rocks along the shore. It was like this for a while until she felt bold enough to approach the blond-haired boy. Ever since she'd found Iun's drowned pocket watch and left it on a rock for him to claim, they'd struck up a friendship: human and sea maiden. What began as mere companionship soon developed into something more, so much so that she couldn't remember when he had stolen her heart. She only knew that he had. And the more she got to know him, the more his words echoed inside her chest. *If only you were human.* If only. What would it be like to have legs and go to him?

Merri was certain that if she could walk, then they could finally be together. Isn't that what Iun had wished for?

"I shall ask you again, young one. What are you willing to risk? All magic comes with a price." Darya narrowed her eyes and crossed her arms, all the while never letting Merri go.

The maiden swallowed, resolved in her answer despite finding it hard to breathe. "My tail. I'm…I'm willing to risk…leaving the ocean behind for…for love on shore."

Darya cracked a smile, something sinister in its uptilt. "Your tail is hardly worth the risk. It is not enough to simply exchange one mode of movement for another. No, you must be willing to give something most precious."

Merri's stomach dipped.

Darya got up from her seat, her eel-like tail tightening its hold around her. *Like what?* The words lodged somewhere in Merri's throat.

"Like your hair," Darya said, eyeing the wave of her strawberry-blonde tresses. She moved closer until she was a handbreadth away. "Or your ears." She reached out her fingers and grabbed Merri's chin, tilting it upward. "Or your voice."

Merri squirmed. "Are there no other options?"

"No." Darya smirked. She seemed to enjoy this.

The sea witch was cruel. How could Merri go to Iun without hair or ears? He'd take one look at her and be completely repulsed; if it came to that, she'd rather have her tail. But her voice? At least she'd look the same on the outside. She wouldn't be able to tell him what had happened, but maybe he wouldn't care that she could no longer sing to him. Given the fact that she would be human, maybe that would be enough.

"If I give up my voice, will I ever…get it back?" she asked.

"If you knew that answer, it wouldn't be considered a risk now, would it?"

Merri weighed this. Her family was estranged and left much to be desired in the way of love. Her three older sisters were preoccupied and off chasing suitors—some things never changed—and her father was distant; he hardly paid attention to where Merri went most days, including the surface. Maybe it was because his beloved wife died when Merri was only three, leaving his daughters motherless and him with all the responsibility to raise them alone. Not to mention, her friendship with Prince Olivander had ended years ago. But Eldarwielle…could she actually leave him? She'd miss the whale terribly, but she'd regret never following her heart even more. Iun loved her; she knew he did. Why else would he wish for her to be human?

"Okay," she said, suddenly bold. "I'll do it."

Darya looked pleased, if not surprised. She smiled, revealing a full mouth of sharp, white teeth. "Very well. Come this way, young one." She moved toward the cave wall arrayed in colors, the vials practically jumping off the shelves as if vying to be used. Reaching a hand upward, she secured a bottle of gold liquid and pulled a knife down from off the wall. "Yours is not the first tail I have transformed, you know," she said when she faced the girl.

Merri's eyes widened at the sharp object, and apprehension knotted in her middle. *I may not be the first, but maybe I was too hasty. Maybe I should go back.* She swallowed, her eyes crossing to the bridge of her nose as the glinting metal in the witch's hand drew near. *And what is she planning to do with that knife?*

Darya's tail tightened its hold once more. "Time to meet your love, young one. This will only hurt a little."

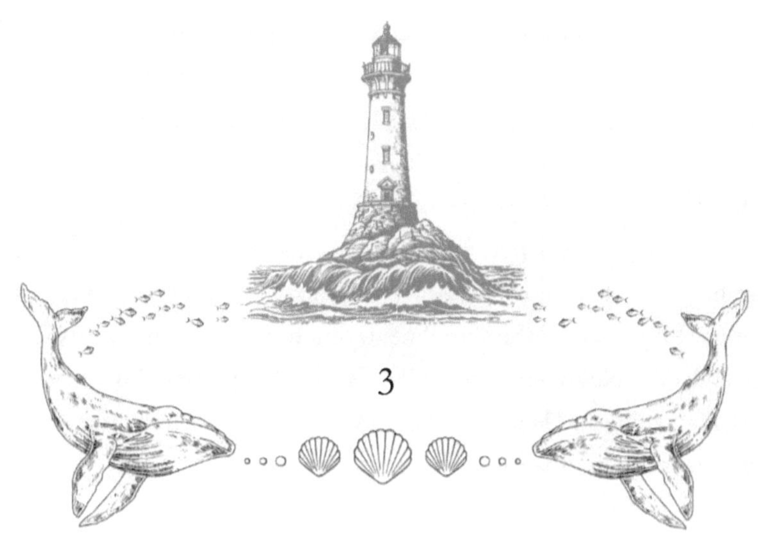

3

SPEECHLESS

Merri

Windkeep, Chaera
Maunt 1198

WARM BLOOD. DOUBLE VISION. SQUEEZING LUNGS. Merri had never experienced the like before. Her entire body felt ill, as if she'd just contrived the worst sea sickness in all of Chaera. And she hadn't anticipated the pain.

Once Darya had given her the potion, it was as if time froze, and Merri watched life swim by in slow motion. Eventually, her whole body grew numb, and she fell asleep where she floated, unable to see the finished product of Darya's powers and what she ended up doing with the knife…

Merri had forgotten her purpose for visiting the sea witch.

Until she awoke on shore.

Her vision stung as she cracked open sand-caked eyelids and was immediately blinded by the brilliance of the sun now hanging high in the sky above her. *The next day. I've slept through an entire night.* The feeling of her skin was warm without the relief of the bay. And every muscle in her body ached. Every nerve was on fire.

Looking around her, Merri noted she was once more on her familiar strip of Kerilow Bay, the rocky alcove only a little to her right. Her gaze cast toward the shoreline, trying to recall recent events when she stilled. She blinked once, twice. *My tail…* An excited tingle trailed down her spine and landed on her new toes. She watched them wiggle, her eyes widening the more she moved them.

It worked. It actually worked!

But how had she ended up back *here* when Darya's cave was so far away?

Just as suddenly, a searing pain began throbbing somewhere in her mouth. Gums sore, jaw tight, it was as if she'd bitten something incredibly hard and unyielding. She reached a hand toward her lips and drew it back when her fingertips touched something dried and caked along her lips. *Blood.*

Bile climbed her throat. Something was wrong.

With a heart beating like an erratic school of fish trying to evade a predator, Merri tried sticking out her tongue…only to find it missing. All that was left was a cauterized stump where the muscle used to be, the massacred thing a remnant of what once was.

"All magic comes with a price." Darya's words came back afresh, haunting her where she sat.

No. No, no, no! Tears gathered in Merri's eyes and trickled down her cheeks. A muted scream escaped her lips, muffling only a portion of her horrification. To trade her voice… She hadn't imagined it would cost her her tongue. If only she had heeded the warning about seeking out the sea witch. If only she had sought Esias first and confided in Eldarwielle. Surely they would have steered her to better waters than *this*.

What have I done?

"Miss, are you all right?"

Merri jumped. She hadn't heard anyone draw near. Lifting her chin, she faced whoever stood beside her and sighed inwardly, relieved to see it was only Calla, Iun's youngest and blondest sister. But how must she look to the little one?

Horror filled her anew.

"My brother sent me over to you. He would have come himself, but…" Her gaze locked on the sand while her fingers ruffled the hem of her pink dress, as if trying to avoid looking at Merri fully.

It was then that Merri realized she wasn't wearing any clothes. *Keeper's Heights*. Darya really had made a fool of her.

"Here." Calla deposited some sort of cream-colored robe beside Merri. It smelled like cinnamon and the sea. "It's my mother's."

Merri tried uttering her thanks before she realized she couldn't. It came out as a strange garble instead.

Calla nodded, stepping back slowly before running away. She soon disappeared to where Merri assumed Iun and the others waited for her.

Merri expelled a breath, grateful for Iun's discretion. He must have seen her and assumed the worst. Which wasn't far off. She gathered the fabric around her body, using a length of rope she found tucked in the folds to secure the garment about her waist. The tunic was a bit baggy and the fabric made her skin itch, but it would more than suffice.

What am I to do now? Iun's thoughtfulness sent heat to her already red face. Maybe there was hope for this situation, after all. He happened to be at the bay today, *and* he had seen her in distress. If this wasn't the makings of a happily-ever-after, then she was more trout than human.

Merri wiped her tear-streaked cheeks with her hand, dabbing her mouth and leaky nose with the collar of her tunic. When she pulled it back, the dried blood had dyed the fabric crimson. She was maimed. She was broken. But she had her heart; that's why she had bargained with Darya in the first place.

Hang on, Merri. Don't give up yet. She'd repeat the mantra until she believed it. She had no other choice. *Maybe it won't be as bad as I fear.* Despite her pain, Merri was surprised not to be feeling even worse. Whether by accident or on purpose, Darya's wicked magic seemed to have healed the wound she had inflicted. Merri was grateful that the stump, though tender, wasn't near as excruciating as it could be.

Pushing up from the ground, she tried standing, only to fall flat on her face. It took her a few seconds to realize what happened. Legs were strange, feet even more so. *How do humans do it?* She tried once more, her legs wobbly and unsteady like the young children she'd seen tripping along the shore. Merri was only able to take a few steps before her legs gave out again, but this time, someone caught her.

"I've got you. It's okay." The voice was distinctly male. And she knew to whom it belonged in a heartbeat. Iun had come for her. He steadied her with a hand on her elbow, and when he took in her face, his eyes widened. "It's you!" He glanced at her feet, then back at her face again. "You're human!"

Merri blushed, about to say *I am*, until she realized she couldn't. Panic crept up her throat. What would he think about her inability to talk? Her fears were soon replaced with nerves, for she was taken aback by Iun's nearness. Up close, he was even more handsome than she realized; his gray eyes, blond hair, chiseled jaw. In that moment, she wished more than anything that she could speak to him.

His brow furrowed. "How? How did this happen?" He looked out to the sea as if that would give him the answers, but what he sought he wouldn't find. Darya's cave was well hidden and couldn't be found in daylight. It was also in a completely different direction. Seeming at a loss, he looked once more at her. "Your mouth is bleeding! Are you hurt?"

Merri nodded, but she felt better with him holding her against the folds of his light brown tunic. It was as if she truly belonged right here. With him.

"Let me take you to my mother. She's a healer and can fix you up quickly."

Merri nodded again, touched by his kindness. His family would finally get to know her, for their friendship had endured months of secrecy. Thank Esias, now that would be over.

"And once you're feeling better, perhaps you can sing for us. I know everyone would love to hear your voice. Especially me." Iun smiled at her as if it was the greatest idea he'd ever had.

Her stomach dropped, dread flaring like a burning inferno in her middle. *Sing for us.* Should she open her mouth and show him she couldn't? But what would he think then?

Before Merri could blink, she found herself, speechless and tailless, being ushered to the home of the one she loved. But instead of hope, all she felt was despair reaching its spindly fingers around her ribs.

She shook it off. At least, she tried to.

Maybe everything will turn out well.

Maybe Iun will love me still.

Please.

Maybe it was worth losing her tongue if it meant she could keep her heart.

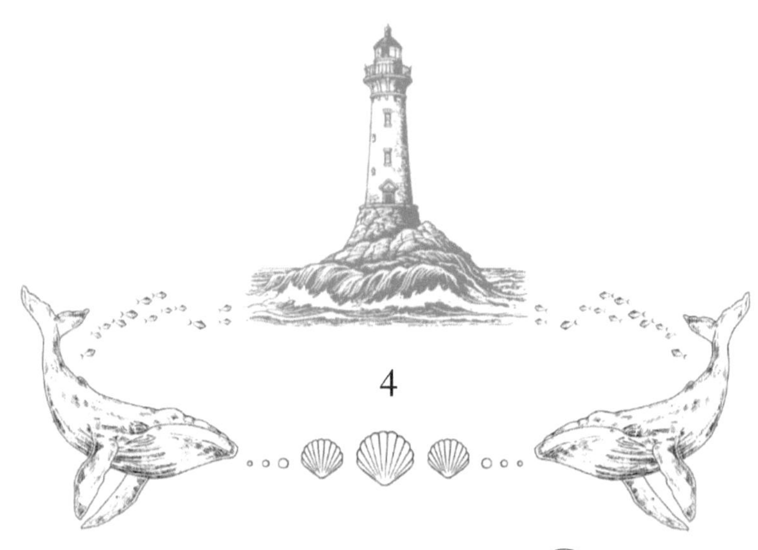

4

SPARRING IN THE DARK

Olivander

Windkeep, Chaera
Maunt 1198

"IT IS LATE. YOU SHOULD BE SLEEPING."

Lord Alyward found Olivander outside in the training arena and was now occupying the prince's time yet again; it was dark, the moon had awoken, and Olivander just wanted some blasted peace after a long day of preparations, preferably with his broad sword and a wooden dummy. The weapon had been a gift from his father when he'd turned thirteen, and not a day went by where he hadn't unsheathed the blade and sent it cutting through the air. The Captain of the Guard didn't care when the prince practiced, only that he did. And the Winderplume simply enhanced his skill, not charmed his sword to do the work for him. Sometimes Olivander liked to escape into the twilight and fillet a dummy, unleashing all his frustrations from the day without interruption. Like he was now. His sword was the one thing he *could* control.

"Couldn't sleep." Olivander arched his arms back and brought the sword low, slicing the sharp edge alongside the dummy's shoulder. Purple Winderplume sparks exploded in the air as a splitting crack echoed off the white walls of the citadel, reverberating until it dissipated into nothing.

All was quiet as the dust settled on the earthen floor.

Lord Alyward cleared his throat and tugged the collar of his fitted black jacket closer to his neck. "As much as it is commendable that Windkeep's future king is keeping up his daily practice by charming his sword, I do not think one needs to stab weapons in the dark to prove his strength. Seems rather pointless." He sighed, eyeing the prince reproachfully. "Especially without a shirt."

Olivander's knuckles cracked as his grip tightened on the hilt, muscles tensing. "Nothing to prove, Alyward. Just practicing."

The regent crossed his arms and narrowed his eyes. "I see. I won't argue to that end; that is not why I have come anyway."

"Then what's the honor this time?" Olivander turned his forearm up and sent the dummy an undercut, slicing its wooden stomach from navel to throat with the tip of his sword as more purple sparks flew.

"I would advise you not to question my authority in public, Your Highness. Nor Prophecy Keeper Reve's." His words caught Olivander off guard as he dealt another blow to the wooden figure, nicking the side of his shoulder rather than the whole arm as intended. "How will that reflect upon me as regent? They will think I am weak, and—"

"One shouldn't have to hide from others' opinions in order to appear strong, Alyward."

"Using another one of your father's witticisms, I see."

"He always had the right answers for everything." Olivander's stomach clenched. Would *he* make as good of a king as his father had been?

"Even so," Lord Alyward said, disrupting his thoughts, "the citadel needs to see their future king as one who respects his elders. As one who will make good decisions, of course, but will also listen to others' ideas."

"Right. Like you have with mine." Olivander swung his sword again, this time striking the dummy straight across the skull. An explosion of purple dust burst into the air as he wiped beads of sweat off his brow.

Lord Alyward pursed his lips.

"I'm not questioning Reve, Alyward, but the man's only had one prophecy since he took up Lysander's mantle, and it never amounted to anything," Olivander continued. "What if these aren't as important as we're making them out to be? What if we have placed too much power in mere words and the contents of my prophecy aren't even true?"

A look the prince had never seen before crossed the regent's face. Was that fear? "You would do well to keep these opinions to yourself, Your Highness. To question a prophecy is to question Esias. Doubts are like seeds; they easily spread and crop up like filthy weeds. And the last thing Windkeep needs is to have doubts about the safety of their kingdom and their future *leader* being the one to incite them. What is inked in red might as well be etched with Esias' blood."

Olivander groused internally. The regent was getting on his last nerve, and it was far too easy not to bite his tongue these days. "I just think there could be a better solution. Why not try the Winderplume? And why get Suntower and Rainhold involved when it's only Windkeep the prophecy addresses? I have a hard time believing Sulmaane would be willing to send Liora and Lark away so carelessly." The Daws and Sulmaanes had visited each other often enough for

Olivander to know their family well; it was as tight knit as his own had been.

"It is not carelessness which motivates him," Lord Alyward snapped.

"Fleet is fortunate to only have sons," Olivander gave an impatient snort. He had visited Rainhold as well. Zaker was four years his senior and Thadrick only two. Even though Olivander was closer with the latter—everyone loved Thadrick—he had spent the bulk of his growing up years with the Sulmaanes.

Lord Alyward's lips pinched. "We are a large nation with close borders. If a prophecy affects one of the three, it is bound to affect the rest. A powerful kingdom knows the extent to which they will go in order to protect what lies within; they are not averse to it. You should learn that well, seeing as you will soon be king."

Olivander shook his head. "You made this decision to send the maidens away without further consultation, and now you ask the whole citadel to follow it blindly, not to mention our neighbors. What kind of leadership is that?"

Lord Alyward's nostrils flared. "One your father trusted without a second thought. One *he* appointed to watch over his only child should he pass away. Are you to question your own father's judgment? And I *did* consult another—my whole advisory, for that matter—and their guidance was sound."

Guilt pooled in Olivander's stomach. He hadn't realized questioning the regent would equate to questioning his father, the man he never doubted for a second.

But was Lord Alyward being reasonable? And had the council really agreed to this? He'd placed more faith in his late father's advisors—Werthen, Reve, Kilner, and Servel—than to come up with something this foolhardy. Not to mention Suntower and Rainhold? He still couldn't believe what he was hearing.

"Well then my apologies." Olivander said the words through gritted teeth and sheathed his blade, the weapon snapping into place its own retort. He respected who his father had appointed, but that didn't mean he had to like him right now.

Lord Alyward straightened his jacket and stood taller. "You know I do this for your safety, Your Highness. I promised your father I would look out for you, and that is what I intend to do."

Olivander grabbed his shirt from off one of the benches and headed for the oaken door leading back into the citadel. He'd heard enough. Every conversation with the regent of late made him feel small. Inferior. And this one was no different.

The regent nodded. "Good. Seems like we are on the same page once more."

Think what you want.

In Olivander's mind, he was as far away from Lord Alyward's foolish plans as a goatherd was from the bay.

There had to be a more reasonable solution to saving his life, the prophecy be hanged.

"This will work, Your Highness. Do not look so glum. Windkeep needs to see their future king in good spirits come the pre-coronation feast. Think of your subjects, if nothing else."

The door banged shut behind Olivander, drowning out the last of the regent's words as he tugged on his shirt and stormed to his bed chambers.

They're all I can think about.

And after Lord Alyward's decree, he wasn't too sure they'd be happy with him.

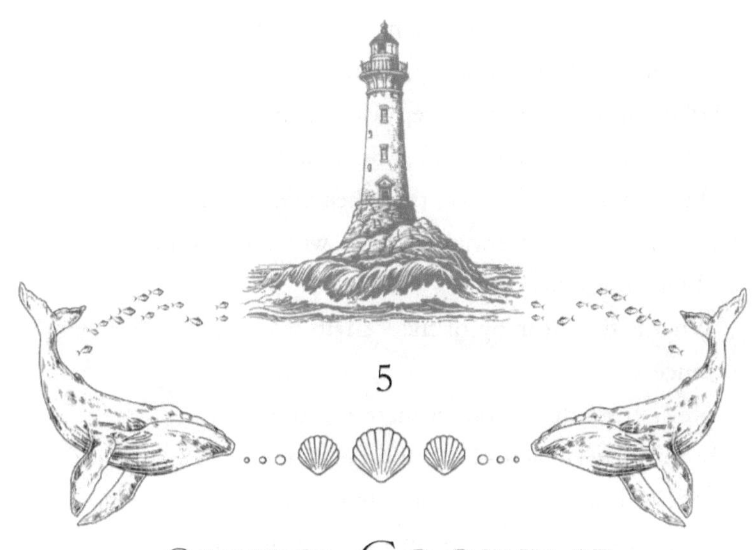

5

BITTER GOODBYE

Merri

Windkeep, Chaera
Maunt 1198

MERRI AWOKE THE FOLLOWING MORNING TO a pounding on the front door and behind her temples. She blinked a few times at the sunlight filtering in through the window, yesterday's events flooding her memory in rampant waves. She'd bargained with the sea witch. Iun had rescued her and brought her to his parents' home. And now she rested on a cot beneath a window in their living room, wearing one of Luci's burgundy dresses. The embers of a crackling fire burned low in the hearth across from her, keeping the small space warm.

More pounding shook her from her thoughts. "Open up in the name of our future king," came a terse, muffled voice from the other side of the door.

Shuffling could be heard from above her as footsteps descended the stairwell. It was Iun's father, Arth Hatch, who looked like he had just woken up from a deep sleep with his blond hair askew and gray shirtsleeves wrinkled. He opened the door, his brow dipping when he saw a burly guard standing on the other side. The man was dressed in dark blue; a bright white wind emblem with a sword piercing through it was branded on his chest.

"What is the meaning of this?" Arth asked, his tone ringing with impatience.

"News from the citadel. A matter of urgency."

By this time, Iylan—Iun's mother—was by her husband's side. She grabbed hold of his hand and tugged her linen robe close to her body. "What could be so urgent that you need to wake the town at four in the morning?" Unlike her spouse, her brunette hair was in a neat coif, but tired lines beneath her eyes revealed her exhaustion.

The guard continued, "A new sentence has gone out that all maidens between the ages of fifteen and twenty-three be sent away. I came to Daall to see if any fit that requirement." Despite the early hour, the man looked alert and ready for action, his blue uniform crisply pressed and no bags beneath his eyes.

Horror washed over the room, but it was Iylan who spoke first. "I'm not sure I understand…"

The guard sighed, as if tired from having to answer the same questions. "Prince Olivander is taking safety precautions because of his prophecy. In the name of protecting your future king, I insist you comply swiftly."

Prince Olivander. It hadn't even been a full day, and already he'd come up twice. *He* was the reason for all of this? Merri's head throbbed even more.

"Prophecy! How does the prince's prophecy affect *our family*?" Arth raised his voice.

"All questions can be saved for His Royal Majesty post coronation, when he holds court next month in Verd. Now, are there any maidens here that fit the age requirements?" The guard's gaze shot past the Hatches and landed on the cot where Merri sat. He lifted a brow.

His Royal Majesty. But he was only turning eighteen! *That must mean… When had Olivander's father died?* What of his mother? This was news to Merri, and it chipped at her already-weak exterior.

Iylan, terror in her eyes, pulled her husband deeper into the room and away from the guard. "We can't have them take her, Arth!" Conviction laced every whispered word, loud enough that Merri could still hear.

We can't have them take her. Unexpected warmth threaded its way through Merri's chest; Iun had only introduced her to them yesterday morning, and already they were trying to protect her? She hadn't anticipated such a quick acceptance into their family. Especially after they had learned she couldn't speak.

Iun seemed to take the news the hardest, though, and had hardly glanced at her all night. Perhaps that would change this morning, now that he had had a chance to sleep on that reality.

"What's all the commotion about?" Iun and Luci descended the stairs, rubbing their sleepy eyes, one in a robe, the other in a nightgown.

Iun stopped short when he saw the guard, his gaze shifting between his parents and the man clad in uniform. "What's going on?"

The guard ignored him, his gaze now lingering on Luci. "I'll ask again: Are there any females here between the ages of fifteen and twenty-three."

Iylan looked like she was ready to bolt, a wild look in her eyes.

Luci stepped forward. "I'm sixteen."

"No!" her mother screamed. She barricaded Luci before the guard by putting herself between them. "You aren't taking my daughter."

Arth fisted his hands and stood taller, a human shield himself.

It became clear to Merri now. She hadn't realized Luci was that old. Her parents had only been trying to protect one of their own. Why had Merri hoped they'd do the same for her?

"Ma, what's going on? Why are they taking Luci?" Iun asked.

"And you," the guard interrupted, addressing Merri sitting on the cot. "What is your age?"

She swallowed, grateful she couldn't answer. Maybe that would be her saving grace. The only one who knew her age was Iun. But he wouldn't...

"She's seventeen," he filled in for her, his brow furrowed even deeper. "Why?"

Merri's stomach dropped.

"Are there any others?" It didn't take long for the guard to have his answer. It was only Luci and Merri, but to the Hatches, one daughter was too many.

Before taking his leave, the man informed the family that the girls would be picked up the following morning. It would do no good to hide or run off; after taking their names, they were now listed along with their residence, and failure to comply would result in harsh consequences. They should pack their belongings and say their goodbyes. The end.

Merri's heart was on the verge of breaking. She'd risked much to come ashore, and now she would be forced to leave it all behind.

The sun began its ascent by the time Merri and Luci were on the road. Their carriage was upholstered in blue velvet with white curtains framing the windows, and it smelled faintly of sandalwood and the sea.

Though it was comfortable, both girls still had tear streaks down their faces, albeit for much different reasons.

Merri kept replaying the memory of their disparaging departure over and over again in her head.

"I guess this is goodbye." Iun toed the loose stones by his front door, watching his parents hug Luci by the awaiting carriage. His expression was grim.

I wish I could say something to you, Merri thought. *I wish more than anything I could stay here.*

"I'm glad you became human," he said.

Merri's heart soared. Maybe all wasn't lost if Iun wasn't upset with her anymore. *This* was what she'd been hoping for, a conversation about their feelings. If only she didn't have to leave. But maybe once the year was over, then she could come back. Surely, Iun would wait for her, wouldn't he?

He cleared his throat, his voice sounding thick. *"I'm glad you became human so my sister didn't have to leave here alone. You're a sweet person, Merri. She's too young for this. Stick by her, okay?"*

Merri's heart felt like it was shrinking beneath the tightening of her ribs. *A sweet person,* not an *I love you.*

"I'm only too sorry that she never heard you sing."

Merri hadn't heard the rest of his parting words for the tears had fallen faster than she could stop them. She'd never recover from this.

The Hatches had gathered around Luci, hugging her and giving her bundles of letters and mementos while Merri stood by crying in silence. The family had bid her farewell, packed her a parcel of kippers and eggs—she'd yet to try eating without her tongue—and had allowed her to wear Luci's burgundy dress for the journey. But unlike their daughter, she didn't possess their affections. And it was this news which shattered her the most. Iun had shown her kindness, but he didn't love her. And now he never would.

Their carriage suddenly jolted to a halt.

"What's going on?" Luci perked up, pushing back overgrown brunette bangs from her forehead and wiping away tears with her coral dress sleeve. Hope lit her features, and Merri guessed her thoughts for they echoed her own: maybe the guards changed their minds and were letting them go.

They both pulled aside the white curtain and looked out the window. Merri watched as a group of men on the side of the road, all dressed in royal blue uniforms, stood conversing in a half circle.

One of them looked in their direction. A lift of the chin. "How many do you have in there?" His voice sounded muffled through the glass.

"Only two," the coachman of their carriage responded. "I can take one more. Two if they're small. What news of Suntower and Rainhold? Have they rounded up their lot yet?"

The guard nodded. "They're going north to Croastan or Geshal instead of crossing through Windkeep to go west like us. I've heard that Oclein won't have them."

The coachman didn't say anything else, and Merri's hope was depleted. They weren't being released; the guards were only taking inventory. She'd never felt so small, and as someone who'd grown up in the sea, that said a lot.

She was about to turn away from the window when someone else caught her attention. A young man was walking down a steep hill; he was tall with short, light brown curls, and he was dressed in a white and gold tunic with a royal blue cape across his broad shoulders. Her stomach dropped; she recognized him instantly despite the long years. He was an older version of the young teen she once knew, and it looked as if he came directly from the citadel.

Luci gasped and pressed her nose to the glass. "It's Prince Olivander!"

Prince Olivander. His name spoken aloud again sent a bitter pang through Merri's chest. So this was what happened to her friend, the prince of the prophecy who was sending them all away. He looked miserable.

"He's so handsome." Luci let out a dreamy sigh.

"*Gogden maurn,* Your Highness," one of the guards said outside, bowing.

The prince frowned. "I wouldn't call it good."

Me neither. Merri moved her face closer so that her nose pressed against the glass.

"Even so, we're glad that you're here to offer your people your support," the guard responded.

He shook his head. "That's not why I'm here. Lord Alyward is handling some affairs back at the citadel, so he sent me in his stead."

The guard nodded. "Well, your timing is paramount. We're trying to see how many maidens can fit in one carriage. To maximize the space."

"Right, like cattle stuffed inside a barn," Prince Olivander scoffed.

"Tell us then"—the guard crossed his arms over his chest—"what does His Royal Highness suggest we do instead?"

The prince scowled. "What does it matter? The lives of others' apparently aren't any of my concern."

The guard chuckled. "They will be next week. In the meantime, you'd do well to show your compliance."

"You want my compliance? Is that what everyone wants?" A muscle pulsed in the prince's jaw. "Fine. Then stuff the carriages full. Send mothers and grandmothers along, too, for that matter!"

The guard's mouth hung open. "Your Highness—"

"Just get them out of my sight. The sooner this is over with, the better." The prince turned on his heel before the guard could finish his sentence.

Merri held her breath as she watched him go, feeling her insides burn. How *dare* he.

"Bay's Depths! What's gotten into him?" Luci said, eyes wide. "He might be good-looking, but he sure is a grump."

Whoever this Prince Olivander was, he wasn't the childhood friend Merri remembered. What happened to the green-eyed boy she once knew? Had he really no concern for the lives of his people? He must not if he was so willingly sending them away. He only cared about himself and that dreaded prophecy, whatever it said.

She watched him storm off, his mood as tremulous as the sea. The last of him disappeared over the hill, his cape billowing in his wake.

Merri had always hoped to see him again one day, to understand why he never returned to the shore. To have some sort of closure. But now she regretted it.

Olivander had *changed*.

She felt the sting of his betrayal anew.

He was the reason she was being sent away. *It doesn't matter that I've sacrificed much to get here.*

He was the reason Iun did not love her. *In time, maybe he would have.*

He was the reason her heart had broken in the first place. *He left me as if I was nothing.*

And she wouldn't soon forget it.

6

WEIGHT OF DUTY

Olivander

Windkeep, Chaera
Maunt 1198

IRATE, OLIVANDER PACED AROUND HIS BED chambers, vest off and hands already running through his hair. Had forty of the citadel's carriages truly carried away all the maidens of Windkeep? Suntower and Rainhold had taken care of their lot, per Lord Alyward's request. He'd promised them additional Winderplume for their compliance, and somehow hadn't received much pushback, from what Olivander could tell. Had no one a shred of humanity?

It seemed only Olivander cared enough to say something, but there he stood, watching the carriages tear apart families and doing nothing to stop it; not like he could have even if he tried. And he'd *tried.* Though not hard enough, apparently. That knowledge alone had made him ill-tempered with the guards. Those unfortunate families, all without their daughters and mothers for a whole year… He shook his head. Despite what Lord Alyward thought, *this* was not the way he wanted to start his reign as king, with his people remembering such a catastrophe.

If only his poor father knew, he'd be trying to dig himself out of his royal crypt.

Olivander huffed out a breath and plunked down on the edge of his bed, pinching the bridge of his nose. "I'm a clodpole. A certified muttonhead. A third rate—"

"Excuse me, Your Highness."

Olivander jumped, taken aback to see someone standing in his room. It was only his manservant, Jasper Clyffton, but still, he hadn't heard him come in.

"Yes, Jasper," Olivander began, regarding the older man who was more family than staff. He was dressed like he always was, with a dark blue tailored jacket and matching pants, and some sort of cleaning cloth draped over his left shoulder. "What is it?"

He cleared his throat. "If I may be so bold. I have been tasked with looking out for you. To knock some sense into those who seek to do you harm."

Olivander nodded.

"Then you will forgive me." The manservant approached him, whacking Olivander across the head with his shoulder rag. "But the same rule applies to yourself. Please do not speak ill of our future king."

Olivander tasted dust before his mouth dropped open. And then he laughed, loud and clear and strong. He'd never been pummeled by one of his staff before, and he found he quite enjoyed it. "Thank you, Jasper. I've just decided you need to hit me more often."

"Happily, Your Highness." Jasper bowed.

But the momentary lightness he felt at the rebuttal soon dissipated once more. His guards and the regent may not care to listen to him, but Jasper would. If he could confide in anyone, it would be him. "Do you think we made the right decision in sending them away?"

Jasper stroked his chin. "Do I think sending innocent maidens away from their families and disrupting their livelihoods for a year is fair? No. Is it wise? That is yet to be determined. But I am on no side that chooses to play the role of Esias."

Olivander soaked in his words. Jasper wasn't merely a manservant; he was part mentor as well, reminding him of truth time and time again, especially when the world had grown too dark to remember it himself.

"Do you really believe a single maiden will take down all of Windkeep, killing *me* in the process? What would be her motive?" *Prophecies should come with an interpreter.* Olivander rested his chin in his hands. Maybe this was worth bringing up to the keeper. Reve might be able to tell him more.

"If I knew that, I would be a lot wiser." Jasper chuckled. "But the truth is, we don't always get the answers we seek. But we do have a choice: to choose faith or to follow the path of fear."

"And you think Alyward has chosen the path of fear."

"I think to act upon one's own will in order to avoid something else is foolish. Prophecies have a way of coming true regardless of intervention. In my opinion, I would have kept the maidens here and figured out another solution. But who am I but your humble manservant? I trust that it was ultimately Alyward's desire to protect *you* which overruled any other reasoning. He has not meant to cause you pain in the process."

Olivander nodded, remembering the regent had said the same thing.

"Let that be enough, Your Highness." Jasper reached a hand out and placed it on the prince's shoulder. "I suggest focusing your energies elsewhere. You cannot change what has been done, but you can decide what you will do next. Let Windkeep see their future king as someone who *listens* and heeds their concerns and then *fights* to maintain them. I have no doubts you will be great at it since that is one of your best qualities."

The prince sighed, and some tension drained from his shoulders. *Thank Esias for Jasper.* "I can always count on you to keep my head on straight."

"And from it getting too big and tumbling off, don't forget." Jasper winked. "Need I remind you that I have known you since you were a young boy and have more than enough stories to keep you humble."

Olivander mused at the prospect. "I have no doubts."

"Come, Your Highness." Jasper moved toward the door. "Go outside and get some fresh air. You will want enough energy to write that speech of yours for the pre-coronation feast next week. If I may venture a guess, I believe you have not touched your quill in an age."

Guilty.

He'd been too busy playing Hobsmatch with Gabe and trying to avoid Lord Alyward to sit down and focus on something so important. With all the preparations about the citadel, he'd needed to retreat and soak in these last few days of simplicity. As much as Olivander wanted to claim his late father's throne and be taken seriously as Windkeep's leader, there was still a part of him that was nervous in doing so.

It was a lot to have a whole kingdom weighing on one person's shoulders. *His* shoulders. He wasn't sure if he could carry that weight without crumbling.

"Do you always know everything, Jasper?"

The manservant smiled. "I know enough to keep me humble." And then he slipped out the door, leaving Olivander to himself.

The room felt emptier without his presence, but the weight of dismay had dissipated somewhat upon his exit. Though Olivander was encouraged, he knew it would be hard not to ruminate on his own fears and failings if he remained in his bedroom. He'd go for a walk outside, fill his lungs with fresh air, and then he'd write that gray-inked speech. He'd remind all of Windkeep of his capabilities at the pre-coronation feast. Perhaps he could even send the maidens home sooner as his first mandate as king.

And he'd trust Esias with wherever that put him next.

A mussel left Olivander's hand with a flick of the wrist, skimming the water and jumping over the gentle waves with a trail of purple dust behind. It floated briefly before falling victim to the tide, sinking to the sandy ground below.

He breathed in the brine and let the wind tousle his mop of short-cropped curls. He'd forgone his cloak and pushed up his shirtsleeves, if only to feel the caress of the breeze on his bare forearms. Nothing calmed his soul like the sea. Though his guilt had made him forget that.

As a child, he'd often go to Kerilow Bay with his parents. He missed them every day, wishing they were still alive, and had to fight against the bitter regret that seemed to batter his heart whenever he thought of them. He'd learned quickly that one could never spend too much time with those who had died far too soon.

He stood at the edge of the bay in a spot he hadn't visited since their passing—a rocky outcropping in the shallows, sequestered off behind large boulders—which provided the best place for solitude. It was a hidden cove all to his own, and though he could see the world outside, they couldn't see him. He hadn't meant to come here, but he needed to be in a place where the memories of his parents were the fullest, even if that meant revisiting what was lost.

And he'd lost more than just them.

Scanning the sand for another mussel, a small purple stone caught his eye, glistening in the sunlight in all its iridescent glory. It was the same shade as the dust which hung around his neck. *Merri.* Flashes of a lavender fin flitted across his mind. And a bright smile. His favorite smile.

Not a day went by that Olivander hadn't thought about her, too. He'd first befriended the sea maiden in this very spot, but he hadn't spoken to her in years; it would mark three come the summertime. When his parents passed in the month of *Sollun*, it had been too painful to visit this place, the reins of grief still so fresh with its claws sunken deep. And then Lord Alyward's grip had tightened. *"A prince must learn his trade. The throne will be yours in only three years."* So he'd put in the work and trained hard…and their friendship sorely paid the price because of it. When he thought about visiting her again, too much time had passed that he feared it would be awkward. And the more he put it off, time only seemed to stretch the distance between them even more.

The familiar sting of remorse pooled in Olivander's stomach. She'd been his first non-royal friend, his *best* friend, and he'd just cast her aside because of some guilt. He never even got the chance to tell her how he felt. *Still* felt.

I'm a coward.

Olivander sighed and pocketed the purple stone. He picked up another mussel from off the ground to chuck across the water, but he paused and turned it over in his hand instead. *"Two halves that make a whole. And spring in between."* His chest constricted at the memory of Merri's words ringing in his ears; what would she think of him now? Would she have understood the reason for his long absence? That he wished more than anything to make it right?

The mussel fell from his hand.

"Merri?" he called across the deep. The need to see her suddenly eclipsed all. How could he have stayed away for so long? "Merri, are you out there?" Nothing. He ran toward the back of the rocky cave and dropped to his knees. He shifted aside some stones before digging through the sand. "Where is it?" *It should be here.* He dug on. And on. But the orange coral was nowhere to be found. Had he forgotten to bury it? Had someone stolen it? *No.* He sat back on his heels and groaned. "I'm an idiot." Merri always found the coral he threw into the ocean, and *he* was the one who brought it back to shore until their next visit. And he'd forgotten to take it from her last time.

He shook his head and pushed to his feet, not even bothering to dust the sand off his knees. *It's too late.* Finding another mussel, he grabbed more Winderplume and skimmed it atop the retreating tide with a forceful grunt, watching the shell practically fly over the water. When he was crowned king, he'd have to make it a point to come here more often. He needed to find Merri and apologize. He owed her that much.

Olivander picked his way over the sand, grabbing more mussels and skimming them with Winderplume dust in turn. He felt some of his frustration go with each release. Despite not having visited here in recent years, he was glad he lived close to the coast. The white limestone fortress of Windkeep Citadel was perched on a high cliff that overlooked these waters, which proved only a short carriage ride or half hour's walk away. But with all the carriages being used elsewhere…

He grimaced, remembering them lined up like a wooden snake, being sent across the kingdoms filled to the brim with helpless maidens. And he'd let it happen.

Olivander grunted; the purpose of this walk was to clear his mind, not to dwell on such things and his inability to maintain friendships. *Too late for that as well.*

"I'm done." *Ridiculous prophecies be hanged.* He skimmed another purple-trailed mussel into the churning surf, trying hard to redirect his thoughts, but it wasn't working. "Finished." *Being useless has grown old.* He threw another mussel, watching its lavender flight across the water. *Why do I keep messing everything up?* "Enough!" He chucked a final shell the furthest it had ever gone and watched as the waves carried its purple remnants out to sea, his vial of near-empty Winderplume swinging like a pendulum around his neck.

A spout of water shot into the air only a little distance beyond his now-sinking mussel, and a low, somber cry rang out from the deep. Its haunting song carried over the waves and danced in the air, wrapping around Olivander's ribs and squeezing them.

A whale.

He'd never seen one this close to shore before, though in all his years of knowing Merri, she'd told him her whale friend was never far away. Was this the same one? What had his name been? *Elderfin? Alderwhile?* He couldn't recall, but he found himself mesmerized by the music. The song was sad. Heart-wrenching. Real. There was meaning in those few, deep notes—more so than in the songs written by man, though he wouldn't tell the Croastan musicians visiting the citadel that. Even without words, the whale's cry conveyed some profound feeling. Almost as if it was mourning the loss of a loved one.

Who are you mourning?

Olivander's eyes glossed over. It began slowly at first. The whale's song moved him, compelled him, and he soon realized that, like the melody, his tears were real, too.

He wept for what once was—his parents' deaths and a lost friend. What was now—the feeling of invisibility. And what would be—the weight of his kingly duties.

He'd come to the bay for a chance at remembering and found a kindred spirit instead. It had only taken a whale to remind him he wasn't alone. That there was purpose in the broken places, hard though they may be.

Olivander wiped stray tears from his eyes and nodded toward the waters, the whale's song lingering on. A bittersweet pang arrested his soul with a subtle thread of understanding infiltrating his tumultuous heart. It was as if the whale knew what he needed.

He wondered about the creature.

What did it need? What made it sing such a mournful song?

He only hoped it would find what it was looking for.

And he hoped, more than anything, that Merri was okay.

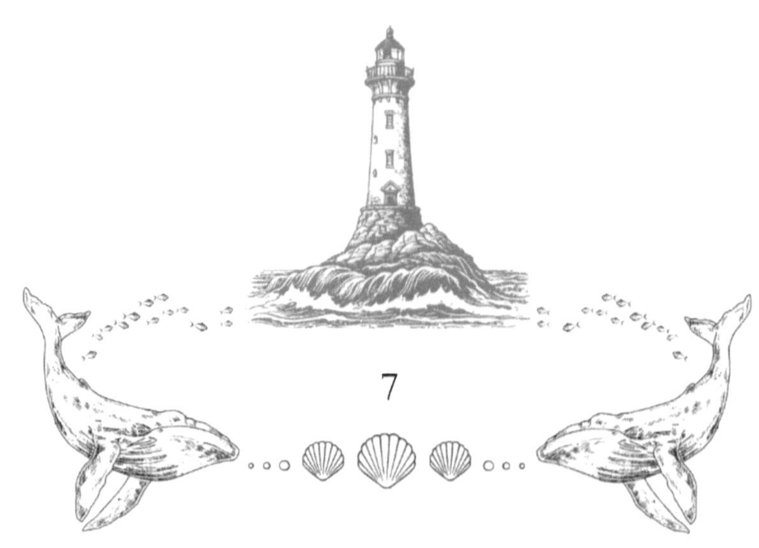

7

BATESONS FARM

Merri

Lisethoorn, Hollms
Maunt 1198

MERRI WAS NOT OKAY.

Days strolled by in an endless blur of browns and greens. The world was waking up from winter's slumber, and that meant much was still growing. Much still appeared dead.

It was like this for the full duration of the carriage ride, and Merri, throat tight and eyes thoroughly dry, longed for something blue. How she wished she were back in Kerilow Bay, swimming through the cool waters with careless abandon. Not trapped inside this four-wheeled cage with an endless view of dirt. With no idea when she'd get out.

Breathe. Think about something else.

The one consolation to this carriage ride was that no one else had been added to the already cramped space. She wasn't sure how they'd managed it, but it was a blessing all the same with just her and Luci…though Merri was beginning to wonder if having a third person would have been better.

Luci sat on the opposite side of the carriage, hardly paying her any mind. Their acquaintance had started out decently at first, but once she remembered Merri couldn't respond to anything she said, she stopped trying. Instead, she took to complaining openly, for she garnered no rebuke from Merri.

"I hate it in here. Now I'll never get married!" Luci crossed her arms over her chest in a dramatic fashion, a glistening tear rolling down her cheek.

As usual, Merri didn't say a word.

"I miss my family. And I know they miss me, too," she carried on. "I'd give absolutely *anything* just to be with them again and not stuck inside here!"

Merri grimaced at her choice of words. She once bargained that frivolously, too, but how things had changed. *Esias, forgive me.*

Luci sighed and leaned her head on the upholstered seat. She sighed again, this time louder, and finally glanced in Merri's direction. "Do open a window, Merri, and rid the stifling carriage of this tepid air."

This was new. Now instead of trying to converse, she was ordering Merri about. But at least Merri didn't feel invisible anymore.

Merri tried the latch, frowning when it wouldn't budge. In truth, she wasn't sure what she was doing at all.

"Oh, you're useless!" Luci thrust her aside and opened the window herself, allowing in a waft of putrid wind. "Bay's Depths!" she cried, trying to close it. "We must be passing a farm!"

Merri tried not to gag. The carriage was already hot and stuffy, and now it smelt downright disgusting. There would be no improvement after this.

"Are we almost there?" Luci asked, pounding on the ceiling of the carriage. Apparently, that was how one communicated with the coachman.

Unfortunately for them, he hadn't heard her.

Luci huffed out a breath and crossed her arms. "I wonder where we are. We've been on the road for forever, and I'm ready to lay down on a soft, clean bed!"

Again, Merri couldn't reply, but she shared similar sentiments. Except, the bed she was used to was one of seaweed and a giant oyster shell. Why had she thought coming on shore would solve all her problems? Chasing love was a foolhardy fancy. It had only made matters worse, and now she couldn't even say why.

Suddenly, their carriage began to slow, and both girls looked outside once more. On the side of the road was a sign, with characters Merri couldn't discern. She knew they were letters, but she'd never learnt how to read; there wasn't much use for such things beneath the waves.

"Lisethoorn, Hollms. But that might as well be on the other side of the world!" Luci exclaimed, reading it aloud. Merri didn't know where Lisethoorn was, had never even heard of it, but surely it couldn't be *that* far away. "Now I'll never get back home!" Tears sprang anew like little rivers down Luci's face, and Merri's heart twisted with compassion.

It wasn't Luci's fault that she had grown terse and unfriendly over the course of their journey. It was hard being stripped of one's home, especially by force. Merri had *chosen* to leave hers for a chance at love, and now the decision had cost her greatly. Regardless, neither of them had prepared for this.

They soon pulled into a rocky drive that led up to an oddly shaped building—the same putrid smell now growing stronger—and came to a stop beside a long stretch of fencing. Strange black-and-white spotted animals grazed on some grass, large fluffy white-hooved creatures filled an entire pasture, and winged beasts with red combs on their heads pecked at something in the dirt.

What is this place?

The carriage door opened, and their coachman ushered them out. Luci went first, and Merri followed on her heels. "Welcome to Batesons Farm!" he said.

Both girls gasped at the sight before them. They stood in a far-reaching green valley with giant mountains wrapped all around it in a half moon. In the valley itself was an expansive piece of land—a farm—with enough animals to form its own country.

But while Merri's gasp was in awe of such a strange place, Luci's was one of revulsion. "We're stopping here? A *farm*? The air smells of dung. I want to go home!" She cried even harder.

The coachman tried to console her. "Just because you're not close to the sea anymore doesn't mean this place can't be pleasant. Give it enough time and its charm will grow on you."

Merri's wonder faltered. *Not close to the sea.*

"That just makes this infinitely worse!" Luci screamed.

Not close to the sea anymore. Was it possible to drown in the air? Only now did Merri realize how suffocated she had been. How desperately she needed to be near the waters which birthed her. Near Eldarwielle and his companionable comfort.

She agreed with Luci. She couldn't live here.

"Be that as it may, I'm afraid this is to be your quarters for the duration of Prince Olivander's eighteenth year. So best to get comfortable while you can." The coachman retrieved Luci's large luggage bag and Merri's salted herring from the carriage and brought it over. "Don't forget to give them this missive from Windkeep." He withdrew a letter from his pocket, closed with a wax seal that matched

Windkeep's crest, and handed it to Merri before climbing back onto his post. *It's from the citadel.* "Head inside. They'll be expecting you." He tipped his hat and set off.

"No, wait! Come back!" Luci wailed, running after him, but she didn't get very far. She tripped on a lace from her boot and sprawled out flat on her face. It was too late anyway; the horses had already turned the corner and were back on the main road. "Come back!" she cried again, spitting out bits of gravel, her cheeks streaked with tears and dirt.

Merri walked over and helped Luci back to her feet. Though she couldn't offer words of comfort, she could still be there for her like Iun had wanted, even while her own heart broke, too.

"Thanks," Luci said, receiving Merri's help and brushing the grime off her skirts when she stood. "I can't believe it. Just like that, we're dropped off somewhere foreign without a care in the world." She trudged over to her luggage and heaved it up a bit before dropping it. She tried again, and couldn't budge the thing more than a couple of inches. "Just great," she said, still wiping stray tears off her face. "No matter, I'll have someone inside take care of it." She stormed toward the large building, Merri following closely behind her. "What are the odds a place like *this* has decent bathing quarters?"

Merri wasn't certain, but all she knew was that it didn't matter. Once they were settled inside, she wouldn't be staying long.

She already had plans to leave before the moon burned bright in the sky.

A mysterious ticking sound reverberated through the darkened room, lit only by a single-flamed candle on the windowsill. Merri had never been this close to fire before, but it was mesmerizing in its dance. It moved like the waves, back and forth, back and forth, except this element shouldn't be touched.

How she longed for the coolness of the water.

The ticking continued, and Merri remembered it belonged to some sort of mechanical device with numbers. *A clock*, Luci had told her, but that meant nothing to Merri. She charted the passing of time by the position of the sun. Who needed clocks when nature told you the hour?

She lay tucked in bed in her new room, the covers pulled up to her neck. Had Iun wanted to marry her, she would have learned to be comfortable beneath linens and cushions and frilly things. But seeing as she was on her own now, her skin crawled whenever she touched these unfamiliar textures.

Who needed blankets when one's blanket was the sea?

Not to mention, the dark-paneled walls covered in knickknacks and pictures were overwhelming to look at, especially when they cast so many strange shadows in the flickering candlelight. She was used to the calming waters of the bay, sand, and clam shells. The power of one's imagination loomed bigger in the night.

The owners of the farm were a middle-aged, married couple, Llana and Len Bateson, and by way of a letter from the citadel had received news to house two unassuming girls for an entire year. They didn't seem thrilled by the prospect, but they had dutifully prepared a room each for Luci and Merri anyway. It was a kindness, though forced, but Merri wouldn't stay to see how long it endured.

In fact, she was leaving now.

Merri pulled back her covers and slipped on the pair of shoes Llana had reluctantly lent her. She'd only wear them to protect her feet, and then she'd cast them off forever. She grabbed what remained of the kippers, an extra cloak dangling from a peg behind her door, and stealthily slipped into the darkened corridor of the house.

With legs still unused to standing, she wobbled a bit and bumped into things she couldn't see, but when she accidentally knocked over something fragile and heard the ear-shattering crash which followed, she ran like she'd never run before.

Keeper's Heights! I can't let them catch me.

Desperation was a great motivator. She clung to it like the cloak about her shoulders as she fled into the dark under a blanket of stars. The air still smelled of manure, but the coolness of the night kept the worst of the stench at bay. It was far better than being caged indoors.

Voices echoed behind her, and lights flared in her peripherals. *More flames.* She rushed onward. *They're coming for me.*

She hadn't meant to, but she'd overheard a conversation from the Batesons when she should have been sleeping. Her room was near the kitchen, and try as she might to avoid it, the walls were paper thin. They were discussing the contents of the letter.

"'Should any maiden seek to flee, you're held responsible for detaining them by any means possible, or else answer to the throne of Windkeep should they come back here too soon.'" She scoffed. "Well, that's a real comfort."

"Sure could use some Winderplume for babysitting the two of 'em 'til next Maunt. Least the kingdom could do after sending a threat like that. The local farmstand barely has enough to sell these days," Len said.

Lucky for them and the beloved prince, Merri wasn't headed in *his* direction. Mortification washed over her simply at the thought. What would he think if she showed up on his doorstep after all these years?

She was headed for the bay, wherever that may be. And she wouldn't stop until she found it.

"Merri!" voices called behind her. "Slow down at once! Come back!"

She ignored them, running up the long drive and out into the road, her booted feet fumbling on the uneven ground.

"Merri!" They were gaining on her.

Guilt gnawed at the back of her mind that she was putting their lives in danger, but she knew their persistence was one of obligation, not love. And she felt it in every cadence of their pursuit. She couldn't stay. She didn't belong here.

Head pounding, adrenaline coursing through her veins, she pressed on. Rounding a bend here, climbing a hill there, tripping occasionally, only to catch herself before pressing onward. She was careful to dodge holes lest she turn an ankle. But with one glance over her shoulder, her heart leapt to her throat at her pursuers' nearness, and when she turned back, she tripped.

Her torso met earth hard and fast, the momentum carrying her rolling body down a hill and into a tangle of trees and overgrowth. She came to a pitiful stop and lay there panting and breathless amongst the leaves and detritus, wondering if she was still alive.

The voices nearby told her she was, and she counted the seconds in her head, holding her breath as they approached. They soon passed over her, and she realized why. Thank Esias for her cloak; its dark fibers helped her blend into the night.

Lifting her head, Merri watched as the torches dissipated into the gloom, and she ran in the other direction. She didn't know where she was going, but that didn't stop her. The moon was her guide. She'd follow its light, and then she'd finally be home.

8

HOME OF THE WINDERPLUME

Olivander

Windkeep, Chaera
Maunt 1198

"Are you sure I have to wear these things? I look like a bruise, not a soon-to-be king." Olivander groaned at his reflection, watching himself pose like an awkward peacock in the mirror. The white, royal blue, and deep plum looked decent enough together, but it was a bit depressing. And the Winderplume-infused golden threads only made him look even more like a gilded fool.

"They are only robes, Your Highness. If these are concerning you, then you should wait until the ones you have to wear tomorrow," Jasper said with a chuckle.

"I can't imagine anything worse than this." Olivander pulled on the fabric of his sleeve before running a hand through his freshly coiffed locks, yanking on the strands. He was used to the simple blue and white of the citadel, not additional colors to signify higher rank.

"The pre-coronation feast is within two hours, Your Highness. I suggest you run a comb through that mop of yours before partaking in the roasted pheasant. And especially before giving your speech." Jasper held out a comb for him to take.

Bay's Depths. He'd nearly forgotten about the speech; at least, he'd tried to put it far from his mind. Olivander knew he should be readier than he felt, but suddenly eighteen years felt too young to lead an entire kingdom.

Only one more day. He swallowed hard at the thought. He wanted to be a great king like his father, and there was much he wanted to improve, but that didn't mean taking the position was any less daunting. His father had led tirelessly with peace and wisdom, a remarkable feat according to Windkeep's history…and all Olivander had to his name was skill in wielding a sword.

His free hand absentmindedly found his pocket and began turning over the stone he'd snagged along the shore. He didn't know why its presence calmed him, but it did. Maybe it was because Merri had always believed he'd be a great king, even when he doubted it himself. He took out the stone and held it up toward the light before placing it on a tray alongside a purple feather, a purple shell, and a purple piece of sea glass.

"More to add to your collection, Your Highness?" Olivander hadn't realized Jasper was still watching him. He eyed the prince curiously. "She must be someone special."

Olivander reddened. "I don't know what you're talk—"

Jasper pointed to the almost-empty bottle of purple dust hanging from Olivander's neck, and the prince snapped his mouth shut. He hadn't thought it was that obvious. Then again, his manservant had eyes that rivaled the astuteness of Lord Alyward's.

"I would wager a guess that there is more on your mind than just your disdain for regalia and your monochromatic tastes." Jasper raised an eyebrow as he studied the prince.

Olivander pressed his lips together to form a thin line and grabbed the offending comb Jasper still held. He was too tired to talk about it and felt like he'd been exposed. He rolled his neck to ease his nerves before turning to face the mirror again. Hopefully his manservant would take the hint.

Jasper nodded in silence, and the prince watched his reflection as he moved to the door, grasped its handle, and paused. He cleared his throat. "You will make a good king, Vander."

Olivander jolted. It wasn't often Jasper addressed him so casually, especially with the name only he chose to call him.

"And a great one as you grow into it." Then he left him. And Olivander felt a few inches taller in his wake.

The prince looked at the comb in his grasp and puffed out a breath. *One doesn't comb through curls.* Another look in the mirror. *But anything will be better than this.*

Bolstered by Jasper's encouraging words, Olivander found himself climbing the long stairwell to the citadel's utmost tower, the place he tried to visit as often as time allowed. His boots thudded along the gray stone steps, the fire sconces quaking as he walked past. When he finally reached a set of oaken doors, inlaid with Windkeep's crest of a wind emblem speared through with a sword, he paused. The royal crypt stood on the other side.

Olivander sighed, then pushed open the heavy doors and entered, the space warm and aglow with candlelight reflecting off the wall of lancet windows. The room was inviting even though it housed the dead. Lord Alyward always made sure the candles remained lit, much to the regent's credit.

It was in this tower where the late king and queen rested, their bodies set in a place of honor in Windkeep, where the wind could actually *keep* them, a memorial fit for a beloved royal couple.

Still, coming here always sent a pang of longing through the prince's chest.

He knelt at his parents' tombs, brushing a hand across the engraved letters with a thread of solemnity. *Our beloved King, Matteo Armadeus Soryn Daws, 39. Our beloved Queen, Firan Lou Gossard Daws, 38. Rulers of Windkeep, Chaera for twenty-one years. Devoted parents and leaders. Loyal to Esias. Departed too soon in the month of Sollun, 1195. 'Tha lun skeul ealni wef cnaw fryth.'*

Two of the most selfless people he'd ever known.

Olivander stared at the last line for a time, feeling the words pierce him anew. *This land shall always know peace.*

"Tomorrow's almost come," he whispered to deaf ears. He was used to talking aloud, knowing full well his parents weren't listening, but being near their graves brought some comfort. "I'll finally become king." Though the weight of that word still felt too heavy for someone his age. He'd thought he'd have at least a few more turnings. But like his father, it seemed Olivander, too, would be claiming the kingship when he turned eighteen. "I hope I don't disappoint you."

Olivander lingered a while longer, praying to Esias for strength and fortitude for the days ahead. He didn't feel ready, but that didn't matter. Jasper believed in him. So did Merri. Now if only he could believe in himself.

He pushed to his feet and exited the crypt before time wore on and the night got away from him. He couldn't miss tonight's feast, no matter how tempting that was. It wouldn't look good for a king not to attend his own party.

Though he had one more stop before then.

Olivander retraced his steps down the stairwell that led to the ground floor, pausing at an offshoot of the spiral tower. He looked down the singular corridor that he'd passed on his way to the crypt and lifted his gaze. Carved into the stone-white archway were the words *In Honor of Chaera's Liberation, Home of the Winderplume*. But that wasn't what caught his attention. It was the door at the end of the hall. He'd seen Nole standing guard earlier, but now the hallway was empty.

Maybe he's inside.

Olivander covered the ground of the short corridor in seconds. He reached for the knob and turned, not surprised to find it unlocked, though he had expected someone else on the other side. Pushing the door open, he first saw the back of Keeper Reve's dark head and his royal blue robe trailing behind him on the floor. The man was hunched over a table littered with stacks of books and paper, and he appeared to be intently studying something.

Olivander didn't want to startle him, so he cleared his throat.

Reve jumped anyway, slamming shut whatever he'd been engrossed in. "Your Highness! You frightened me."

So much for trying to be considerate. "My apologies."

"I'm surprised to see you here," he said.

Olivander held up his bottle of dwindling Winderplume. "I came back for a refill." He'd used most of it on training sessions and skimming mussels.

The keeper nodded. "Seems we are of the same mind." He started putting books back on shelves and shuffling papers, gathering the chaotic mess together in a way that seemed like regimented order, and moved to the small dais in the center of the room which held the Winderplume. The glistening iridescence swirled within the glass dome in a mesmerizing waltz, reflecting off the windows of the circular room. This was the sister tower to the crypt, so they were nearly identical in all regards but height.

Reve donned a pair of gloves and rotated a portion of the glass encasement, causing a small opening to form on the outside. Almost instantly, the dust settled as if it were merely sand upon a shore. He scooped up and poured some of the contents into an opaque jar resting on a nearby table. As soon as the sparkling dust touched the lid, Olivander could have sworn it turned the color of rainfall.

Quick as a flash, the keeper replaced the scooper, rotated the panel, and the Winderplume resumed its beautiful dance once more. "These prophecies will not write themselves." He nodded, holding up the jar.

Olivander looked around the room, remembering his question from earlier. "Where's Nole?" Usually, it was Nole or Hektor who guarded the Winderplume in shifts. They kept a running tally of how often residents came for refills, and they reported it to the regent at the end of the month. And neither man was present. "I thought he would be inside."

The keeper nodded. "He should be, but Lord Alyward required him elsewhere. He is concerned for your safety and has the courtyard heavily guarded for tonight's feast. But Nole was kind enough to give me the key. Perks of being the Keeper of Prophecies, is it not?" One of his blue eyes winked.

The prince chuckled. Maybe this would work in his favor. He could ask the keeper about the life-threatening words that had sent the maidens away; surely he could interpret the prophecy better than anyone else. Tell him if it was really necessary.

"If you will excuse me, Your Highness, I am needed elsewhere." Reve bowed and moved around him, pausing at the threshold. He glanced over his shoulder. "As are you, do not forget. The prince cannot be late for his own coronation feast." Then Reve flung him the key and winked once more. "Lock up when you are through."

The keeper left Olivander with his questions still lodged in his throat. The prince sighed. He would just have to ask them later.

He walked toward the Winderplume and filled his vial in much the same way Reve had filled his jar. The glistening grains crashed and swirled, turning a sparkling lavender once they touched the glass.

Olivander had accomplished what he'd come here for, and he should head back. *The prince can't be late for his own coronation feast.* But he walked deeper into the room instead. It had been some time since he'd last been here and even longer since he'd last opened any of these books. He surveyed the spines Reve had been looking at, his gaze moving left to right at the shelf on the wall. *The Old Archives. Vol. 1* had a paper sticking out of it, almost as if it were a bookmark, and Olivander was too curious not to take a look. He carefully opened to the marked page and read over the words written in gray ink.

Many ages ago, when the moon was young and had only a few turnings, Chaera was both budding and in decline. It struggled to flourish, as if infested with an unseen sickness—trees withering, water infected, the people as ill as the ground they walked upon. It was then that a phenomenon came over the sea.

One chilly Ekorm, on the winter solstice, a plume of dust purer than snow blew in from over the waters and covered the land in glimmering iridescence. Not cold nor warm to the touch, the layer didn't dissolve. Instead, the dying land began to revive. Trees grew fuller, water flowed clearer, and its inhabitants began populating the land in droves. And what was once a withering village became a thriving kingdom in a matter of weeks.

And still, the dust had not moved.

Magic had covered the land in unshakable repose, given by Esias Himself.

The people of Chaera took care by donning gloves and gathered up the dust to preserve it, wondering what to do with such a gift. Though some remained wary of the substance, most cherished it and wanted to see it protected. Three leaders came forth from the masses—Torrance Suntower, Ronan Rainhold, and Alastair

Windkeep—and together forged a plan.

"We should sell it for a high price and make a hefty profit. Chaera will become a rich and powerful nation. Incite envy in our neighbors. Everyone will want to be like us," Suntower said.

"Ne," disagreed Rainhold. "We should keep it to ourselves. Hoard it away. No one should know about this or else we lose the greater advantage. There is power in secrecy. In keeping what is ours."

"How about we settle somewhere in between?" Windkeep suggested. "We both keep it safe and sell it at a reasonable cost. For something this powerful shouldn't be held under lock and key, nor should it be given away frivolously. It would not be right to charge so high a price for a gift freely bestowed nor bury it away to never see the light of day."

The three men went back and forth, but they could not come to an agreement.

"How about we make a deal?" Windkeep, the oldest of the group, proposed. "We will divide the land into thirds—Suntower, Rainhold, and Windkeep. Whoever can build a fortress worthy enough to hold this magicked dust is the one who gets to claim it and do as they please with it."

The men shook hands and went their separate ways. Little did they know it would become the beginning of an age-long dispute.

Suntower's palace was constructed too close to the sun; they feared it would catch fire and burn. Rainhold's castle was built beneath a perpetual storm cloud which mucked the land. But Windkeep's citadel was strong, designed for defense and protection, the fortress unmovable on the edge of a windy cliff. When they cast the people's vote, everyone chose the eldest as the winner.

Windkeep claimed the mysterious magic, and as tribute to the miracle that blew in upon the waters of the winter solstice, coined the phenomenon Wyndsmeoca—Winderplume, we call it today. There, in the citadel's high tower, it would reside. And as long as the dust wasn't exhausted in a single use, its swirling iridescence promised a never-ending supply.

It was determined then that Windkeep's province would forever be the strongest of the three, while Suntower and Rainhold would appear the weaker.

And that was only the beginning of the ages-long fight for peace.

Olivander stifled a yawn when he finished the long passage. This was nothing new. Everyone learned the history of Chaera and the Winderplume in their youth, the original text having been copied and translated from Old Chaeran to Common Englasi, which was then distributed to the masses; the citadel was fortunate to have both. Though this event happened many turnings ago, this was why his father had worked so hard to maintain what he believed. As a descendant of Windkeep, he fought to uphold the first king's original goal, and by doing so, had encouraged peace between the provinces for years. In turn, Suntower and Rainhold had received Winderplume for a fair price. And they still could do what they saw fit with their share.

Olivander turned the page and saw *Winderplume's Gift and Signs* scrawled across the top. He read the paragraph below.

How does the Winderplume work, and what can it do? It only takes a heart bent on seeing goodness flourish and a pinch—sprinkling—of the dust over the desired place or object in order to enact change. No words are necessary, for the dust, once bonded with its host, already knows its purpose. Aside from its obvious healing properties, Winderplume is also known to make crops grow twice as fast if added to the watering, has given people clarity if ingested in food or drink, and can make objects fly for a time. It also can cast subtle illusions, can change the color of one's ink depending on motive and position, can change the property of fire, and has been used to make everyday tasks easier for mankind—amongst many other things. It truly seems limitless, aside from its ability only to perform what would be considered "small" magic. Time cannot be altered, nor can one be brought back from the dead.

Olivander bit his tongue. This was something he was still trying to reason out. His father had been sick, and if the Winderplume was known for healing, why didn't it save him? Save his mother, too? It couldn't stop the inevitable sting of death, but countless others who'd been far worse than his parents—including those who'd suffered the Bitter Blight before Olivander was born—were still walking the citadel's halls today. *Why didn't it work for them?*

He finished the paragraph.

There are many unique traits about this plume of dust, one of the most prominent being that the iridescent grains turn a different color depending on the person who carries it. The change is activated by one's touch or simply if placed in a jar already beholden to the plume. Most say it is a reflection of their soul or what matters most to them and changes color accordingly. For some, the color remains the same until the day they die. Regardless of the shade, the Winderplume's characteristics do not alter; the color serves more as a means of identification rather than one's skill, though some would argue they are one in the same. This occurrence is known as 'The Mark of the Dust.' (See section Of Winderplume and Further Properties for more.)

Olivander reached for his vial of restocked Winderplume. His color hadn't changed from lavender ever since he'd first gotten it. That was five years ago now. *Merri.* He guessed his heart still pined for the impossible.

He flipped through the rest of the book and stopped when he got to the desired heading—*Of Winderplume and Further Properties*—and read the words beneath.

Can the purest of Winderplume be ill-used? Though the dust was given to Chaera as a gift, some have forsaken it for a curse. What was originally meant for good can quickly turn immoral should it fall into the hands of a corrupted soul. Like with all magic, there are risks.

And what of the remnants? What happens should someone take what has already been bonded with another and use it as their own? As mentioned previously, once the Winderplume color is set, it will only work as intended for its initial host. Otherwise, that same dust remains useless in the hands of another, mere scraps discarded like carrion. Impure, so to speak. Should someone attempt the impossible and seek to claim this bonded dust as their own, it becomes its own mark: one of corruption. A fissuring of one's soul with consequences unimaginable. Hence the importance of not claiming the Winderplume solely for one person and thus rendering it unusable for the masses.

It takes a steady mind—one bent toward Esias—to remember this gift for what it is, unless one allows darkness to overtake all reasoning. It is not worth detailing an account of these grievous ways, but those who have let pride, bitterness, greed, and fear root in their hearts…take heed, lest you fall, too.

Even though the warning wasn't new, a chill climbed the prince's spine. This reality had frightened him as a child, but his father had often said it was a good thing to be reminded of one's need for grace. That no human was ever truly safe from a darkening soul, but with a little humility, self-denial, and an ever-pressing reliance on Esias, much could be mastered.

Olivander was grateful Windkeep seemed to uphold his father's ideals and Esias' truth.

But he wasn't a fool. He knew blackened souls still walked, or *swam*, Chaera's land. Darya. Though plenty was still hearsay and rumors, that wicked sea witch had done much to become what she was today. Regardless of *why* or *how* or whatever her connection to the Winderplume was, it was widespread knowledge that her choices were a good reminder of where unchecked darkness could lead.

Olivander brought his gaze back to the book and found a familiar poem a few pages later. It was an anonymous writer's work labeled *The Gray Inkwell.*

Green for peace
Purple for might
Black for perfidy
Red for sight
Orange for wrath
Blue for doom
White for hope
Writ' Winderplume

A large nick was at the top of the paper, close to the spine, as if someone had thought about ripping it out but changed their mind. Olivander's eyes traveled toward the bottom and paused when they saw deep indents just to the right of the gray-inked poem. It looked like someone had written on top of the old book, and the pressure from their pen had creased the page below.

As long as a guard stood watch, anyone working in the citadel was allowed to enter this room should they not only need more Winderplume but also desire to read up on Chaera's history. Not tear out pages. Not copy them.

Olivander sighed. *Utter carelessness.* But the question still lingered in his mind: *Why? Did someone try to copy the poem? Or was it something more sinister?* The marks didn't look new, so he didn't know how long they had been there for.

He studied the text again. "'Writ' Winderplume,'" he read aloud. As mentioned earlier in the book, Winderplume dust could change a person's inkwell into one of the seven colors listed in the poem, though it was rare. One's motivation or position largely determined the color; most people either didn't have enough to move beyond gray, *or* they chose not to use the dust for fear of their thoughts being revealed in the first place. Regardless of how the dust was used, the majority of Chaera's letters, books, and speeches were written in gray. Safe. Boring. Predictable. Aside from some of his father's missives; Olivander remembered glimpses of green and purple ink-stained pages strewn across the desk in his study when growing up.

Then there were the Keepers of Prophecies. The gift of sight marking their words red. No one else had the ability to write crimson even if they tried, especially not while the appointed keepers still lived or willingly kept their positions. And there were currently two in Chaera—one in Windkeep and the other in Suntower; Rainhold's keeper had been dead for decades with no one to take his place.

Years ago, Oli's father had chosen Lysander for Windkeep, and when he passed, Reve was the obvious next choice. In turn, their pens would turn red anytime they wrote. That was the power of the sacred dust. It knew the intentions of the writer, and that was how every keeper for generations had been solidified.

And that's how it would be for years to come.

From somewhere in the citadel, a loud ding echoed throughout the limestone walls, snapping Olivander out of his revisit with Chaera's history. It was the clock, and it was chiming the hour. The prince had lingered too long and couldn't waste another moment. He replaced the book on the shelf and latched the door before taking the stairs two at a time.

He couldn't be late for his first speech as almost-king.

9

NOWHERE TO BELONG

Merri

The Edge of the Sea, Somewhere
Maunt 1198

MERRI STOOD AT THE EDGE OF THE SEA, her burgundy dress swaying by her ankles, borrowed boots and cloak now resting in the sand beside her. Her bare feet were only steps away from touching the water for the first time since becoming human. She wasn't sure *which* ocean she was near, whether it was part of Kerilow Bay or somewhere new, but that didn't matter. Didn't all waters connect anyway?

She breathed in the salty air. *Eldarwielle, I hope you're waiting for me.*

After running and searching blindly in the dark, she'd finally found it. Her ocean. Her home. She assumed the Batesons had taken to the road, trying to catch her on her way back to Chaera, but little did they know she wasn't born of land.

She was born of water.

Swallowing her hurt over a love lost, Merri stepped forward, feeling the chill of the water seep through her skin and into her bones. A shiver crawled up her spine. Odd. As a sea maiden, she'd never felt the cold, but now, that was all she could feel. The sensation climbed her legs and settled in her middle the deeper she went in. Tiny pinpricks of fire, almost like the dancing flames on her windowsill.

It will get better. It will feel normal soon.

Only, it didn't. When she dove beneath the waves and came up sputtering, Merri realized something was truly wrong. Her feet couldn't touch the ground. And that's what frightened her the most.

I have to get back to shore.

Her arms flailed and her useless legs kicked beneath her, hardly moving. Wave after wave forced her downward, and salty water coated her throat. She was worse than stuck. She was sinking.

She coughed up water and sucked in a gulp of air when her head penetrated the surf. Panic gripped her chest, and tears mingled with her silent cries of desperation. She'd sacrificed much for love only to lose it all. And now her ocean home would no longer keep her.

She couldn't swim. She was drowning.

Help! If only someone could hear her thoughts. *Esias, help me!*

Down, down, down she went. The brine stung her eyes when she opened them. Her heart pounded. She clawed at the water, but it did nothing. Her last supply of oxygen was running out, and she knew there would be no returning to the surface after this. It was too far away.

Somewhere in the distance, a low cry resounded. Merri looked out to deeper water and saw a glowing shape approaching, its silhouette dancing in the light of the waxing moon. Its song reverberated through the tide, the melody wrapping around Merri's heart.

Eldarvielle. She'd know his voice anywhere. *He came for me.*

Warmth spread through her limbs as he drew nearer, his large upper jaw brushing the tips of her fingers as a sign to hold on. Merri clung to him with her remaining energy and let him carry her skyward. They cut through the water in a wink, his powerful fluke doing what she no longer could.

She gasped, spitting out water once they cleared the surf. Her chest heaved in ragged bursts, her body spent, but she was alive. She could breathe. The whale saved her.

Thank you, Eldarwielle. Thank you, Esias.

The night air was a welcome relief after tasting death, and yet, it suddenly felt unfamiliar in all the ways it shouldn't. And so did the sea.

Merri's stomach churned. She didn't fit here. She didn't fit anywhere. She'd tried to belong to two worlds and found she belonged to none.

Oh, Eldarwielle, what am I to do?

She didn't release her hold on him, relishing in his familiar comfort. He was the one thing that still felt right in this sad tale. But even so, their companionship had changed. For she could no longer speak to her dearest friend.

Could he still read her thoughts? Or had Darya taken that from her, too? A new panic gripped her.

"I can, dear one. There is no cause to fear."

Merri's pulse slowed. Her mind revisited an old conversation she'd had with Eldarwielle a few hours after she'd rescued him. "I can hear all the thoughts and speech of sea and land-kind, Merriweather. You can only hear mine because I'm indebted to you. A gift I'm glad we share."

"You are safe, daughter of the sea." His reverberating voice came gently even now, a warm timbre echoing in her head, welcome amid the combative silence. It was so sweet she began to cry. She hadn't lost everything, after all.

"What did Darya do to you, child?"

Merri told him about the bargain and her broken heart, expecting to receive the chastisement that was her due, yet Eldarwielle simply listened, his deep whale-song the only signs of his distress.

"That wretched witch. I wish you never went to her, Merriweather."

She wished she hadn't either. She wished more than anything that she'd stayed away.

What am I to do now? She repeated the same question from before. *I'm being chased by people I hardly know, I can't go back to Chaera, and I can no longer live in the sea. I don't belong anywhere.* She bit her lip to keep the sobs at bay.

"You only feel that way because you believe it. But there is a place that will keep you, though it will take some time to get there. Another must arrive before you, who is only a few paces behind. That is paramount."

Merri frowned at the whale's riddle. *What do you mean about another?*

"Do you trust me?" Eldarwielle asked.

I trust you more than I trust myself. If she had only talked to him before, then she might not be in this situation. *But where am I going?*

Eldarwielle's song rang anew, deep and unfathomable like the sea. *"To a place where no one can harm you."*

Merri liked how that sounded. *I could live somewhere like that.*

Eldarwielle hummed and clicked. *"Do not misunderstand me. It would only be for a time. You will know when you are ready to return, for it is I who will bring you back. All of you."*

All of us? Come back? Merri wasn't sure what that meant either. *But there's nothing for me here. Why would I return unless it's you whose side I'm next to?*

"The sea is no home for a human, Merriweather, no matter how much one wishes for it to be. But running away will not solve anything either. Eventually, you must face the road you have chosen, but for now, you must go elsewhere. Before it is too late." Eldarwielle's hum deepened. *"Are you ready, child?"*

Was she? Where would Eldarwielle take her?

I think so. Merri trusted him with her life, but that didn't mean she wasn't worried. She still had so many questions.

"Then close your eyes. This will take but a moment."

Before Merri could do what he asked, she was alone once again. Panic gripped her, already beginning to feel the pull of the sea below. She looked around before sucking in a final breath. *Be still, Merri. You can trust him.* Her racing heart told her otherwise as she submerged beneath the waves, wondering where he went.

But all she knew was darkness as a large mouth enveloped her. And spinning, spinning, spinning in an endless stream of brine.

A scream lodged somewhere in her throat at the realization.

Eldarwielle, her dearest friend, had eaten her.

10

THE PRE-CORONATION FEAST

Olivander

Windkeep, Chaera
Maunt 1198

"WYLECUMAN, CHAERANS, FELLOW STAFF, residents of the citadel, and those living within our province. And an extended welcome to those from Suntower and Rainhold, who have made the journey to attend tonight's feast!" Lord Alyward, dressed in a royal blue robe, stood on a raised platform, addressing a large courtyard filled to the brim with tables, chairs, and people. His advisors—Werthen, Reve, Kilner, and Servel, dressed in royal blue robes of their own—were seated behind him, while Olivander joined their line and sat at the end. A handful of guards flanked them on all sides, not to mention those positioned around the courtyard's perimeter.

Reve was right. Every square inch is guarded.

The flickering lanterns hanging from topiaries, jars of candles burning overhead as a makeshift ceiling of stars, and a pleasant aroma of seasonings and spices swirling about the cool night air made the outdoor space enchanting. A moderate ensemble of Croastan musicians—violins, cellos, violas, and singers—stood off to the side, waiting for the command to resume their music.

Olivander still felt ridiculous in his regalia. But there was little he could do about that. He turned the smooth purple stone over and over again in his hands, an attempt to soothe away lingering nerves. He'd repocketed the treasure as soon as Jasper had left his room.

"It is truly a testament to Windkeep's good fortune to have its peoples, and those beyond, here on the pre-coronation of Prince Olivander," Lord Alyward continued.

"Bring us back our daughters!" hollered a voice from somewhere in the courtyard.

"We're only here to get some answers!" another chimed in.

Olivander thought he saw Lord Alyward pale, but the regent simply held up his hand, seemingly at ease with the citadel guards flanking his sides. "There will be a time and place for your future king to answer your questions about his decree, but tonight is not that night. For now, we celebrate!"

The blood drained from Olivander's face. *My* decree?

"He's no king of ours!" another person shouted from the back.

More protests echoed amidst the crowd, but with one nod from the regent, guards removed the protestors from the outdoor enclosure.

"Whose idea was it to invite such lowlifes amongst the gentry?" one of the advisors muttered under his breath.

Olivander set his jaw and balled his hands into fists, holding fast to his stone. He squeezed it so hard he was certain it would leave a lasting imprint on his skin. Had Lord Alyward lied to all of Chaera about their daughters? Saying it was Windkeep's future king who had sent them away and *not* the regent? *Why?*

Olivander had been wrong. His subjects weren't unhappy with him; they were *furious*. If he were in their position, he'd be livid, too. It was another reminder of why he needed to assume his new role. Now. And why Lord Alyward shouldn't have made such a ludicrous decision in the first place. *So much for beginning my reign with peace. I'm sorry, Father.*

"As I was saying…" the regent resumed, as if nothing were amiss. "Before we partake in the meal, Prince Olivander will give his speech."

Boos issued from the crowd as all eyes looked in the prince's direction. His shoulders tightened, but instead of nerves, anger coursed through him. Why would Alyward do this? Determined to set things right, Olivander stood from his seat as the regent took his. He unclenched his fists and reminded himself of Jasper's words: He was made for this very opportunity and would lead these people as best he could, even if he had to grow into the role.

It can be done.

Olivander pocketed the stone and reached for the parchment hidden within the folds of his tricolor robe. He paused. He'd planned a speech, but the gray-inked words didn't seem fitting anymore. He'd been too nervous to use the Winderplume at the time, but if he were to write something with it now, he was sure the words would blaze orange. He had to clear his name, regardless of Lord Alyward's intent.

They'll remember me as the young man with big dreams. Dreams to see Windkeep thrive and bring Chaera's daughters home. Not the one who sent them away.

Olivander cleared his throat, nodded, and began. "My fellow citizens of Chaera. Fathers, mothers, brothers, sisters—" He choked a little on the last one. "Those from afar and those near. Two-legged or four." He nodded toward the one dog in attendance, which surprisingly garnered some chuckles from those nearby. The scruffy mutt lived on the citadel grounds because he kept the mice away. "Wylecuman." He continued onward, growing in confidence with every point he wanted to make. "I am uncertain of what you have heard before today, but it was not I who sent your daughters away. I would never dream of such a thing; is a king's life more important than the lives of his people? Should one prophecy cause such disruption?" Some people nodded; some still scowled. "I will do my best to bring them back. And swiftly. You have my word."

"Yeah, the word of a liar," someone snickered.

A muscle in Olivander's jaw twitched. His adrenaline was petering out as he continued talking, his uncertainty growing as he finally neared the speech's end. "In short, a king is not a king without his people. And by Esias' grace and wisdom, I aim to lead you as best as I am able. *Panci eoullym*—thank you."

A scant applause resounded in the expansive courtyard as Olivander reclaimed his seat. Most people stared daggers in his direction, with arms crossed or scowls lingering. He thought he even caught someone muttering, "He's nothing like this father."

He glanced at Lord Alyward. The regent's expression was unreadable. *What's his motive? Is this some vain attempt to put me in my place after our disagreement?* Olivander would have some harsh words with the man once tonight's banquet was over.

Keeper Reve stood from his seat. "And now, we feast!" His hands came together in one resounding clap, signaling for the waiters to bring out the food. The musicians started up their tunes once more, and the evening was blanketed in reverie.

Olivander wanted to feel relieved that his part was done, but he worried it was just beginning. It was as if he'd swallowed the rock in his pocket, all appetite lost.

A waiter approached his table and placed a steaming trencher of herbed pheasant, roasted ground plums, and caramelized sweet onions in front of him. Normally, he'd want to devour the entire plate, but now he couldn't stomach the thought. Instead, he pushed the food aside and reached for his chalice.

"Not eating, Your Highness?" Lord Alyward said, only a few seats away. He had some nerve to talk to the prince after what he'd done. "Cook prepared the dish in your honor. It would be a shame to disappoint her and her staff."

It smelled otherworldly, Olivander admitted, with the rosemary and sage blending into the melted butter and fat. Pheasant, duck, and even mutton weren't as common as the fish they often received from Daall. Living on the edge of the sea provided most of their meals, so tonight's feast was a rare one indeed.

But he couldn't enjoy it. Not after what the regent had done.

Olivander watched as people carved into their poultry and tucked in, savoring the aromatic flavors dancing on their tongues. *I'll remember this night for the rest of my life. The way Alyward made a fool of their new king.* He vice-gripped his chalice as he brought it to his lips, downing its contents within seconds. The cordial was perfectly cool and refreshing against his throat, taking the edge off of his anger.

But something about it tasted strange. Metal lingered on his tongue.

Maybe they chose a new import this year.

Olivander surveyed the room and watched the people watching him. It seemed he wasn't the only one not partaking of the meal. He grimaced. *Would that I could change things.*

A gentle throb began pounding behind his eyes. Massaging the random fuzziness pulsing at his temples, he blinked and lifted his gaze to the strung candles above. *A headache. Now?* The timing couldn't be worse. Though maybe he'd use this as an excuse to leave the feast early. That way he wouldn't have to avoid conversation with the regent all night. He pulled at his collar, tugging the fabric away from his neck.

Why had the courtyard turned impossibly hot? Had someone lit the fire pits? *No.* They were outside, and it was nighttime on the edge of spring. *Am I growing ill?*

Olivander stood, hoping to get something else to drink and shake off this heat and dizziness. But then the room spun, everything swirling to black.

"Your Highness?" Somewhere in the amassing fog, he thought he heard someone say his name.

He was falling, tumbling, and spinning. The heat was so intense, his temples set to burst; it felt like hours, maybe days, had passed. It wasn't until his head collided with something hard that the burning stopped.

All was cool and clear once again.

What just happened?

Olivander cracked open heavy-lidded eyes and stared blankly. The room tilted sideways. Looking up and down, he realized why; his ear was pressed against the floor. He appeared to be in a courtyard of sorts, that much he could tell. But there were so many people. Too many.

Where am I?

He pushed himself up, wobbly on unsteady legs beneath him, and dusted off the grime from his robes. *What am I wearing?*

A scream pierced the air, forcing his gaze to the mass of people. A woman stood, pointing in his direction, horror written in every crease on her face. "Imposter!" she shouted, her eyes wide.

Why is she pointing at me?

"Who is this man who wears the robes of a king?" someone else shouted behind her.

What king?

Rough arms seized him from behind. Before he could utter a word, he was yanked off the platform where he stood and taken inside what looked like a giant castle. Something solid smashed against his back, and he realized he'd just been pushed up against a wall.

"Who are you?" a man dressed in some sort of guard's uniform asked, scowling.

He opened his mouth to answer and frowned. Why didn't he know how to respond?

"I said, who are you?" The guard pressed his body into the wall even harder. The back of his head collided with stone.

"I—" he began. "I don't know." *What's going on?*

"I will take it from here, Vigil." A man in a royal blue robe strode forward, determination in his gait. He released the guard and watched him leave before turning back around. He narrowed his eyes, then spoke. "Come with me."

Where are we going? He followed the strange man through winding corridors and down spiral staircases laced with white-stoned walls and gray-stoned floors, his confusion mounting with each step. He'd woken up from some curious dream only to find he knew nothing, no one, and couldn't recall his own name.

"Almost there," the robed man said, his voice terse.

They descended more flights of stairs, the fiery sconces flickering as they went past, casting their shadows across the walls and floor. A door stood just ahead, and the robed man grabbed a torch to the right of it before pushing him through it. "Walk," he commanded. They were in a tunnel now; the walls were made of solid rock and glistening wet, smelling strongly of mildew and salt. And just when he thought it would never end, they exited the mouth of a cave onto a deserted beach. A little boat lay nestled under a tangle of seaweed, beneath a twilight sky. It would have been a peaceful sight, if not for the adrenaline coursing through his body. And the fact that he still didn't know what in the blast was going on.

The robed man walked toward the boat and hauled it up to the sandbank. Then he reached behind a rock and thrust a bag inside. "Some food, should you survive."

Should you survive? Hairs rose on the back of his neck at the implication. "What do you mean?" Suddenly, his arms were being tied behind his back, and his legs soon followed. His muscles didn't regain the strength to fight until it was too late, and by then he was already sitting in the bow of the small vessel in nothing but his undershirt and trousers.

"You will find out soon enough," the robed man said, edging the prow into the water. "And you won't be needing *this*"—he clutched the vial hanging around the young man's neck and snapped the corded rope clean through—"any longer." He kicked the boat until its bottom left the sand.

"Wait," he croaked, "there must be some mistake. I don't—I don't remember anything."

"Precisely." The robed man grabbed an oar and used it to push the vessel beyond the whitecaps. "No one will remember you after today." He smiled deviously. "You won't even remember yourself."

Something in the way the robed man said this raised small bumps across his skin. "But you do, don't you? You know who I am."

The robed man smirked. "And the secret will die with me." He gave one final push and sent the small boat out to sea.

No. "There must be some mistake!" He'd never felt so lost and confused in his life. What he could recall of it, at least. He knew nothing aside from this moment. "Take me back. Row me to shore. I only need some time to figure all this out," he shouted.

The robed man crossed his arms over his chest. "Time cannot help you now, I'm afraid. But I suggest you hold onto that bag should you ride out the storm; it might just be your salvation."

Storm? Apprehension turned his stomach. "What storm?" he hollered. The ocean was the last place one should be if the weather turned fierce. He needed to get off this boat. But try as he might, he couldn't loosen the ropes.

The robed man shook his head. "By tomorrow, you won't even remember this conversation," he responded. "That is, if the storm doesn't kill you first." The robed man tipped his head before retreating into the mouth of the cave as if he was never there to begin with.

"What storm?" he cried, but his question bore no response.

Now he was truly and utterly alone, for he didn't even know himself.

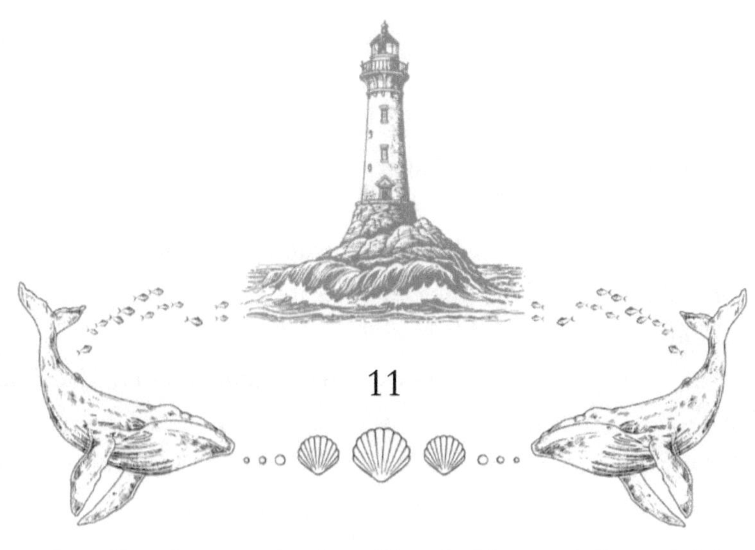

11

A SLIP INTO NOTHINGNESS

Nameless

Kerilow Bay, Chaera
Maunt 1198

Who am I? Why can't I remember?

The boat rocked beneath him, carrying him farther out to sea. His bonds were tight, his stomach was growling, and the rising sun was already beginning to feel a little too warm.

He'd been out on these waters all night and was now too far away from the coast to tell if any land was on the horizon. His voice was hoarse from calling for help for endless hours, praying someone would hear him, but his efforts were useless. If he thought about things too much, he started to feel himself dip into lunacy.

Perhaps I already am insane.

What had that robed man meant about a storm? The seas were as still as glass, aside from the occasional ripple. He'd spotted a turtle surfacing for air a few minutes ago, and then a fin which looked to belong to some larger fish.

Aside from that, all was quiet.

How did I end up here?

He tried recalling the events leading up to now, but his mind was a haze, like he was attempting to navigate a dark, unfamiliar room blindfolded.

The hours passed by as he slowly baked under the sun. The more time he spent out here on this vessel, the more he started believing he had always meant to climb aboard it. His past was a distant memory now, and all he had was the bow beneath him and a steady sunrise in his future.

What will happen when I get back home?

He didn't know where home was, but he figured he'd know it when he came to it.

That's right. I only went for a turn about the sea. I've merely gotten lost.

"I'll find my way back," he said, speaking aloud for the first time in a while. His throat was dry, having no one but himself to talk to on this voyage.

But he found he didn't care.

The only thing troubling him was the ropes on his wrists and ankles. He hadn't recalled being tied up, and he wondered what purpose they served him on this jaunt across the ocean. Hadn't he come out here to enjoy the sunrise?

"When I get back, I'll simply have them removed." He shrugged off the feeling that someone had done this to him on purpose. After all, what purpose would it serve to tie up an unassuming man?

He squinted into the distance, relief flooding his body upon seeing what looked like a ridge of mountains. *Home. At last.* He just prayed this boat would bring him there safely without an oar.

It seemed his wish was coming true; either he was getting closer, or the mountains were drawing nearer.

His stomach dropped. *Wait. Mountains don't move.*

With his gaze fixed on the horizon, he realized something was wrong. He couldn't be moving more than a few centimeters at a time, and the mountains were growing exponentially in size.

Those aren't mountains.

A massive wave rolled beneath his boat, sending his small vessel careening left and right. Another one followed and smashed into him with so much force, he almost fell overboard. The breath left his lungs, and his clothes puckered against his skin. It took him a few seconds to realize the hull had filled up to his knees with water, and was now precariously leaning on its starboard side. It wouldn't be long before the ocean claimed the vessel whole.

"Help!" he yelled, calling out to deaf ears. He was alone. There was nothing out here but his capsizing boat.

But this was only the beginning.

Wave after pounding wave smashed into him, turning the once-glassy sea into a writhing pool of chaos. He clung to what he could of the boat in one hand, his bag of provisions clutched tightly in the other.

But it was no use.

He was going to die.

A storm had come.

And with one last wave, his boat was cloven in two. The strength of the water sent a sliver of wood in his direction, severing his bonds and slicing his hand.

And down he went.

Down to the deep.

No amount of swimming would save him now.

I feel so cold.

The sun has grown dark.

I'm slipping farther away from the light.

Water traveled down his throat, stinging his desperate lungs. Every part of him ached with the need for air.

Is this what it feels like to die?

His eyes bulged, seeking purchase in the dark waters, his entire body tremoring from the chill.

Who am I? Am I to disappear from the world without even knowing my name?

Despair flooded his core.

Is it possible to grieve the future? When it's stripped away along with my very essence?

Down he sank, descending like a millstone without a destination.

Rigid muscles slowly gave way to the ocean's tempting caress. Succumbing to the limpness and simply *forgetting.*

I already do forget.

I forget it all.

I don't remember anything.

Who am I?

A haunting melody rippled through the waters as a fuller darkness enveloped him in shadow. And before he could swim away, he was devoured by a giant beast carrying him away to a deeper grave.

Who am I?

Who am I?

Who am...I?

Who am...

Who...

...

FORGOTTEN

12

THE MADMAN OF TENBY

Jac

Tenby, Wales
August 1996

IS THIS WHAT IT FEELS LIKE TO DIE?

Massive jaws closed around Jac's drowning body, and a strangled cry rent his throat as his eyes shot open. He expected to see darkness within the belly of the beast that devoured him, but instead, light filled his vision. He wasn't in the water at all.

It was only a nightmare.

I fell asleep. Again.

He sat up and lifted his watch lying limp on the blanket beside him to read the hour. *And for a long time, too.* 10:35 a.m. blinked across the screen.

Jac swung his legs over his bed and rested his head in his hands, allowing himself to breathe. He pushed aside the light brown curls that hung over his forehead, registering the sound of crashing waves nearby. His pulse slowed. When living in a lighthouse on the cusp of the sea, it was no wonder its creatures infiltrated his dreams.

This wasn't the first time.

A shiver crawled beneath his skin. He had a vivid enough imagination during the day, but it got even worse at night. He couldn't recall when the dreams started, really, but they began slowly at first. Now, every time he fell asleep, unless he could avoid it, peoples and places he'd never heard of filled his thoughts, making him wonder if he was truly losing his mind.

That or he was supposed to be a writer. Wasn't that how most authors started out? Imaging characters inside their heads?

Though faces were blurred and landmarks were fuzzy, he'd dreamt enough about a man named Prince Olivander and a land called Chaera to write a novel. But he had no idea where they came from. Not to mention the beast that kept trying to eat him whenever he dreamt of the sea.

Jac heaved a sigh and looked at his nightstand. The surface was stacked high with books and atlases, his most recent read atop the pile. He assumed he'd spent another night too long amidst the pages of Melville's *Moby Dick*, to the point that it made last night's dream *worse*. His gaze scanned the rest of his small room. Towering stacks of books lined the curved walls in various heights, another stack on his windowsill. There wasn't much else in the way of decor save for a painting of a ship above his bed, a trunk to store his clothes, and a table in the center of the room.

Reading consumed the majority of his day. What else was he to do whilst avoiding sleep and keeping an eye out for ships along Tenby's coast? Aside from checking the functionality of the halide lamp and Fresnel lens, logging the weather, and maintaining the warning horn—that thing was *loud*—his post was rather boring. Books kept him busy and sharpened his mind during those endless nights.

Something to pass the time. Something to keep the nightmares at bay. Or maybe, provide some answers.

He pushed himself up from his creaky bed and walked to the arched window across his circular tower room. Squinting into the late August morning, he hoisted himself onto its ledge and sat beside the pile of books. He watched as herring gulls swooped into his line of sight and down the rocky cliffs, squawking over a cod from *Bae Caerfyrddin*. He looked right and could just make out the docks jutting out into the sea from Tenby's harbor, the pastel townhomes providing a colorful backdrop to the schooners bobbing gently in the surf.

How simple was this life.

My life.

"Another day," he said to no one in particular, his gaze cast out to sea. Jac loved the ocean, even with all its hauntings in the night, and couldn't imagine living anywhere else. But even so, his days were filled with monotony. Though Nain always seemed to find things for him to do. Speaking of his grandmother…

"Jac? Are you up yet?" her weathered voice called from downstairs. Nain was never one to sleep in, preferring to ascend before the sun could beat her to it. And by at least noon thrice a week, she'd make it a point to bake and ready baskets of bread rolls to be handed out to the locals.

He'd forgotten that today was one of those days.

They weren't wealthy by any means, but that never stopped Nain from being charitable. "Kindness isn't dependent upon whether you've a spare pound or two in your pocket. Give willingly or give nothing at all," she'd said every time he saw their food stores running low. And whenever Jac quirked a brow at the empty tin can in the cupboard, save for a button and a mote of dust, Nain would just shake her head and dig her rolling pin into the dough even harder. "I won't allow any Scrooges in this house."

She was stubborn, but her heart was as gentle as a lamb. Jac loved that about her, though he couldn't help his concern. Nain's husband had been the original lighthouse keeper of the *Telor Pendu*, but with his passing a few years back, she'd finally sought another caretaker in his stead. That's where Jac came in. As an orphan, Nain adopted him like he was her own grandchild—it didn't matter that they had only known each other since May—and he'd helped run the place ever since. His position as Tenby's lighthouse keeper provided some income, though it wasn't much. Thankfully, they were both pretty hale, but if Nain's rheumatism got worse… There wasn't a lot of wiggle room to spare.

"Jac?" her voice came again, this time more pressing.

He took one last glance at the horizon before hopping back down into the shadows. "Coming!" he shouted. It was hard pulling himself away from the sea, especially on mornings after disturbing dreams, but in the end, the smell of warm, buttered *baps* won out. Not to mention the brusque scolding Nain would give him if he lingered too long.

He tugged on a pair of jeans and a cream-colored t-shirt before descending the spiral staircase to the floor below. At the landing, he passed the small room that belonged to his grandmother and walked into the round kitchen. Paint chipped off the white cabinets, grout cracked behind the laminate counters, and the wooden floorboards were warped by the sea. A small table and four chairs rested in the center of the room. Character and history were woven into every fiber of this place.

The Telor Pendu was an average-sized lighthouse, with just enough space for the two of them. The *ystafell ymolchi* required a brief walk outside in an adjacent building, but unlike the main tower, the bathroom was unheated. The black roof—or blackcap, as it was named for—of both structures helped provide some warmth, though the white-stone and concrete walls did the opposite. The middle of winter knew this keenly.

"Took you long enough," Nain said upon his arrival. She winked up at him, and Jac couldn't help smiling back. When standing, she was at least two heads shorter than he, nevermind when she was sitting down. Her bob looked extra gray this morning, as if the previous brown had been dipped in ashes, and the tanned skin surrounding her emerald eyes was never short of wrinkle lines. The woman always bore some sort of expression, most often mock exasperation when it came to Jac, so whenever Nain chose to wink instead of scowl, he knew it'd be a good day.

"You're looking well this morning, Nain. Is that a new dress?" He reached for one of the baps on the counter and crammed the entire thing in his mouth, swallowing the bread faster than he chewed it. Within seconds, he washed the roll down with a glass of water.

"Surprised you noticed when your head is stuck inside books and the refrigerator most of the time." She laughed, crossing her arms over the light blue material. "Finished sewing it last night, I'll have you know."

"I'm amazed you have the patience for it."

"And *I'm* amazed you don't get tired of all those words." She watched as Jac brought another roll to his mouth. "And the same fare day in and day out."

"How could I ever tire of your baking, Nain? Mmm. Delicious." He wiped his mouth with his arm and reached for a third roll.

Nain slapped his hand away before he even picked it up. "Leave some for the rest of *Cymru*, would you?" She chuckled. "You act like you haven't seen a speck of food in weeks. Which I know isn't true because I watched you eat a whole plate of *Aberffraw* biscuits last night."

"A feat I'm quite proud of."

"I swear, you youths are built with ever-expanding stomachs. I can't keep up." She threw her hands up in defeat before grabbing the handles of six small baskets off the table and giving them to him. "Now off with you, before you wreak more havoc on the few baps we have left. The addresses are on top." She ushered him toward the lancet-shaped front door, walking as fast as one could with aching joints.

Jac had just enough time to snag his messenger bag before Nain practically pushed him in the direction of town. He had plans to visit the library before returning home.

Feeling like a pack mule with all his baskets, Jac strategically placed them in the crate on the back of his red vintage Schwinn so as not to flatten the rolls. As usual, it was a tight fit. He suppressed a small groan; this wasn't the first time he wished they could afford a car. He picked up one of the address cards and read it aloud. "Adara Goff. 4 Steeple Street." He knew Adara from church—her father was the bishop. "Easy enough."

Long shadows spread across the ground, and he glanced upward, noticing the dark clouds overtaking the once-sunny skies. Wales was like that; sunny one day, cloudy the next—even nearing the end of August. *All the more reason to own a vehicle.*

Jac hopped on his bicycle and pedaled the few miles into the heart of Tenby. If he was lucky, he'd get this errand done before the approaching storm.

Sure enough, today's batch was quick, and the townsfolk grateful. "Give my love to Nain, would you?" was said on more than one account. And by the time the skies had fully darkened, he only had one more basket left to deliver.

"Orsin Locke. Keeper's Rock." Jac snorted at the rhyme despite the tightening of his ribs. Had Nain really sent him to deliver a basket to the Madman of Tenby? Everyone knew Orsin. Enough to stay far away from him, anyway. Well, everyone except Nain, apparently.

Jac huffed out a long breath. "Better get this over with." Thunder cracked in the distance as he hopped on his bike. *And before it rains, too.*

He pedaled back in the direction of the lighthouse, but instead of taking a right toward the sea, he kept going straight. *Clustog Fair*—Mary's Pillow—lined his path, the pink perennial a common sight along Wales' coast. They waved their long, stemmy stalks as he went by, unaware he was delivering baps to a madman.

The rocky path soon gave way to dirt and sand, and Jac could just make out a small shanty sitting alone in the distance on the edge of a large cliff. The nearer he got, the tighter his shoulders felt. *Has Orsin always lived this close?* Aside from their lighthouse, not many homes were situated on the fringes overlooking the bay. Not to mention, not many people were Orsin. Jac had heard enough rumors about the man to know he didn't want to stay long.

If he was fortunate, Orsin wouldn't even be home.

Jac leaned his bicycle against a crumbling stone wall, grabbed the remaining basket, and took the short, overgrown trail to the house. *Everything* was overgrown; ivy climbed the chimney and shutters, paint chipped off the shiplap, a few cracks spider-webbed the foundation… It reminded him of some gothic novel. He half expected Heathcliffe to emerge out of nowhere as if just walking in from the foggy moors. When Jac reached the front door, he contemplated leaving the basket on the steps and walking away, but Nain's voice rang in his ears. *"Be sure they see it. Otherwise, leave a note."*

He wasn't one for writing letters to crazy men.

Jac rapped his knuckles on the black door and held his breath, counting the seconds. Heavy footfalls sounded from within the house, and Jac braced himself when the door opened.

Orsin stood on the threshold, overgrown himself. He was dressed in a plaid shirt with tan slacks. His graying beard hid the majority of his neck, and the hair atop his head was only a few inches shorter than that. Jac suddenly felt like he needed to shave.

"*Alright*, uh, this is for you." Jac extended the basket of bread and took a step back.

"*Diolch*," Orsin said, his voice deep and hearty. Though his beard was thick, it was easy to tell the man was smiling. His eyes were the most telling of all; they seemed to pierce Jac's entire being with their blue gaze. "You're Jac, correct? Nain's told me a lot about you."

Jac nodded, unsure what to say. He hadn't planned on speaking much at all. Like Orsin, everyone knew Nain. But it was for far better reasons.

The old man opened his mouth as if to speak again, but Jac wasn't one for lingering. He was afraid to, if he was honest. He backed down the short steps and made his escape.

"*Hwyl*. Have a nice day," he called over his shoulder, running the path back to his bike as large raindrops pelted him from above. The skies had finally opened, which meant the library would have to wait until later. He sprung onto his means of escape before he could hear Orsin's reply and sped toward home.

If he was lucky, he'd never have to come back here again.

The rain hadn't let up in days; the steady droplets reverberated as Jac leaned up against the glass of his tower window. He'd already read every book he owned and was in desperate need of something new. But with the trek back into Tenby's bustling square, and with only his Schwinn as a means of getting him there, he'd have to wait until the skies cleared.

No use checking out new books only to have them waterlogged.

Jac could go and stay at the library, but Nain had fallen last night, and he didn't like the thought of leaving her alone for too long while she recovered.

So it would be another day stuck inside the lighthouse, puzzling out his dreams.

He flipped once more through the atlas on his lap, his research proving futile. Scanning over a map of the world, he bit his lip in concentration. "Maybe Chaera isn't a country; it could be a city instead. What about Windkeep?" He remembered saying the same thing weeks ago. His dreams had only mentioned the place, not exactly what it was. Like always, everything was *vague*, as if looking through a fogged glass. But where would it be? He knew there was a castle—citadel, rather—and some sort of monarchy. "It has to be somewhere in Europe." Other countries' politics looked a bit different than the United Kingdom, and Chaera didn't strike him as capitalist or socialist.

The pages blurred past in a wash of color as Jac continued to flip through. He scoured the contents, bringing the book closer to his face to read the fine print. If determination had a name, Jac would assume the moniker. He was at it for hours, locations and coordinates mocking his vain attempts at getting answers. It wasn't until the distant foghorn of a passing barge brought him back to reality.

Nothing. Again. No matter how often he looked, it didn't change a thing. Chaera was nowhere to be found.

He slammed the book shut and restrained himself from throwing it across the room. He'd have to return the atlas to the library soon, and he didn't relish the thought of owing precious pounds for property damage.

What now? Hope seemed a petty thing.

A sudden thought struck him. *Maybe I heard of Chaera from a story.*

"I can always start with mythology," he said aloud. He'd been so focused on trying to fit Chaera into his own world that it never occurred to him to look for it elsewhere. His purpose for going to the library now felt even more preeminent.

He looked out the window.

If only it would stop raining.

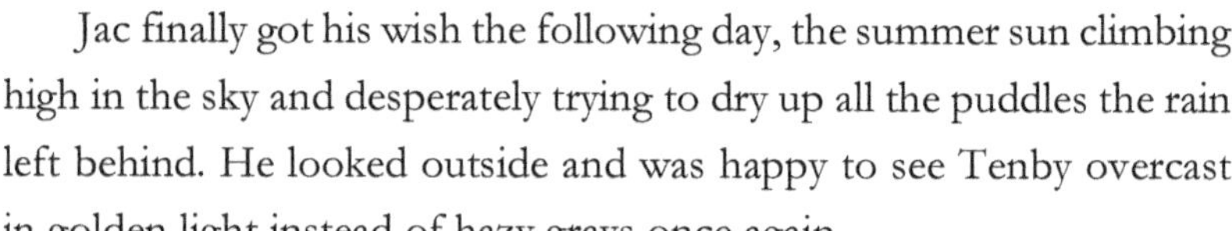

Jac finally got his wish the following day, the summer sun climbing high in the sky and desperately trying to dry up all the puddles the rain left behind. He looked outside and was happy to see Tenby overcast in golden light instead of hazy grays once again.

In his excitement, Jac rushed down the stairs and nearly plowed straight into Nain, who would have tumbled over if not for his steadying hands on her elbows.

"*Lesgyrn!* Watch where your feet are at, Jac. You'll send me to my grave sooner than I'd like." She laughed, giving him a peck on the cheek. "Now be a dear and help me to the table."

Jac reddened. "*Sori.*" This wouldn't be the first time his haste for literature almost caused someone physical pain. "Why aren't you using your cane today?"

She sat down and adjusted her brown skirt over her legs, waving a hand in the air as if batting away his suggestion. "Do I look like an invalid to you?"

"But your leg—"

"It was only a fall, Jac. These bones have many years to live yet, Lord willing, and they won't be made any better by walking with a rod of wood all day." She huffed and grabbed a gooseberry from the bowl in the center of the table, sticking the whole thing in her mouth. Some people preferred to peel the skin off, but not Nain. She closed her eyes, sighed, and wiped her fingers on the napkin in front of her. "There's nothing quite like a good *eirin Mair* this time of year."

Jac had to agree. They were his favorite fruit, and he was only too glad they grew along the path leading up to the Telor Pendu.

"So tell me, where are you off to in such a hurry, now that it's stopped raining old women and sticks?" she asked.

"The library."

"Ah."

"What? I want to get a few more things to read."

"'Course you do. And bring the whole Telor Pendu down on us." She laughed. "I haven't been up to your room in weeks, Jac, but even I can tell the floor is practically sagging from the weight of all your many tomes." She gathered two more gooseberries in her hands.

"One can never have too many books, Nain." Jac smiled and crossed his arms over his chest. He loved the library; most often, he just borrowed books, but anytime they had a sale, he was sure to grab a few at a discounted price. "What about you? What are you baking today?"

She winked. "Not a thing! I've got the day off. But Alban is picking me up in his car soon to take me into town."

Jac lifted one of his brows and smirked. "Alban, you say?"

Nain swatted at him. "Oh, out with you! You know it's not like that."

"Maybe not yet, but he definitely thinks otherwise." Nain wasn't only well known in all of Tenby, but she was sought after by most of the widowers. One taste of her Welsh cakes, and they were practically proclaiming their love for her on bended knee.

Nain shrugged. "If a man wants to bring me to town in his car so I can buy some more flour, who am I to refuse?"

Jac shook his head and walked toward the door. "If you say so. Do you need more pounds? I have a few spare coins in my room—"

Ouch. A gooseberry struck his temple.

"Jac Elis Hughes, you will do no such thing." Nain scowled, though there was a mischievous glint in her eyes. "Now go before I think of some errand to send you on instead of letting you go to your second home."

He chuckled, grabbed his messenger bag, and stepped outside into the sunshine. He hopped onto his bike and cast his gaze toward the glistening bay. The sea breeze tousled his hair and clothes as he pedaled, the smell of salt tickling his nose. He breathed it in. On days like these, it was a little easier to be thankful for what he had instead of what he didn't. A bike allowed a better view of the sea, anyway. He didn't think he could ever live far away from the water, not when he was so used to living on its edge.

Jac continued into town, the purpose of his visit settling on him afresh. He visited the library at least twice a week, if not more. This time, though, it felt different. He was ready for more information, and he had high hopes the endless shelves of books would hold the answers.

Town was bustling today, with people walking along narrow, cobbled streets and shop owners trying to entice them into their stores with flashy signs. Tenby was known as a tourist destination, especially now during the warmer months. But unluckily for them, Jac wouldn't be purchasing anything. That was the beauty of the library; even the poorer folk, or those with little means, could afford to read.

He parked his bike beside a tan building that had *T E N B Y L I B R A R Y* engraved on a large plaque above the doorway. Locking his Schwinn up so it wouldn't get stolen, Jac walked the short stretch of pavement and through the large glass front door. He breathed deep. Like the sea, the library had a distinct smell: a mixture of paper, ink, and dust.

"*Croeso nôl*, Jac!" A pretty brunette in a white blouse and jeans stood at the front desk and waved him over, patrons already milling about the library.

He smiled as he approached. "Alright, Bronny."

"I was wondering if I'd see you today! Give me a few." She disappeared through a door and, within a matter of seconds, came back with a small tower of books. "I've had these waiting out back just in case. I picked them out myself!" Her golden eyes beamed as she placed the stack on the counter and pushed them toward him. Jac spent so much time here that the workers knew him by name and his reading preferences. This wasn't the first stack Bronny Vaughan had made him.

"Thanks." He perused the titles, smiling when he saw *The Fellowship of the Ring*. He'd read that one, and the rest of the trilogy, at least twice already. He also saw Bronny had added *The Wind in the Willows* and *Ivanhoe*, and since he hadn't read those yet, he selected them from the pile.

"Anything I can look up for you today?" she asked.

Chaera. But the internet had never been useful whenever he'd researched the location. "Actually, I was interested in checking out some mythology books."

She perked up. "Oh! One of my favorite genres!" Jumping on her computer, Bronny began clacking away on the keys. "Anything in particular?"

Jac shrugged. "Not really. I guess I just need a place to start."

She nodded and leaned closer to the computer screen. "Let's see… It looks like the majority of books are in at the moment. I'll take you over to that area."

Bronny led Jac to the mythology section, letting him know how they were alphabetized and the different subcategories under the broader genre. And if there was a specific book he was looking for, he need only tell her and she could order it later. "But I bet you already know all of this since you practically live here." She laughed. "Just let me know if you need anything else."

"Thanks, Bronny," he said. Then she left to wait on other patrons.

Jac preferred it this way; he could focus better when exploring the books himself.

Approaching the shelves, he scanned countless titles and recognized a few. His memory was decent some days, but in regards to his past or what happened years ago, it tended to be a little foggy. The local doctor said it was due to partial amnesia, since he had no problem recalling the present, and asked him if he'd ever gotten into an accident. The problem was, Jac couldn't remember. What he wouldn't give to have kept a journal all those years; it would save him the headache now.

"Maybe I read about Chaera in one of these…" *I know I've read about it somewhere. I must have.* Why else would the same place keep occurring in his dreams?

He grabbed a book off the shelf titled *The Odyssey* and flipped through its pages. He'd read the story a few weeks back but couldn't remember much. He also picked up *One Thousand and One Nights*, *The Iliad*, and *The Epic of Gilgamesh*. He'd check these out and read through them at home. Hopefully they'd share the location he dreamt about, and if he was lucky, maybe even mention the prince. And if not, he'd scour the shelves again before starting in general fiction.

He was about to leave when his eyes roamed the section adjacent to mythology. "Lore and Legends," he read aloud. *Similar, but different.* He scanned the shelves, stopping when his gaze landed on a gold-embossed spine with ivory flukes, bear claws, and wings surrounding the title. He pulled the book out and read the name: *Tales of a Lost World: Sea, Land & Sky* by Gerard Platt. The title alone piqued his interest.

Maybe when he needed a break from all the ancient stuff, he could dive into some lore. Despite his frightening dreams, he never tired of the mysterious ocean or learning about new creatures. "More nightmare fuel, I guess." He chuckled to himself as he added the book to his stack and headed back to the front desk.

"Found everything you were looking for?" Bronny asked, taking the books from him.

Jac nodded. "I think so." While Bronny checked out his books, his gaze roved around the library. A few patrons were scattered about the place, some standing at shelves while others sat down with their finds. One in particular was reading a newspaper in a tattered armchair.

Jac was about to turn around when he did a double take, his eyes trained on the front page news article. *Is that…?* He hadn't expected to see a familiar face, especially one so youthful, but he'd remember those eyes from anywhere.

"Jac? Hello?" His ears finally registered Bronny's voice.

"Sori, what?" he asked, still not turning around.

"I said your books are ready. What are you looking at?"

He swallowed. "That newspaper. How old is it?"

"Oh, that? It's from a while back; I can't recall the date. Apparently, some patrons still like to check them out. Not sure why since all that information is old news."

Old news. Jac needed to know more. He was hungry for information from the past. "Do you have an extra copy?"

Bronny lifted one of her brows. "Uh. Sure." She reached under the desk and rifled through a stack, pulling out the desired one before scanning the barcode affixed to the top and handing it to him. "These unfortunately have a shorter lending time, so make sure you bring it back within the week."

"Thanks." Jac nodded, grabbing all his belongings and heading out the door.

He had some reading to do, but even more pressing, he wanted to know why the Madman of Tenby had landed the front page news.

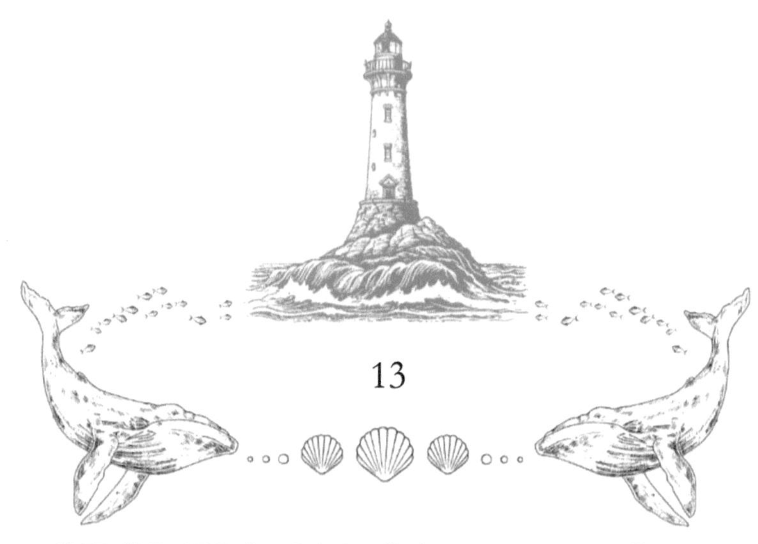

13

SECRETS BY CANDLELIGHT

Jac

Tenby, Wales
August 1996

JAC STOOD UP, WIPING THE SWEAT off his brow and eyeing the rows of freshly planted vegetables. "Another summer, another autumn harvest," he said. He'd been outside turning the soil for the seasonal crop rotation and fixing the chicken wire the past couple of days, digging up withered remnants from early summer and pulling out overgrown weeds. The raised beds were now filled with broccoli, winter squash, cucumber, rutabaga, turnip, and carrot seeds.

All that was left was to water them.

The Telor Pendu wasn't just good for protecting ships; its residence also boasted fertile soil. Ever since Jac had come to the lighthouse three months ago, the vegetable garden was bountiful. Nain said her late husband's green thumb was the envy of all of Tenby, a mantle she had tried to carry in his stead. And once she hired Jac, he took it upon himself to maintain it in turn. And rightly so; what they sometimes struggled with financially, they made up for in their garden by selling the produce for additional income. Always a plentiful harvest every year, it was rumored the sea air made the plants grow extra hale.

"Alright, Jac!" someone called to him from the dusty road. He turned and saw that it was the local fishmonger, Barti Morgan, from town. He owned a portion of the docks in North Beach's harbor, often taking tourists out on his boat for deep sea fishing. The middle-aged man got out of his rusty truck and strolled up the sandy path toward the lighthouse.

"Alright, Barti, how's it going?"

They shook hands.

"Can't complain. The weather's been a bit stormy, but the catch is good." He smiled and adjusted his fishing cap. His gaze landed on the vegetable garden and Jac's dirt-smudged jeans. "Nain's got you busy, I see."

It was true. Though Jac had willingly taken up the yard work, it was often Nain who prompted him when to do it. Which just so happened to be when he'd returned home from the library two days ago. She'd left him a note on the counter, asking if he'd "be a doll and get the new harvest growing."

She hadn't been lying when she said she'd find him a job to do.

But that meant his books hadn't been touched. He'd been too busy and too tired to read much of anything these past few days. He figured it was all the physical labor, not to mention he'd fallen asleep earlier in recent nights, trying as he might to avoid it.

Last night he'd dreamt of Prince Olivander again, had felt his sorrow as he stood at the edge of the sea, and thought he even heard distant whale-song when he brushed the sleep from his eyes come morning. It was getting harder to differentiate between what was real and what was not.

"She does it to keep me out of trouble." Jac chuckled, refocusing his thoughts on the present. "You know how Nain is."

"Sure do!" Barti agreed, chuckling too. "Speaking of, is she home? The wife's been begging for her *bara brith* recipe ever since she broke her foot. It's cracking good. She'd be over to get it herself if she was well enough."

Jac smiled. Nain's fruit loaf was one of her specialties. "She's currently out—"

"Not anymore." Sure enough, Nain was walking the path their visitor had just trod toward the Telor Pendu, the arthritis clearly showing signs in her hip even with her cane. But her smile was bright. "*S'mae*, Barti."

"Nice to see you again, Nain."

"Where'd you come from?" Jac interjected. "Don't tell me you walked all the way home." He looked at her bad hip and recently injured leg, raising an eyebrow.

"Oh posh. I told Cadell to drop me off so I could enjoy a *ling di long*. It's a perfect day for a stroll." Nain waved her hand in the air. "You worry too much about me, Jac."

First Alban. Now Cadell. Who's next to try their hand with Nain?

She turned her attention to their guest. "Now, Barti, to what do we owe this pleasure?"

"The wife's been asking about you."

"Elaine's a sweet one." Nain smiled, now standing between them. "Did she send you all the way out here?"

Barti nodded. "Wanted to get one of your recipes."

"As does the rest of Tenby, I suppose." She laughed and gestured for him to follow. "Come along, then." Barti escorted her up the lighthouse stairs so the two of them could go in and chat.

Jac stood alone, grateful to be done with the outdoor tasks. But now something was troubling him. It was more than just seeing Nain pushing herself beyond her means; that woman had more grit than aches. It was something else.

The car that had come for Nain earlier had driven her into town, so why then had she walked home from the other direction? More specifically, from the direction of where the Madman of Tenby lived?

Gooseflesh prickled his skin, and it wasn't just from the sea winds. Suddenly, it felt even more pressing to read that newspaper article.

After a much-needed shower in the outhouse, Jac sat once more in his tower loft, the newspaper smoothed out across his lap. The date read 1966. Bronny had mentioned it was old, but Jac didn't realize it was *thirty* years old. Unsurprisingly, Orsin's picture looked vastly different from the version Jac had seen standing in the doorway of his house. His beard had been shorter and darker back then, and it was full and grayer now. Only the sharp look in his blue eyes remained the same.

"'The Madman of Tenby: Is He Truly Mad?'" Jac read the headline aloud, wondering the same thing himself. It was well known across Wales that Orsin wasn't fit for proper company, but it was never really stated *why*.

Jac assumed that, over the years, the reasoning had gotten watered down or forgotten, and now everyone just kept their distance due to the rumors. But that reasoning no longer suited him. His curiosity demanded more. What was wrong with the strange man?

He read the opening lines, preparing himself for the worst.

Everyone loves a good story, but what happens when you think you're in one? Fact or fiction, truth or make-believe? Some lines are blurrier than others, and for The Madman of Tenby, that's truer than most. All last week, a weather-beaten man in strange attire was seen walking the shoreline morning until night, muttering under his breath and refusing to do much else aside from munch on seaweed and drink water out of a clam shell. When approached by the local journalist, he avoided the reporter entirely, refusing to give his name or state his purpose. It wasn't until a man and his wife, a Mr. and Mrs. Hughes—local and well-beloved to the town of Tenby—approached the shore-walker and finally learned of his name: Orsin L. Locke.
But it doesn't end there.

Jac paused his reading, his gaze skimming over the lines once more. *Mr. and Mrs. Hughes?* His mind sped like a turbulent wave. *His* last name was Hughes, having adopted it from Nain herself after she'd taken him in. Was this some sort of coincidence?

He kept reading.

When Mrs. Hughes asked the man if he was from around here, he questioned where 'here' was. He went on to say how the look, smell, and air was not that of his home.
When Mr. Hughes inquired if the man needed some help finding his way back, he said he had tried but there was no going back to be had. The sea would not take him; it wouldn't let him pass.
The Hugheses left Orsin soon after, but the mystery of the man still remains. Though he no longer walks the water's edge every day, one can still find him mumbling in his secluded seaside cottage on the edge of Tenby's coast.
Will we ever find the answers to this enigma? Maybe not, but for now, it's best to keep one's distance should the man turn wild.

If he came from the sea like he claims, then there's something far fishier here than mere fancy.

Jac scanned the words again. Once, twice, three times. *What did I just read?* The article left him with more questions than he'd started out with. Orsin really *was* mad, or so it seemed. Had the man truly come from the sea? What did he mean by 'it wouldn't take him'?

Jac's head spun, and he gripped the newspaper harder than he meant to. When he removed his hands, his fingerprints left behind ink smudges on the paper's edges. An unwelcome present for the librarians when he got around to returning it.

Bronny's gonna kill me.

He needed to speak with Nain. For at the moment, she was as much of an enigma as Orsin himself.

Jac couldn't remember the last time he'd spent all afternoon helping Nain about the kitchen. Baking breads and cakes, sweeping, and dusting the places she couldn't reach. He wished he could say he was doing this purely out of the goodness of his heart, but he would be lying if he denied his motives. Nain was more apt to talk if she wasn't on her feet all day, and he wanted to be sure she'd had plenty of "rest" before he peppered her with questions about Orsin.

Besides, the movement was good for his muscles. After another fitful night's sleep that included more troubling dreams of the prince, Jac needed to take his mind off of them. But it wasn't always successful.

"Watch what you're about, Jac!" Nain interrupted him from her seat at the table. "You'll not only wipe the coating off, but you'll wear a hole right through the metal!"

He looked down, the pot in his hands innocent against his vigorous ministrations. He'd been thinking about his dream again, about how poorly Olivander had been treated and how confusing it was when his memory was stripped away like it was nothing… He hadn't realized what he was doing.

I really need to find some answers. Or start writing a book.

After a few more hours of working himself stiff, Jac finally pulled over a chair and sat next to Nain, who was happily sewing by the light of a burning candle—she preferred this to the electric bulb overhead, saying it was easier on her eyes. The sun had set, the moon had shed its cloak, and their cozy home of the Telor Pendu was quiet. Only the distant sound of the thundering waves down by the rocks echoed in the background.

"Can't tell you how good it feels to be sitting this long." Nain smiled at him. "But don't spoil me, Jac. These limbs shouldn't stay useless forever. You'll send me to my grave much too soon."

"What is it about me that's always sending you to an early grave, Nain? Am I really that much trouble?" Jac jested, popping one of the mini Welsh cakes he'd baked into his mouth.

"The best men are." She winked. "I should know. Alun topped them all. Oh, how I miss the old *cwtiar.*" She sighed, adding more stitches to the sock she aimed to fix.

With the mention of her late husband, Jac figured now was as good a time as any to bring up the news article. He sucked in a breath and jumped in before Nain had a chance to steer the conversation elsewhere. He cleared his throat. "I stumbled across an old newspaper in the library." He paused, gauging Nain's reaction. She kept sewing and didn't seem bothered, so he pressed on. "It mentioned the Madman of Tenby, and a married couple with the last name Hughes."

Still, no reaction.

"And I figured that maybe…" He paused again, not sure why

words were so difficult all of a sudden. "Well, I was wondering if—"

"What are you getting at, Jac?" Nain dropped her hands into her lap, looking him in the eye. He swallowed, pulling the newspaper out from beneath the table. Her eyebrows rose. "Since when did you put that there?"

"I wanted to know if the article was talking about you." He finally spat it out, placing the newspaper in front of her. "I know there are a lot of Hugheses in Wales, but I don't know, it just seemed like something you would do—approach a strange man and all that."

"You think Alun and I talked to Orsin?" Nain asked, raising an eyebrow again.

Jac nodded, feeling hopeful. But maybe he shouldn't. After all, it probably was wisest to keep his distance from the man, not unearth the reason for his madness.

Nain's stern façade cracked, and then she smiled, the candlelight casting flickering shadows over her wrinkles. "I was wondering how long it'd take you to find that out."

"Wait. What?" Whatever he expected, it wasn't this.

"I know how often you go to the library, Jac. It was only a matter of time until you read every piece of written material in that place." She chuckled. "I figured you'd eventually put two and two together, and then you'd come seeking answers."

Am I that predictable?

"The question is, what is it that you would like to know?" Nain leaned in closer, studying him.

Jac hesitated only a moment before unfolding the newspaper and pointing to Orsin's picture. "I want to know if he's truly as mad as everyone says he is." He glanced up at Nain. "And if so, I want to know why you visited his house the other day when you'd previously headed into town." The last part was more of a stretch, considering he didn't *know* Nain had gone to Orsin's, but he ventured a guess anyway.

"Ha!" She set her sewing down on the table, a glimmer in her eyes. "Nothing gets by you, does it, Jac?" She grabbed the news article, looked at it briefly, and nodded before setting it aside. "Now, I'll ask you a question first. Just because someone looks or behaves differently than you, does that mean you treat them poorly?"

Jac didn't have to think very hard. "Well, no. That'd be ridiculous."

Nain nodded. "That's right. Oftentimes, there are reasons beyond any of our understanding that prompt a person to act a certain way. And it doesn't always mean madness."

He considered this, wondering if that was true in Orsin's case.

Nain continued, "Humanity is a messy, sinful business, and it's an unfortunate reality that people thrive off of rumors. The rush of 'belonging' to something at another's expense. If a person can make something out to be bigger than it is, *without* seeking to understand it in the first place, to cast judgment before understanding"—Nain tsked, shaking her head—"then that's a madness all on its own."

"Are you saying Orsin has his reasons then?"

"Everyone does, Jac. And to understand them, all one has to do is ask."

"And you did, didn't you?"

Nain smiled. "That I did. What the news article doesn't say is that my husband and I invited Orsin to the Telor Pendu for tea that same day. Over the years, him and Alun became fast friends, but since Alun's passing, I've made it a point to go over there on occasion to visit Orsin when I'm feeling well enough. That wasn't the first time I'd been to his home, Jac."

"Nor the last, I can imagine." He felt like he was seeing his grandmother for the first time. "So what's his story, then? Why does everyone still think he's mad?"

"Ah." She grabbed her sewing and resumed her task. "As to that, you'll have to ask him yourself. It's not my place to tell someone else's story when they are alive enough to tell it for themselves."

He should have known. Nain was always close-lipped when it came to others' affairs. Was he desperate enough to find the answers on his own? Maybe desperate wasn't the right word, but he sure was curious.

"I'll think about it," Jac said, taking the newspaper and folding it in his lap. Orsin still seemed an enigma, if not more so. Could he be trusted? He may not be the crazy person all of Tenby made him out to be, but that still didn't mean Jac wanted to talk to him.

Jac stifled a yawn. It was getting late, and there was still that book from the library he wanted to start. He should go upstairs.

"Do you remember the day you came to live here? The day I adopted you as one of my own?" Nain asked, stopping him from getting up.

Jac nodded, though some of it was a bit hazy. But why bring it up now?

"It was nearing the end of May when you had recently come to town. All you had for belongings were a bag with your name card and some waterlogged pieces of bread. No one knew you, and poor dear, you didn't even seem to know yourself. You were Jac Rooks then, and thank the good Lord above, you're Jac Hughes now."

He smiled. "Still one of the best days of my life." He was grateful to have some place to call home after feeling lost for so long. "But what has this to do with Orsin?"

"It takes courage to pursue a course of action you know little about," Nain continued. "To seek the good when others choose not to."

Jac stared at her. How did he fit into this picture?

"The point is, Jac, it only takes one person to make someone feel welcome. Like they belong. Courage is going against the masses. I sought the goodness in Orsin, much the same way I did with you—inviting you to live here as one of my own. You see, the two of you aren't so different from one another, I think. Seeing as you were once homeless and alone, I would think you'd understand him better than most."

Guilt niggled Jac's conscience as Nain's words washed over him. She was right. How had he not seen it before? *I'm a hypocrite.* Silence enshrouded the room as he mulled over their conversation, trying to figure out what to say next.

A clock hanging on the wall chimed the late hour of 10:00 p.m.

"I think that's enough for tonight," Nain said, as if reading his thoughts. "I'm fading fast, and my bed is calling my name." She stood on shaky legs and bent down to kiss his forehead. "You're a good man, Jac. I know you'll make the right decision."

She left him alone in the candle-lit kitchen. Thoughts of Orsin and courage and the sea's secrets dancing about his head like the flickering flames.

Courage is going against the masses. Nain's words pulsed like a vein in his body. The sentiment touched somewhere deep inside him, as if it had been an anthem he'd once sung but was just too long forgotten. Snuffed out from disuse. He then recalled the prince from his dreams, who longed for the same courage to stand up against the regent and his guards but was unable to make a difference.

Jac shook his head, chuckling. *What are men but cut from the same cloth.* But *he* would make a difference. Or at the very least, he could try.

Standing from his seat, he blew out the candle and headed for the tower.

It wasn't a question anymore. It was only a matter of when.

He knew what he was going to do.

He'd visit the Madman of Tenby.

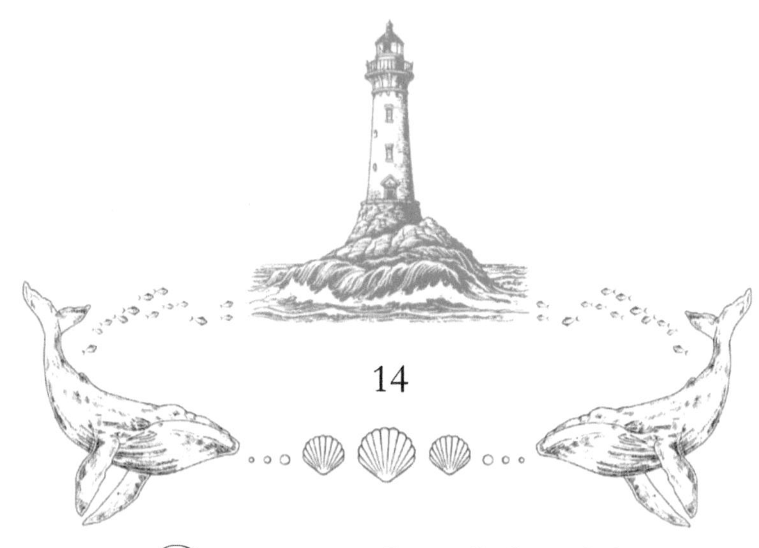

14

DREAM OF SONGS

Merri

The Edge of the Sea, Somewhere
August 1996

MERRI STRETCHED HER WEARY LIMBS, not yet ready to wake up. Her eyes remained shut, and her slumbering gave way to dreams. Hazy at first, and then vividly clear.

A fragile girl stood at the edge of the sea, her thin gown billowing in the breeze behind her. Every crease in her brow spoke of how she was all alone and forgotten. Uncertain. Afraid. She stepped into the surf and waded out to deeper waters. Her feet began to slip.

Though she was sinking, she didn't drown.

Where am I? she wondered as the waves carried her deeper. The space was soft, both cold and warm, reminding her of *something*.

How long shall I remain here? It was cozy in her dark cavern, a low lullaby echoing all around her, enticing her to close her eyes and sleep.

A deep song echoed in her ear. *"There is a place that will keep you, though it will take some time to get there."*

Who are you? she thought. How long would time stretch in her dark cocoon beneath the waves? *Where am I going?*

"Another must arrive before you, who is only a few paces behind," the song came again.

The girl tried prying open her heavy eyelids, but she found she no longer could.

Another? A few paces behind? She was so tired that even forming thoughts was becoming an impossible task.

"That is paramount," the singer of songs replied.

Why? Whatever did these waters mean?

How much longer?

"Much time has passed," the voice sang once more, *"and now the time has finally come."*

How much time? She suddenly stirred, no longer sleepy.

"Wake up, child. Awake."

Merri's eyes shot open.

15

A BODY IN THE BAY

Jac

Tenby, Wales
August 1996

THE BAY WAS DARK BENEATH THE MIDNIGHT sky. Jac glanced out the tower window from where he sat on its ledge, watching the waves crash to shore and feeling the warm breeze slip in through the opened pane above. He came here to think more times than he could count, and he'd been here for hours following his conversation with Nain. The same pile of books rested beside him, the new mythology ones from the library at the top. He'd already read a few chapters of each, but had no luck. Chaera still wasn't mentioned.

Jac checked his wrist watch and read the time: 3:00 a.m. *Good.* He'd avoided sleep this long. He could avoid it longer still. But now he craved something different to occupy his mind.

Tales of a Lost World: Sea, Land & Sky leaned against the pane of glass, as if reading his thoughts, beckoning him to draw nearer. He picked up the tome and opened to the first section, "Sea," and saw it addressed mythical beings painted in watercolors. Moonlight illuminated the pages.

"Sea maidens, sirens, selkies, sea nymphs," he read aloud, switching to read the rest in his head for fear of waking up Nain.

Seekers of souls, daughters of the deep. Though often confused for one another, all four have very distinct qualities and features.

Speeding through the descriptions, he finally came to the end of the section.

Though fictional to most, these mythological beings had to come from somewhere; a fisherman's offshore sighting, a haunting melody drifting over the waters, a mysterious woman shrouded in fog at the edge of the sea... So be on the lookout. Some tales may hold more truth than you think.

He shook his head. Perhaps that's why Orsin was seen along the shore all those years ago; maybe he was looking for a mermaid.

I'll know for certain soon enough. Jac thumbed through more pages on sunken underwater cities and another on the mysterious disappearances of ships in the ocean. *Skip.* He'd read about these before and didn't feel like revisiting them now.

His hand stilled when he saw *Lore of Sea Beasts* in bold letters scrawled across a two-page spread, drawing his attention to the painting in the background. It was of a kraken, with eight tentacles wrapped around a sinking ship as the creature guided it toward its gaping maw. The image made his stomach churn, but he expected no less from a book like this.

He flipped the page. A Leviathan graced the verso in all its massive, vicious glory. Next came the Loch Ness Monster; though a lake-dweller, it was equally as mysterious as the first two. More beasts made appearances as he continued diving deeper into the book, but none made him pause long enough to read on.

Until he came to a new heading labeled *Ivory Keepers & Their Unique Giftings—Sea, Land & Sky.*

Ivory Keepers?

The singular sentence below read:

Some animals serve more important roles than others.

His gaze traveled down the page and landed on the first animal he saw, a watercolor painting of a pearlescent humpback whale. It resembled its more colorful brothers but was albino. *Fascinating.* A quick turn of the following pages revealed a white bear—it looked like a regular black bear for all but its color—and an alabaster raven, which seemed like something out of a fantasy book. *Interesting.* Maybe it was Jac's affinity with the sea, but something about the whale compelled him to turn back and read the beast's description before moving forward.

His gaze zeroed in on the text, and he read the first couple words aloud. "Legend states—"

A low cry resounded from somewhere outside, and he almost dropped the book. Jac looked out the window and scanned the sea. He wondered if a ship had gotten too close to shore or, possibly, if two vessels had come to a head and one sounded a horn. But he didn't see anything. Maybe it was a distant gull caught in a fisherman's trap.

He picked up the book and tried resuming his reading. But the low cry came once more.

"What's going on?" Hopping off the window's ledge, he went to the center of his room and climbed the second set of stairs that led to the watch room above. He went up here at least once a day to check on the halide lamp, clean the lens, and log the weather conditions—wind speed, temperature, and visibility—to aid in navigation. But every so often, he'd venture to the outside gallery to view the stars in their full glory. Well, as best as one could when surrounded by a giant rotating light.

At the top, he leaned against the part of the railing that faced the bay, the warm, salty wind whipping against his skin. He squinted into the early morning, watching as the waters went from black to dark blue whenever the Fresnel lens bent the light to shine upon the surface. As the beam hit the water, it revealed what was once hidden in shadow.

Still, he saw nothing.

The cry came again, and Jac's heart thudded in his ears. It appeared nearer and louder this time. *This is no seagull.*

It almost sounded like...

Not too far away, Jac saw a spray of water shoot into the air and glisten like jewels in the moonlight. A caudal fin followed, milky white like a beacon of light itself, as the fluke sliced through the water and disappeared in a graceful arc.

A whale. There's a whale this close to shore!

A shiver ran down his spine as he remembered his book. Was it mere coincidence? Maybe he should go back to reading it to make sure. But he couldn't tear his gaze away from the sight. He watched as the magnificent creature resurfaced and disappeared again, all the while still crying into the night.

It sounded...distressed. Maybe it had lost its mate. Or perhaps it was simply lost.

Jac leaned closer. Or maybe it was something else entirely. What was that near the whale's nose? It almost looked like...a body.

The Fresnel lens rotated again and again, the light shining boldly upon the sea. The hairs on the back of his neck rose as a vein pulsed by his ear.

It is *a body!*

Jac bolted down the flights of stairs and out into the twilight once more. If there was half a chance that the body was still breathing, he'd do everything in his power to ensure it stayed alive.

He took to the rocks and climbed down the precarious coastline as fast as he was able, careful not to pierce his feet on any jagged edges. In his haste, he'd forgotten to put on shoes.

The whale's cry was even clearer now, the closer he got to shore. Only a little ways until he would finally touch the water. Every step was one of determination; a lighthouse keeper's duty was to make sure people survived along the coast, even if said people were being propelled forward by whales.

He wasn't concerned about the beast itself. Whales didn't eat humans. But he was curious as to how someone had ended up in the bay and why a whale was rescuing them in the first place. Especially during this time of day.

When he reached the edge of the sea, he plunged right in up to his torso like he'd done countless times before, though he'd never done so fully clothed. A shiver snaked up his spine at the sudden change in temperature, and though the waters were warmer this time of year, his skin was ice, his nerves fire. He took a steadying breath and went deeper, submerging himself up to his neck as he began swimming toward the creature. The beast shifted and headed in Jac's direction, as if knowing his intentions.

The beast's cry rang out in the deep, and Jac swam on. Water sprayed in his eyes with each vigorous stroke forward, the waves pushing him down as he broke through the surf. His body was slowly acclimating to the water, which was a relief. He was nearly there.

Soft skin brushed against his fingertips as he grabbed hold of the floundering body. It was a woman, he could tell that much, but with her hair matted against her face and the waves tossing them about, he couldn't determine if she was breathing.

He grabbed her arms and wrapped them around his neck, wondering how on earth he would swim, when the whale pushed them both in the direction of the rocks. Jac gasped in surprise, almost forgetting the creature was there, hidden beneath the waves. But he couldn't think about that right now. He had to get back to shore.

The whale did most of the work, and before he knew it, Jac's feet touched solid ground again. Exiting the water was almost as shocking as entering it, with the drastic temperature difference. He gritted his teeth and gathered the woman in his arms, climbing the rocky coast until he found a flat enough rock to lay her on. Lowering her to the ground, he was careful to cradle her head lest he make her situation any worse than it already was.

Please be breathing. It was hard to tell in the moonlight, especially here where the lighthouse's beam didn't reach. He pressed his ear against her chest, praying he wasn't too late. The gentle rise and fall eased his worries, reminding him to expel his own breath. *Thank God.*

Whale-song called him back to the waters, and he could just make out the glistening humped back and dorsal fin of the large creature waiting near the shallows. The low notes reverberated up the rocks, and for some reason, Jac felt as if the whale was thanking him.

The mammal wouldn't see him, but he nodded toward it anyway. Whales were smart, but knowing when to rescue someone in distress… Jac had never seen the like before.

A small groan brought his attention back to the girl. She was stirring, which was a good thing, but he needed to bring her inside. And soon. He didn't know how long she'd been in the bay or how much water she'd swallowed, but she looked exhausted and chilled to the bone.

By the time he reached the lighthouse, Nain was already there, waiting at the door.

"How did you—"

"Your footsteps could wake all of Pembrokeshire, Jac." She opened the door farther. "Quick now, bring her inside." Nain was like that; she didn't ask questions. Just saw a situation that needed fixing and stepped in to help as best she could. "Heat up some bone broth and ready the tea kettle, would you?"

He nodded. Leaving the girl in Nain's care, he busied himself doing what she asked, grateful for the chance to be useful.

He prayed that the girl would make it through the rest of the night.

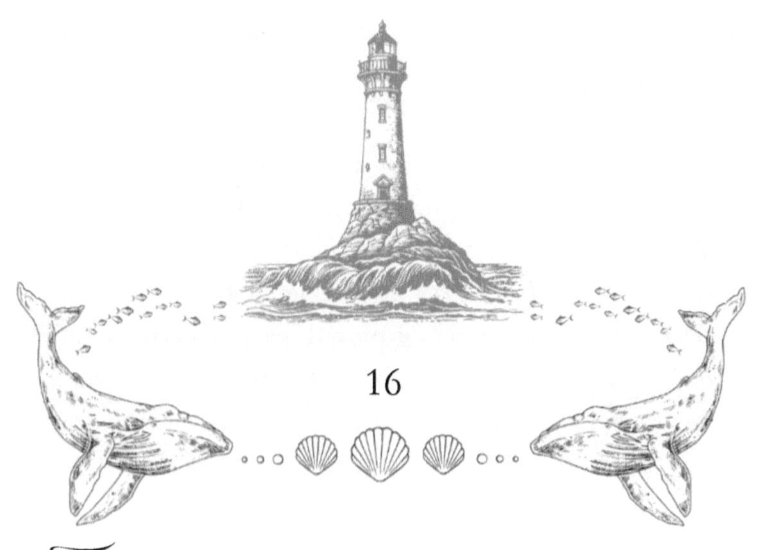

16

THE FAMILIAR STRANGER

Merri

Tenby, Wales
August 1996

"WAKE UP, CHILD. AWAKE."

Merri gasped for air beneath the pounding waves. She couldn't breathe. She couldn't swim. She couldn't find her way. Everything came flooding back—the ocean, the sinking, the memories. *Eldarwielle ate me. My dearest friend. He asked me to trust him and then swallowed me whole.*

She clawed at the water, desperation in every attempt…only to find she was clawing her way through fabric. She rubbed her eyes open and sat up, realization settling in. *I'm all right. I'm not drowning.* Her body relaxed, and her heart rate slowed as her breathing regulated. *I'm still alive.* Her hands fell from her face and rested on the quilted green-and-blue blanket she'd wrestled with moments ago, the material soft between her fingers. There was a pillow behind her back. She pulled it forward and hugged it to her chest, the smell of sandalwood and the sea easing some of her nerves. A yawn escaped her lips as she rolled back her shoulders, her limbs tight from disuse.

How long was I asleep for? She surveyed her surroundings. *And where am I?* A knot twisted in her middle as she remembered her flight from the Batesons. *Am I back at that farm?* One look at the circular room told her otherwise, unless they'd moved her to someplace different. *No. It's brighter here.* This room was small with enough morning light shining through the window that she felt as if she was touching the sky. And there was no more manure, only the smell of something cooking and the familiar scent of brine.

But what is this place?

Merri didn't know much in the way of humans, but even she was familiar with books. Whoever lived here loved to read. A lot. She looked at the towering stacks lining the white stone walls and focused on the ones beside her on the table. She turned her head, frowning when she couldn't comprehend the words on the spines. *Would that I could read.*

"You should check on the young lady." A woman's voice broke through the silence. She sounded nearby, though Merri couldn't tell from where exactly. "See if she needs anything." *Below me?* A set of stairs ran from the middle of the room in both directions, one set leading up and another leading down. She figured maybe someone was downstairs.

Her guess was confirmed when she heard footsteps echoing upward from the ground floor. She wrung her hands, anticipating the unknown. *All will be well.* She reminded herself not to be afraid; a cruel person wouldn't have given her a warm bed, would they? It was only Darya who had treated her so poorly, but a voice kept prodding in the back of her mind, telling her that she was unwanted and easily forgotten, and now someone who Iun would never love.

Why should anyone else care? *It was a foolish bargain, Merri.*

She jumped when she saw a pair of green eyes peeking through one of the slats in the stairs, looking in her direction. "Oh good, you're awake!" It was a man. He climbed the rest of the way and entered the room. It was hard to tell what he looked like with a towering stack of books in his hands, though the way in which he carried himself was familiar. He went to the window across the room and placed the stack on its ledge, adjusting the spines to ensure they wouldn't fall. "Sori if I scared you." His back was still to her, the only thing visible about his appearance being a head of light brown curls. "I wanted to make sure you were decent before I came in."

She blinked, struck by his tone. There was a slight accent; even still, it was recognizable. But surely it wasn't...

"I found you in the bay last night. My grandmother dried you off and gave you one of her dresses. Your other one is in the laundry."

Merri looked down and finally noted what she was wearing. It was a strange fabric, but the pattern was a comfort: little seagulls and starfish. When she lifted her head, she found the man had jumped onto the window's ledge and was now looking in her direction.

Merri stifled a sudden gasp. She stared at the familiar face before her and grew dizzy. *But... It can't be.*

The man continued, "I'm relieved you're alive. I wasn't sure if you'd make it or not."

Her stomach rolled like a tidal wave. *Why are we in the same room?*

"You wouldn't believe it, but I think a whale saved your life."

A whale. Merri's mind flicked back to the bay. *Eldarwielle.* Of course he did. If he *had* eaten her like she feared, then how had she ended up here? The realization mended one of the cracks in her distrusting heart. He'd helped her like he promised, even if his methods were questionable. But where exactly was *here?*

"I'm Jac Hughes, by the way," the man said, drawing her attention back to him. "What's your name?"

It took her a moment to register what he said. *No. No, it's not. And why are you asking me my name? Has it been so long that you don't remember me?* She rubbed her spinning head, trying to make sense of everything. Her fingers found a tender bump from where she must have hit it during her night in the sea. She grimaced.

"Are you hurt?" His brow dipped.

Merri thought back to when Iun had asked her the same question only a few days ago. The answer was yes. She was hurt in more ways than one. But now she was even more confused. Why didn't this man know who she was?

He jumped off the windowsill and walked toward the stairs. "Hold on. I'll be right back." He disappeared for a few minutes, and when she heard his footsteps returning, he had a glass of water in his hand. "Here, drink this. It'll help."

She nodded, accepting the drink from him. Their fingers brushed for a brief moment, and she looked up to see if her touch sparked any recognition. He remained clueless. Maybe when Eldarwielle had swallowed her, she'd lost some of her sanity in the process. Surely Jac was simply Jac, wasn't he? The water was cool and refreshing as it coated her throat, reminding her of the sea. But the room suddenly fell quiet, as if a weight of silence had grown eyes and was boring into her soul. She looked up to see Jac staring at her much in the same way.

"Your tongue," he said, pointing to his own mouth. "It…it's gone."

Heights Above. How had he noticed?

The tears Merri had been holding back finally escaped, and she averted her gaze, embarrassment flooding to her core. First he'd forgotten who she was, and now all he could see was her brokenness.

"I'm an idiot." Merri felt the bed sag beneath her, and she

assumed he had sat down. "Sori. I didn't mean to make you uncomfortable. I just—" She looked up to see him run a scarred hand through his hair, his expression pained. "I wanted to make sure you were okay."

He did? She didn't feel okay at all.

"Can you talk?" he asked.

Merri shook her head, wiping the tears from her eyes. She thought she heard him mutter something under his breath.

"Do you know where you are?" he asked.

She shook her head again. He was acting stranger by the minute. But she was grateful his questions were making things a lot easier for her.

"You're in Tenby."

Her brow furrowed. *What's a Tenby?*

"In Wales," he continued.

Merri's eyes grew round. *Eldarwielle?* Had he swallowed her for a second time?

"Oh. Not an actual whale!" He laughed. "You're in the southern UK."

What in Kerilow Bay did he mean?

He sighed. "I'm guessing you're not a local, then."

Merri shook her head in response. She feared she'd disappointed him. Oh, how she wished she could talk. It had been this way with Iun and his family, too. They asked her question after question until she moved her head or mouthed short words, but her actions could only communicate so much. Aside from Iun, they hadn't realized she was from a different world, that there were many things beyond her understanding.

In regard to the man who stood before her, he should already know that. But it seemed he held no recollection of her at all. Why wasn't he back in his precious home, glowering in his misery and only caring for himself?

He snapped his fingers. "Wait a minute!" He got up, and when he returned, he handed her some sort of book with a lot of colors and words she couldn't decipher. "It's an atlas," he said, pointing to a strange-looking shape, floating in what looked like the ocean. "This is where we are. See, it says Wales."

But she couldn't see. She couldn't read; that was the problem. She'd never learned. *Breathe*, she told herself. There was nothing worse than feeling like her body was a cage, and she was the one trapped inside it with no way out.

She shook her head and handed back the book.

Jac hesitated. "Can you not read?"

Merri hadn't known such mortification. There had been no need as a sea maiden. She shook her head again, lips trembling. When she gathered the courage to look him in the eyes, he didn't seem angry. Instead, he was pacing the room and stroking his chin as if in thought.

He glanced down at her. "But you can understand me, right?" His tone sounded hopeful.

Merri nodded, trying to figure him out. *Why isn't he scowling?* This new version of the man she once knew was confusing in many ways. Her gaze traveled to his clothes; she'd never seen someone in blue pants and whatever type of shirt that revealed so much of one's arms before. She was used to the palace uniforms or commoner's garbs, not something so...casual.

"Then maybe all you have to do is write down your responses. Then we can figure out who you are."

Her ribs tightened. *Write down my responses.* That was like asking a fish to walk on land, and she'd learned that the only way to do so would be to bargain with a sea witch. And it wasn't worth it. When she looked at him, his face fell. That was answer enough.

"Okay, so we are out of options it seems." He went back to

pacing, and Merri watched him. "At least for the time being," he clarified.

Time being?

He walked the length of the circular room, peering out the window before turning around once more. "Wait." His eyes lit up as he faced her. "How would you like to become literate? I could teach you how to read and write. Open a whole world of possibilities for you."

He'll teach me?

"I've got plenty of material here as resources. Plus, we have a library in town."

Merri looked at all the books in the room, wondering if it was possible. As a Dorsaleene, learning came naturally. But she was human now. She didn't know if Darya's curse took that ability away, too. But if it worked, she'd finally be able to communicate. She wouldn't be trapped with only her thoughts.

Merri wanted that freedom. So very much.

But her stomach knotted. *What if he grows tired of teaching me? What if I become a burden to him instead?* He'd already left her behind once— why wouldn't he again? Surely an offer this kind wouldn't last for long.

As if reading her thoughts, he smiled. "I promise I'll be a patient teacher. I can assure you it'll be fun."

She nodded hesitantly, her eagerness betraying her fear and confusion. Her eyes began to sting.

"Great. I'll bring you up some breakfast. Then maybe we can get started tomorrow, after you've had some time to rest. Sound good?"

She nodded again, and he left, taking his smile with him.

In his wake, the tears began to fall. It was as if a lifetime worth of memories came flooding back, mixed with confusion and gratitude over his generosity. How was she to process all of this? She tried blinking them away. But alas, she was a girl whose tears leaked like the sea.

Keep it together, Merri. Her mind was quite the muddle.

She recalled Iun's attentiveness upon their first meeting, and her eyelids grew hot at the thought. He and his family were courteous to take her in when they didn't have to. But they had so easily let her go. Whereas the farmer couple back in Lisethoorn hadn't wanted her in the first place and had tried to chase her down when she fled. All because of the prince's prophecy and the ridiculous mandate to send the maidens away.

She recalled him standing there with a wrinkle in his brow and his unwillingness to act. *He* was the reason for this mess in the first place. If not for him, she'd still be cozy in Iun's home, getting to know him and his family.

But that confused her all the more.

Now she was somewhere she didn't know with the very person who had sent her away in the first place. The very person who had ruined so much of her future. Who had first broken her heart when he left her behind almost three years ago.

And he had no clue who she was.

Why did he leave? Why doesn't he remember me? Why is he helping me now? Why, why, why?

She swallowed, her eyes stinging and most definitely bloodshot.

Why did Eldarwielle bring me to someplace where Prince Olivander is, too?

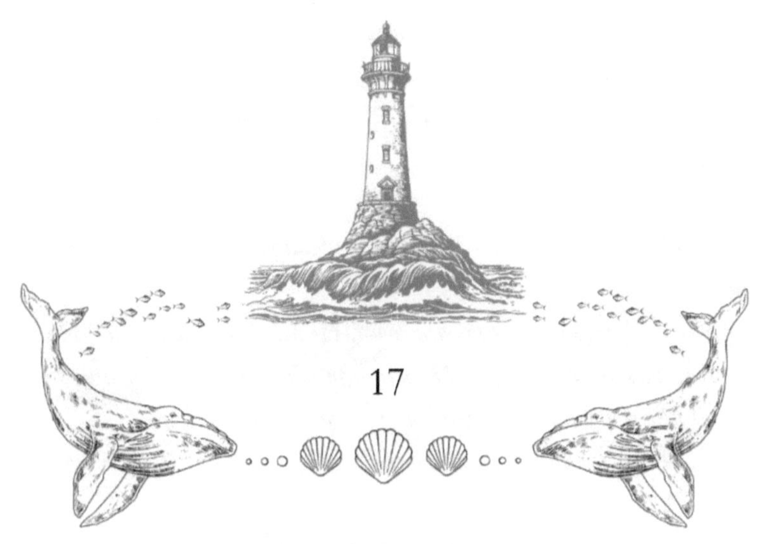

17

A MERRY MEETING

Jac

Kerilow Bay, Chaera
Nosh 1188

A YOUNG BOY STOOD AT THE EDGE OF THE SEA, *his toes wiggling in the sand. Water swirled around his ankles, and he giggled at the biting coolness. He was used to coming here in the warmer months, not on the brink of winter. His parents had said to stock up on the sunshine and lingering colors of* Ondin *and* Nosh *before the first snowfall coated everything in grays, so to the ocean they came.*

He picked up a jagged piece of bone and examined it, feeling like he'd discovered a pirate's discarded treasure.

"Won't Da be proud?" he thought aloud. Even at eight years old, he was trying to perform his duties as prince, hoping his keen eye would serve the kingdom well.

"Oli!" a voice called to him. "Oh, where has that boy gone now?" It was his

mother, and she was looking up from her chair, a crease in her brow.

"He'll be okay, Firan. Let our son adventure all he wants now." His father placed a reassuring hand on her shoulder. "Esias knows the years will pass all too quickly."

"But Matteo—"

"Besides"—he chuckled—"I can see his head poking out by those rocks over there."

Oli smiled, making sure to duck lower. He was hiding in a small rocky cave only a few paces away. He'd reveal himself soon, if only to calm his mother's nerves; he didn't like seeing her so worried. But he also wasn't done exploring.

His current search was for shark teeth.

"Hello."

Oli glanced down at the tooth in his hand, his eyes growing wide. Since when have teeth learned to speak without a mouth?

"Not there, silly. Here!" The voice came again, and this time, Oli cast his gaze toward the water. Two cerulean blue eyes stared back at him beneath a tangle of orangey-looking hair and freckled skin. A purple fin flopped out of the water, up and down, up and down, and Oli watched in wonder. A sea maiden! Her top was a twisting of leafy vines covering most of her torso, studded with small shells along the neckline. And she leaned on a rock, only a little way off shore.

"Hello," Oli said back to her. "Aren't you cold?"

"Only as cold as you are standing there on land," she said. "The water's quite nice."

"Geia, for my feet." Oli pointed to them. "Not for the rest of me."

"How would you know unless you tried?"

Oli tilted his head. "My mother always says to wait until late summer to go swimming. She's afraid I'll catch a cold."

It was the sea maiden's turn to tilt her head. "How does one catch something that you can only feel?"

Oli wasn't sure. "Maybe it's like the game of Seek."

"You play Seek, too?" The sea maiden's eyes lit up.

He shrugged. "Everyone knows how to play Seek."

It didn't take the two of them long to begin playing the game. Oli threw something precious in the water, only for the sea maiden to search for it, find it, and bring it back. And the sea maiden threw something on land, only to have Oli do the same. They were at this for hours, laughing and trying to outsmart the one whose turn it was to close their eyes, all the while enjoying each other's company.

"Hey, you're peeking!" the sea maiden said.

"Am not," Oli replied through slitted fingers, his eyes snapping shut when she looked his way. He wasn't trying to cheat; he just liked watching her feathery tail slice through the waves.

Oli had never made a friend so quickly before, and he was determined to make this newfound friendship last forever. But after a few more rounds, they finally took a break.

"What's your name?" the sea maiden asked, her head resting on her arms. She'd resumed her place on the rock while Oli remained seated on the sand.

"Prince Olivander Soryn Daws," he began. "But you can just call me Oli. Or Vander." He preferred those to his longer title.

"A prince!" She sat up straighter. "I've always wondered what it'd be like to live in a castle. Tell me, is it awfully romantic?"

"If you count eating with two different forks during dinner and always wearing a cravat romantic, then geia, it's truly awful."

"What's a cravat?"

"Like I know."

The two of them giggled.

"But I do get to train with wooden swords and learn how to fight," he added.

"What for?"

"My father says it's to defend our kingdom one day. I don't know what from, though. But one day I'll be king, too."

"When's that supposed to happen?"

He shrugged. "He says if he passes away before I'm old enough, then some regent will serve in his place until I'm eighteen. But I'll probably become king once *he dies when he's older." Oli wouldn't worry about that now; it was difficult to explain. "So, uh, what's your name?"*

The sea maiden's bright smile diminished, the lines around her mouth smoothing. "It's kind of long. And weird."

"Now you have to tell me."

"You promise not to laugh?"

He nodded. "Unless it's really, really weird."

"What?" Her eyes widened.

"I'm only kidding. So...what is it?"

The sea maiden ducked her head, fiddling with a shell the waves had brought her. "It's Merriweather Lea-Finna Caspiana Dorsaleene."

Oli's mouth dropped open. "Wow. That's... It's really..."

"But everyone calls me Merri."

"Merri." That was a lot easier. "I like it."

The sea maiden brightened once more. "And I like Oli."

He tilted his head. "What's it like down there? Where you live."

"Well," she began, "it's really open. And there are many pods of sea maidens and sea gents in my reef."

"Are all of them as shiny as you?" He looked at her tail.

She nodded. "And every tail color is known for a different ability. The Finnilows have green and blue tails and are good at growing plants and befriending animals. The Tidallyns have yellow, orange, and red tails and are good at strategy and tinkering, which is another way of saying they make and fix things. And then there's us, the Dorsaleenes, with our purple, pink, and gray ones, known for good memories and quick learning."

Oli's eyes widened. "All of that goes on down there?" He leaned forward on his knees, trying to see beneath the waves.

Merri laughed. "It's like a vibrant rainbow! We don't know our last names until we're four; our tail won't choose its color until then."

"You aren't born with a last name?" That was hard for Oli to wrap his head around.

"Well," she amended, "I guess it's not a last name. At least, not the way you humans have them. But everyone's pod gets added on at the end. I'm the only Dorsaleene in my family."

"I want to know more." Oli scooted closer to the waves.

The two continued talking, both sharing stories about their lives and asking questions. Oli had never had so much fun in his life. But eventually, his parents called him away. Their time at the ocean had come to a close, but he promised Merri he'd be back to visit as often as he could.

"Goodbye, Prince Oli of the double forks!" Merri saluted him.

"And goodbye, Sea Maiden Merri of the very long name." Oli bowed.

Then he waved, wondering when he'd see her next.

He hoped it would be soon.

18

THE DISTRUSTING GUEST

Jac

Tenby, Wales
August 1996

"You're telling me you told a girl you just met that you'd do *what?*"

Jac shifted uncomfortably on his feet. It was the following day, and their visitor had spent her second night in the lighthouse. But he'd only just broken the news to his grandmother. "To read and write."

"*And* that she could do so while staying here, don't forget." He opened his mouth to respond again, but Nain cut him off, wielding her wooden spoon like a fly ribbon. "What part of your eighteen-year-old brain told you that was a good idea? You don't know a thing about her, Jac, and you're just going to keep her in the Telor Pendu?" She put the other hand on her hip, ruffling the folds of her apron, and eyed him carefully.

"I don't know." He shrugged. "I guess I just wanted to help."

"Where will you sleep? We're tight like herrings in the salt as it is. She's already claimed your room, and my bedroom floor isn't going to work out, not with you waking and screaming in the night."

Jac reddened. Nain was right; he'd had another nightmare last night—the one of Prince Olivander meeting his death amidst a churning sea. But then…he'd dreamt for a second time as soon as his head hit the pillow. Something *new*. It was of a young sea maiden, though he couldn't see much in the way of detail. But the young girl reminded him of the one they had upstairs. Had rescuing her triggered such a strange dream?

"I'll sleep in the outhouse." He shrugged again. "But this girl…" He paused, not quite sure how to explain what he was feeling. "She looks terrified. Something's happened to her, and she can't even speak to let anyone know what it is. Part of me is afraid she's lost her memory or something."

Nain folded her arms across her chest, studying him. "People might ask questions, Jac."

"Then let them. I thought that *you*, of all people, would understand. To help someone who needs it most. You're the last person I'd expect to send someone away."

She held his gaze with her chin lifted high and stepped away from the kitchen counter. She stopped inches from his chest, her head not close to meeting his shoulder. "Are you certain you want to go through with this?"

When their visitor looked at Jac as if a mere touch would break her, something inside him broke, too. He needed to help her. And a small part of him thought she reminded him of *someone*, even if only from his dream. "Yes," he said. It wasn't even a question.

Nain smiled. "That's my Jac." She squeezed his arm.

"And if you disagree—" *Huh?* He lifted an eyebrow.

"You've got a good heart, Jac. I just wanted to see how long it would hold. Seems I've taught you a few things, after all." Nain winked, resuming her place at the cutting board and throwing chopped vegetables into a boiling pot on the stove.

Jac chuckled. "So she can stay? For how long?"

"Of course! And if you don't mind the cold, as long as she needs. Our home is always open, tight as we are. You know that."

Jac nodded, grateful for his grandmother's generosity. He sniffed the air, eyeing the meal she was preparing. "Isn't it a little early for cawl?"

She waved his remark away, throwing more veggies in the pot. "I'm of a firm mind that meals aren't seasonal: we only choose to make them that way because we can. Cawl is as good on a warm day in Tenby as a cold one. Besides, our visitor could use something to thaw her bones. Who knows how long she was in that bay." Nain shook her head, amusement glinting in the upturn of her mouth. "But that whale friend of hers…what do you make of that? Must be a remarkable beast."

He'd told her about the creature the other night. It was so remarkable, it was still hard to believe. How had it known to push them toward the shore? But that wasn't the only thing that shocked him. "There's something else, Nain." Jac swallowed, rubbing a hand along the backside of his head. "She, uh…she doesn't have a tongue."

Nain tsked and nodded. "I figured that out when I fed her the broth." Reclaiming her wooden spoon, she stirred the contents of the stew. "The poor dear. The world can be cruel."

Heartless, more like. He wondered how it happened. Had someone cut it out? Who would do that to a helpless girl?

"That's it. Just tilt your hand a little more to the right." Jac watched as the girl traced some words on a piece of paper. They were in his room, sitting at the small table riddled with books and ink-scratched paper between them, she diligently working and Jac trying to encourage her progress. They'd been at it for hours, having covered vowels and consonants before moving on to a few oceanic terms with the letter *W*. His aim was to expedite the process of figuring out why she was in the bay to begin with, and so far, the page was littered with the words waves, water, and the one she was currently tracing now: whale.

She smiled briefly when he told her what the last one said.

The ideal thing to work on was her name. But for now, he was trying to explain the alphabet and their corresponding sounds, enough for it to make sense for her to figure out on her own. It was much harder teaching someone how to spell their name who couldn't speak it aloud in the first place.

The girl looked up after she'd finished the page, sliding it toward him with a knitted brow. When he reached for the paper, she shrank back, studying him from a distance as if he too were a word needing copying.

I don't get it.

She had seemed eager to learn, but he couldn't help feeling like she didn't fully trust him. Which made sense given the circumstances. Trust took time to build, but he only wished she wouldn't stare at him like she was scrutinizing a piece of week-old bara brith for mold spores. He truly meant her no harm.

"This is really good progress," he said, looking at her letters, the pen's ink not straying from the penciled ones beneath. "You've got a steady hand."

She bit her lip.

"It's a good thing, don't worry."

The girl nodded, glancing toward the waning sunlight filtering through the pane of glass.

"Would you like to take a break? I could get you something to drink." He watched her carefully, hoping to glean a little more from her mannerisms. She'd been up and about since yesterday afternoon, but had mostly kept to herself or had gravitated toward Nain; that he understood. But was she still tired? Enjoying this? Did she think him a poor teacher? He hoped that tomorrow they could pick up where they left off; figuring imagery might be the next best step to learning the words, he wanted to show her some research books with lots of pictures. But if she needed more time, he didn't want to push her…

She nodded and got up from her seat before walking to the window, her gaze cast out to sea. Her fingers went toward the latch, but they fumbled with the fastenings, as if they had never once tried opening a lock.

"Here, let me get that." Jac walked over, letting in a gust of warm sea air as he opened the window. "It gets a little stuck sometimes. I tend to keep it shut so the books don't absorb part of the sea." He laughed, hoping to get one out of her, too, but she only inched farther away from him. Which meant his proximity was probably making her uncomfortable.

He stepped back, raking a hand through his hair. "Right. Well, uh, I've got an errand to run." He looked around for something that would legitimize his departure. His gaze settled on the newspaper with Orsin's article, and he tucked it into his messenger bag that lay sprawled on the floor. It wasn't yet due, but Bronny would have his head if this wasn't returned on time. "I'm going to the library." Nevermind that it was nearing closing time.

Should I invite her to come with me?

The girl dipped her head and turned her back to him once more, seemingly more interested in the ocean than him. Which was understandable, he guessed.

"Right. Be back later." He left the tower with his bag, wondering if teaching a girl who wanted nothing to do with him was actually a good idea, after all.

"Back so soon, Jac?" Bronny leaned over the counter, her smile wide when he entered the building. "This isn't like you to come by so late, not with only an hour left to browse."

He smiled at her, some of the tension leaving his shoulders. Bronny's welcoming presence was a night and day difference to the girl's who was currently occupying his room. Which reminded him, he'd forgotten to bring some extra bedding down to the outhouse earlier; he'd be sleeping next to the toilet for the foreseeable future. Thankfully, the place had been updated in recent years to have indoor plumbing.

"I came to bring this back." He extracted the newspaper from his bag and placed it on the counter.

"Find what you were looking for?"

"I guess you could say that." His mind was currently too occupied with thoughts of a mysterious girl and her life-saving whale to linger much on Orsin. Now he had even more unanswered questions than before.

"Is something bothering you? You seem distracted." Bronny studied him.

Did he want to talk about it? It had only been two days, so maybe all their guest needed was time. Still, Bronny was a girl; maybe she'd have something to offer in the way of advice.

"Well, now that you mention it. There's kind of a situation at the

Telor Pendu—"

"Is it Nain?" She stiffened. "Is she okay?"

Jac chuckled. "No, she's fine. That woman's made of tougher stuff than steel." He looked down at his maroon *daps*, trying to figure out how to go about this. Maybe getting too specific wouldn't help. Maybe he needed to seem a little more detached. "I have this friend who, uh, he's trying to help this girl who doesn't seem to like him."

Bronny tilted her head. "This friend of yours, is he a nice fella?"

Jac felt himself redden. "I would hope so."

"How do you not know? Don't you know your friends, Jac?" Bronny laughed.

"Right. He's nice, or at least, he tries to be."

"Then why wouldn't this girl like him?"

"That's the thing. They just met, and he's only ever tried to help her. But she doesn't seem to trust him."

"Well, trust thrives by growing roots."

"I know that. I mean, he knows that," Jac corrected.

Bronny's lip twitched. "Has your friend tried talking to her about this?"

"She, uh…" Jac ran a hand along the back of his neck. "She can't talk."

"She's mute?" Bronny's eyes widened.

Something like that.

"That definitely complicates things, then."

He nodded. "What would you suggest I—my friend—do?"

Bronny leaned forward, looking a little more serious. "Typically, people don't just choose to dislike someone without a reason. There are reasons for everything, Jac. So maybe this 'friend' of yours just needs to be patient enough to prove to this girl that he's not who she's afraid he is. Or at least, give her time to come around."

Time. Why did everything always come back to time?

Jac nodded. "Thanks for the advice." He wasn't sure what to do with it, but he could be patient. He was a lighthouse keeper who watched the same tide rolling in day after day; it was ingrained in him to be enduring. "This helped."

"What are friends for?" She smiled, and the bell above the library entrance chimed. They both looked to see another patron walk through the door and head toward them. "Sori to cut this short, but it looks like I've got to get back to work."

Jac nodded. "No problem." He headed for the exit, but before he made it outside, Bronny called back to him.

"Don't worry, Jac. She'll come around to you. Just keep your head up!" She winked and began waiting on the newcomer.

Jac left the building ten degrees warmer, Bronny's intuition something he hadn't expected. He was only too glad for the coolness of the night and the sea breeze that reminded him to relax.

Now all that lay before him was the ride home and a mysterious girl he hoped would come to trust him.

When Jac pulled his bicycle up alongside the Telor Pendu, he paused and strained his ears into the wind. Was someone singing? He followed the melody around the lighthouse to where the vegetable garden in the front stretched to a small, empty plot of grass in the back. The sight took him by surprise.

Beneath the fading sunlight stood Nain with their guest by her side, the two of them pinning clothes on the clothesline. It was growing dark, and the two were having as much fun as if they were taking a stroll down the beach.

"I didn't know you sang," Jac said to Nain, observing them in wonder, Nain in her blue dress and the girl in the one his grandmother had lent her earlier; she was smiling. It looked good on her.

"I don't. Not well, anyway." Nain chortled, clipping a pair of his boxers next to one of her compression stockings. Some sights he would never get used to. Much like a car, he wished they had a washer and dryer. But some appliances were more important than others, he supposed.

Though he wasn't too keen on the fact that his underwear now hung mere inches above a pretty girl's face.

"So, uh, you both been out here long?" He tried to ignore the hanging clothes and eyed the basket of wet laundry instead, noticing there were still a lot of items left in it.

Nain shook her head. "Just got outside but a few minutes ago. But this sweet one here offered to help with the washing." She looked at the girl and smiled.

Jac swallowed. *Great.* Now their guest of only forty-eight hours had not only seen his underwear, but cleaned them, too. He started backing away. It was kind of her to help Nain, but he'd rather not stick around to watch his mortification get pinned to the clothesline.

"You know, Jac, now that you're here, why don't you take over for me? I just remembered a letter that needs responding before tomorrow's post." Nain shuffled slowly toward the front of the lighthouse, but not before patting him on the shoulder and looking at the girl once more. "Thank you again, *annwyl*," she said, then disappeared inside.

Now it was just Jac and their guest, and a sopping wet pile of embarrassment.

The girl stared at him, not having moved much since Nain left. Her smile was only a ghost of what it once had been.

What should I say?

"Do you enjoy doing laundry?" *Really, Jac?* He wished he'd bitten his tongue. Instead, he rifled through the basket to find his clothes. If

Nain was going to have him hang wet laundry with their guest, he wanted to make this as least awkward as possible. For *both* of them.

She looked his way and then at the basket by their feet, nodding.

"It's really nice of you to help out and all, but you're a guest here. It's not required of you."

The girl shook her head and mouthed the words, "I want to." Which shouldn't have surprised him, but it did. Maybe this was a promising start.

The girl reached into the laundry basket and drew out something long and burgundy. It resembled some sort of peasant's dress, and Jac recalled that's what she'd been wearing the night he rescued her. Tenby didn't make clothes like that, nor did anywhere in their current generation, unless it was a costume for *Nos Galen Gaeaf. Where on earth did she come from?*

Jac kept hanging articles of clothing while glancing at the girl in his peripheral. He smiled when she looked his way, but beyond that, he didn't know what else to say. Bronny's words, only spoken a few hours ago, still bounced around in his mind: *"Trust thrives by growing roots."* He didn't know how much time he'd have with their guest, but he wanted her to feel comfortable here. To trust that he only wanted to help her for as long as she remained. Having a woman's presence like Nain was probably doing more good for that resolve than anything, though.

"Nain told me you had a bump on your head." Jac paused mid-clip of a pair of his jeans while she hung one of his grandmother's aprons farther down the line. "Is it feeling any better?"

The corner of her lips pulled into a smile, and she nodded, seeming grateful to have been asked.

"Good. I'm glad." His smile matched her own, and the two of them continued working their way down the line in silence. By the time they finished, the stars started to peel back their covering, revealing little dancing sparks about the moon. "Woah, would you look at that?" His gaze was glued skyward, one hand shielding his forehead like a baseball cap from the Fresnel lens rotating above. "Orion's out. And it's only August."

The girl looked up and squinted, trying to see what he saw. Apparently, she couldn't find it because she walked over to him and tried looking from where he stood.

"It's right there. A line of three stars straight across, and then four surrounding him, two for the hands, and two for the feet." She squinted some more, and Jac helped her by shielding her face from the lighthouse's strong beam. "Do you see it?"

She fixed her eyes to the sky, searching. An eagerness to see what he saw.

"It's faint, so it might be difficult to tell."

Then she nodded, pointing with her finger in the direction she'd finally spotted the constellation. Her beautiful smile was back.

He grinned. "You've been in Tenby for two days and you've already seen something unheard of." He'd read enough about the stars to know which seasons they showed up best and where. By all accounts, Orion should still be sleeping. "This is a winter constellation, and it's still the end of summer." He sighed, marveling once more at the ethereal sight. "Something special, that's for sure."

The girl kept looking at the sky, and Jac couldn't help glancing at her.

He had a feeling she was something special, too.

19

EIRIN MAIR

Merri

Tenby, Wales
August 1996

A WEEK HAD PASSED AND STILL, she couldn't make sense of it. Every time Merri looked at Jac's face, she saw Prince Olivander. And every time she thought of the prince, casting off a years-long friendship and standing outside her carriage without a care in the world, the more he acted less and less like Jac. How could two people look the same and yet be so different?

Why does he call himself by a different name?

Why is he here?

Where exactly is here?

It was in the middle of Maunt when she'd left Chaera, but it currently felt like the underbelly of Sollun or Attol. *How is that possible?*

She didn't trust what she saw in Tenby, Wales—wherever that was. And she didn't trust Jac. He wasn't who he said he was. How could he be in two places at once, single-handedly destroying her chance at love in one location, and then finding a way to mend the cracks of her brokenness in another? All the while not even knowing who *she* was. Had their friendship meant nothing to him all those years? It was as if the old Prince Olivander had disappeared entirely and became someone new in the form of a man going by the name Jac Hughes.

Merri rubbed her head, a steady pain growing in her temples. She wasn't used to this much thinking.

All she knew was that until she figured out what was going on, she'd keep her distance from him, no matter the fact that he saved her life and was currently helping her get her voice back through the written word. No matter that he had shown her the brilliance of the stars.

She swallowed, guilt niggling the back of her mind. He was being so kind, and she didn't know what to do about it. Except push him away.

Esias, help me.

Maybe I'm mistaken.

To be fair, it had been nearly three years since they last interacted… But hadn't she seen him brooding outside her carriage only the other day? He was as recognizable as the sun.

"How's it going?" Jac asked.

Merri startled, her clumsy grip sending the pen tumbling from her hand and clattering loudly. They'd started the lessons again this morning the same way they did with all the others, the table between them once more scattered with ink-stained pages, opened books, and some half-finished breakfast pastries and *crempogs.*

"Sori to scare you. Everything's looking really good. And it's only been a week," he encouraged.

When she looked up, she saw a smile stretching across his sun-kissed face. He appeared sincere.

She was surprised by her progress, grateful to hear she wasn't utterly failing like she'd feared. *Darya didn't take everything from me, after all. I'm still a Dorsaleene.*

And…there was no use trying to deny it any longer. She studied his features more thoroughly, fully convinced; Jac and the prince were one in the same. But what a contrast a smile versus a scowl did to his demeanor. The former lit up his green eyes while the other darkened them.

"What? Is…is something on my face?" he asked, lifting a hand to wipe the corners of his mouth. "Nain tells me I eat like a slob, so I'm not surprised."

Keeper's Heights. Had she been caught staring at him again?

Heat climbed her neck. She shook her head, averting her gaze. She still couldn't look at him without her heart twisting. When she saw him, she felt his betrayal and Iun's parting words anew. And her head spun from bewilderment.

"Well, that's a relief. I wouldn't want you thinking your teacher was a barbarian or something." He winked at her.

Now her cheeks were aflame. She watched him get up from his seat and walk to the window. Despite how her chest ached, she found herself wishing for the past and wondering what their friendship would have looked like if he'd never left. Would she still have fallen in love with Iun? Sacrificed her voice to get a pair of ridiculous legs?

Merri swallowed the growing bitterness creeping up her throat. Some things she would never know.

As much as she appreciated Jac taking the time to teach her, it was hard being in his presence. Harder still that he had no memory of her. It made her want to run and fight her way back to the sea. Land was a strange place, and though she was quickly learning the ways of humans, there was still so much to discover. *Too much.* The prospect was overwhelming.

She missed having a permanent home.

She missed Iun and the life they could have had.

She missed the Prince Olivander of her youth.

She missed Eldarwielle worst of all. Her one comfort was knowing that he had somehow sent her here for a purpose. But how would she get back? Part of her longed to wade into the cool waters of the ocean, but another part of her was afraid. She wasn't certain if she'd be rescued a second time should she drown.

Her head continued to spin in circles. *Will my life be an unending yearning for what once was? Simply because I made the wrong choice?* She kept her gaze focused on her hands as her vision blurred. *These horrid emotions.* She wasn't used to others, or even herself, seeing her tears when they usually blended into the sea. *Blink. Blink them gone.*

"Would you like to go for a walk today?" Jac asked.

She glanced up to find him still looking outside, unaware of her inner turmoil. *Thank Esias.*

"I can take you around town, or maybe we can discover more ways to help you know where you are."

A walk sounded lovely. She wasn't used to being inside so much, and though the lighthouse proved the least constricting home thus far, she craved the salty air.

He turned to face her, and she nodded, pushing up from her seat. Since her harrowing rescue in the bay, she hadn't had much energy for anything aside from studying and moving around the lighthouse. Now, she was more than ready to stretch her fragile legs over a longer distance.

"Great, let me grab my wallet."

Wallet?

When he got downstairs, Jac walked to the kitchen counter and stuffed an odd, square-shaped thing in his back pocket. "You ready?" He looked over his shoulder, frowning when he saw Merri still climbing down the steps.

She dipped her head, trying her best to hide how her limbs shook. She'd only descended this staircase when she had to, mostly when no one was watching. Stairs weren't easy to navigate; she'd rather walk or run. Increasing her pace, Merri took the last couple steps and tripped, pitching forward. Jac thrusted an arm out to break her fall.

"Caref—*oof.*" Her momentum collided into his chest, sending both of them careening backward.

Jac grunted when his back hit the wooden floor. And when Merri landed on top of him, he let out another stilted groan.

This can't be happening!

An awkward moment of silence, and then a croaked "Are you okay?" escaped Jac's winded throat. He lifted his head to look at her, his eyebrows wedged together in concern.

Are you *okay?* She nodded, her face impossibly hot. His hand was pressed gently against her back to keep her from falling farther.

"Good. No harm done, then." He laughed. "This isn't the first time I've ended up on the floor, and it won't be the last, I assure you."

"Everything okay out here?" Jac's grandmother stepped out of her bedroom and into the kitchen. When she saw them sprawled out on the ground, she chuckled. "Showing the young lass how you mop the floors, Jac?"

He groaned. "That was one time, Nain."

"Still, it's a memory I'll never let you forget. When one's mop breaks, one typically doesn't lay down and use the shirt off their back to clean the floors."

Merri wasn't sure what they were talking about, but they were laughing. And not at her. She cracked a nervous smile, pushing herself off of Jac and to her feet, nerves still pulsing. Unlike him, Nain had been easier to trust; she liked the older woman instantly. Merri took a step in her direction and paused… Though, it would probably be rude if she didn't help Jac up since she'd just knocked him over. She extended a hand instead.

His eyes widened, and he only hesitated a moment before taking it. "Thanks."

She nodded, ducking her head. She wished she could apologize for being so clumsy.

"Where are you both off to this morning?" Nain asked, amusement still on her wrinkly face.

"I wanted to show Eirin Mair around Tenby." Jac grabbed a bag hanging by the front door.

Eirin Mair? Merri frowned. She hoped that in time she'd learn how to write her name…or have Jac remember it, but it seemed he was growing impatient and had decided to give her one himself. Though part of it did sound like her name to begin with.

Nain gave a knowing smile before messing about the kitchen. "Have fun."

Jac held the door open for Merri as they exited the lighthouse, a lightness in his step that she hadn't seen before. It was as if the sunlight fueled him and the ocean air filled him with life.

She felt it, too. The sea beckoned to her as the salt danced under her nose. She breathed it in deeply, not bothering to hide her smile. *Freedom. That's what the ocean is. Even if I can't be in it, I can still be close.*

Something orangey-red flashed before her eyes. When she looked down, Jac held out a strange-looking object in his hand for her to take.

"Eirin Mair," he said, one side of his smile lifting higher than the other. "I hope you don't mind the nickname, but your red hair," he paused, glancing at the flowing strands brushing across Merri's cheeks. "It reminds me of our gooseberries—the Whinham variety. We call them eirin Mair here. They're, uh, one of my favorites."

Merri's middle warmed despite her efforts to the contrary. There were worse things to be named after, she guessed. Though her hair wasn't *that* red. Maybe it would suffice in the meantime.

"I promise once I learn who you are, I won't refer to you as a fruit anymore. But calling you *something* feels more humane than nothing."

Once I learn, not *once I remember.*

She nodded while her heart bruised anew. *"Names are important,"* Eldarwielle had often said to her, *"and should be used in full, not halves."* Hence why he always called her Merriweather. Names gave purpose and meaning. Built trust. When she'd learned Eldarwielle's, their friendship had grown deeper. The same had happened with Iun.

A pang ripped through her chest at the thought of him. *It's done, Merri.*

She'd once learned Prince Olivander's name, too, and he'd learned hers… She swallowed another pulsing ache. *Don't think about that now. Just take the eirin Mair.*

Merri reached for the gooseberry, careful not to touch Jac in the process. She had too many questions and was tired of not being able to ask them. The most pressing of which stood before her in the form of her childhood friend. But she couldn't deny his thoughtfulness. Maybe it would do her some good to try and forget her problems, if only for a day.

Starting with the fruit.

"The skin is edible," he said, watching her. "Some don't prefer it, but it actually tastes pretty good. Though I'm not sure if you—"

She bit into it all the same, a muted sour sweetness stinging the insides of her cheeks. She knew what Jac was about to say, and he was right. Flavors were vastly different now without her tongue. But if she thought hard enough, she could still taste *something,* be it only in her imagination.

Maybe that's what her life would be like from now on: muted joys. Things weren't as bright and beautiful as they once were when her heart had been whole, but she knew Esias had a way of breathing life into the lost and hurt places. *Can He do the same for me?* Maybe it was *choosing* to see the good, even if it took time to find.

And her heart sorely needed that right now.

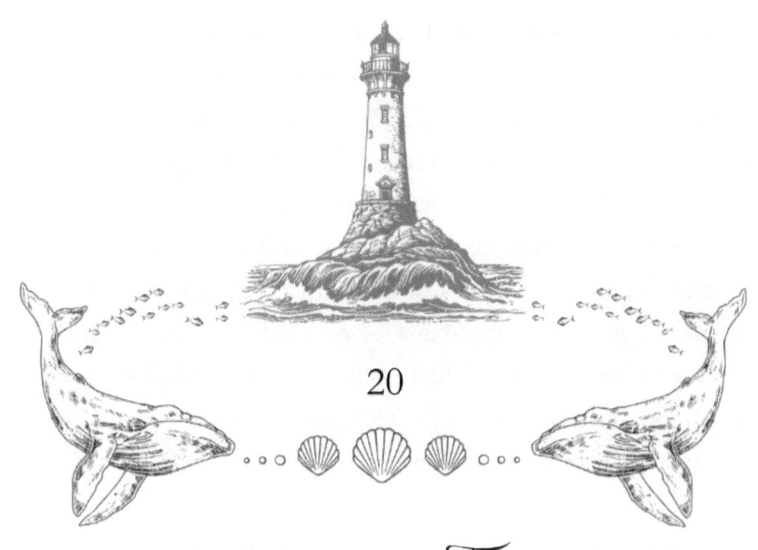

20

EXPLORING TOWN

Merri

Tenby, Wales
August 1996

NARROW WALLS PRESSED IN around Merri as she followed Jac through the winding streets of Tenby. They passed brightly colored doors and windows with flower boxes affixed beneath the glass, rock walls with greenery growing in overabundance through the cracks, and the smell of something sweet dancing in the salty air.

She picked her way carefully over a cobbled road, hoping not to trip again, for her recent fall in the lighthouse still lingered fresh in her mind—the way Jac had cradled her, had asked if she was okay even before he assessed himself. The memory did strange things to her middle, and she wasn't sure what to make of it. *He was just being friendly, Merri.*

She focused on the path ahead. *Where is he taking me?*

They soon emerged into an open area—Jac told her it was a shopping plaza—which was ablaze in sunlight. Today was warm, too warm, and apparently a record high for Tenby, whatever that meant.

It didn't take her long to start sweating.

Spring isn't this oppressive. Why does it already feel like Attol?

She thought the carriage ride back in Chaera had been stifling, but whatever Nain's dress was made of currently felt worse, like coarse sand against her skin. It was thick, itchy, and way too hot to be wearing beneath the sweltering sun. *Why didn't I wear Luci's dress instead?* Though that garment had more material than this one did, even if it was thinner.

She stepped into a patch of shade and stopped to fan herself, suddenly feeling faint. *Heights Above,* how she wished she was back in the water. *Why is it so hot between all these buildings?*

"And this is where the tourists come to—" It took Jac a second to realize she was no longer by his side. He looked around him, his confused brow leveling out when he saw her. "Are you okay?" He walked over to her.

How was she to tell him she was slowly roasting like a beached whale? *Sorry, Eldarvielle.* She tugged on the sleeve of the dress and pointed to the sky, hoping he would understand she needed a few minutes to cool down.

Jac's eyes grew round as he looked at what she was wearing. "O! I didn't even realize. It's been a hot summer, and an even hotter August. You must be dying in that!"

Summer? August? She assumed that word meant a month, but it was one she'd never heard of before. Had so much time passed already? How was that even possible? She hadn't been asleep for *that* long, had she?

"Eirin Mair?" Jac asked.

She nodded, her gaze flitting back to his, suddenly self-conscious.

"There are plenty of shops around. Why don't you get something else to wear." He took his wallet out of his pocket and handed her something colorful. "It's on me."

Merri stared at him. What in Kerilow Bay did he mean? *Do people just get new clothes whenever they want?* She looked at what he'd just given her. *And with paper?*

"Here." He pointed to one of the shops. "I know someone who works inside. She'll be happy to help you." Jac led her to a yellow-painted door with a clear pane of glass in its middle. He pushed it inward, and before she had a chance to walk through, he bent to whisper in her ear. "And don't worry about talking," he assured her. "She asks a lot of questions, but you won't get a word in edgewise."

Merri nodded, more unbidden warmth winding through her middle. She was a fish out of water, but no one else had to know that. When she stepped inside the building, a wash of cool air smacked her in the face, sending a chill down her spine. *What in Kerilow? It's freezing in here!* She began rubbing her arms, making her second-guess her need for new clothes, after all.

Jac must have read her mind. "Sori about that. We don't have AC back in the lighthouse, so the contrast is kind of—well, it's a lot." He laughed, rubbing a hand along the back of his neck.

I don't know what AC is.

"How can I help you both today?" An older lady with short, unnaturally plum hair and red-rimmed glasses approached them. Her smile was almost as bright as her blue eyes. "Ah, *bore da*, Jac! Good to see you again!"

"Good morning to you, too, Iris." He nodded at the woman. "I, uh…I have a friend here who could use something else to wear. It's a bit hot outside."

Iris glanced at Merri, assessing her dress like one would a precious shell on the shoreline. "*Ie*, I see what you mean. Come come, right this way, annwyl."

Before Merri knew what was happening, she was ushered toward the back of the shop and away from Jac.

"I'll just be waiting outside," he said.

"No problem. We'll have a tidy time!"

Tidy?

"Now, let's see. You're about my height, though a little slimmer. I'd say a small would be right and tidy. How do you feel about lime green?" Iris held up a vibrant dress that stung Merri's eyes. "No? Too bold? Let's try something else."

Jac was right. Iris liked to talk; she hopped from one topic to the next, not bothering to hear the answers to her questions, which boded well for Merri.

After sifting through copious other options, Iris finally stilled. "Ah. There's lovely. This is the one; of that, I am certain!" She ushered Merri into a small room with the designated dress. The door closed behind Merri, but she couldn't take her eyes off of the garment. She reached tentative fingers toward the fabric, letting them brush against the soft lavender material. A lump formed in the back of her throat. Her tail had once been the same shade. *I'll never swim again.*

"When you've put it on, we'll ring you up so you can wear it out of the store." Iris's voice grew distant, so Merri assumed she was walking away. She gulped. Why did people speak so strangely here?

By the time Merri left the shop, she was much cooler and only slightly mortified. Iris had been kind when Merri handed over Jac's colorful paper, even when she didn't understand how paying for things worked. Back in Kerilow Bay, if someone was in need, they bargained for necessities with shells and oyster pearls. But she now had a pretty dress and a complimentary tote bag that apparently said "I Heart Wales" with a picture of a humpback on it.

"All set?" Jac asked from behind a book. He didn't so much as glance up.

Merri nodded, her light purple dress ruffled gently in the wind, feeling infinitely better than Nain's heavy one, which now resided in her new bag. She'd never worn its like before, with its dainty cap sleeves and flowy skirt that fell just below her knees. It was difficult at first, but after putting it on and looking in the mirror, it was almost as if nothing had changed. She'd found the land version of her tail and couldn't resist giving it a little twirl.

"How would you like to go—" Jac paused, his unfinished sentence hanging in the air.

Go where? Merri stopped mid-spin to find him staring at her with his book still open, his eyes wide. She caught her breath. *Why is he looking at me like that?* Pulse climbing. *Does he remember after all?*

He cleared his throat. "You look…that dress…" He cleared his throat again. "The color suits you, Eirin Mair."

Her shoulders drooped. *No. He does not.* But that didn't stop her cheeks from growing even warmer. He was still looking at her with those *eyes*, something unspoken behind them. And she was confused. *Am I always to blush around Jac Hughes? Even if I don't trust him?* She wasn't used to all this attention. Though she'd be lying with herself if she didn't enjoy it.

"Right, well, uh…" He finally blinked and put his book inside his bag before gesturing toward the ocean. "Let's head to the harbor. There's someone there I'd like you to meet."

Merri followed Jac over more stone-laden streets and between pastel-colored houses, away from the center of town and toward the sea. Her spirits lifted with each intake of salty breath.

This is home.

"This is Harbor Beach," Jac said as Merri's feet touched the blessed sand. She eagerly cast off her sandals—another gift from Nain—and wiggled her toes through the tiny grains, reveling in their sun-kissed warmth. "North Beach is on our left—it's something else, really, with its golden sand and the Goscar rock; it's also, uh, close to where I'd found you in the bay." His grin turned sheepish, but he continued, "And up there on Castle Hill"—he pointed to a large mound of rock and earth on his right—"are the infamous ruins of Tenby Castle. There's a museum up there, too."

What's a museum?

"And on the other side is Castle Beach." Jac chuckled. "Wales really likes their castles."

And beaches, Merri added.

"St. Catherine's Island is just a little ways off shore, but you can't really see it from here. It's only accessible at low tide, which makes for a fun adventure."

I think I've had enough adventure for quite some time.

"I don't expect you to remember all of this, by the way." Jac ran a hand along the back of his neck like he was prone to do. "I just love where I live, on the edge of the sea and all."

On the edge of the sea. She sighed, a tingling rising in her middle. *I used to be* in *it.* To be so near the ocean, to stand on the coastline and know its waters stretched for miles upon miles to distant places she'd never see again. She wanted to run into it and splash around, but an even bigger part of her was afraid to.

How would it feel to enter a world again that would no longer keep her?

Oh, Eldarwielle, I hope you won't forget about me.

But Merri trusted him. He'd sent her here for a purpose, even if she'd yet to figure it out. Present company notwithstanding.

And she trusted Esias even more. He was known to form beauty in the dark places, like pearls in the deep. Maybe He'd do the same with her. But had her reckless decision made her too broken to love? What if He never forgave her? And what if she ended up making a rash decision again? What then?

So many questions swirling like the tide in her mind, and being so close to one's home and yet knowing it could never be… It was almost too much to bear. A salty tear trickled down her cheek, reminding her she was still made of the sea.

"The ocean—it's special to you, too."

Merri snapped her head up, almost forgetting Jac stood beside her. His gaze was cast out toward the waters before he looked at her.

She nodded. *Yes. It's where I once belonged. I was a sea maiden, don't you remember?* But of course he wouldn't.

"Is that why I found you in the bay? The night I rescued you?"

No. There are so many things I wish I could say. But how to remind you when I can't even write my own name? Merri shrugged. It was easier than trying to explain.

"Chin up, Eirin Mair. You'll learn how to write soon enough, and then I can help you solve this mystery. Then we can get you home."

Home. The word tugged on her heartstrings like the kelp beds in a current. *There is no home for me. Not anymore.*

"Alright, Jac! Didn't expect to see you today." A middle-aged man with a fishing hat and what looked like rubber boots came striding down the nearest dock and over to where they stood. Hanging from the side of his pants was a rusted putty knife, a tool Merri had seen cast along the ocean floor a time or two.

Jac shook his hand. "Alright, Barti. We were just coming to see you."

"I can see that." The man turned and smiled warmly at Merri. "Now who's this pretty little *geneth* you've got with you today?"

Merri blushed.

"This is my friend, Eirin Mair. I'm just showing her around Tenby. I thought it'd be fun to bring her on your boat."

Boat? Merri suddenly felt unsteady.

Barti smirked in Jac's direction before he focused on Merri. "Right. Nice to meet you, *friend* of Jac. Be that as it may, the *Gwylan Môr* isn't running today. Been due for a good barnacle scraping, and I've only just taken a short break to grab some lunch."

Merri's nerves settled a touch. She loved the water, but she wasn't so sure how she'd feel being stuck inside a vessel that carried her over the waves. Would it be torturous to be so near and yet so far?

"That's okay. Maybe another time."

"My gangplank is always waiting." Barti smiled before walking away, whistling a jaunty tune to the rhythm of the echoing waves.

Jac glanced at his wristwatch with a sigh. "He's right. It's after one o'clock. We should head back to the Telor Pendu and grab something there."

Merri nodded, feeling the ache of hunger gnawing against her ribs. Had so much time passed since breakfast? She looked once more at the ocean, not wanting to tear her gaze from it and yet too hesitant to draw nearer.

I can always look. And I can always come back again.

"We can come back another time," Jac said, as if reading her thoughts.

She nodded, trying to forget the way the sea cloaked her like the smoothest garment, wrapping her in its gentle embrace. She needn't think about all she had lost.

They retraced their steps back toward the center of Tenby, Jac pointing to new landmarks and commenting on this and that. All the while, she tried to remain interested. It was hard when the song of the crashing waves commandeered her senses and beckoned to her.

Taunting her with impossibilities.

A muted scream left Merri's throat as a strange metal carriage zipped past her on the road. She clung to Jac's arm without thinking, her heart throbbing somewhere in her stomach as she watched the contraption speed away.

What is that thing?

Jac chuckled. "You look as if you've never seen a car before."

I haven't. And I'm not sure I like it.

"Typically, they don't run tourists over, but you can never be too careful." His smile turned into a frown when he looked at Merri's startled face. He placed his hand atop the one she still had locked around his bicep, and she stilled instantly. "I promise you're safe here, Eirin Mair."

Safe?

Here?

With Jac Hughes?

"You can trust me on that," he said, giving her hand a gentle squeeze.

Trust?

But he was Prince Olivander.

He abandoned their friendship years ago.

He dashed her hopes upon the rocks of Kerilow Bay.

He took her far away from her one chance at love.

He hadn't stopped those carriages.

But he was also Jac Hughes.

He had saved her from drowning.

He had invited her into his home.

He had shown her the stars.

He had brought her around Tenby.

He had bought her a pretty dress.

He was teaching her how to read and write.

Safe. Here. With Jac Hughes.

Trust me.

"But just to be sure, walk on my other side from now on, the one furthest from the road," he said.

Merri swallowed, releasing her hold on his arm at once and putting some distance between them as she went to his other side. Her fingers went cold after letting go of his warmth, and her middle danced like the waves.

Safe. Here. With Jac Hughes.

She was safer than she'd been in a long time. And that's what scared her the most.

Trust me.

She hadn't meant to—hadn't even wanted to—but how easy it was to slip back into the past after so long. She'd told herself "no," and all the while he was slowly chipping away at her exterior with his kindness. *He's Olivander, after all.* But it wasn't wise to start trusting someone who had cast their friendship aside so easily. Who was living a double life.

Despite it all, she found that she was beginning to.

What's wrong with you, Merri? She chided herself for being too soft. For always wishing things could go back to the way they were before. *For once, can you not get involved?*

Maybe there was a reason. For all of this. Didn't Esias have plans far greater than anyone could fathom? Even grander than the very depths that were once her home?

But why doesn't Jac call himself Olivander? Doesn't he know he's a prince? Maybe *he* was the one who needed help, and not herself.

Merri's head started to ache again. Too many emotions and all of them conflicting. But one thing was clear. After she learned how to write her name, she was bent on getting some answers.

Starting with this one: *What happened to make you forget who I am?*

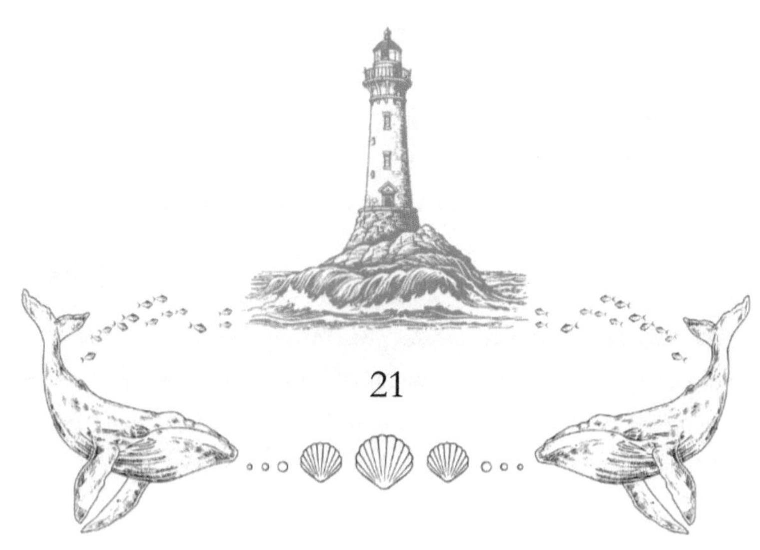

21

∆ND SPRING IN BETWEEN

Jac

Kerilow Bay, Chaera
Kipp 1189

"I HOPE YOU LIKE IT. I picked it since it was dying," Merri said. "Plus, it sort of looks like a fish."

Oli laughed, looking at it closer. He wasn't sure how she saw a fish, but perhaps her imagination was more creative than his. "Yeah, sort of." He took the orange piece of coral from her and buried it beneath some stones toward the back of their rock enclosure. "And now when I throw it in the water, you'll know I'm here, waiting for you."

She nodded. "And I'll bring it back every time. Kind of like Seek."

The two of them smiled in agreement, and Oli moved to the cave's exit.

"Where are you going?" Merri asked.

"To get my parents. They've never met a sea maiden before."

"What?" Merri's eyes grew round. "I'm not sure that's such a good idea."

"Why not?" Oli crossed his arms over his chest. It had only been a few days since they'd last seen one another; after a long winter of remaining indoors, Oli and his parents had resumed their biweekly visits to the beach. It was spring now, and that meant he was a whole year older…which he hoped also meant a whole year wiser. And he thought introducing his parents to Merri was a good idea. "My parents know all my friends. They'll like you, I promise!"

Oli rounded the entrance and shouted, "Mum, Da, come he—ouch!" His hand flew to his head. A small pebble lay at his feet that wasn't there a moment ago. He turned and found Merri glowering at him, her eyes full of fright and hurt.

"Oli! What are you doing?" she gritted through clenched teeth. "I told you this wasn't a good idea."

"What do you mean?" His pulse quickened. He'd never seen someone look so afraid before. "What's wrong?"

"Don't you understand? I'm part of the sea, Oli. Around here, most people think we're scum. Unsuitable playmates for children and friends. It's dangerous to come to shore as often as I do, but it's only because my father doesn't seem to care."

What? Oli had no idea. "My parents aren't like that. They can't be…"

"And now they'll pull you away from me, and we'll never be friends again."

Oli's insides squirmed. "How…how do you know?"

Merri sighed and slumped lower into the waves. "It happened to me once before. And to an acquaintance from another pod. Humans don't like what they don't understand. At least that's what my father always says."

"Oli? Are you in there?" His own father's voice carried over the booming waves, making Oli's pulse beat even faster.

"Uh oh." Oli bit his lip. They were getting closer.

Merri withdrew farther into the ocean. "It's too late. I have to go—"

"So this is where you've been hiding—oh!" His mother made eye contact with Merri. "Haelen—hello—is this your friend, Oli?" Her voice was gentle and sweet as she entered the mouth of the rocky enclosure. Inviting and full of life, like he'd always known. There was no way his parents would make him say goodbye to

Merri forever, would they?

Oli nodded.

His mother knelt along the ocean's edge as his father stood only a few paces away. Oli watched as Merri's eyes darted between the kneeling queen and himself, the fear and uncertainty still there. "Are you who our son has been spending all his time with?"

Merri nodded slowly.

"What is your name, daughter of the sea?"

"M-Merri," the sea maiden said, bowing as much as one could in the water.

"It is nice to meet you, young Merri. I am Queen Firan." The queen smiled and stood to her full height once more. "And this is King Matteo." She gestured to Oli's father behind her.

"A pleasure!" He tipped his head. "Any friend of Olivander's is a friend of ours. As is everyone else in our kingdom, even those in the sea." He smiled warmly. "Is your family nearby?"

Merri nodded again. "Our pod isn't too far from the shore."

"Well, I look forward to meeting them one day. For now, we will not let two adults dampen your fun." He chuckled and then looked at Oli. "Son, mind your manners and do not run too far, all right? You will give your mother another conniption." He winked at the woman by his side.

"Matteo!" The queen lightly slapped his arm before holding fast to his hand. "I just like knowing where you are, Oli."

"Geia, Da. Mum." A smile pulled on the corner of his lips. His parents joked like this all the time, and it was funny to watch.

"We hope to see you again, Merri." Oli's mother waved to the sea maiden and kissed her son's head before walking with her husband back to their spots on the beach.

Oli sat and threaded his toes in the grains of sand, hoping his new friend wasn't too mad at him anymore. He'd thought the conversation went well, but maybe he was wrong.

"Are you sure they're the king and queen?" Merri asked once they were out

of earshot, reclaiming her spot on her rock.

"Of course!" He laughed. "Why?"

"Because they're the nicest people I've ever met!"

"Oh. Yes, they are." Oli's heart lightened; she wasn't mad at him, after all. "But you don't know them like I do. My mother makes me eat beets and puts them back in the larder for morning's breakfast if I can't finish them at supper."

Merri stuck out her tongue and made a noise of disgust.

"And my father tells me men don't cry over silly things…not like I cry anyway." He made sure to add that last part.

"Well, my father snores in his sleep," Merri said.

"And what about your mother?"

She shook her head and studied her hands. "I don't know. She died when I was three. I don't remember much."

Oli frowned. A sudden weight came upon him. "I'm sorry."

She looked up and smiled. "It's okay. It hurts my sisters more since they're older."

"You have siblings?" Oli sat up straighter. He was an only child and always wondered what it would be like to have built-in friends. "What's it like?"

"Well, we get along most days. But I'm the youngest of four, and they sometimes forget I exist." Merri shrugged like it was no big deal, but Oli could tell it bothered her.

"Do they like to play Seek?" he asked.

Merri scoffed. "No. Jade's too busy liking boys now that she's all grown up and thirteen. So she's always with Kitt and Lara, our older sisters. They used to play with me, though."

"How old are you?" Oli asked, curious.

"I'll be nine in a few months. My birthday is at the end of spring."

"And mine's at the beginning." Oli smiled.

"Oh! Like a mussel shell."

Oli raised a brow.

"You know, a mussel shell?"

"I know what a mussel is, Merri. I just don't get what you're saying."

She laughed. "Wait a second." She dove below the surface of the water and came back with something dark in her hand. She held it out for him to take. "We're like this mussel," she said. "Each a part of the shell—from Maunt to Sol, *you* one side and *me* the other—and the rest of spring is between us, the gooey thing you eat."

"People eat these?"

"That's not the point, Oli!" Merri crossed her arms.

"Sorry, so we're like this shell?"

She nodded. "Two halves that make a whole. And spring in between."

He looked at the mussel, turning it over in his hands. How had she gotten that out of this thing? He studied it even closer. He'd never felt like he'd belonged somewhere so easily before. With shoes too big to fill in the citadel, it was nice finding a friend along the shore. One that seemed to like being around him as much as he liked being around her. Maybe that's what she meant.

Oli glanced up and smiled at the sea maiden. "I like that."

She smiled back. "Me too."

22

IT'S NOT A DATE

Jac

ONLY FIVE DAYS HAD PASSED since Jac took Eirin Mair into town, and he was already growing restless. Staying cooped up with a pretty girl was the stuff of dreams, but he found he wanted to *do* things. Take her places. Not just stay in the tower and stare at words all day.

How ironic. All I do is read anyway.

He often replayed their interactions in his head, when she'd fallen on him in the kitchen or gripped his arm on the side of the road. It was rather cute. And then the times when she'd stare off in the distance and seem almost lost, the sunlight highlighting the tears dotting her cheeks. He hated to see her that way.

So last night when Nain had asked him to pick more gooseberries the following morning, he jumped at the chance. It was the perfect opportunity to invite Eirin Mair. She was learning well; surely she wouldn't mind taking another break, would she? Besides, he was still trying to earn her trust, to tear those walls down—or rather, construct an opening she would allow him to walk through.

For reasons he couldn't explain, her opinion of him mattered. And he still couldn't shake off the feeling that something about her seemed familiar. Maybe it was his dreams again… He'd had another last night. That sea maiden returned, and she'd met the prince's parents. Like all the rest, details were limited, blurred, and hazy, but the sea maiden kept reminding him of Eirin Mair.

Jac quickly showered and got dressed for the day, his nerves ricocheting throughout his body as he exited the outhouse to see her. *Relax, Jac.* When he finally reached the front door of the Telor Pendu, he opened it a crack and stopped in his tracks.

"Fold the dough like so. That's it; you're a natural, annwyl!" Nain's joy reverberated through the ground floor, warm and inviting. He assumed she was talking to Eirin Mair. "You know, it's quite nice having another woman about the place. Jac's a love, don't get me wrong, but your company has been such a sweet one these past couple of weeks. I've never seen my boy so happy, truth be told."

Jac's pulse thrummed impossibly hot in his ears at the mention of his name.

"He's always got his nose stuck in a book," she continued. "Not much has changed, mind you, but you being here seems to have given him purpose again. Life as a lighthouse keeper can be sort of, well, dull, which is why I usually send him on so many errands." Nain chuckled, and a warm ember burgeoned in Jac's chest. Sometimes he took it for granted how much she cared for him.

"So thank you, annwyl, for giving some life back to my Jac. He's grown quite fond of you."

Nain. Now Jac's entire face was on fire.

Silence lingered between them, but he assumed Eirin Mair had responded in her own way.

"Now look at you, blushing like a Mary's Pillow," Nain said, and Jac could only guess how much this conversation was mortifying Eirin Mair. She was all the things Nain had said, but that didn't mean she was comfortable hearing it.

He had better go in and rescue her.

When Jac pushed open the door all the way, he saw Eirin Mair standing beside Nain, an apron tied around her waist. She was a few inches taller than his grandmother, who seemed to be shrinking on the daily, and they were currently sticking a tray of baps into the oven. Her cheeks had a healthy glow to them—most likely from embarrassment—and she was smiling. *Smiling at me.*

Jac's stomach flipped a little.

"Well, look who decided to finally join us this morning," Nain said with a wink. "Been standing there long, Jac?"

He nearly tripped over his own feet. "Nope, just got here." He walked into the kitchen. "Though I'm surprised to see you already enlisted some help this morning. What did you do? Drag poor Eirin Mair out of bed?" He chuckled and leaned against the counter, his back pressed up against it so he could see their faces better.

"Don't be cheeky, Jac. Our darling guest came down to get some water and wanted to help me instead. Have I ever been known to turn away a helping hand?"

"*Na.*" He laughed. "But you've swatted *me* out of the kitchen more times than I can count."

"Only to keep you from stuffing your gullet and jilting the locals. You're a different story entirely." Nain's guffaw filled the room, and Eirin Mair's smile stretched even wider.

"I help with quality control. Making sure everything tastes good before all of Tenby gets a bite. Quite chivalrous, really."

Nain ignored him and leaned in closer to Eirin Mair, whispering, though Jac still heard her. "He says this, but I haven't changed my recipe in over thirty years. Quality control my rump!" The two of them laughed some more.

"Right, well seeing as it's two against one this morning, I came here to see if Eirin Mair would like to join me in gathering some gooseberries." He looked at the strawberry-blonde woman covered in flour and smiled. "What do you say? Would you like to increase my odds and join forces with me?" He cringed at how cheesy that sounded.

She blushed again and looked to Nain as if asking for permission to leave.

Nain waved her off. "Oh, go ahead, annwyl. You've helped me more than enough this morning."

Eirin Mair nodded and took off her apron. She hung it on a coat hook by the door and grabbed one of the baskets Jac held out for her.

"Be back later," he called over his shoulder.

Nain nodded, and the two of them retreated to the outdoors. The tail end of August was still warm, but thankfully, this morning was more bearable than the past couple of days. Besides, September was only two days away with its coming promise of autumn.

Jac led Eirin Mair down the winding lighthouse path and stopped at one of the many bushes lining the walkway. "We can begin here if you'd like."

She nodded, eyeing him carefully.

"Gooseberries tend to fall off easily, so just be careful when you pull. They may burst." Jac demonstrated how to harvest the fruits, plucking them off one right after the other.

Eirin Mair did the same, though the first one she pulled off exploded in her hands. Jac hid his smile and pretended like he hadn't noticed, giving her the space to try again. The next attempt was successful, and that seemed to instill in her the confidence to keep going.

They gathered the fruit in silence as the minutes ticked on. Jac was unsure what to say, so he observed her when she wasn't looking instead. She wore her lavender dress again—now dotted with flour—and Jac was in his typical jeans and t-shirt. The smell of gooseberries tinged the air with sweetness and stained their fingers as they continued to fill their baskets full. Funny how he was surrounded by *eirin Mairs*.

The name was silly, he had to admit, but it suited her well. And the way that lavender dress complimented her strawberry-blonde hair and blue eyes… He couldn't get the image out of his head when he'd first seen her in it. Jac glanced her way again and watched as another gooseberry burst in her grip, the corner of his mouth tugging into a smile. The front pieces of her hair were pulled back into a low bun while the rest remained long and curled beneath like gentle waves. If radiance had a face…

She looked his way, and he averted his gaze just as quickly, fixing his attention on the bush before him.

It had been worth using what little money he had just to see her a bit more comfortable; he already had plans to get her a few other outfits once the weather cooled down. He had no idea how long she'd be staying with them, but he found himself wishing it would be a long while. He liked making her smile; it was such a fleeting thing most days, and he was determined to make it stay.

"How many have you got?" Jac asked after a time.

She looked in her basket and shrugged.

He made his way over to her, popping a freshly plucked gooseberry in his mouth. She held her basket out for him to look inside. "Wow, more than me." *Probably because I spent all my time staring at you. Yikes. I sound like a creep.* Since when had he become so enamored? He had a few friends who were girls—all of them pretty in their own way—but there was just *something* about Eirin Mair which made him want to be near her.

After another half hour of picking berries, they both headed back inside. Nain was no longer in the kitchen, but there were baskets filled with warm baps still cooling on the counter, the smell of butter and yeast a cheerful welcome. And a note for Jac, asking if he would be a dear and deliver them.

He sighed inwardly. He had hoped to hang out with Eirin Mair longer, and trekking all across Tenby with baskets of gluten wasn't what he had in mind. But maybe once he was finished...

"Would you like to go out tonight?"

Her head snapped up, her eyes wide and questioning to match his own.

Did I really just ask her that? It sounded like a date. Truthfully, he just wanted to take her somewhere new. He loved seeing the way her demeanor changed when she relaxed, letting a smile or two show on her lips when she thought he wasn't looking. Besides, he knew she loved the ocean, and he hadn't been able to take her back since their first adventure.

"Uh—" He cleared his throat. "It doesn't have to be anywhere fancy. I just wanted to show you around Tenby some more."

Eirin Mair looked at him carefully like she had with the gooseberries, as if contemplating what to do with his words. Like she was treading cautiously lest she get hurt. Then she nodded.

"Great, then it's a..." He swallowed. "I look forward to it."

After Jac finished delivering the bread in town, he'd gotten back to the Telor Pendu only to spend the majority of the afternoon in the kitchen. Eirin Mair worked diligently in the tower above on another lesson while Nain had joined him, watching from the table. But she retired a few minutes ago, waggling her eyebrows with a *look* he wasn't used to. "You two have fun tonight," she'd said as she shuffled into her room, smirking before closing the door.

He shook his head and chuckled. *What Nain would give to be a gnat on the paint.* The window above the sink showcased a slowly darkening sky, and he looked at his watch to check the time: 6:15 p.m. He couldn't wait any longer. He already had a plan up his sleeve.

Climbing the staircase, he found Eirin Mair hunched over a book, biting a pencil while concentrating extra hard. She'd been practicing her reading today, just simple books he'd borrowed from the children's section of the library, and he'd set up a CD player with the books on audio to help her copy the text and sound out the words.

"*Helo.* How's it going?" he asked, walking over to her.

She glanced at him and pressed pause on the machine, waving her book in the air like a white flag. Sighing, she slid a piece of paper toward him.

"That bad, huh?" He chuckled and scanned over her words talking about discolored eggs and ham. In hindsight, maybe Dr. Seuss wasn't the best option. But the letters were well formed and legible; she was a star pupil in the making. "He was a master in his own right, I suppose," Jac said, alluding to the author. "This looks great, by the way." He was proud of her, and truth be told, he was proud of himself for getting her this far. It was exciting to see someone learn a completely new skill from scratch. He gave the paper back to her. "So, I was thinking we could head out soon, if you'd like."

Eirin Mair looked relieved. She scribbled something on a piece of paper and handed it to him: *"Where?"*

Jac suppressed a smile. "You'll find out soon enough. Come on!"

He grabbed his jacket and wallet from off the table and headed for the door leading down to the spiral staircase. She followed him, curiosity brightening her eyes.

In the kitchen, he grabbed a basket off the kitchen counter and opened the front door for her. "Ready?" he asked.

She looked at the basket in his hands and then at him. She tilted her head as if asking a question.

"Oh, this?" Jac didn't want to spoil the surprise. "I have more bread to deliver, that's all."

They walked down the lighthouse path and onto the paved street heading into town, Eirin Mair keeping a respectable distance and Jac's adrenaline making him uncommonly warm. He wished more than anything that she could talk to him, if only to hear her thoughts and the sound of her voice. The silence made him fidgety and gave his mind too much space to think.

"So, uh, it's a nice night, isn't it?" *The weather, Jac? Really?*

She gave him a timid smile and nodded, looking up at the sky.

He followed her gaze. It was a cloudless night, and the stars were already poking their heads out. And he knew the perfect place to bring her to view them in all their glory. She seemed to like them the first time.

They continued to pick their way over a mixture of paved roads and cobbled streets. Finally, when they hit the outskirts of town, Jac veered left and moved aside some coastal straw, revealing a hidden path he was all too familiar with. He motioned with his head for Eirin Mair to follow. "Over here."

She looked at the path and then his face, biting her lip as if uncertain.

"I promise it'll be worth it, Eirin Mair." He wanted to assure her that she was safe with him, but he hoped it would be something she'd determine herself.

Tentatively, she stepped forward and followed Jac down the path, all the while his heart swelled in his chest. He'd never taken anyone here before, seeing as he discovered this secret path only last month. He was sure some of the locals knew about it, but that didn't diminish its appeal. And where it opened up to…well, he just hoped Eirin Mair would like it as much as he did.

"Close your eyes," he said, taking her hand so she wouldn't stumble. He didn't anticipate how it would make his insides feel like a blazing volcano, especially when she didn't pull away. "We're almost there."

A few more steps, and their feet went from walking on dirt to walking on sand. The strong smell of salt clung to his nostrils as waves echoed in the distance, and he wondered if Eirin Mair guessed where they were. He led her over to one of his favorite spots and stopped. "Okay, just give me a second. I'll tell you when you can look."

She stood there with her eyes closed while he went to work.

He glanced up in the middle of unfurling a blanket, double-checking to make sure his surprise wasn't spoiled. "You aren't peeking, are you?"

She shook her head, but he could have sworn he saw one of her eyelids flutter closed as if it had just been opened a crack. He chuckled to himself as he finished up what he was doing. Standing back, he was quite pleased with it. "Okay, I'm done. You can open your eyes now."

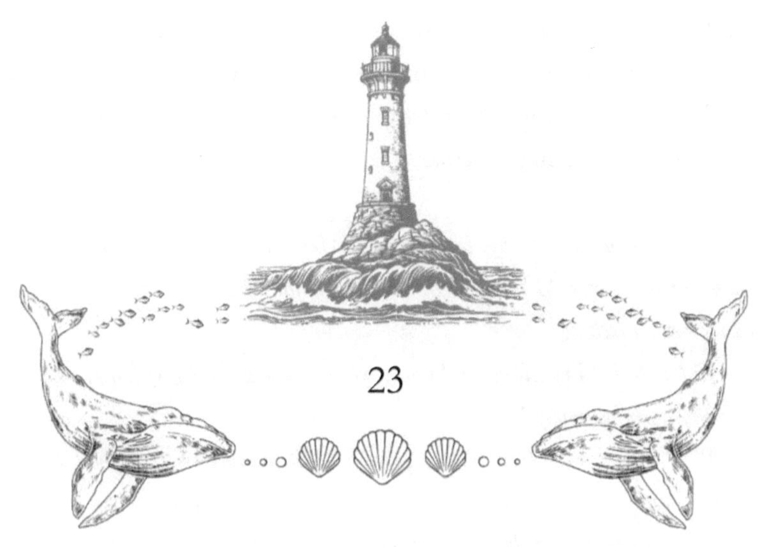

23

A PICNIC FOR FRIENDS

Merri

Tenby, Wales
August 1996

WHEN MERRI OPENED HER EYES, she had to blink a few times to make sure she was seeing things right. A blanket lay spread out in the sand by her feet with Jac's basket now uncovered, showcasing a plethora of food. And the best part? They were by the ocean, very close to the shore, just the two of them tucked away in a little alcove amongst rocks, sand dunes, and a waning sun.

Did Jac do all of this for me?

"It's not much," he said. "But I know you've been wanting to go back to the beach, so I figured taking you here might be just what you needed."

Merri looked at him. *Not much?* If she had the ability to speak, she wouldn't even know what to say. This was such a kind gesture, one that sent a bittersweet pang rippling through her chest. It reminded her all too well of their friendship along the shore of Kerilow Bay, especially one time in particular.

"You brought something, didn't you?" Merri asked, trying to spy the object hidden in Oli's arms. "I told you this meal was for you. That means you didn't need to bring anything."

Oli laughed. "Try telling that to my mother. She always says not to go empty-handed to a dinner party."

"Well, I guess it's okay." Merri shrugged. "If you don't like seafood, then it's probably better to have something you like anyway." She was still so excited to show her very best friend the kinds of meals one could have in the ocean. She just hoped he didn't think it was too weird. "Okay, give me a few minutes, and I'll bring everything up!"

Merri left Oli and swam to her home nearby. She'd spent all day mixing and baking and filleting, and now it was finally time. Surprisingly, her oldest sister had helped her with the hard parts, seeing as she was only eleven and sometimes bungled the steps, but it had been worth it. She hoped.

Placing all the food in large oyster shells and half-domed brain corals, she made quick work of bringing it to Oli.

"I'm back!" She started setting out the food on a rock he'd dragged over to her, the slab acting as a makeshift table.

"You made all of this?" Oli touched one of the dishes as if inspecting it, something like a thin filament stretching over the meals. "I'm impressed."

"Just wait, it tastes even better than it looks!"

They both claimed their spots around the rock, Oli sitting in an inch of water along the shore and Merri mostly in the shallows. He opened his parcel and revealed a round loaf with a swirl in the middle, still steaming, and placed it next to one of the seafood-filled shells.

"We've got shrimp sandwiches, krill pancakes, and crab soup." She pointed

to each of the food items, her mouth already salivating. "And your...?"

"Wind Cake. It's supposed to resemble Windkeep's crest with the raspberry line. It's an old recipe Cook likes to make."

Merri smiled. "Wind Cake it is!"

Oli gestured to the table. "How do you keep everything from getting soggy?"

"Easy." Merri grabbed something sharp and poked the tops of each of the dishes, both of them watching as the thin filament burst. "Airfilm. Crafted by the Tidallyns. It helps preserve food. Ready to dive in?" she asked, chuckling at her pun.

"I don't know where to begin," Oli confessed. "What do you suggest?"

"Hmm." She tapped her chin. "Krill pancakes for sure. They're my favorite, and I have a feeling you'll like them, too."

Oli nodded and put a few on his plate, which happened to be another slab of stone, and Merri watched nervously as he took his first bite. What if he hated it? What if he thought she was a poor cook? Then his eyes lit up, and he promptly had a second bite, and then a third.

Merri tugged on his arm. "Slow down, Oli! You'll choke."

"Where have you been all my life, Mer?" Oli shoveled more pancakes into his mouth, and she couldn't keep from laughing, her middle warmed by his words. "I'm telling you, these have the power to end wars. Or start them. Mind if I have some more?"

She slid the oyster shell in his direction, her nerves from earlier completely gone. "They're all yours."

Merri snapped back to reality, the memory fresh in her mind as if it had only been yesterday. But instead of baking Oli krill pancakes, here was Jac who'd made dinner for her instead.

It was as if a shorebird had alighted in her chest and was flapping its wings beneath her ribs. She ignored the strange feeling and sat down, fingering the folds of the blanket. Jac joined her.

He pulled out a lantern from the basket and lit it with a match, the little flame flickering and then shining clearly within the panes of glass. "It's getting dark. Figured we'd probably want to see what we're eating."

Merri surveyed the spread before her, noticing some sort of red-sauced dish, a bowl of fruit, what she guessed was some sort of cake, and more of Nain's bread rolls. *When in Kerilow did he have time to make all of this?*

"So, uh, we have ravioli. Italian, I know, but I can't get enough of the stuff," Jac began. "And then there's the gooseberries you helped me pick this morning, two slices of bara brith—trust me when I say Nain's recipe is the best in all of Tenby—and then some of her baps, which you know a thing or two about." He winked at the last part and handed her a dish and napkin. "Help yourself."

Even though she couldn't taste much, Merri still needed to eat. She took the plate from him and sat there, not having the slightest idea about what he'd just said, but there was that telltale ember warming her middle whenever Jac showed her kindness. He hadn't stopped since the night he rescued her, and it was doing confusing things to her nerves. Had Nain told the truth when she said he'd grown fond of her?

Heat scorched her cheeks at the thought.

Merri spooned some of the square-shaped pastas onto her plate, careful not to drip any sauce onto her dress, and grabbed one of Nain's rolls. She picked up a fork and took a bite, trying to still her gallivanting heart by fixing her gaze on the ocean only a little ways in front of her.

Roll. Crash. Splash. Their rhythm was soothing. Predictable. *Don't think about why Jac brought you here. On a picnic.* Her gaze shot toward the sky. *Beneath the stars. Alone.*

A cool breeze blew their way and ruffled her hair and dress, raising little bumps on her bare arms and legs. It was a good reminder to breathe.

They continued to eat in silence as the quiet stretched between them, ebbing and flowing like the tides, and she wondered what he was thinking. If only she could ask him questions.

"This is North Beach, by the way," Jac finally said, causing Merri to jump internally. "Tourists have been visiting here for years."

She remembered him talking about this beach a few days ago.

"We're in a hidden location, though. So, not many people come this way too often," he continued, picking at the blanket between his legs. He leaned back on one hand while his plate of food rested on his lap. He glanced her way. "Do you go to the beach often, where you're from?"

Merri looked at him, wondering how to answer. Though his questions were usually "yes" and "no" ones, they required more complex answers than she was able to give him. She nodded anyway.

"I can see why. It's one of my favorite places. I could sit and hear the waves crash all day." He took a bite of food and nodded at the sea.

Me too. More than anything.

As if in response to Jac's statement, the waves continued their cascading dances, their tumbling and breaking noises filling the empty spaces with a peaceful rhythm. Aside from the ocean, all else was quiet, with the waxing twilight and a chilly breeze blowing in from over the water. A perfect night…if only Merri's stomach would stop twisting and dipping like the gulls.

There was so much she wanted to say—so many emotions she was trying to make sense of.

"You ever feel like you were made for something, and you just haven't found it yet?"

The question took her by surprise. When she turned to look at him, Jac's gaze was still fixed on the sea. "Like you're happy with where you are and all, but you can't help wondering if there's something else. Something *more.*"

Merri swallowed. She'd once thought the same thing, had even made efforts to attain the unattainable…and much good that got her. But unlike her sad story, Jac's was different. *There is something more for you.* Her pulse pounded in her ears; it was so loud that she swore he could hear it, as if it was reaching out to him as a plea. *You're a prince, Oli. The prince of Windkeep. You were always made for great things.*

"Sori." Jac let out a nervous chuckle. "I didn't mean to get so deep all of a sudden. The ocean does that to me, I guess." He ran a hand through his hair before taking another bite of food.

She wished more than anything that he would continue.

"Oh! I almost forgot." He wiped the corner of his mouth with a napkin before reaching into his jacket pocket. "I wanted to give you something." He pulled out a small glass jar and held it up toward the light. The material reflected the lantern's warm glow, showcasing the glass in muted oranges and yellows. "North Beach is known for its golden sand, and I thought that since the ocean is so special to you, taking some of its sand with you would bring you some comfort." When he handed her the jar, his fingertips brushed her own, and it sent her stomach flip flopping.

She glanced at his face but noticed he wasn't really looking at her. Or rather, he *had been*, but he'd just looked away to pick once more at the blanket between his legs. *Is he nervous?*

"You don't have to keep it if you don't want to."

After all the years of being his friend, she'd always known Oli was thoughtful, so it didn't surprise her to find Jac was the same way. But for some reason, it made her insides feel like jelly. *He thought of me. Again. I'm definitely going to keep it.*

She uncorked the top and scooped some sand into the little jar, squinting to see the little grains filling it up. She would treasure this for the rest of her life, if only to remember her time here…with *Jac.* When he finally made eye contact with her, she mouthed the words "thank you," hoping he would be able to read her lips.

Jac smiled. "You're welcome." He glanced at her fully now, as if more confident. His expression dipped into concern. "You're shivering."

I am? Because all Merri felt being this near to Jac was warmth burning through her veins.

He shrugged out of his light jacket and scooted closer to her until his side was practically bumping against hers. He wrapped the warm fabric around her shoulders. His hands stilled when they pulled the collar around her neck, his face a mere breath away. "Is that any better?" he asked, his voice huskier than normal.

Merri was a little *too* warm now, but it wasn't from the jacket's comforting embrace. She nodded, her eyes traveling briefly to his mouth. *Why am I thinking of kissing Jac Hughes?*

"Good," he said, looking into her eyes, all traces of his nerves gone. He was so close. A stray hair blew across her face, and he reached out, tucking it behind one of her ears. Merri's middle might as well have been a whole nest of shorebirds at this point, their wings fluttering beyond belief. "I feel like I've met you before, somewhere…" he continued, his hand still by her ear. "Which is crazy, I know."

No. Not crazy at all.

"There's just something about you that seems familiar. I know you're not from around here, but…I wish you were." His thumb brushed lightly against her jaw, cupping her chin ever so gently. "I'm really glad you're here, Eirin Mair."

Merri couldn't help it anymore. If Jac wasn't going to kiss her already, then she would kiss him. Part of him remembered her; he had to. Why else would she seem familiar to a man she'd just met? Maybe it would be like a fairy tale from one of Jac's books—he'd read enough of them out loud for her to remember some of the stories. Maybe all it took was a kiss to break whatever memory-bound spell held him captive.

She closed her eyes and leaned forward, pressing her lips to his as quickly as a fin slapping the water. When she pulled back, she was startled to see Jac staring at her, his eyes wide and mouth agape.

Keeper's Heights! What did I just do? Embarrassment flooded her from head to toe and her cheeks became flames once more, but this time for another reason entirely.

She pushed to her feet, but Jac stilled her retreat by grabbing her hand. "Wait. No. Don't go!"

Merri reclaimed her seat, her rapid pulse telling her she was a fool. *Ridiculous, heart. Why can't you ever listen?*

"It's okay, I'm not upset. In fact, I was contemplating kissing you first before you went ahead and just did it. Call me a coward, but I didn't want to make you uncomfortable."

Merri's stomach was all sorts of twisty seaweed knots as his words sunk in. *Jac wanted to kiss me.*

He cleared his throat. "Is it okay if I kiss you back?"

Jac wants to kiss me again.

She nodded, her heart soaring.

He bridged the gap between them easily, his hand cradling her head as his lips met hers. It was gentle and sweet, a thing of dreams.

I'm kissing Oli. She felt like she was flying. She felt like she could overcome anything. Maybe this was why Eldarwielle sent her here. She was a flickering flame in the midst of a darkened sky.

He still doesn't remember me.

Uncertainty suddenly eclipsed joy as dread wormed its way into her core, climbing her spine and settling about her temples. She was a smoldering wick amongst shadows.

He doesn't even know my name.

How had she thought kissing Jac would solve anything? It only made matters worse. He didn't know she was his best friend from Kerilow Bay. If he did, would that change things? Would he be kissing her the same way he was now?

This was a mistake.

Merri pulled away and shoved him back. She hadn't meant to, but she needed distance. Desperately.

She stood and bolted beneath a sky studded with stars. She ran back the way they came, ignoring Jac's cries for her to slow down. The light from the lighthouse in the distance was her guide to lead her home.

Home. She scoffed again at the word, a mere taunting of what she could never have. Not here. Not with Jac. Never with Oli.

She just wished this could all be forgotten by tomorrow morning, or else she feared she'd need to find a new place to stay. But knowing Jac and his kindness, he wouldn't make it awkward. It was only if her fragile heart could handle such a misstep.

And she wasn't sure it could.

PART 3

KNOWN

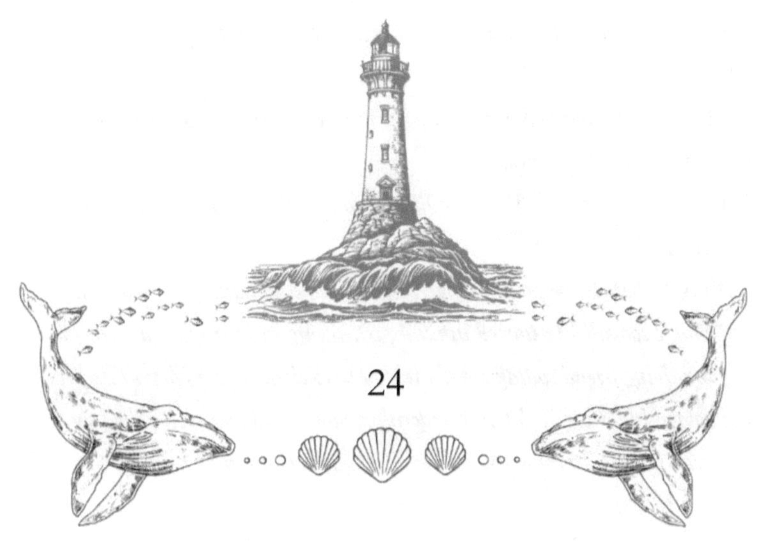

24

A Gift in the Sea

Jac

Kerilow Bay, Chaera
Sol 1193

"Close your eyes, Merri."

"What? Why? What are you doing, Oli?" The sea maiden held her arms close to her body as she leaned against her rock, the orange, fish-shaped coral resting in her hands.

"I'm too old for that nickname now, Merri. And because…"

"Because why, Oli?" she protested, ignoring his objection.

Olivander sighed. "Can't I just surprise you and have that be enough?"

"What's the surprise?"

"Merri!"

"Fine, fine." She brought one of her hands up over her face.

"Thank you. Now no peeking!" He studied her, wondering if she was looking *through her fingers. Her hair glowed beneath the warmth of the almost-summer sun.*

"We're not playing Seek again, are we? We're midfoots *now, Oli. I think the time for childish games is over."*

Olivander laughed. "I'm a midfoot. You still have another week left of being a dawnling*."*

"That's beside the point!" Merri let her hand fall and glowered at him.

"Don't look!" He turned around fast, trying to hide what was in his hands so his conniving friend couldn't see. He'd been excited to give Merri this present for a while now. He'd used a lot of Winderplume on it and had even asked the citadel's blacksmith to teach him a few things. But part of him was nervous. What if she thought it was silly?

"Okay, okay." Merri covered her face again. Silence lingered between them. "You're not planning to scare me, are you?"

Olivander laughed, stepping foot into the water. "If I wanted to scare you, this wouldn't be how I'd do it." The weight of the object in his hand felt like an anvil.

"Why do you sound like you're getting closer?" she asked.

"Probably because I am."

"Wait. Oli, what are you doing?"

"Just relax, Mer. After all these years, don't you trust me?"

Merri harrumphed. "Not fair. You know I trust you. I just might not like what you're doing. Eldarwielle won't be too happy if he hears me scream."

Olivander walked closer, the waves now up to his calves. Almost there. "Oh, don't worry about that. You'll like this." I hope. "You'll be telling him how great of a friend I am." Though Olivander had never seen the whale, he knew all about him; he was never too far away.

"I'm not so sure—"

Olivander covered the distance between them in two long strides, his pants now soaked through to his thighs. When he reached Merri, he placed the object on her head and grabbed the orange coral from her hand before backing away a step. "You can open your eyes now."

Merri didn't waste another second. Her eyes snapped open, her gaze searching his own. "Brilliant, Oli. How am I to see what you've put on my head?" She laughed, about to take it off.

"No, wait!" Olivander pulled a hand mirror from his back pocket, holding it before the sea maiden.

She gasped, her hands flying to cover her mouth. "What in Kerilow?" Her cheeks turned blush pink, and she reached a tentative hand toward her head in wonder. "This is for me?"

Olivander nodded. "I hope you like it. I know you've always wondered what being in a palace was like, so I figured I'd bring it to you. A princess usually wears a crown."

"Oli, I…"

"I kind of made it myself, so it's a bit rough. It's okay if you don't like it," he said hurriedly.

"Like it? I love it!" She continued to stare at the crown's reflection in the mirror, and Olivander watched as the purple gemstones glimmered alongside the strawberry blonde of her hair, the perfect complement to her features. "I've never received a gift like this before. Thank you so much, Oli!" She threw the mirror and jumped toward him, embracing him.

He dropped the coral in the waves and brought his arms around her. He was sopping wet now. Not that he minded. The contact sent his heart skittering against his ribs as he hugged her close. He'd never held her like this before, and he found he rather liked it. He nearly fell over into the water, but he didn't care. She liked his gift, and that's all that mattered. "Happy early birthday, Mer."

She hugged him even tighter. When she finally pulled back, her eyes strayed from his face to the object hanging around his neck, lighting up when she realized what it was. "You finally got one!" She seemed almost as excited for him as she had been about receiving her crown.

Olivander nodded. "For turning thirteen. My father said I'd earned my Winderplume now that I'm one step closer to becoming an adult."

"I remember you telling me about it and how you couldn't wait to get yours.

I've never seen one up close before." She picked the vial up with her fingers and brought it to her eye-level. "It's lavender like my tail!"

Olivander rubbed a hand along the back of his neck. His face heated. "Yeah." He was relieved he never told her the reasons for the colors, them being a mirror to one's heart and all.

"What's it do?" she asked.

"Well, a lot of things. Small things. Magic makes a lot of tasks easier. For example, I can now eat food twice as fast."

Merri snorted. "Why would you want that?"

"So I can eat more."

"What else?"

"I don't know. I haven't really tried much out yet." Aside from making that crown.

"Think it can make me swim faster?"

Olivander laughed. "I guess we'll have to find out."

25

THIEVERY

Jac

Tenby, Wales
September 1996

THE SCENT OF *CIF* ALL-PURPOSE CLEANER and lemons tickled Jac's nose. He blinked. A blanket of peace enveloped him, with the distant waves echoing in the background and the cool breeze blowing in from the window.

What a difference the temperature was from last month. Now that August had come and gone, so had the tourists and the heat wave. Late September was one of Jac's favorite times of year, being more temperate and a calm transition into autumn. Plus, the cooler nights made sleeping easier without AC.

But that wasn't the only thing. His dreams as of late had made sleeping easier, too.

He glanced at his watch; it blinked 9:35 a.m. After he'd finished his routine maintenance checks of the lighthouse and bid everyone goodnight, it had been close to 10:00 p.m. when he sat down to read. But sleep must have claimed him swiftly, for the book lay sprawled open across his chest, and he recalled little of its contents. Jac couldn't remember the last time that had happened.

It was strange. Ever since Eirin Mair showed up in the bay, his dreams had shifted. Instead of nightmares of the drowning prince in Chaera, he dreamt of a young Olivander and a sea maiden named Merri, who still reminded him of their guest.

The muscles in his hands twitched. Not only did she captivate all his attention during the day, but she occupied his subconscious. Again and again and again. Maybe it was because he was with her every day…and he couldn't stop thinking about her whenever he wasn't.

His stomach dipped. *Or maybe it's because of our kiss a few weeks ago.* He hadn't planned on acting on it, considering they'd only known each other for a short time, but she'd kissed him first. He couldn't deny the growing attraction he felt—she was beautiful, achingly so—nor this sense that he already knew her from somewhere and couldn't place *why*. But it was more than that. It was hard to explain, but it was as if her heart seemed to beat in tune with his, which only confused him further. But it didn't matter. He'd kissed her and she'd fled, leaving him alone at North Beach with more questions than answers. He'd wanted to apologize for making her uncomfortable, but he had a strange feeling she would rather him not bring up the subject at all.

So he hadn't, and he tried his hardest to push it to the back of his memory. Still, part of him kept replaying the event over in his mind to figure out what went wrong.

He slipped his thick blanket off his shoulders and stretched, trying to avoid whacking his arms against the tub. Nain, bless her. Ever since Jac had decided to sleep in the outhouse, she'd scrubbed the place clean from top to bottom, including the tub he now slept in.

The basin was surprisingly comfortable, and though he was tall, there was plenty of space to fold his legs. He definitely missed his own—much warmer—room, but it was worth the sacrifice to help Eirin Mair.

A little over a month had passed since the whale sang its song and he'd jumped into the bay to rescue her. Before the kiss, he could tell she was warming up to him like a slow thaw, but now, their interactions were like a winter freeze. It felt like she was keeping him at arm's length again, no matter how much he tried helping her.

At least they were making progress in her studies. He was certain she was close to being able to tell him her name. Which would help matters some.

A knock sounded on the outhouse door. "Jac, are you up?" Nain's voice came muffled on the other side. "I've got to use the privy."

Of course. That was one of the negatives of bedding down in the bathroom. He had to leave the space whenever anyone had to use it. Even in the middle of the night.

"I'll be right out!" Jac shouted. He stood and grabbed his sheets and pillow before stuffing them inside a cotton bag on the floor. He leaned it up against the wall and made for the door. "Good morning," he said, opening it wide. The cool, salty breeze he'd felt earlier tugged on his curls and beckoned him to breathe a little deeper.

"Bore da, Jac!" Nain said, brushing past him. "How'd you sleep?"

"Really good, actually." He yawned and stretched in the doorframe. "Been sleeping better these days."

"You're telling me all it took for you to get a good night's rest was for you to be near the toilet?" Nain chortled. "We should have sent you here months ago."

"I guess so." He shrugged and stepped in the direction of the lighthouse. Jac doubted it was the new location versus *who* occupied the old one that had anything to do with it. His mind had been full of countless other things than his usual research. Which made sense, he supposed.

He should go check on Eirin Mair and see if she'd eaten breakfast yet. Maybe they could do something fun in town today.

"Oh, Jac." Nain poked her head out the door, slowing his retreating figure. "It's bread day again. Please deliver the baps before noon."

It seemed Nain already had half his day planned.

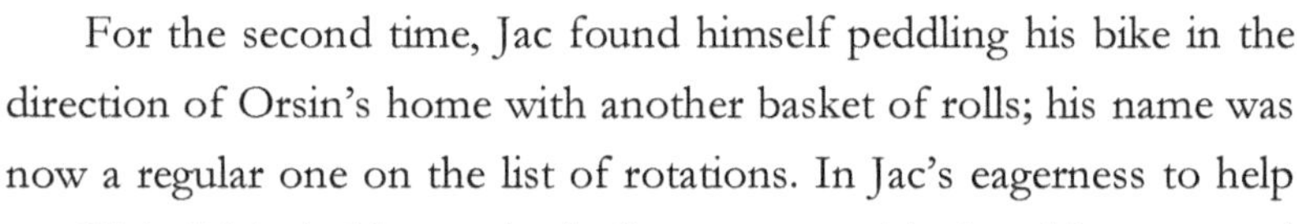

For the second time, Jac found himself peddling his bike in the direction of Orsin's home with another basket of rolls; his name was now a regular one on the list of rotations. In Jac's eagerness to help out Eirin Mair, he'd completely forgotten to visit the older man and ask him about the news article he'd found so pressing earlier.

But now that Jac was practically on Orsin's doorstep, he began second-guessing his decision. What if Orsin truly *was* mad like all of Tenby said he was? Was it safe to spend more time in his company?

Changing your opinion of someone so quickly—*willingly*—was a conscious decision that he hadn't exercised as of late.

Relax, Jac. Nain visits him. You can, too.

But just in case, he decided to go alone instead of bringing Eirin Mair, saying he'd be back soon to do more exploring. He didn't need someone watching him make a fool of himself when he finally asked all the questions spinning around in his head. Even if Nain was already scolding him for taking so long in doing so, be it only in word.

Dearest Jac,

It's about time you visited Orsin again. He could use another man's company; he misses Alun's—don't we all? Make sure to give him the largest basket, would you? And don't let the naysayers get inside your head. He's safe. As are you.

All my love, Nain

Jac supposed he should thank her. Without this "kick in the pants," he wasn't sure when he'd remember to visit Orsin on his own.

When his house came into view, it only took Jac a few minutes to lean his bike against the stone wall, grab the bread, and step up to the recluse's threshold. He raised his hand to knock, but his fist met air as the door flew inward without any prompting.

"Bore da, Jac," Orsin said, standing nonchalantly in the doorway. He wiped his brow, his hands stained with…

Is that blood? Jac's stomach dropped. "How'd—how did you—?"

He chuckled. "I have windows, you know."

"Right." Jac swallowed some of his nerves. He could do this. "Nain baked you more baps."

Orsin smiled. "So I see. Why don't you bring them inside?" He indicated the interior of his home, and Jac's insides knotted even tighter. "The kitchen is to the left, the living room toward the back. I only have to finish something up. I'll join you shortly."

And with that, Orsin left him, not really giving Jac much of a choice.

Tentatively, he stepped over the threshold. Even though about eighty-five percent of him believed Orsin was sane, the other fifteen percent accounted for him leaving the front door ajar. If things got strange, Jac wanted to make sure his exit was clear.

As Jac walked deeper into the house, he found his shoulders relaxing. It wasn't a big space by any means, but it was breezy and light with open windows and white-paneled walls. And neat. Aside from a few paintings on the walls, there wasn't much in the way of clutter or household objects. It sort of resembled an art gallery.

He found the kitchen and placed the basket on the counter. He knew Nain's bread-receivers usually returned the baskets within the week, but he saw a few of them piled up in a stack to the right of the sink. A note was affixed to the bottom one. *Get these to Nain, ye old coot.*

Jac chuckled. It seemed Orsin didn't have the best memory either.

He made his way to the living room and paused. A couch sat in the middle of the room, and across from it rested two brown leather armchairs flanking a fireplace. Apart from the seating, there wasn't much else decorating the room, aside from a ship on the mantel, more watercolor portraits on the walls, and a coffee table with a few books.

Jac plunked down on an armchair and picked one up, leafing through the pages as he waited. The words were written by a neat— cursive—hand, so he assumed it was a diary of sorts, though the dates at the top were scribed in a way he'd never seen before. But what stuck out to him the most was the ink. Not many wrote in red unless they were a teacher grading papers.

I should put it back. But his eyes were faster. Jac realized quickly that the words didn't belong to a diary as much as to a story, and it didn't take him long to be swept away.

Not every morning did one find themselves rocked by a cradle of death.

Savage waves tossed a fishing boat as if it was a featherweight out in the middle of the sea. There was no rain, only massive whitecaps seemingly coming out of nowhere. And a young man was left to fend for himself at the helm.

"Reading anything good?" Orsin entered the room, wiping his hands on a towel.

Jac jumped out of his skin, slamming the book shut as it fell on his lap. His pulse pounded behind his temples.

"It's okay, son. It's there for a reason." Orsin winked and went into the kitchen, which gave Jac a moment to collect himself and replace the book. When the bearded man reentered the room, he brought the basket of Nain's bread and a server on which rested plates, butter, and two mugs of tea. "Help yourself," he said, taking a seat on the couch and already tucking in.

Jac didn't think twice. It made him feel less awkward having something to do. Sure, he'd wanted to talk to Orsin over a month ago, but now that he was finally alone with the man, he found himself unsure how to begin. Or how to act.

Especially when the man was staring at him so intently.

"Where did you say you're from?" Orsin asked. "I know you've only been at the Telor Pendu for a few months now. Since May, correct?"

Jac nodded and swallowed his bite of food. "I honestly couldn't tell you. Doctors said I have partial amnesia and can't recall much of my past. But I like to think Tenby was always meant to be my home."

Orsin hummed before taking a bite of his roll. "I see. Nain tells me you're a big help over there."

She has? "Uh, yeah. I hope so."

"She's quite the woman, that one. Not paying much heed to naysayers and the like."

Maybe talking to Orsin would be easier than Jac thought, when the older man lobbed him such an easy gateway into his next topic. "About that"—Jac swallowed as fast as he could—"Nain and I were talking a little while ago. And I, uh—" How was he to put this delicately? "I stumbled across an old news article in the library, published in 1966. It sparked some questions."

"Ah." Orsin nodded. "I see."

Jac shifted uncomfortably in his seat. *You do?*

"And did you get the answers you were hoping for?" he asked, taking a sip from his mug.

"Well, uh…" Jac fiddled with the remaining bap on his plate. "I guess I walked away with even more."

"Questions?"

Jac nodded and took a bite of his roll.

"Then you've come to the right place." Orsin smiled, and the tension in Jac's shoulders dissipated a little more. "There have been many news articles written over the years, but only one has ever brought people to my doorstep. I assume my arrival to Tenby is of which you speak?"

Jac nodded again.

"Well, what is it you would like to know? I don't pride myself on keeping secrets. It's only that a very few are willing to learn them."

"I guess that's what I want to know the most. Those secrets…or the truth, rather." Jac stuffed the rest of the bap in his mouth and made quick work of it. He was getting closer. "What really happened that day when the news reporter found you along the coast?"

"You mean, what happened to make them coin me 'The Madman of Tenby'?"

Jac paled.

"Chin up, son. I live on the edge of a cliff, not under a rock." Orsin chuckled. "The news reporter got the gist of what happened that day. I *was* patrolling North Beach like I'd lost my mind, determined to make sense of my situation, but that's what happens when you're a little water-logged, I suppose."

"Water-logged?" Jac leaned forward and grabbed his mug. "Had you almost drowned?" He sipped the tea as his mind went back to Eirin Mair and her near encounter with the bay's gravitational pull.

"Not likely, though it makes folks around here more comfortable than saying I'd been spat out by a fish."

Jac spat out his drink in turn. "A *what?*"

"I know, I know. A modern-day Jonah." Orsin raised his mug and took a long sip.

"Wh-what kind of fish?"

Orsin lowered his mug and placed it on the table. "Oh, did I say fish?" He shook his head, chuckling to himself. "The longer I'm away, the more the details fade, I suppose."

"Sir?"

"Sori, son. Don't mind the jabbers of a muttering man; I've had a long day writing in my study." Jac noticed Orsin's hands again; though the red dye wasn't as prominent as when he'd opened the door, parts of his fingers were still stained crimson. Jac's mind flashed back to the book on the coffee table. *Had he written the story inside it?* "I tend to get some details muddled when my head's been in books all day."

"That's okay." Jac couldn't recall details on a good day, and he was *years* younger than the man who sat before him. "So if it wasn't a fish, then what was it?"

Orsin leaned forward and smiled. "It was a whale."

Jac pedaled back to the Telor Pendu with a stack of Nain's baskets jostling in his crate and a heavier messenger bag than when he'd left. He hadn't realized the time and wished he could have stayed at the cottage longer, but he'd promised Eirin Mair he'd be back soon, and it was already nearing three o'clock in the afternoon.

Like his conversation with Nain, he'd left Orsin's with even more questions. His mind swam with secrets, confusing dreams, and whales. But he had a feeling some of that would change. Or at least that was the hope.

When he arrived at the lighthouse, Jac parked his bike out front and heaved his bag onto his lap. He sucked in a breath and pulled out the book hidden under some old cheesecloth, marveling as it rested in his hands. Guilt pricked the back of his conscience as he fanned through the pages, the familiar sight of red ink staring back at him.

He only hoped Orsin didn't notice it missing.

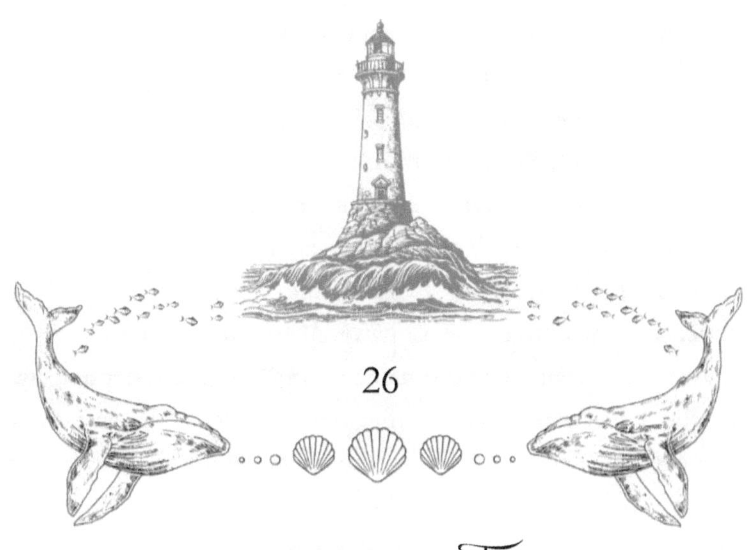

26

A FICTIONAL TRUTH

Merri

Tenby, Wales
September 1996

WHY IS WRITING SO DIFFICULT? Merri gripped the pen between her fingers as she'd done countless times before, letting the instrument carry her hand over the paper like a wave upon the sea. *Sound it out, Merri. Just write your name.* Jac had tried teaching her the vowels, and for some reason, she couldn't remember what sound belonged to which one; a few of them sounded the same to her. How was she to write what she didn't know? Her family had only ever spoken her name aloud; she'd never seen it in print before.

So much for being a Dorsaleene. What's the use if this is harder than it should be?

But she was getting closer. And Jac always told her she was

learning quickly, so she'd have to take his word for it.

The *M* was easy. No other letter made that sound. And she understood there was at least one *R* in her name. But goodness, those pesky vowels would be the death of her.

"More…" Jac read over her shoulder. "More what? I'd be happy to get something for you if you need it, Eirin Mair."

Merri shook her head, crossing the word out. *Right.* *O* was definitely not the correct vowel. *Think, Merri. You can do this.*

"Are you working on your name again?" he asked, stepping away from the table and going to the window's ledge to retrieve his messenger bag. They were back in the tower room this morning after yesterday's outing to Tenby's center, and the cooler weather was a welcome balm indeed, especially with a light blanket draped across her shoulders.

She nodded, determined to figure this out.

Being called Eirin Mair was taking a toll, especially when it was Jac who kept saying it. It was a daily reminder that he'd not only left her behind, but he'd forgotten her, too. *A month and a half of this. Can I handle any more with No-Longer-Prince-Olivander?* She swallowed and looked about the room, her eyes flitting to Jac's before returning to her paper. *Yes.* Despite it all, she liked it here. Which surprised her. Secrets and unanswered questions cloaked both of them like a shrouded garment.

Not to mention that kiss…

Shame coiled like a sea serpent around her ribs. She was only too glad he hadn't brought it up, even though things were now a little stilted between them. It haunted her enough without needing to feel the mortification all over again. All the better to pretend like nothing happened. Though her heart told her otherwise.

"Well, I'll leave you to it. I think my staring over your shoulder is making you nervous again." Jac chuckled and headed for the stairs.

Merri couldn't help but crack a smile at his candor. He wasn't far off, but what he didn't realize was that he was making her nervous for entirely different reasons. She couldn't care less if he watched her write down words.

"See you soon." He raised his bag in a wave and left Merri to solve the riddle of her name on her own.

He'd taught her the basics, had left her countless charts and examples on the table, pointing to pictures and explaining the spellings and pronunciations of the images depicted. Plus, that CD player was now a dear friend. He'd done so much work to prepare her for this moment, and she was determined to see it through.

It was her goal to have her name written neatly on a piece of paper by the time Jac returned.

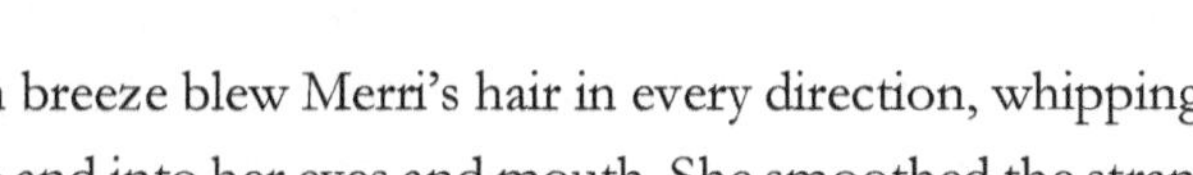

The ocean breeze blew Merri's hair in every direction, whipping it across her face and into her eyes and mouth. She smoothed the strands behind her ears, only to have the same thing happen all over again. She didn't mind, though. It made her feel alive.

A sleek slab of rock warmed by the waning sun's light held her on the cusp of the sea as she sat facing the bay. The Telor Pendu stood like a beacon higher up on the cliff behind her, only a few yards away.

Hours had passed, and there was still no sign of Jac. But Merri wasn't in a rush. She'd done it. Or at least, she *thought* she'd figured it out. Back in the tower room, there lay scrawled across a fresh white slip of paper a slew of names, and she felt confident that when Jac came back, he'd pronounce one of them correctly. The way her name sounded.

Heights Above, her joints ached from writing all morning.

She massaged the appendage and fixed her gaze once more on the sea. To her right in the distance, she watched as people walked along the sand of North Beach, the town only a little ways behind that—if she recalled correctly. She wondered if she could see the little alcove Jac had taken her to from here. Maybe he was there even now. An uncomfortable weight pressed on her stomach at the thought.

Merri blinked and looked to the horizon, thinking about Eldarwielle instead. The waves rolled atop one another, kissing the shoreline, only to retreat again. The sun glistened upon the waters, even in its descent, reminding her of happier times. *I miss you, dear friend.* Breathing deeply of the salt and seaweed, the familiar smells of home wrapped around her lungs and tugged. *So much.*

A lone tear slipped down her cheek, and she hastily swiped it away. She needn't cry again.

She focused her attention on her lap, where a book lay snuggled in the blanket she'd brought from the lighthouse. She'd found the tome amongst Jac's stacks on the windowsill and was instantly captivated by the gold lettering and whale fins. It had something to do with legends and myths and a lost world—she could tell that much by the title. And though the book had many words, it also had a lot of pictures, so she hoped it would make deciphering it a bit easier.

Flipping open to a section in the front, images of sea beasts she'd never seen before and expansive underwater worlds graced the pages, making Merri ache for the ocean's depths only a leap away, lapping at the rocks and her toes.

She flipped the next couple of pages and stopped when her gaze landed on a painting of a white humpback whale. *Eldarwielle. It looks just like him.*

She brought her legs closer to her chest, tugging the large blanket even tighter around her shoulders. *"The sea is no home for a human, Merriweather. No matter how much one wishes for it to be."* Eldarwielle's words came rushing back to her as if they'd been spoken only a moment ago. More weight pressed against her ribs while her stomach twisted into a knot. Oh, how she missed the familiar world she'd grown up in, even if she could never swim beside her whale friend again.

The book now rested atop her knees as she flipped through the first couple pages for something different. Her next breath caught in her throat. Images of sea maidens in all their full-tailed glory smiled back at her, as if taunting Merri with what she no longer had. *It's me. Or what I used to be.* She traced one of the watercolor fins with her pointer finger, marveling at the shiny scales and the feathery softness of the tail, reminiscing about what it felt like to glide through ocean currents. She longed to feel this beautiful. This whole.

Why did I trade it all for love? Remorse swam in her stomach when she thought about seeking out Darya that fateful night. But if-only's would only haunt her at this point.

Merri glanced once more at the sea maidens depicted in the book, studying them closer, until she brought her focus to the text below. It took her a minute, but she deciphered a few of the words:

Though fictional to most, these…beings had to come from somewhere.

Fictional? As in, not real? But everyone knew sea maidens existed. Though many viewed dwellers of the deep as scum, most didn't pay them much heed. Or they didn't care to. Prince Olivander's parents were the exception, and she'd hoped Iun's family would be, too, but he'd never introduced her to anyone…until she became human.

Her stomach soured at the thought. Had Iun been ashamed of her all that time? Was he *still* ashamed of her? She shook her head to get rid of him, focusing once more on the singular word blaring black and bold in front of her. *Fictional.*

It made her wonder where exactly Tenby was. This whole time, she thought maybe it was a distant land in the same world as Chaera, but now she wasn't too sure. *Where am I?*

Merri turned the page and saw sirens, selkies, and sea nymphs on the verso. Her brow dipped low at the images. She'd seen all of them back in Kerilow Bay, had even befriended a sea nymph once and crossed paths with a siren and a selkie a time or two. They were in here as well?

What sort of book is this? Were there no sea maidens or nymphs in Tenby's oceans? No talking whales or creatures?

Merri's mind raced.

What if she told Jac the truth and he didn't believe her? If he no longer remembered Merri, let alone his old identity, then he probably wouldn't believe sea maidens were real either. Now that she had a way to reveal her identity, to potentially remind him or spark some sort of memory…her courage faltered. *Isn't this what I've been looking for? A way to make it easier?* But the idea sounded less and less feasible the longer she sat there and stared at that awful word. *Fictional.*

If she told him, what would he think of her then? Scum? As easily forgettable as before? Crazy?

Would he regret their kiss? *I hope not.*

Why does his opinion still matter so much to me?

Her mind went back to a moment when she'd asked this same question, except she'd voiced it aloud to Eldarwielle:

"Why do I care so much even after all this time? Why does his opinion still matter to me?" Merri swam in the cool waters of Kerilow Bay alongside her whale friend, spilling out her frustrations over Prince Olivander. It had been a year since they'd last spoken; she was now sixteen and just as hurt and confused as when she was fifteen.

"You care about others deeply, Merriweather. Even when they do not return it. That is not something to be ashamed of." *Eldarwielle glided calmly beside her, his deep voice reverberating all around them.* "It is a thing of admiration. And it is that very care which rescued me. That very care which yearns to make others feel known and loved."

Merri stilled, her eyes growing wide. "Loved?" That's all she'd ever wanted herself. But it seemed her father no longer remembered what that looked like since her mother had passed almost thirteen years ago now. Her absence stung, though she wished it stung more.

Eldarwielle hummed. "Yes, child. Loved." *He kept swimming in slow circles around Merri's floating form.* "And it hurts even worse because you have lost someone who you felt could love you back."

She blanched. "Love me back? But that would mean—"

"Yes, Merriweather. I think a part of you has always loved your prince. Even when you did not realize it. And that is why you still care."

The memory came flooding back like a tidal wave, drenching her in its emotional torrent. How had she remembered that? *How had I forgotten?* Part of being a Dorsaleene was to carry the burden of memory, both good and bad; they didn't have the luxury to pick and choose. When Eldarwielle had told her she loved Olivander, she'd pushed it to the deepest recesses of her mind. Trying to forget, like he'd forgotten about her. But to no avail.

She'd been so young. What good was it to fall in love with a human on the shore anyway? It wouldn't have worked. That's why she sought out Darya. When she befriended Iun, she hoped *his* love would be worth the risk of losing her fin.

And now, she had no one.

Oh, Esias, what am I to do? Merri slammed the book shut and put it on the rock beside her. She drew her legs even closer to her chest and rested her quivering chin on her knees. Another tear slipped down her cheek, and this time, she didn't bother hiding it. *Can You even hear me, wherever I am?*

Not only was she forgotten, but according to the book, she was no longer real.

"I think a part of you has always loved your prince." Eldarwielle's words haunted her.

Your prince.

Not anymore.

She'd never felt so alone.

27

TO BECOME KING

Jac

Kerilow Bay, Chaera
Sol 1195

"DO YOU THINK I'LL EVER BE ABLE *to see where you live?" Olivander asked Merri, watching her purple tail flick up and down in the waves as she leaned on her rock. The orange piece of coral sat beside him, half-sinking into the sand. Many springs had come and gone since they first met at Kerilow Bay, and because her birthday had passed only last week, it was now the beginning of summer and they were both the same age: fifteen.*

"I don't know. How long can you hold your breath for?" she returned, cocking her head to the side.

"About seven minutes."

Merri snorted. "Then I'm afraid you'd drown before you even make it inside my house. Can't your Winderplume help?"

Olivander huffed. "Seven minutes is *with the Winderplume, Merri. Believe me, I've tried." He spread his legs out and draped an arm over his knee. "I wish I could show you the citadel then. How long can you remain out of the water?"*

"Only an hour, remember? And with your Winderplume, ninety minutes." Merri shook her head. "Trust me, whenever you leave here, I see if I can go longer, but I start shriveling up like a starfish."

He shook his head. "I'd rather have you alive, thank you." The smile on his lips wilted into a straight line, his gaze now cast on his finger drawing shapes in the sand. He knew Merri's gaze was still on him.

"What's wrong?" she asked.

"Nothing."

"I don't believe you."

"You can believe what you'd like." Though he didn't really mean that. What was the point of Winderplume if it couldn't do big magic? If it couldn't change anything?

"What's bothering you today, Oli? Why's visiting each other's homes so important to you all of a sudden?"

He finally looked up and shrugged. "I don't know. We've known each other for seven years now, and I feel bad that all we can do is sit on a beach."

"But I like where we sit." She sounded hurt.

"I do, too, don't get me wrong." Olivander shook his head. "I just wish we could see more of each other's worlds, you know? It's one thing to tell you about Jasper and the way the halls glisten in the morning light. Or the gardens my mother loves and the stables. But to see it all for yourself…" I guess I just want to share that with you. Before it's too late.

Merri held her arms close to her chest. "I'm sorry."

Olivander snapped his gaze up. "What? Why are you apologizing?"

"For not being a friend you can bring places." She sniffled. "For living somewhere you can't see either."

He shook his head. "No, Mer. That's not it." Why had he even brought this up? He couldn't explain himself well, and now he'd just made his best friend cry.

How could he tell her that being with her, regardless of their location, mattered the most? It was just that…he wanted to give her more, and he wasn't sure if he'd even get a chance to do that. Their spot by the ocean was special, but was it so wrong that he wished to create other memories with her? Before his duties as king came first?

His father was sick, and Olivander wasn't sure how much longer he had to live. The physicians worked tirelessly to restore him back to good health, but there hadn't been much improvement yet. And to make matters worse, his mother wasn't eating, too worried over her sick husband.

What was Olivander to do? He was told to live life as normal, but how could he? His duties as a son trumped his declining childhood. Not to mention, if his father passed soon, he'd be crowned king once he turned eighteen.

"Then what is it?" Merri didn't take her eyes off of him. "Why are you acting so strangely?"

Olivander groaned inwardly. He couldn't face the truth right now. Not when it showed how weak he felt. "It's nothing."

"Oli, we're best friends. I thought we told each other everything."

He looked up and his gaze took in Merri's beautiful eyes and perfect smile before finding its place on the sand again. His pounding heart betrayed him. Not everything. At least, not yet. *But most things, yes. She was right, though. She deserved to hear what was bothering him.*

"I don't know if I can do it," he finally said.

"Do what?"

"Become king."

Her brow furrowed. "But that won't be for a long time, right? You have plenty of time to get ready before then."

He shook his head. "My father's sick. I don't know how long he has left." It was hard not thinking of the consequences of death when its cold fingers gripped someone you loved by their throat. Even the Winderplume couldn't stop death, though it could keep it at bay. He'd pray to Esias and hope the magicked dust would be enough.

"How long has he been sick for?" Merri's words were gentle, as if she was afraid to ask the wrong question.

"Months. Maybe even years. Many turnings." Time had a way of blurring everything together. "It's hard to recall."

"Oli, I'm so sorry." Merri swam over to him and grabbed one of his hands. "I had no idea it was that bad. You never said anything."

He shrugged. "He seemed to be doing better for a time, so I didn't think it was worth mentioning. I think we're all just waiting for the Winderplume to save him."

They sat in silence, and Olivander didn't let go of her hand, thankful for the way it anchored him to reality.

"Why do you think you won't make a good king?" she asked quietly.

He kept his gaze on the horizon, watching the dipping gulls and glistening waves like little dots in the distance. Images of his parents bringing him to the bay paraded before his memory; his father somehow always put family first even when he was in charge of an entire kingdom. "My father—" He swallowed a rise of unexpected emotion. "Well, he's the best. One of the best kings Chaera has ever known. He's secured peace for generations, fought for it with every ounce of his strength, only he hasn't needed to form a political alliance to do so. He's given the Winderplume to commoners and neighboring countries, sharing it willingly the way it had first been shared with us. Peace has been kept since. That was almost unheard of hundreds of years ago." He took a breath. "My father's strong of character, as stoic as iron, but he has a heart of compassion, too. Like grit that's weathered much of life and turned the better for it. He's ruled his people well for years."

Merri squeezed his hand. "He sounds a lot like you."

Olivander raised an eyebrow. "Me? I haven't done half of those things, Merri, and I hate public speaking."

"One's ability to speak in public doesn't determine if they're fit to rule."

"But it does make a difference." Olivander stood, dropping her hand in the process, and started pacing along the shore. "Don't you see, Merri? I'm not as *confident as him. I might be better at wielding a sword, but what good will that do in a land that thrives best under peace? What if I can't maintain it? I can't negotiate like my father. What if my leadership causes Windkeep to fall and everyone suffers because of it? I couldn't bear that."*

"Do you hear yourself, Oli?" Merri retorted. "None of this is true, and you know it!"

"Well, it sure as the depths feels like it." He kicked a loose stone and sent it kerplunking somewhere into the shallows. Watching it disappear and the ripples overtaken by the breaking waves, he felt the fight drain out of him in much the same way. He reclaimed his seat on the sand and heaved a sigh toward the sky before shaking his head. "I'm sorry, Mer."

"For what?"

"I've been under a lot of stress lately. I didn't mean for you to see me like this."

"I'll take you in any form, Oli. Happy, annoying, angry…you get the idea. But fearful? I didn't think you'd let its hooks sink so deep into your heart to the point that you're fighting its release." She reached for his hand once more, and Olivander let her. "If you allow it to remain, I'm afraid it'll begin to fester and feed you lies until that's all you can see."

Olivander raked his other hand through his hair and expelled a long breath. "You honestly believe I can do this? When the time comes?"

She sat up straighter and nodded. "I've never doubted it. Since the moment I first met you, I knew you'd make a great king." She squeezed his fingers. "You're already a great friend."

Olivander stared at her, letting her words sink in. Would he truly make as great of a king as she thought? He hoped so. There were too many to disappoint otherwise. He squeezed her hand back before letting go and leaned forward, his forearms on his knees. It was a sunny day today, and they sat in silence for a few moments beneath its rays, the waves the only sound between them. The wind blew gently across the sea, and Olivander watched as it tousled Merri's mane and sent a couple strands across her face like little tongues of flame. One corner of his mouth lifted higher than the other.

"What? Why are you smiling like that?" she asked, tilting her head to the side.

"No reason."

"Oli!"

He laughed. "All right. If you must know, it's your hair. It almost looks like fire in the sunlight. Fitting, seeing as it matches your personality."

Her eyes widened. "That is completely off topic. And no, I'm as docile as a clam."

He laughed. "It's very pretty, Mer. As are you."

She huffed, hiding the reddening of her cheeks. "Fine. But just know, the next time I try to cheer you up, I won't be wasting as much breath." A full smile spread wide, pulling her cheeks toward her ears, trying as she might to hide it.

And that was all the encouragement his heart needed.

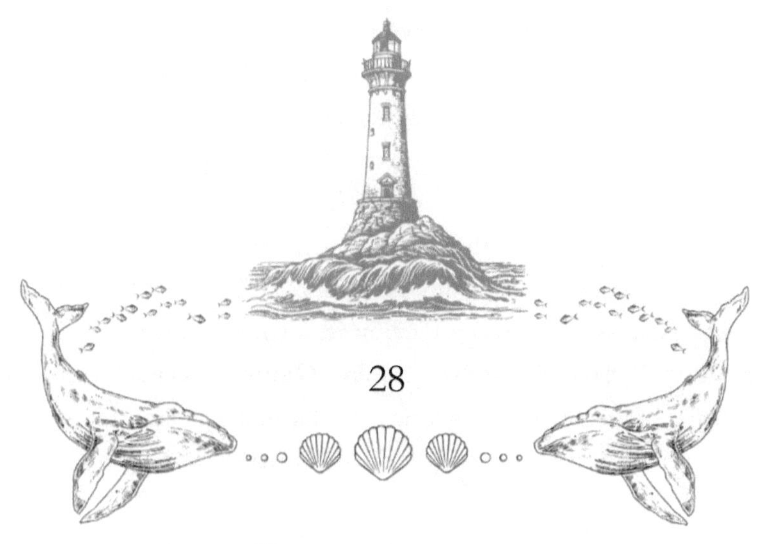

28

HER NAME IS MERRI

Jac

I'M A THIEF. A NO-GOOD, DIRTY, ROTTEN THIEF.

After he'd left Eirin Mair for the afternoon, he'd given her some space so she could work in peace...*and* so he could find a secluded spot to read Orsin's story. But no matter how much Jac tried to fan through the pages and read more of the scribbled red ink, the guilt from taking the book to begin with magnified tenfold. It was one thing to read it inside the house to which it belonged; it was another matter entirely when he tried reading it elsewhere.

What was I thinking?

He should have asked to borrow it, not stolen it like some petulant child when the man wasn't looking.

And now he was too ashamed to face anyone. Which was part of the reason why he'd stayed away for so long. That, and because of the tide. He'd made his way to St. Catherine's Island and had fallen asleep in the shadows of the towering fort. One of the perks was knowing the workers; they allowed him past roped-off areas. And when he awoke, it was much later than he'd thought, high tide now at its peak.

There was no escaping any time soon, so it forced Jac to reason out his most recent dream. Once more, a young prince and a young sea maiden had paraded across his mind, Olivander telling Merri about his fears of becoming king one day. Something about it seemed reminiscent of a time gone by, but that confused him all the more.

Why do these dreams keep happening?

First, he'd only dreamt of Chaera and Prince Olivander: blurry faces and poor details, never fully grasping the whole picture, but picking up enough on certain elements to know the dreams were consistent. And then came the nightmares: sea monsters that swallowed people. Drowning. Getting lost. Random storms. Death. Now, it was of a youthful prince and a sea maiden, still blurry, but redolent of...*something*. It was like an itch he couldn't scratch.

Am I vitamin deficient? Stressed?

Or perhaps he just had a lot on his mind.

"I'm a lighthouse keeper; what could possibly be on my mind?" Jac shook his head and buried it in his hands. "What's wrong with me?" Did anyone else dream of places and people the way he did? It didn't make sense. Was there something he was missing?

Jac's mind went back to Orsin. "Maybe *I'm* the Madman of Tenby." His dreams definitely weren't improving, and now, he'd stolen a book.

He groaned. He may not get to hear Eirin Mair's thoughts, but he had a feeling she'd think he was crazy and be disappointed. And for some reason, that bothered him. Not to mention what Nain would think if *she* found out.

Jac looked upward and faced the darkening sky. *Forgive me*, he pleaded. What a mess. "I need to bring this book back." He stood abruptly. "Now."

He left the fort behind and made his way to the base of St. Catherine's Island and surveyed the damage before him. By the light of the waning sun, he could tell the sandbar was still buried beneath feet of water. Which meant…he wouldn't be stepping foot on the mainland dry.

But that didn't matter. Once he left this island with the blasted book burning a hole in his bag, he'd retrieve his bike before stopping by the Telor Pendu. He wanted to bring Orsin some more of Nain's baps. Nothing seemed to smooth things over like her baked goods.

Jac hoped it would be enough to earn himself some forgiveness.

"What on earth happened to you, Jac? Why are you wet as a drowned rat?" Nain's eyes widened when he stormed through the lighthouse door and began rummaging around in the kitchen.

He hadn't a moment to lose. His limbs were sore, not to mention he'd only swum with one arm so his other could keep his bag above the waves…everything felt a little *off.* "Do we have any baps left, Nain?" Jac flung open cabinets and lifted lids off of jars, trying to remain steady on his feet.

"No. Tomorrow's bread day. We're all out at the moment," she said from her seated position at the table, her knitting falling into her lap.

"Do we have *anything*?" he asked.

"What am I, a bakery?"

"I just need something. Doesn't need to be big. Do we have any bara brith, some pudding?" A soft hand came down on his shoulder as he headed toward the refrigerator, stopping him in his tracks.

"Now what's going on, Jac? Why are you acting so strange all of a sudden?"

He cursed under his breath. *I'm an idiot.* He hadn't considered how his haste would come across. And he didn't feel like spewing his sins before his grandmother. "I'm just really hungry," he said, finally opening the fridge and spotting a leftover bowl of cawl pushed toward the back. *Perfect.* He grabbed the meal and ripped off the cling film before sticking it in the microwave.

"Are you sure that's it?"

Jac nodded, his guilt twisting into an even tighter knot. *Now I'm a liar.*

"Men and their stomachs." Nain shook her head and shuffled back to her seat, still giving him a questioning look.

When the timer beeped, Jac retrieved the cawl and headed for the door once more.

"Jac?"

"Hmm?" He paused on the threshold, the porcelain nearly singeing his fingertips as he held fast to the bowl. *In hindsight, maybe I should have waited to heat this up.*

"Where are you off to at this hour? It's nearly nine o'clock."

"Oh." Again, he hadn't thought this through. His only aim was to make things right, forget whatever else happened in between. He hadn't realized the time. Would Orsin still be awake? "I want to get a good look at the stars," Jac said, shrugging. No lie there; he would do so as he walked.

"What about your Eirin Mair? Can't you view them up there with her?" Nain leaned forward and placed her knitting on the table. "She's been alone all afternoon, only coming down for supper before heading out to the rocks. I don't know when she came back in, but she's been waiting for you, wherever you were off to." Jac felt his urgency leave him. *Eirin Mair.* How had he forgotten about checking in on her? "It's not like you to leave others behind."

No. It isn't. He'd left her with the intention of coming back to see her progress on her name and how she was doing. And instead he'd abandoned her for what felt like an entire day. Some tutor he was.

"You're right. I'll go." He was about to head for the stairs.

"Jac, your clothes." Nain looked him up and down, reminding him that he was utterly bedraggled and dripping water all over the floor.

"Right." He grimaced. "Be back in a minute." He made for the outhouse to grab fresh clothes, only pausing to glance in the direction of Orsin's home. He sighed, then took a sip of the cawl. That visit would have to wait until tomorrow.

Jac headed toward the stairs, his guilt now as heavy as his wet clothes sitting in a sodden pile in the hamper. He felt like the rudest, thieving guttersnipe alive. And now he felt ridiculous for using the word guttersnipe.

He climbed the stairs carefully, wondering if Eirin Mair was asleep or not. He didn't want to wake her if she was. As he neared the landing, he noticed light coming from the door that stood ajar. Relief pushed some of the guilt away; at least he could set things right with one person tonight. He took a steadying breath and knocked before edging the door open all the way.

Eirin Mair was on the windowsill, her knees drawn to her chest as she looked out over the dark waters. She hadn't even heard him come in.

He cleared his throat. "Helo," he said, stepping over the threshold. She didn't turn around. Why did he suddenly feel so awkward in his own room? *Because you're an idiot, Jac.* Right. "I'm sori I didn't come back sooner; I got distrac—" He paused at the table when he saw a list of names on a white piece of paper; a smile tugged on his lips. "Did you write all of these?"

Eirin Mair nodded, finally pulling her gaze away from the ocean. Her eyes looked puffy, like she'd been crying, and the smile he'd grown accustomed to seeing as of late was no longer there. What on earth happened while he was away?

"Is everything okay?"

She hopped off the windowsill, ignoring his question, and headed for the table which stood between them. Picking up the paper, she handed it to him, pressing it toward his chest.

"You want me to read these?" he asked, studying the page and then her face. Her features were schooled as if she was attempting not to cry again.

She nodded again, opening her mouth to pretend like she was speaking.

"Out loud?"

One more nod.

He understood. If he read the names to her, then she could confirm if one of them sounded like hers. Then he'd find out what was troubling her afterward. "Okay, here goes. Marie," he began.

She shook her head.

"Mary."

Another shake.

"Mari."

Not that one either.

He continued down the list and each name he said, Eirin Mair kept shaking her head and biting her lip. He hoped for her sake that at least one of these was right. She seemed eager, desperate even. Like everything depended on *this* moment. He was nearing the list's end when an expanding feeling in his chest overtook him as he stared at one of the remaining names. *Merri.* The word rooted itself in his very being and got stuck there. For some reason, he already knew the answer. *It's this one.*

"Me—" He cleared his throat and tried pushing the word out. "Merri."

Her eyes widened, and there was a look in them he couldn't read. It was as if she'd finally tasted water after being parched for so long. Like a sun breaking through storm clouds. She nodded vigorously, her eyes glazing over.

"Your name is Merri." It wasn't a question, but more of a statement. The name felt strangely familiar on his tongue.

A smile overtook her features. Was that a glimmer of hope in her irises?

"Merri," he said again, finding the name both recognizable and foreign. Lyrical and confusing. Was it a coincidence that she shared the same name as the sea maiden from his dream? It would be even stranger if she had a tail… He cleared his throat a third time, feeling oddly lightheaded. "It's a beautiful name. I've never heard it before." Which was true; aside from his dream, no one he knew shared it.

Her smile faltered, and the look of hope that was once kindled in her eyes was doused. She took a tentative step back, then another, and her cerulean eyes became even more glossy than before. The wall Jac had seen slowly coming down over the course of the past couple of weeks was now reconstructed once again.

The realization did something strange to his chest.

Suddenly, a book was thrust into his hands, and when he looked down, he saw a piece of paper sticking out of the top as if to mark the page.

Then she fled. Again. Merri disappeared from the lighthouse and into the night.

She left him all alone in his tower, and he'd only just learned her name.

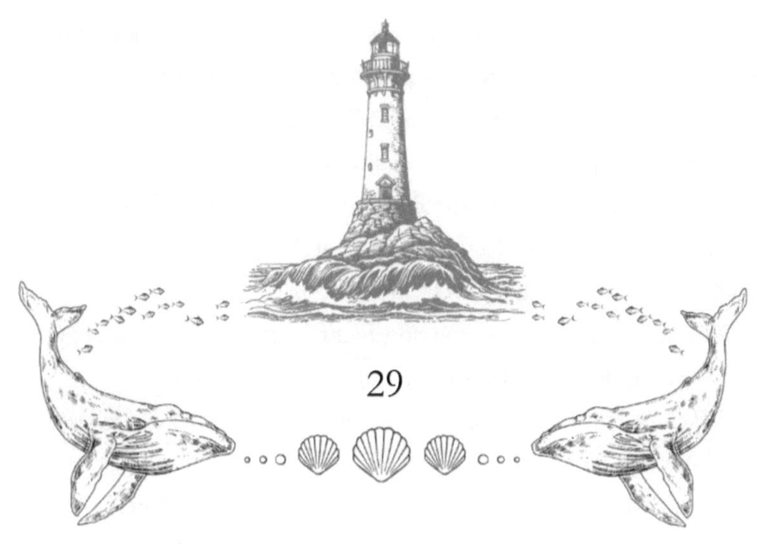

29

TEARS IN THE SAND

Merri

Tenby, Wales
September 1996

I CAN'T DO THIS. I CAN'T DO THIS.

Merri ran away again. When one lost their ability to speak, it was easier just to flee. She didn't have a particular destination in mind, only that she remained near the coast. And she wouldn't stop until the tears stopped first.

I can't do this.

I thought I could. But I can't.

Not anymore.

She thought that hearing Jac call her Eirin Mair was hard, but she was wrong. Oh, so wrong. When her real name slipped past his lips, she was transported to Kerilow Bay close to three years ago, remembering fifteen-year-old Prince Olivander on the edge of the sea, looking at her as if she meant something to him. But now, when he'd called her by name without any recollection…it was her undoing. The last shard of hope she carried was shattered. Utterly and completely.

She'd never loved Iun, she realized. Only the thought of him. That maybe someone could love her back and wouldn't leave her if she became what he wanted. *You're a fool, Merri!*

The tears kept falling, making it difficult to see and navigate the rocks leading down to the shore. But she ran on.

Why did Eldarwielle send me here? Why did Esias make me with these ridiculous emotions?

Merri had wondered if Jac was the one who needed help, but there was nothing left to offer. Her fragile heart couldn't take it anymore. She wasn't made for tough things.

I kissed Oli. And he doesn't even know who I am.

Her toe snagged on one of the rocks, and she went tumbling, the hard jagged edges melding into the soft parts of her body. A silent scream tugged on her throat as the rocks scraped and scratched her exposed skin, rolling over sand and stone until her body came to a painful stop.

She didn't even attempt to move. With her face pressed against the tiny grains, she sobbed even harder.

Esias, take this pain away. Help me not to feel.

Her tears mingled with the sand, caking onto her skin.

I loved him. I still love him. And I've never stopped.

Gentle and firm arms gathered her up, and when she opened her eyes, she saw she was sobbing against Jac's chest.

"I've got you, Merri. It's okay." He held her tighter. "Everything is going to be okay."

She buried her face into the folds of his shirt, gripping the material with her fingers. The tears wouldn't stop flowing, her heart wouldn't stop hurting, and she was so incredibly weak.

"It's gonna be okay," he said again, rubbing small circles on her back.

How will it be okay?

The man she loved was holding her so tenderly, and he didn't remember anything about her. He never would.

Merri had never let herself cry so much before. The wracking coughs and uncontrollable shaking—it exhausted her beyond words. She heaved mighty breaths, nearly choking on sobs as her energy waned. And without even knowing, she drifted off to sleep.

Something tickled Merri's cheek, and when she opened her eyes, she was startled to see a piece of coastal straw inches from her face. She was resting amongst sand dunes with a jacket draped over her, the morning sun climbing the orange-hued sky and the sound of the crashing waves only footsteps away. Sandpipers skittered about her feet, chirping their pre-migratory flights.

It was morning.

I must have fallen asleep outside. She yawned, but then snapped her mouth shut. *Why am I outside?*

The previous night and its hauntings came back in a rush. *Jac knows my name. I ran away. I fell.*

Unbidden warmth welled up in her middle. *He came after me.*

She tilted her head skyward and caught her breath. He was still here even now, holding her. His back pressed up against a mound of sand while his arms cradled her weary body. He'd come looking for her, had comforted her, and had never left. Merri was mortified for having fallen asleep on him, forcing him to remain outside, but he looked almost…peaceful. As if he wouldn't have wanted to be anywhere else.

Was it possible to feel such joy alongside so much suffering?

The wise thing to do would be to get up and put some distance between them. She was no stronger this morning than she had been last night, though the sun seemed to chase away the shadows better than the moon had.

Call her a glutton for misery, but she took a moment to stare up at him, drinking in his features now that there was daylight and she was so close. His jaw was strong and smooth, only the subtlest of hair shadowing his chin. His skin was tan from being outside so much, and he still looked very much like he had when they'd last seen each other back in Chaera all those years ago, albeit a more mature version.

My Oli. Without thinking, her hand lifted to touch his cheek. And that's when Jac woke up.

Keeper's Heights. She pulled it back. *I shouldn't have done that.* Her neck and ears grew impossibly hot, her breaths rushed. *He's not mine.* He blinked a few times as if trying to register what had just happened. She pushed herself away from him, the jacket dropping from her shoulders, but he grabbed her hand, holding it firmly in his.

"Wait, Merri. Don't run away again. Please."

She stilled at the sound of her name. Was that concern in his eyes? She nodded, but Jac kept hold of her hand as if he was afraid she'd still disappear.

"Are you feeling any better this morning?"

Her insides were in knots. Her eyes felt puffy, her body ached, but after examining her arms and legs, she realized she wasn't as cut up and bloody as she had thought. But it wasn't the physical she was worried about as much as it was her heart. She'd finally admitted she loved him, and for some reason, that changed everything.

"I wish you could tell me what's going on," Jac said. "Then I'd be able to properly help you." He shook his head, as if annoyed with himself. "Do you miss home? Is that it? Have you felt like you've stayed here too long and want to find your family? I wouldn't blame you if you did."

That was part of it, yes. But there was so much more. *So much.*

"I'm really sori I left you all alone yesterday."

Merri shook her head. He shouldn't have to apologize for that. She didn't need constant attention, nor was that his responsibility. It was only that his absence made her deep loneliness all the more pressing. And that wasn't entirely his fault.

Why don't you remember me? If she could find the answer to this burning question, she had a feeling it would help her to move on. Heal some of the brokenness. And then she could find Eldarwielle and go back to Chaera. Tenby was proving to be more dangerous for her, after all.

She looked at him as if offering an apology, unsure how to proceed.

"Don't look at me like that, Merri. As if you're some burden to bear. I invited you to stay here because I *wanted* you to. It's been a lot of fun teaching you this past month and a half—it gives me something else to look forward to every day."

Her heart swelled despite telling herself to keep fortifying the walls surrounding it.

"And knowing you, you're probably worried about last night. Don't be." *He's still holding my hand.* His grip had gentled, his thumb running over a few of her bloodied knuckles. "After you fell asleep, I carried you somewhere more comfortable, but I didn't want to wake you. So I figured I'd hold you until morning." Was that embarrassment coloring his cheeks?

Merri's vision blurred. *Not again with the tears.* Why was Jac being so kind? Even after she'd run away multiple times. Didn't he realize what it was doing to her?

"I hope you'll forgive me if I did something to offend you. Is this—" he said, his gaze suddenly vulnerable. "Is this about our kiss?"

Merri's pulse jumped. *Our kiss.* She shook her head despite everything screaming *yes*. It played a big role, but she couldn't face that right now. Not yet.

"I just wish I knew what to do." Jac sighed.

It seemed like he really cared for her, that somehow he wasn't just saying these things to make her feel better. But why?

Because that's the kind of man Prince Olivander is. The kind of king he will be one day. Suddenly, his demeanor at the carriages back in Chaera made sense. He hadn't been careless like she'd once thought. He'd been angry because he couldn't do anything. His inability to act made him feel useless, which was probably how he was feeling now.

Merri silently chastised herself. *Oli has a heart of gold, and I've been so selfish to think only of myself.* If only it were possible to forget her sorrows and help him. Windkeep needed their future king, and here she'd been so concerned about her own affairs and happiness. The aching was keen, but it didn't compare to an entire kingdom's loss.

He cleared his throat. "When you ran away last night, I was afraid I'd never see you again. Just learning your name, all you left me with was an overdue library book thrust against my chest—"

Merri squeezed his hand. *The book!* How had she forgotten about the book? She'd given it to Jac with the hope that he'd read it instead of coming after her. But that clearly hadn't worked. She was both terrified and eager for him to see what she wrote inside. But maybe it could help. Standing fast, she pulled him to his feet. *Where did he put it?*

"What is it?" He retrieved his jacket and dusted off the sand. "Was it something I said?"

She nodded. If only she could get him to open the book, then maybe he could understand part of this sordid tale. Maybe it would lead to more questions, and she could somehow tell him he was a prince. Prince Olivander. What was the worst that could happen? Jac would leave her entirely? He'd already forgotten about her, so if he chose not to believe her, what did it matter?

The loss would heal with time. *I hope.*

Merri pulled him along, back to the lighthouse, running the path the same way in which she'd fled.

It was time Jac learned the truth.

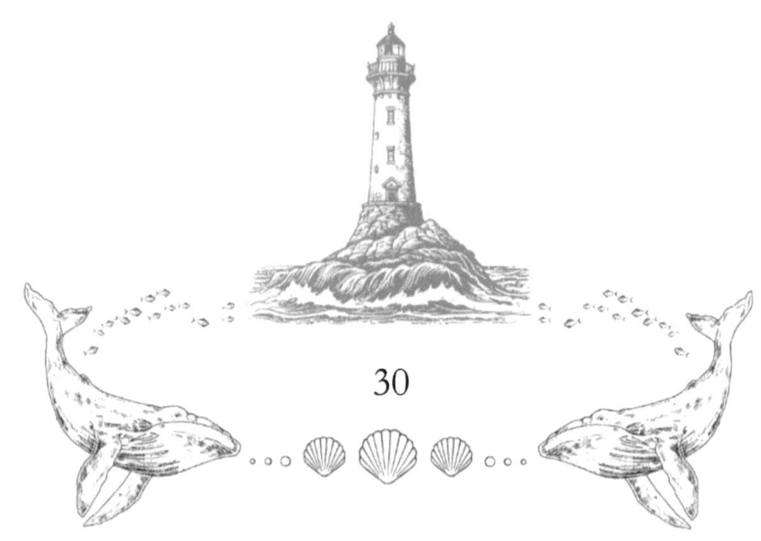

30

A SEA MAIDEN AND A PRINCE

Jac

Tenby, Wales
September 1996

JAC LOOKED DOWN AT THE PIECE of paper stuck between the pages of the book and then back up at the woman standing before him. Her strawberry-blonde hair curled gently down her shoulders, looking like one of the rays of light currently beaming in through the lighthouse window. She'd written something on the paper, just three simple words with an arrow pointing to one of the pictures in the book: *This is me.* He swallowed the words he'd failed to say earlier and tried again. "You're a *sea maiden*?"

Merri's cheeks were the color of flames. She nodded as she bit her lip. Was she serious? It didn't look like she was joking.

"But…how is this possible?" Jac shook his head. "They…they

don't exist."

She reared back, hugging her arms tighter around her middle. Had she been afraid he'd say that?

Jac's mind flashed once more to his dreams, of a young sea maiden named Merri on the edge of the ocean, with an equally as young Prince Olivander. Was it merely coincidence anymore? Were the two girls one and the same? But how had this dream Merri ended up here…and with *legs*? And who was the prince?

He stumbled back a few paces, his head growing impossibly light. *What's happening to me?* His vision tunneled on the sides, and before he knew it, he was falling. He thought he heard a muted scream or a whispered name from somewhere when suddenly, images flashed before his mind, causing his head to spin even more.

He was standing on the edge of the sea, only this time, he wasn't the prince. He was Jac Hughes. The wind was blustery and whipping around him, and in the water was a sea maiden, with a shimmering lavender tail flashing in the waves.

When he looked into her eyes, he saw Merri's as clear as the dawn, the brilliant blue rimmed by red and puffy underskin. She'd been crying, and she was directing her pain at Jac.

"You left me" were the only words she said, her grief as wide as the ocean. *"You left me."*

Jac's stomach dropped to his feet. *"I didn't mean to."* But did he? He had no idea where he was or what the sea maiden meant. *You left me.* Her voice rang in his ears. But how could he leave what he didn't remember?

Her image disappeared like a mist, and past dreams flooded his mind. Of little Merri and the prince meeting for the first time, then of Olivander introducing her to his parents. Next came the one where he'd given her a crown, and most recently, when he'd told her about his fears of becoming king. All the while, countless other visions of their time spent together filled in the gaps. The images paraded and flashed their taunting stories in his mind on repeat, more vibrant than they'd ever been before, though only Merri's face showed clearly for what it was. The two were one and the same.

The visions faded, and all he could see was light warming the space behind his eyelids.

When Jac opened his eyes, Merri was leaning over him, and he realized his head was resting somewhere in her lap. *What on earth just happened? What* was *that?*

She stared down at him with those same cerulean blue eyes, her brow pulled low as if to ask "Are you okay?"

"I'm good." He rubbed his head, massaging his temples as he held her gaze. She'd just screamed at him and accused him a moment ago. *But no.* That had been a dream. It never happened. Jac hadn't stepped foot on that beach before, and he'd never beheld a sea maiden…until recently. "Are you okay?" he asked, almost unblinking. His mind was still trying to play catch-up.

She nodded. Like she always did.

Was the woman before him an actual sea maiden? If not, then why did he keep dreaming…*thinking* about her as if she was? *Something weird is going on here.*

A sudden thought struck him. His mind went through the catalog of his dreams and decided on the best one. Using his core, he rocked forward to a sitting position and turned around to face her. He needed to test his theory.

"Merri." The use of her name sent a jolt through his limbs; it still felt familiar in all the ways it shouldn't. "Did you ever receive a crown as a gift?"

Her eyes widened as if in surprise, and Jac faltered. Maybe it was a stupid question. But then she nodded, and his pulse quickened. He pressed on. "Was it from someone…" *Here it goes. If I say his name, I'll no longer be the only one who knows about him.* "Someone named Prince Olivander?"

Merri stood back, her eyes even wider than before. Was that excitement? Surprise? Fear?

Have I just proven myself crazy?

She nodded again, a slow smile spreading across her face. And then she pointed at him. At Jac. And she wouldn't stop.

"So you know of a prince named Olivander?" Were Jac's two worlds colliding? Was he finally losing his mind? *What's happening?*

Merri moved even closer.

"What is it?" he asked her. "I believe that you're a sea maiden. I don't know how it's possible, but I believe you."

Merri didn't stop pointing at him, her finger now inches from his chest.

Jac grabbed her whole hand and held it there. "What are you trying to tell me?"

She waved her other arm around, pointing and gesturing, but Jac wasn't following. Then she stood up straight, as if struck by a sudden thought, and pulled away before running to the table still scattered with writing utensils and books from yesterday's lessons.

Scribbling furiously over the paper, Merri crossed words out, tore up sections only to begin again, all the while biting her lip in concentration. Jac walked over to her, curious what she might be doing. Her writing had improved greatly since they'd first begun, but even so, her vocabulary was pretty limited. How would she succeed in getting her point across?

Finally, when she was done, she thrust the paper toward him and made him grasp it with both hands. A feeling of déjà vu enveloped every sense in his body. When he trained his eyes on the paper, he saw words and a drawing, a combination that sent his heart rate through the lighthouse roof.

There was a picture of a crown, similar to the one Prince Olivander had given to Merri in his strange dream. And right next to it were four printed words that would change his life forever:

You are the prince.

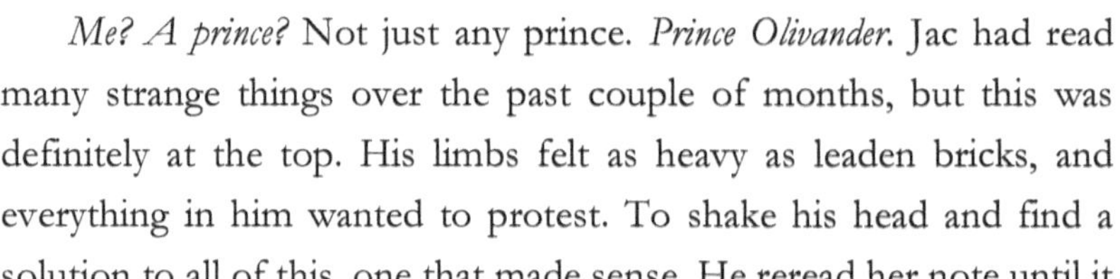

Me? A prince? Not just any prince. *Prince Olivander.* Jac had read many strange things over the past couple of months, but this was definitely at the top. His limbs felt as heavy as leaden bricks, and everything in him wanted to protest. To shake his head and find a solution to all of this, one that made sense. He reread her note until it was all he could see.

There was no way he was this prince Merri was talking about. It wasn't possible. He was a lighthouse keeper. He knew nothing about how to run a kingdom. He lived in Tenby, not some distant land of Chaera.

Chaera. Why did that word suddenly feel so incriminating? As if it were the final nail driven into his crazy coffin? If none of this was true, then why else would he be dreaming of such a place if it didn't exist? If he wasn't the very man Merri deemed him to be?

Jac's mind screamed. He'd thought he was getting a headache earlier, and now he had a full-blown migraine. *This can't be right.* He was pacing the tower room of the Telor Pendu, Merri watching him with curious and fearful eyes. It pained him to see her like that; she didn't deserve to be treated like she was a liar, no matter how much he was struggling to believe her.

"I'm not upset with you, Merri," he said, still pacing. "I don't believe you have a reason to lie to me, but this is a lot to wrap my mind around. I mean, *me?* A *prince?*" He shook his head. "You can trust me when I say I'm processing this as best as I can." Truly, how else was one to digest the news that they were a forgotten royal of a make-believe kingdom? Typically, he'd laugh at such a notion, but his dreams told him otherwise.

My dreams. He glanced up at Merri. *She has no idea I've been dreaming about her this whole time.*

She tilted her head when she looked at him, as if trying to understand what was running through his mind.

He was just as lost. There was so much *he* didn't understand. None of this seemed logical, but…had this accounted for why his memories of the past were so foggy? That it wasn't partial amnesia like the doctor had suggested?

Am I actually considering this as a possibility?

He ran to his nightstand and thrust open the drawer, rifling through its contents. *Where is it? Come on.* Why was he a packrat with so much trash? He moved aside cough drop wrappers and an empty Smith's Snackfood Company bag to find a purple stone buried underneath. He didn't remember where he'd gotten it, but it had been in his pocket when he'd arrived in Tenby. *Maybe that's important.* He replaced the stone before resuming his task. Finally, his hand found what it was looking for and he withdrew the small leather-bound folio. He unclasped it and nearly ripped it open, his eyes scanning the water-damaged paper within.

Name: Jac Elis Rooks. Date of Birth: Middle of spring. Age: 18. Born in:
______.

He squinted hard at the writing. The paper was one of the few items he'd had in his messenger bag when he arrived in Tenby. He hadn't thought much about it at the time; it was enough that he knew his name, though it would have helped to know the actual date of his birth rather than a generalized *middle of spring.* Not to mention, the place he was born in was empty as if it had forgotten to write itself down. He'd been so relieved to find a place to stay that he'd never taken the time to delve into this deeper.

"Are you sure you're not confusing me with someone else?" he asked, looking up from the paper.

She shook her head, all seriousness and little irony.

And that's that. He slammed the folio shut and shoved it back inside the drawer. He'd revisit that later.

"So if I'm this prince, then why am I *here*?" He stood and started pacing again. "Why don't I remember who I am?" For all Jac knew, he had only ever been himself. According to that paper, he'd come to Tenby as Jac Rooks and was just as soon adopted as Jac Hughes. His name had never been Olivander.

"If I'm this prince," he continued, remembering all his dreams, especially those of late, "then that means I'm in charge of a kingdom. That I used to live on the edge of the sea." *Like I do now.* "It also means…" He paused his pacing, looking Merri dead on. "That we know each other. Have known each other for a while." For some reason, he believed that part the most. There was something about Merri which struck him as familiar, though he hadn't been able to figure out why. Was *this* the reason after all?

She nodded, her eyes wide and glossy. She looked shocked at what Jac had just said.

"I know this might be weird to hear, but I've been having dreams. Strange ones." He walked a few steps closer. "Of this prince, and then ever since you arrived, of a sea maiden. I'm starting to think it might not be a coincidence that you and she share the same name. And I learned hers first."

Merri didn't blink, her gaze latched onto his every word. Seeing her look so vulnerable and confused sent a pang through Jac's chest. He'd been drawn to her since the beginning, had felt some sort of connection, but that still didn't mean he was Olivander, did it?

"So, if I'm this prince," he pressed on, swallowing the growing lump in his throat, "then that means I've forgotten about you." He drew even nearer and watched as a few tears trickled down her cheeks. He bridged the gap between them and gently used the pad of his thumb to wipe the freckled skin beneath her eye. "I've hurt you," he said. "I don't know how or why, but I've done this to you. I've been the one making you cry all this time, haven't I?"

Merri sucked in a sharp breath. She didn't nod but averted her gaze to the floor. She didn't need to nod for Jac to understand.

"Then why on earth don't I remember?" He took a step back, raking another hand through his hair. His eyes were stinging now, liquid anguish tempting to spill over. "I'm sori, Merri. I have no idea what's going on." His hand stilled with fingers stuck in his curls as the space against his ribs tightened, making it hard for him to breathe. "I kissed you." He faced her again, mortification filling him like a pitcher to a glass. He could only guess how much his actions had hurt her; it didn't matter that she'd kissed him first. His hand slipped off his head. "Dang it, I kissed you, Merri!" How could he have done that?

She placed a steadying hand on his arm, and when he looked into her eyes, there were tears, yes, but they weren't of the blaming sort. She was trying to comfort him, the cad that he was.

He couldn't help it. He reached both hands up and cupped the sides of her face, looking fiercely into her eyes. "I promise you, Merri, I won't kiss you again until I remember. All of it. No matter how much I would like to. I can't keep hurting you like this." Conviction laced his every word. "You deserve more than that." She deserved the world. His dreams told him of the life they'd once shared back in Chaera, but none of the memories were his own. And he couldn't understand *why*.

He slowly backed away and let her go, feeling the loss keenly. Walking to the window, he fixed his gaze on the bay below. He was finally getting some answers, and he'd never been more confused in his entire life. Jac leaned forward until his forehead banged on the glass, closing his eyes only to open them again and watch the waves crash along the shore.

How was any of this possible?

How did his childhood best friend end up here with all her memories intact while his were gone?

Why Wales? With Merri landing on his doorstep being pushed by the very creature which shared the name of his country.

Whales in Wales. It was almost laughable, really.

Wait. His conversation with Orsin came back to him. Orsin had been spat out by a whale. And then Merri, only last month, had been pushed to shore by one. According to his dreams, hadn't she known one as a friend, too?

Perhaps it was merely a coincidence. But Jac was quickly learning that coincidences held more purpose and truths as of late…

"Merri." He turned to face her, a new idea burgeoning in his mind. She was now sitting on his bed, a silent bystander watching him for the rambling idiot he was. "About the night I rescued you…" He walked over to her. "There was a whale in the water. I feel like that's important. Almost like a clue."

She nodded, though he could tell she wasn't following.

"And I think I know someone who can help us figure out why."

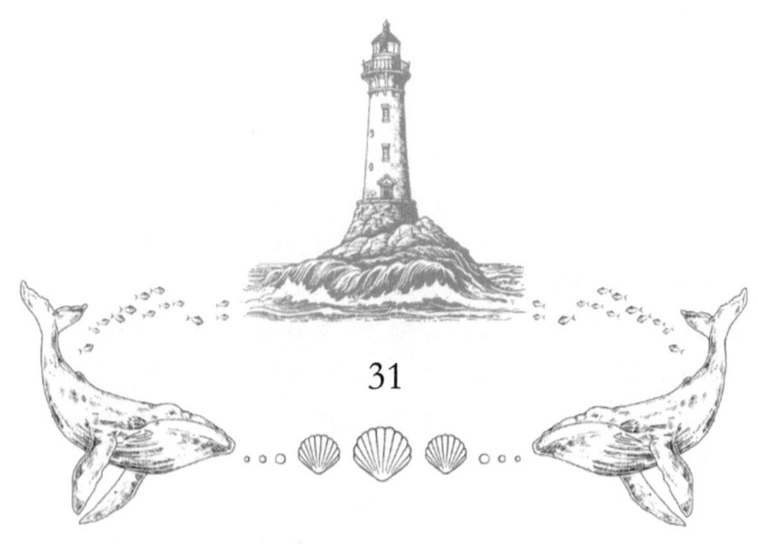

31

A STORY INKED IN RED

Merri

Tenby, Wales
September 1996

"OKAY. I'M ABOUT TO KNOCK," Jac said.

Merri nodded, though she didn't understand why he looked nervous. Since becoming human, she'd seen countless people knock on doors. What made this one any different? Jac's hesitancy set her on edge; he hadn't told her much, only that they needed to go see someone as soon as possible.

She still couldn't believe she'd told him the truth that easily. Honestly, she didn't understand how he'd known to ask those questions in the first place. Then he mentioned his dreams. They'd already revealed to him pieces of this troubling puzzle. *He even dreamt about me.* The thought was embarrassingly encouraging. But despite his dreams, he hadn't realized *he* himself was the prince.

Until now… The truth had come to light in less than a day, and there were still so many questions.

"You ready?" Jac looked at her.

She sucked in a breath and nodded, trying to ignore the rising uncertainty in her gut. If Jac was nervous, then maybe she should be, too. *Who resides on the other side to make him act this way?* She clutched the lore book closer to her chest, having brought it with her from the lighthouse. It was a comfort to simply hold it; knowing there were other sea maidens, even within the pages of a book, helped her feel less alone.

"If you get uncomfortable or anything, just let me know and we can leave, okay?" He fidgeted where he stood, pressing his messenger bag closer to his side.

Is he okay? Merri nodded again, now even more uneasy.

Jac raised his fist and pounded lightly on the door. They waited a few moments in silence until they heard heavy footfalls coming from the other side. When it opened, Jac tensed beside her, and for some reason, it made Merri want to grab his hand. If not for his sake, at least for hers. She reached tentative fingers toward his and warmed when he didn't hesitate threading them between his own. His eyes remained glued on the figure who now stood in the doorway.

"Back so soon, Jac?" the man said, his smile wide beneath a thick, gray beard. He looked at Merri and their clasped hands, eyes twinkling. They were blue like hers, kind and friendly-looking, making her instantly feel at ease in his presence. Jac, on the other hand… "And who have you brought with you?"

"Uh, yes, sir." His hand tightened around hers and lifted it in an introduction. "And this is Merri, sir."

Her heart skipped a beat at the sound of her real name being introduced for the first time. But just as quickly, her hand was released, as if Jac had realized what he was doing.

"You can call me Orsin, son. Same goes for you, Merri. Nice to meet you." He stepped back from the door and gestured inside. "Welcome to my home. You're just in time."

"In time for what?" Jac asked.

Orsin smirked behind his weathered appearance, looking years younger than his age. "For a story."

Aside from Jac's bedroom, Merri had never been inside a place so bare before, but she didn't mind it. The walls were bright with only a few paintings and smelled of the sea, making her feel at ease. But Jac still looked uncomfortable. His eyes kept darting to his bag by his feet while his leg bounced.

Orsin sat across from them both on a couch, a spread of tea things and fresh fruit on the table between them. Plus a couple of books. "Please, dig in," he said, his eyes keen.

Jac nodded and grabbed what looked like an apple, only to turn it over and over again in his hands.

Merri wasn't hungry, her stomach still trying to settle after an emotionally turbulent night and morning.

"So, what brings you both out this early?" Orsin began, looking between them. He took a sip from a teacup and placed it on its matching saucer.

"Well…" Jac shifted in his seat, his gaze tracking Orsin's movements. "We, uh…" His leg started bouncing again. "Well…"

"Cat got your tongue?" Orsin's eyes glimmered.

"No, sir. Uh, I mean, Orsin." Jac shook his head.

Why is Jac acting so strangely?

The older man looked in Merri's direction. "I have not seen you around here before. Are you new to Tenby?" he asked her.

Merri nodded, not able to offer much else. The room swelled once more with silence.

"Rather quiet we are this morning." Orsin chuckled, not looking annoyed or irritated. Simply stating a fact. He fixed his gaze back on Jac. "Are you sure there is nothing you want to tell me, son?"

Tell him? Hadn't they come to this man's house to *ask him* questions?

Jac swallowed, his Adam's apple bobbing like a buoy in the water. "Well, actually…" He bent down to his bag and pulled out some fabric. Merri had no idea what he planned to do with the garment until he started unfolding it, revealing an old book beneath the material. "Part of the reason why we're here is for me to return this." He paled as he slid the book back onto the table in front of him.

Orsin's eyes lit up, a shadow of a smile beneath his beard. "It's hard to return something that was not first lent out, you know."

Jac stole from Orsin? Merri's eyes grew wide.

"I should've asked permission." Jac's jaw became a blotchy red. "I promise I didn't read anything though, aside from the first couple words when I was last here. I'd planned to, but I guess I still have a conscience, after all." He puffed out a single laugh while running a hand along the back of his neck. "I'm sori."

"Don't be." Orsin's small smile grew into a broad grin.

Jac straightened. "You're not mad?"

"On the contrary, I'm quite pleased. A bit shocked, to be frank, but thrilled actually."

"You are?"

He is? Merri looked from Orsin to Jac, trying to follow along.

"Do you know why I leave these books out on the coffee table, Jac? It's not merely for decoration." He leaned in closer. "It's a test."

"Yeah, one I apparently failed." Jac scoffed.

"Not so. You, my son, are actually the only one who has passed."

"You're serious? How?" Jac stared dumbfounded at him, and Merri shared his confusion.

Orsin nodded and reached over to grab the book Jac returned. He opened it and flipped through the pages, and Merri saw what looked like red ink pass by on each turn of the paper. "You see, if anyone were to come over, which does happen more than you may think, I always tell them to make themselves comfortable in my living room while I finish something up in the back. With minimal decor, what else is there to do but pick up a book off the table and flip through the pages?" His eyes glimmered with mischief.

"I don't understand."

"Well, I'm getting to the most important part. For the average person, when they leaf through these books"—he gestured to the one in his hand and the others on the table—"they see merely a blank page. But there are a rare few who actually see words. And it's *those* people I am looking for."

Jac leaned in closer. "But how is that possible?"

Merri's pulse pounded in her neck. She'd seen the red ink, too.

"Because only those from my home country can read the words written by the Keeper of Prophecies."

The Keeper of Prophecies… Why did that sound so familiar? Had Olivander mentioned something about that to her at one time?

Jac frowned. "I'm not sure I follow—"

Orsin cut him off. "It's not customary for the Winderplume to be used on regular script. Quite forbidden where I'm from, actually, but in this case, it was necessary."

Winderplume. How had Merri forgotten about that? Oli used to wear a vial around his neck. Where had it gone?

"Here." Orsin took their silence as a lack of understanding and got up to hand Jac the book he'd just returned. "Read it aloud. I think you'll find it most illuminating."

Merri watched as Jac raised his brows, still looking unsure.

"Go on, son. Though the words may seem harsh, they won't bite."

Jac swallowed and opened the book as Merri leaned in closer, her ears tuned to the sound of his warm timbre. She'd heard him read to her countless times, but never a story only a few people could see. He cleared his throat and sat up straighter, his voice timid at first and then growing in confidence as he continued.

"Not every morning did one find themselves rocked by a cradle of death.

Savage waves tossed a fishing boat as if it were a featherweight out in the middle of the sea. There was no rain, only massive whitecaps seemingly coming out of nowhere. And a young man was left to fend for himself at the helm.

'I must get back to Chaera,' he said, his oar steadying the vessel. 'All of Windkeep depends on it!' He spat out the water that sprung from the depths, his short beard weighted down by the sea. All his will was bent on remaining afloat. To capsize would surely mean his end. The end of a life he so desperately wanted to finish out until the end of his days, Esias willing. What of his wife and children? His daughter was growing too fast to keep up with. His son was just learning how to walk.

And as Keeper of Prophecies, the citadel looked to him for direction. King Matteo and Queen Firan ruled the kingdom, but it was the keeper who kept their spirits light. Who warned them if need be. And with the recent birth of their son...

No. He could not think about such things. Would not. The prophecy was in his keeping, and its words required heeding. Time to implant its truth into the minds of the people.

He would make it back to shore. He had to. But the waves kept pummeling his craft, eager to send him down, down, down. He gripped the sides of his boat harder.

He knew not how it had happened, only that he was asked to leave Windkeep Citadel on urgent business, and had somehow ended up stranded in the middle of

Kerilow Bay, in the midst of one of the worst and strangest storms he had ever seen.

When he aroused, he realized whoever knocked him out had also stolen the red Winderplume from around his neck. The thought made his stomach churn. Why? For what purpose? Little good it would do in the hands of another.

Then his memory recalled something sinister and dark.

Before getting sent out to sea, he had overheard a conversation he was not supposed to. 'Now that the prophecy is set, all that is left is to take care of that filthy child.' *The voice had scoffed.* 'Windkeep needs no prince. Windkeep needs no king.'

Such treason is this. *Prophecy set? No prince? No king?*

Why had he ended up here? Cast out to sea like carrion!

He eyed his satchel sitting idly by his feet, relieved it had not tumbled overboard. The only remnants he had of his Winderplume were the grains of dust in his inkwell, now resting in the bag between his legs. He was not waterproof, but at least the pack was. Thank Esias for that. So much truth written in red. If he passed, so would these words, never to be heeded again. Though he guessed even death could not stop the will of Esias.

He shook his head, swiping a hand over his eyes to clear the water blurring his vision. But it was pointless, for at that moment, a rogue wave decided to attack his boat from beneath him, pushing his craft upward to the point of tipping over.

A desperate cry pierced the air as the man was thrown overboard, only having the foresight to snag his satchel before he hit the water.

'Esias, help me,' *he pleaded, floundering as he struggled in vain to keep himself afloat. But the waves kept pushing him down.*

This is no ordinary storm.

Terror filled his limbs as he was dragged downward, his body suddenly feeling like it was made of lead. His arms flailed. He pushed upward, breaking the surface only long enough to take a short breath. He clutched his satchel tighter, hope still buoying his spirits that he would survive. That this wicked storm would take pity on his battered soul.

But down, down, down he went once more. He cracked open his eyes and saw the surface getting farther away. Fear clogged his throat, making his lungs constrict even more. He tried swimming upward but found that he no longer could. The waves were relentless in keeping him down.

I am going to drown. This is it. I am done for.

He registered movement to his left, and terror struck him anew. Swimming toward him in the deep was an enormous glowing mass that kept growing in size the closer it approached. And it was coming fast.

Esias, hear me now!

But it was too late. His plea went unheard. For all the keeper knew was darkness as the giant creature's mouth opened wide before him, swallowing him whole."

When Jac finally finished, the room had grown uncannily quiet, like the very timbers were holding their breaths. Merri felt it, too, for the whole time he'd been reading, she was full of dread. *King Matteo and Queen Firan. Chaera. The prince and his prophecy. This story…it's about you, Oli!* She lifted her eyes to Jac's, questions multiplying faster than she could count them. But who was the Keeper of Prophecies? And what beast swallowed him?

Jac snapped the book shut, breaking the silence. "Orsin, we need to talk."

32

ORSIN'S TALE

Jac

ORSIN SMILED BENEATH HIS BUSHY BEARD and leaned back on the couch. He crossed his arms over his chest. For an old man, he sure had the relaxed and elusive demeanor down. There was that glimmer in his eyes again which spoke of things he understood, even before Jac opened his mouth. "What is your question, son?"

Jac's mind raced. This story… It talked of a prince, the king and queen of Windkeep, and a shadowed beast swallowing someone in the middle of the sea like in his nightmares. It spiked a cold shiver down his spine. *This story is about me, isn't it?* One look at Merri confirmed it, her subtle nod and wide eyes. His blood coursed through his body like a freight train at full acceleration. *Am I finally getting answers?*

"This story mentions a land called Chaera," Jac began, turning over the book in his hands.

Orsin nodded, eyeing him carefully. "That it does."

"And is it..." Processing all this information was like stuffing flour down a sieve; his thoughts were scattered all over the place. "Is it real?"

"As real as the very breath in your lungs. As real as Tenby is to Wales. And as real as the magic spanning across realms, times, and years."

What? "Magic?"

"Ie." Orsin tipped his head. "Magic."

Jac glanced at Merri and wasn't surprised to see her captivated by the man. She didn't look shocked by his recent proclamation. She was a sea maiden, after all. Her very existence *was* magical.

Orsin continued, "There is both good and bad magic in this world, son. Well, not *here*, specifically, but its remnants linger if brought from somewhere else. Somewhere like Windkeep in Chaera, home of the Winderplume."

The Winder-what? There was that strange word again. Maybe Orsin *was* mad. Jac swallowed. "I don't understand. If Chaera exists, then where is it?"

"Let me first ask you a question of my own." Orsin shifted in his seat, leaning forward so his elbows were propped on his thighs. "What makes you so interested in this foreign land? Why does it seem you already knew about it, even before reading that story?" He glanced at the book in Jac's lap, his eyes like slits.

Jac cast his gaze to the floor, finding the fibers of the rug infinitely more comforting than the man's piercing gaze. "I may have had a dream or two. Of the land, that is."

"Anything else in those dreams of yours?" Orsin prompted.

Jac looked up. "Sir?"

"You can call me Orsin, son."

"Right."

"Have you dreamt of any people? Names and faces you have never heard of before?" Orsin's eyes sparked curiosity.

"Just of a man named Prince Olivander, the rest of his family…and a sea maiden."

Orsin's eyebrows climbed his forehead. "Prince Olivander?"

Jac nodded. "But I've never been able to see his face or anyone else's." *Just Merri's, and that only happened once.* "The dreams blur them out." If they had only granted him that insight, maybe this would be a little easier to digest.

"Interesting." Orsin stroked his chin.

"I know this is wild, but Merri…she says I resemble him. The prince, I mean. Might even be the man himself. " *I am really losing it now.*

"You don't say." Orsin looked at the girl sitting across from Jac. "Now why would you think that, little lady?" he asked her, his smile warm.

Jac cleared his throat. "She can't—" He noticed Merri's cheeks had started turning red. He wished he could hold her hand like she'd done for him, letting her know it would be okay. "She can't speak. Her tongue…it's missing."

Orsin dipped his eyes low and shook his head. "Of all the sori things… How come she believes you are this prince?" He fixed his gaze on Jac once more, his expression somber and searching.

"Do you remember that sea maiden I dreamt about? Well, it was actually Merri." He tossed her a nervous smile and ran a hand along his neck before continuing. "Apparently, we were friends back in Chaera. I don't remember anything—I wish that I could—but I've dreamt about her. About all of it. I thought I was going crazy." *Still do, to be frank.* "Now I'm not so sure what to believe. But you mentioned a whale spat you out when you first came here, and when Merri arrived on Tenby's coast, there was a whale again. Only this time, it was pushing her toward the shore. I figured if anyone would know something, then it might be you." He shrugged like it was nothing, but his thundering pulse said otherwise.

Instead of answering his question, Orsin's eyes traveled once more to Merri, his gaze lingering on something in her hands. "That book of yours…"

"What book?" Jac had just laid it all out on the table, and now the old man was changing topics.

"Mind if I see it, dear?"

Merri nodded, standing up to hand over the tome. Jac hadn't even realized she'd brought it with her, his mind too focused on returning the one he'd stolen. But now it seemed he was to be reminded of his crimes twofold: an overdue library book blaring "Bronny will kill you!" with every gold-embossed sheen as the cover reflected the overhead lights.

"Now let me see," Orsin said, flipping through the book as if it was one of his own, like he'd held it before. "I own a first edition of this tucked away somewhere in my study, but seeing as you have this with you and I don't have time to ransack the whole place to find mine—quite serendipitous, really—it makes my point much easier. Ah, yes, here we are. The Ivory Keepers." He laid the book open like an inked griddle cake, the spine surely cracking, and Jac felt himself die a little inside; Bronny would have a fit and no choice but to fine him. Orsin flipped the book around and handed it to him. The familiar painting of a white humpback whale swirled across the page, and Jac's pulse quickened. *I never finished reading this.* He arched an eyebrow, but all that did was get the book pressed against his chest even harder.

And for the second time, Jac found himself reading aloud. "The sea is best known for its mysteries; little is understood and much is still to be discovered. But all can agree that it inspires the best stories. There have been accounts of those swimming, shipwrecked, or caught in a deadly storm who have presumably died, only to return to shore years later completely hale. Some have even turned up in the middle of the sea. How is this possible, one might ask? Legend states it is the waters, ancient in their comings and goings, which are guardians of transport. So much so that some beasts within possess the key: they are called Keepers of Realms, otherwise known as portal-keepers. And what better creature than one of the largest mammals on earth? The white humpback whale might be more than just a gentle giant of the sea. With a single swallow, they transport people to distant places, so beware when you go swimming, lest you get consumed and end up somewhere else."

What the heck did I just read?

"You see," Orsin began filling in the blanks. "This book is full of hearsays, but they are, in fact, *real.* There are quite a few keepers throughout the worlds—all mostly animals—but Earth has no understanding of them."

"Keepers? Worlds?" A vein in Jac's neck pulsed.

Orsin nodded. "A keeper's role is to do the behest of their Creator; they are messengers or servants, if you will. They have been appointed since the beginning, though many choose to overlook them or have simply forgotten they exist with the passing of time. As for worlds, Tallidoore is but one of them—a realm of magic and folklore, and home of continents *Eobreth*—where Chaera resides—*Mosoa, Letun,* and *Jabor.* White humpbacks are the means by which realms are accessed; they are the portal-keepers of all the worlds, for it is the waters which connect each realm. It's best not to fear their bite. For they ultimately answer to the call of Esias, as should we."

"Esias?" Jac raised a brow, his head spinning. This wasn't the first time Orsin had mentioned Him; the name had been inked red in the story he'd just orated.

"That's right," Orsin said. "Here, you know Him by another name." He got up and left the room, only to return with another book. He placed it on the table and slid it in his direction, understanding dawning when Jac glanced at the title. *Beibl Sanctaidd.* Orsin continued, "Getting swallowed can be frightening at first. I know I was petrified. Thought my life was ending before I had a chance to live out my days. But it seems Esias had other plans for the time when He sent me here." He raised his mug and took a generous swig before placing it back on the table.

"But how…" Jac's mind reeled. "How do these portals work exactly?"

"It isn't a matter of how they work; they just *are.* The same goes for all the keepers; that is how Esias made them. Do you recall C.S. Lewis' wardrobe? Some things are better left experienced than explained."

Jac considered this, remembering his read of *The Magician's Nephew* a few months ago.

"Did you ever have any dreams of being swallowed, Jac?" Orsin asked.

The question took him by surprise and sent a tingle through his skin. *Yes. Devoured.* He nodded. "There was always a storm, too."

"I figured as much." Orsin smiled, his grin spreading wider than usual. "Well, it looks like you have come to my house as a mere lad and are walking away a prince. After all, you are the spitting image of your father, Your Highness."

Jac recoiled. It was odd to know he resembled a man he didn't even remember. *Why hadn't Orsin said something sooner? This can't be real. This can't be happening right now!*

Without any hesitation, Orsin stood and walked over to Jac, pulling him to his feet and into an awkward embrace. "I knew the moment I saw you, but I didn't want you thinking I was truly 'mad,' as they say. You don't understand how great this news is for Windkeep." He stepped back with his face beaming. He gripped Jac by the shoulders. "Ever since that dreadful storm, I feared for your life. I didn't know what would become of you, but I promise, I tried my best to get back. Though I never should have doubted the prophecy. It's all coming to pass as it should. Down to every last detail. Your parents will be so relieved to know you live, my boy."

Jac saw Merri fidget out of the corner of his eye; she looked at her hands and picked at her fingers. He wondered what swam through her mind. *She knows something, and she can't say what it is.*

"Your Highness, it looks like your dreams have simply been your mind reclaiming lost memories. I don't know why you can't recall who you once were, but my guess is that whatever spell was put on you weakened when you came here. Magic is not common to this realm. But by coming to Wales, with Tenby's coastal air, the spell has lost some of its potency. Bet the gits didn't think of that." Orsin mumbled the latter part to himself, backing away to sit once more on the couch.

Who didn't think of what? Jac stared at the old man before he reclaimed his own seat, feeling even stranger to be known when he still knew nothing of himself. And he couldn't get over the fact that Orsin was now addressing him, a humble lighthouse keeper, as royalty. Merri had written it on paper, but it was even more ridiculous when spoken aloud. Was he truly Prince Olivander and had simply forgotten?

"You mentioned a spell." Jac needed information, to fight logic with reasoning, but his penchant for stories told him otherwise. He'd read enough of them, had dreamt enough dreams, and then Merri had shown up on his doorstep like a goddess from the sea, claiming he was from another world. And now Orsin... It was all too much to be coincidental at this point. But was he really cursed? "It's not, like, super bad or anything, right?"

Orsin leaned in close, gaze flitting between Jac and Merri. "In Chaera, there is but one witch, and she lives in the sea. Her curses run deep, are as twisted and dark as tainted blood, and she does anything to get what she desires. A spell cast by her is bad indeed and will not be easily broken."

The hair on the back of Jac's neck stood straight.

"But it *can* be done," Orsin continued, sitting back once more. "What the sea witch doesn't realize is that a curse can only take away the physical—everything that you own, be it a kingdom, a title, a crown. But it can't strip away what's inside of you, those truths endowed by Esias Himself. You see, even the greatest spells can't destroy memory in its entirety. You experienced this yourself. Even now, it has been fading, loosening its hold."

"How…how do you know all this?"

"Did I not tell you? *I* am the Keeper of Prophecies. Orsin Lysander Locke. Winderplume confirmed and all. I have lived in Chaera my whole life and was appointed keeper at Windkeep by your very father, King Matteo Daws, when he came to power at eighteen. I was only five years his senior, but we forged a fast friendship, your father and I. We knew of the dangers Chaera faced with that witch murking the waters, so Matteo sent a few of his men to locate her secret chamber. Each attempt always turned out to be futile. But we figured maybe that was a good thing; she was hard to find. Wicked enchantments were only cast if people went *to* her. She could not do much harm otherwise, being bound to the sea. We thought her threat was limited. But we were wrong. Very wrong."

Jac glanced at Merri, her face drained of color and eyes glued to Orsin's face, unblinking.

"I already mentioned it, but when you were born, there was a prophecy at your birth. You wouldn't know its contents, but it was something *good*. Something that promised hope for our kingdom. Windkeep has received many prophecies over the course of my life, but none so great as yours." The old man threaded his fingers together. "But when the tide pulled me out to sea, I kept hearing these dreadful words on repeat: 'Now that the prophecy is set, all that is left is to take care of that filthy child.' But what did that mean? Aside from the king and his trusted council, no one had a chance to hear what the prophecy said. Even then, I doubt they would recall its contents. I was sent away before the customary reading. Their goal was to drown me, but Esias had other plans.

"I landed on the shores of Tenby and thus began my years' long determination. I knew I couldn't be exiled from Chaera forever, not if I was the only one who knew the truth, even if it would come to pass regardless. But sometimes people need encouragement, and a kingdom sorely does. So I began planning. Writing stories in that book to recount the past, all the while hoping someone would come along and be able to read them. I made some money, bought my house, and slowly started building a new life, ready to leave it all behind at the drop of a hat." Orsin shook his head. "Then one day, something caught my attention. I was rummaging through my bag of prophecies only to find two missing. If you know me, I am meticulous about these sorts of things; never a word out of place. Someone had stolen them, no doubt. But the odd thing is, *yours* still remained." He looked at Jac. "Now why would someone who wished your prophecy harm let it remain in my possession? Why not take it for themselves? My only guess is that they wished the words and I shared the same fate: to simply disappear.

"There are many riddles to this twisty tale, Your Highness, but my hunch is that whoever tried to kill me also planned to kill *you*. It has something to do with the prophecy on your naming day, I stake my life on it. Someone sought out that wicked sea witch in order to bring Windkeep crumbling down."

First a prince and now a prophecy. But the singular word that kept bouncing around in Jac's head was *Why?* If all this was true, then why was his life so important as to bring it to ruins? *This is some sordid fairy tale.* "Why me? Why send me here of all places?"

Orsin chuckled and shook his head. "It's best not to question Esias' ways, son. I did for the first fifteen years I was here, and it has done me no good. I have chosen to believe I'm here for a reason…as are you. And now that you've come, it seems the tide is shifting in our favor. You should be thanking Him; it was His intervention which rescued you from the death you were intended for."

That was all well and good—Jac was grateful to be alive—but the direness of that situation wasn't striking as hard as it should. He hadn't known he was close to death until this moment. And if Jac was truly from another world, shouldn't he return to it? The prospect seemed terrifying. But would his memories come back if he did?

"You mentioned you tried getting back to Chaera. Did it ever work?"

Orsin frowned. "Afraid not. A white humpback is rare to find. It's true I made the attempt, but it only worked a few times. And it was not to Chaera."

"It was a different world?" Jac asked. He knew Orsin had mentioned there were others, but his limited scope was fixated on the Milky Way…and now the land he supposedly was from.

The old man nodded. "To a place called *Igriadran*. A strange land, even stranger creatures, but I only stayed about a week or so. Hard to tell these days. One trip to the ocean, and a whale swallowed me back up and returned me to Tenby, as if it knew I belonged here. Only, time seemed to have stopped completely while I was gone."

"How is that possible?" *Multiple worlds, and Orsin's been to at least three of them.* What else was out there? Jac took a bite of fruit, ruminating on this information as his jaw worked to mask his coursing adrenaline.

"Let me ask you a question first. How old are you, Your Highness? If you can recall such a thing."

Jac's mind went back to the leather-bound folio in his nightstand. Was it even accurate? It was all he had to go by. "I believe I'm eighteen."

Orsin nodded, suddenly grave. "I figured as much, what with the prophecy. Time moves differently within the portal, Your Highness. Sometimes it stops completely, slows down, or speeds on ahead. One might be just a lad in their home country only to find they have aged ten years somewhere else and vice versa. Sometimes it's only hours or days or a week's difference." He scratched the back of his head. "And from what you just told me, I left Chaera eighteen years ago and somehow aged thirty years while in Tenby. By all accounts, I should be forty-seven, but I just turned sixty."

Sixty?

"I'd prefer to stop this fast track to death, if you catch my drift. Which makes heading back to Chaera even more pressing."

Jac nearly choked. "Heading back?" That was actually a possibility? He knew he'd just thought of it a moment ago, but Orsin proclaimed it like there wasn't another option.

"Of course! But first, we must prepare and make a plan." Orsin's eyes glimmered right before he winked at Jac and Merri. "After all, the Locke's are missing a husband and father. The sea is lacking a sea maiden. And Windkeep needs their prince."

33

A LIFE WELL LOVED

Merri

Tenby, Wales
September 1996

DARYA. DARYA DID THIS TO HIM.

Merri knew without a doubt that it was the sea witch who had cursed Olivander's memory and turned him into Jac Hughes. But why? What need did she have to intervene with the royal family? She was cruel, yes, but she typically kept her charms to the sea. Unless…unless someone sought her out first.

The prophecy. Merri didn't know what it entailed, but that's why the guards had sent both Luci and her away from the Hatch's home. Sent all the maidens away from Chaera. She shook her head. It didn't make sense. Orsin had mentioned that Oli's prophecy was *good.* If that was true, then why had the kingdom said he was in danger because of it?

Chills spiked like shards of frozen water along Merri's spine, reminding her not to get too far ahead of herself. Still, with all that just transpired in Orsin's home, all the pieces were coming together, and Merri was simply the messenger. Her role was small; though without her presence here, would Jac have known he was the prince? Maybe in time, Orsin would have told him through his magical red ink, but part of her hoped that somehow her presence had helped speed things along. She'd influenced Jac's dreams, hadn't she? Merri was still shocked that he'd dreamt about her at all, and she was left wondering just how much the sleeping world revealed to him of his past.

Esias, Your footings are sure. Even when I've chosen the wrong ones. Could her rash decision of visiting the sea witch actually be why she was here…helping her heart's true love?

Merri's feet padded along the sandy path back to the Telor Pendu with Jac walking beside her; they'd left Orsin's but moments ago, and he'd hardly said a word. *I don't want to force him to talk.* It was a lot to take in, learning you were a prince and having it confirmed again, and again, and again… His mind wasn't his own, nor were his affections something to claim. He'd kissed her, had wanted to kiss her more, but until his memories returned, he vowed he wouldn't.

But what if he does remember? Remembers everything. Would he want her then or simply be her friend and nothing more? Whispered kisses in Tenby spoke their own truth. But she wasn't sure. He'd never loved her like she loved him all those years ago. *You don't leave someone you love and never return.*

Merri shook away those thoughts. She'd promised not to dwell there, to think only of herself and her discarded dreams. It wasn't Olivander's fault if he never shared the same feelings. Though it did sting. Bristled and spiked at those tender places that longed to be loved.

Enough, Merri. Think about something else.

Orsin mentioned portal-keepers… Out of all the things they talked about, this one seemed to make the most sense. *Eldarwielle. That's how he sent me here. How he, and probably his brethren, sent all of us here.* But there was still that unanswered question looming in the back of her mind like a wall of rocky coast: *Why?*

She fixed her gaze ahead, watching Jac out of the corner of her eye. His attention was drawn to the ground, his hands lost somewhere in his pockets.

He looks so defeated. Like some adrift vessel. It was something Merri could relate to.

Orsin had said they needed to get back to Chaera. And though Merri had longed for the same thing, part of her was afraid to return. What did she have there anymore? She couldn't see her family without drowning first, and Iun's hadn't wanted her either. At least in Tenby, she had a place to stay, a place to call her own, if for a time. Nain seemed to like her, and she enjoyed helping around the Telor Pendu. *I'll miss it here. It's become a sort of home.*

But if they went back to Chaera, would it be enough for Jac's memories to return? That alone would be worth it. His kingdom needed him; she had no idea how it was faring without him. A sudden ache, like a twisted limb, punctured Merri's heart. *He'll realize his father is actually gone. Why haven't I thought about that before? Is his mother dead, too?*

Orsin doesn't know the king died and told Oli his parents would be thrilled to see their son again. Merri didn't have the strength to tell him the truth. Not after all that transpired in such short a time. His burden was already great enough.

"Are you okay?" Jac's voice whispered through her thoughts, causing her to look into his warm, green eyes. They were Oli's eyes, but they didn't look right on a face so distant. So utterly lost.

Merri nodded, wishing she could ask him the same. So she nudged his shoulder, and he seemed to get the hint.

He breathed out a wry chuckle and shook his head. "I don't really know. It's not every day one wakes up only to find they're royalty. Especially from another world."

They continued to walk in silence, the afternoon sun high over their heads. They'd been with Orsin so long the morning had come and gone and, with it, the dewy clouds.

"I didn't doubt you, by the way," Jac said. "About me being a prince and all. But it does help hearing it from someone else, too. I still can't believe it, but what other explanation is there? Maybe I was made for another world besides this one." He kicked at the loose gravel as if he was kicking away his thoughts.

You are, Oli. Even though Tenby would keep you, too.

"For so long I thought I was losing my mind, but then you showed up and everything seemed to get worse." Jac reddened. "That is to say, things got *better*, actually. You made me feel less alone even when my mind took me elsewhere." He looked at her again, having them stop along the sandy path. Merri's nerves tingled when he grabbed her hand. "I don't understand what's happening to me, but it's two against one at this point, so I'm relying on you and Orsin to recall what I cannot. If I really am this prince, which I'm starting to believe against my will, then I can only hope my memories return so I can be who I once was. Who you remember me to be." Jac swallowed. "I can't bear to see you so hurt on my account, especially knowing how close we were." He shook his head. *"Are."*

Merri nodded, squeezing the hand holding hers, her small attempt at comforting him. She deepened her gaze, willing him to read her thoughts. *It'll be okay, Oli. I'm not going anywhere. I've always known you'd be a great king, even when you've doubted yourself. And now is no different. Windkeep needs you...*

I need you.

"Thank you," he said, sucking in a huge breath and releasing it, as if pushing away the tension. "Let's just hope Nain isn't too surprised when Orsin comes tonight for tea and we tell her the news. That woman has seen many things, but even *this* might be too much for her."

Merri laughed to herself. She'd only known Nain for a short time, but it was enough to know the woman spoke her mind more than not. And she didn't take lightly to foolishness.

Which meant there was a good chance she'd call them all crazy before the end of the night.

"This is tidy *Tatws Pum Munud*, Nain. What did you put in it this time?" Orsin asked from his seat at the table. The old man was already working on his second helping.

"Oh, just the usual. Some potatoes and some of Jac's carrots from the garden." Nain said, smiling in his direction. "The harvest came out good. You should be proud."

"Thanks, Nain," Jac said. "Orsin's right, though. Something tastes different. Good, just…*better?*"

Nain guffawed. "I used pancetta instead of bacon, if that's what you're wondering." She swallowed a quick bite and looked at Merri. "Men and their stomachs are something else. Always tasting something different. Keeps my feet light, sure does."

Merri laughed, wishing she could enjoy the taste of the meal like them, but was thankful for a full stomach all the same. What she enjoyed most was the company. Although she had tea with Nain and Jac most nights, this was the first time Orsin joined them, and it felt even more like a family. It made her miss the days of her youth when her family was happier; it made her long for the days ahead filled with a family of her own.

If she ever got back to Chaera, she would miss this. This moment. She wished she could hold onto it forever.

By the time everyone finished their meals, cleared their plates and pushed their bowls aside, the hour grew late. The inky black of an autumnal night leaked through the window above the sink. And Merri soaked it all in. Despite not being able to talk, she was still made to feel included. Another thing she was thankful for.

After finishing a chat on the weather and how they would winterize the garden come the colder months, the conversation switched to discussing Merri and Jac.

"I had two visitors early this morning," Orsin said, drawing everyone's attention to him.

"If heavy feet on stairs and slamming doors before dawn have anything to do with it, I'd guess it was these two sitting right here." Nain took a sip of tea, and Merri felt awful. Until a hand gently squeezed her knee. "It's no issue, Merri." Her spirits lightened upon hearing her real name from Nain's mouth. "I'm a light sleeper and don't get much anyway, annwyl."

She nodded, though her stomach sunk at where this conversation was inevitably turning. It was only a matter of time before Nain learned the truth.

"Sori about the rude awakening," Jac began. "We visited Orsin because we, uh…we had something important to discuss with him."

Nain lowered her cup. "Oh? And what about?"

Orsin shifted in his seat. "Well, you see, Nain…"

The old woman's brow drew together. "Nothing good ever starts with 'well, you see, Nain.'"

He pressed on like he hadn't heard her. "Do you remember that day you found me on North Beach? And you and Alun invited me to your home?"

"Ie…"

"This is about that. About Chaera." A moment's pause. "About Jac." It didn't take him long to fill in the gaps and leave no room for questioning. All the while he spoke, an overall heaviness settled upon Merri's shoulders, especially as she watched Nain's face twitch from trying to subdue her emotions.

Jac seemed to notice, too. He grabbed Merri's hand from under the table and held it. She wasn't sure who needed the comfort more.

When Orsin finished, the very room seemed to hold its breath. Then, like a stone being plunked into a calm streambed, Nain bolted upright from her seat.

"I've never heard such a load of rubbish in all my life!" She began pacing around the kitchen like a mad woman, everyone watching her from the table. The electric lighting they opted for tonight instead of the customary candles Merri had grown used to caused the atmosphere to feel even more charged. Especially when they flickered with every heavy footstep on the wooden floorboards. Nain's eyes turned hard as she counted off her fingers. "First, you invite Orsin to our home last minute—no offense." She glanced at the older man, and he tipped his head as if to acknowledge her apology and offer one of his own. "And then proceed to tell me you're from another *realm*?" She zeroed in on Jac. "I did *not* wake up early this morning just to have the wool pulled over my eyes, you know." Nain huffed as she pointed a finger at the men, starting with Jac and then moving her way to Orsin.

She hadn't pointed at Merri, and the one-time sea maiden guessed it was because she couldn't rightly say anything. Still, she was as much to blame as all of them.

"And you didn't," Orsin chimed in. "Nain, have you ever taken me for a liar?"

She crossed her arms. "Na. But—"

"And you understood the circumstances by which I first arrived here. Both you and Alun did."

"Ie. But—"

"Nain. Jac is from Chaera. Like myself. I know this news is hard to swallow—"

"Hard to swallow!" Nain scoffed, stopping inches before his face. With Orsin sitting down, the two were nearly at eye-level. "Weeks old bara brith is *hard to swallow*." She gestured to the dessert on the table. "North Beach's golden sand is *hard to swallow*; that stuff will clog your arteries right up before you can utter a single word." Her irises blazed like flames. "But *this!*" She sucked in a sharp breath and gestured around her kitchen to anywhere and nowhere. She shook her head and stepped back, resuming her pacing.

Orsin cleared his throat and proceeded carefully. "You know I've been waiting here for years. You've known my isolation like a friend, took me in when others wouldn't..." He stood to his full height and met her as she unknowingly paced her way into his chest. "Nain, you have to believe me when I say I'm not doing this to hurt you. But this is a truth that can no longer be ignored."

Nain pursed her lips, but Merri thought she could see her resolve cracking. *Are those tears?*

"Please." Orsin's singular word seemed to be her undoing.

She shook her head. "But my Jac. I can't lose my boy." Merri watched as Nain's eyes relented, liquid pooling in their corners and slipping down her cheeks. What was even more shocking was she allowed Orsin to hug her. "I can't lose someone else again." She sobbed into his chest.

Merri's heart felt like someone was squeezing it, but maybe that was just her hand. Jac's grip had tightened. They shared a secret glance, and it spoke volumes. The two were shocked to see Nain in this condition. Had Jac ever seen his grandmother cry before?

He got up and walked to the sobbing woman, enveloping her in a hug of his own. He didn't say anything, only rubbed Nain's back as she mumbled, "Not you, *fy machgen*. Not you, too."

"Everything will be okay, Nain," Jac whispered, though it sounded like he didn't believe his own words.

How could he promise something like that? Did Jac know what he was getting himself into? *No.* His life had just turned upside down, but his heart cared for others beyond himself, and it was one of the most beautiful things Merri had ever witnessed.

He was and had always been too good for her. Even when she'd misjudged him.

The kitchen now resonated with quiet sobs and empty plates, as if mocking them that this was their last meal together. And Merri didn't want to linger where so much sorrow rested. She no longer wished to be an outsider looking in on a family soon to be broken apart, partially because of her own doing...

She pushed up from her seat and made for the front door. The Telor Pendu was stifling and the starry night was calling her name. But there was no need to run. A walk allowed time for her racing thoughts to turn over everything. From Darya to wanting legs. From losing Olivander to finding Jac. Broken hearts and broken bodies. Loss upon loss upon loss.

She looked up with heavy-lidded eyes at the midnight expanse stretching above her. Despite it all, the stars still shone through the deep. Tiny pinpricks of light pushing through the impossible.

Merri only stopped moving when the waves along Tenby's coast licked her toes, the sound of the ocean her only company. Pretty soon she'd go back to Chaera...but she wasn't sure what she wanted anymore.

The moon hung in its fixed spot in the sky, its glow illuminating the space around Merri in muted whites and grays. She didn't know how long she sat there by herself on the rocks, but she wasn't surprised to hear footsteps approaching. She'd wondered when he'd come for her. Only… it wasn't Jac.

"Mind if I join you?" Orsin asked.

Merri nodded, finding herself drawing her knees closer to her body. She stared at her bare feet, her toes now sandy, wet, and cold from after feeling the cool breath of the ocean.

"What a lovely night."

She looked up to see Orsin's chin tilted toward the stars. A smile appeared beneath his bushy beard, and Merri felt something inside her ease. She might not know the old man well, but any friend of Oli's parents felt like someone she could trust. Which was sorely needed right now.

"You must love the sea," he said, now looking at the expanse before him. Salt and brine and reverberating echoes of waves and gulls. The ocean was dark and ominous in this lighting, but it was nonetheless striking. Moonlight was its own beauty.

Merri nodded, resting her chin on her knees. *I love it so much.*

"Me too. But I used to hate it, you know."

She raised an eyebrow and faced him more fully.

Orsin chuckled and continued, "It's true. In my eyes, it took away my life. Took me far from my wife and family. From my friends. Sent me to my death. Exiled me from the only land I ever called home. To say I looked upon the ocean with any fondness would be an unmerited kindness. But to make it worse, I blamed Esias. In my grief, He had stolen everything from me."

Merri watched him as his smile dipped into a frown. Pain laced his words.

"But thankfully that changed."

How? What happened?

"As the years wore on, I realized a life-altering truth. Had I been wronged? Yes. But by who? Who was *I* to blame Esias for the events in my life when it was *He* who carried me through, even when death seemed the only outcome? I had blamed the very One who had done more *good* for me than any living man ever could. The waters which attempted to drown me ended up being my salvation. And that is only by Esias' grace."

Esias' grace. Orsin's words were grains of sand slipping through her fingers. It seemed so far away. So unattainable. Especially after what she'd done. She believed Esias was good and caring, but did that still extend to her when she'd maimed who she once was?

"Jac mentioned you can't talk." It was as if Orsin had read her mind. It sent Merri's pulse thumping in her ears. "And he also said you're a sea maiden from Chaera."

Her eyes remained glued to her hands, picking away at her cuticles in order to steady her rising nerves. *Jac says a lot of things.*

"If so, I've never seen a sea maiden this far from home. And definitely not one with legs."

Her face was blossoming petals of fire, her stomach roiling with the weight of her past mistakes. She needn't be reminded of just how low she'd sunk. Just how desperate she was for love and how she'd lost everything. It was one thing to bear the burden of shame herself, but to have someone else pry the lid off of her tightly sealed-away mistakes… It was a mortification she never wished to relive. Tears pricked the corners of her eyes, attempting to overflow should this conversation go any further.

A gentle hand settled on her shoulder, and Merri hesitantly lifted her eyes to meet Orsin's. But instead of the anger or judgment she expected to see, there was only compassion and kindness. "I didn't come here to ridicule you, Merri. I am in no position to do so," he said, his tone calm and gentle. "But I know a Darya enchantment when I see one. Why did she do this to you, child?"

Her eyes leaked liquid sorrow as Orsin's kindness washed over her. He was so much like Eldarwielle, her dearest friend, who saw more than what the eye could behold. It was a comfort, a rare thing, one that Merri hadn't realized she needed. A person to know her secret shame and not toss her away like the outcast she already knew herself to be.

Only, she couldn't say what happened, but that didn't seem to matter to Orsin.

"I'm not as senile as I appear," he continued. "I know Darya's reach only extends when someone seeks her out first. It is the singular code by which she lives. So in order for Olivander's memories to disappear like that"—the old man snapped his fingers—"or for you to exchange your fin for a pair of legs…then something, or some*one*, must have approached her."

Orsin knows. He knows without me even having to say a word.

"You went to her, didn't you?" His question wasn't accusatory, only searching.

Merri averted his gaze and nodded. *Oh, I wish I never did.*

"Why?" he prodded. "What mattered so much to you that you would risk losing yourself to the ways of that conniving witch?"

Love. A life worth living where I could be loved fully as I am. But how could that have happened when she'd stripped away so much of herself to begin with? It wasn't love which prompted that. If she dug deep enough, it was desperation. It was insecurity. It was feeling like she was never good enough to be loved the way Esias had made her. She'd tried so hard to be something else that she'd ended up losing herself completely.

And now I have nothing left.

"Ah." Orsin nodded, making Merri wonder what he saw in her.

"It's complicated, isn't it? The heart wants what the heart wants."

The infuriating organ. I should never have trusted it.

"Would you go back and change things if you could?" he asked.

Yes. But also, if she did, would she have ended up here? With Jac? Eldarwielle might not have brought her to Tenby if she hadn't been drowning that fateful night. Like her inner turmoil, the truth was also complicated. *I wish I never went to Darya. I wish I still had my tail. But these moments in Tenby with Oli have been some of the happiest days of my life.* Despite all the tears…

Orsin nodded at her silence, seeming to understand more than he let on. "You're not alone, Merri." She looked up at the sound of her name. "I may not have sought out Darya, but I've known desperation like a friend. I've cursed Esias, albeit in my heart, for things He never did. I've forged my own way and tried to take matters into my own hands. I'm a man of action; I need answers. It does me no good to remain idle and twiddle my thumbs, despite my climbing years." He shook his head. "But like you, I was wrong. And like you, there was and can be hope."

Hope. Was it possible to still hold onto after it had betrayed her for so long?

"Do you miss home?" he asked.

Merri nodded, not having to think twice. The coral reefs, the colorful schools of fish, the seaweed fields and turtle bales. The rippling tide, her glistening fin, swimming alongside Eldarwielle, and shockingly enough…even her own family. Were they concerned that she'd been gone all this time? It hadn't crossed her mind, considering she'd always felt invisible to them.

"I do, too," Orsin said. "It's been lonely living in a land so far from Chaera. I can't recount to you all those sleepless nights and crying out in agony. The unspeakable scenarios conjured by my mind, those gut-wrenching, dark places—" He shook his head, as if losing himself. "The point is, I learned to accept my fate. Accept that this is where I am supposed to be, especially when all my attempts at changing that failed." He gave a short, throaty chuckle. "But then you and Prince Olivander came along and changed that resolve pretty quickly. A prince must claim his birthright; it's not a matter of whether he must but *when*." There was that gleam in the old man's eyes, sparkling from the light of the moon.

Her chest expanded at his words. The idea of seeing his family again wasn't something Orsin had thought possible…until now. It made her want to reunite them as soon as they could; she couldn't imagine losing something so precious.

Merri pointed to the ocean and mimed the motions of a whale, then she tapped her wrist where Jac usually wore his watch. Finally, she lifted her arms and shrugged as if asking a question. *How will we get back? Maybe I can summon Eldarwielle. He would come. He always comes for me.*

Orsin shook his head. "I'm not sure what you are asking, but the portal-keepers are not wish-granters, I'm afraid. They only show up when the time is right." He looked out to sea once more. "So let us hope time is on our side."

Oh. Her resolve sank. Merri had only known Eldarwielle as a constant companion, but she supposed Orsin was right. The whale wasn't something to be used. If she thought otherwise, then she'd be no better than that wicked sea witch.

Thunderous waves echoed against the rocks, splashing water onto Merri's ankles. Orsin's legs were already in the climbing surf, his pants soaked up to his shins as the silence stretched between them.

"We should probably head back. Before the tide gets even higher." He stood and offered his arm to Merri, patting her hand gently once she grabbed on. They proceeded to pick their way carefully over the rocks back toward the Telor Pendu, her weight of sorrow a lighter burden to carry. But what of those who awaited them inside?

"Nain will be okay, you know," he said.

Merri's eyebrows rose. *Can he read my thoughts, too?*

He chuckled at her expression. "I saw the look in your eyes before you left. It's hard news, but Nain has weathered tougher stuff than this. It's a curse to love so deeply. And when it's taken from you, you're left to mourn on your own."

In the most painful and isolating way. She was shocked Orsin would agree.

"But," he continued, "even more so, it's a gift." His words were filled with sudden warmth. "To feel so much that you can't help but ache at the loss…now *that* is something special. What is love without sacrifice? What is love without knowing you could very well lose it all in but a moment? Does it make it any less worth holding onto? Does that mean you should avoid it altogether?" Orsin shook his head. "No. Love is always worth it, even if it means you have to let it go. And Nain knows this better than most."

Out of all their conversations, this last part hit Merri the hardest. It twisted and pitted out that dark and battered place in her chest, the spot that ached and pined for what she never could have despite having given so much of herself.

She always scolded herself for loving too quickly. Too freely. Too fully. But Orsin… He just said it was a gift. How could loving someone who could never love you back be worth it? What of death? Or, in Orsin and Nain's case, separation?

Hadn't *love* gotten her into this mess in the first place? She'd sacrificed much in order to get it and had received a paltry sum in its place.

He patted her hand again as the spinning light from the Telor Pendu passed over them in its rotation. "Aside from our Creator, we're not promised love in this world. But we sure as anything can give it. Can hold onto it. Keep it close. Feel the ache and sting of it when it's gone." He sighed. "But our affections should not be all consuming and drive us to unfathomable ends. It requires a delicate balance, only achievable with Esias' help. To love Him first and above all else…well, that's when you know your heart will be okay in the end. Despite pain, loss, and death. There is nothing more freeing than that, Merri." He sighed as they finally reached the door of the lighthouse. "There is nothing more freeing than a life well loved."

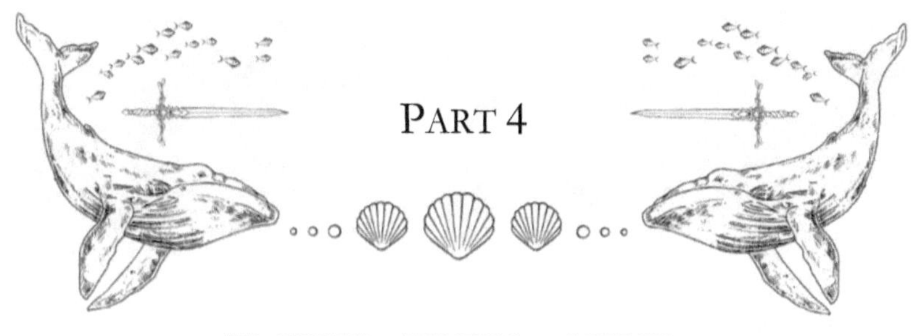

Part 4

REDEEMED

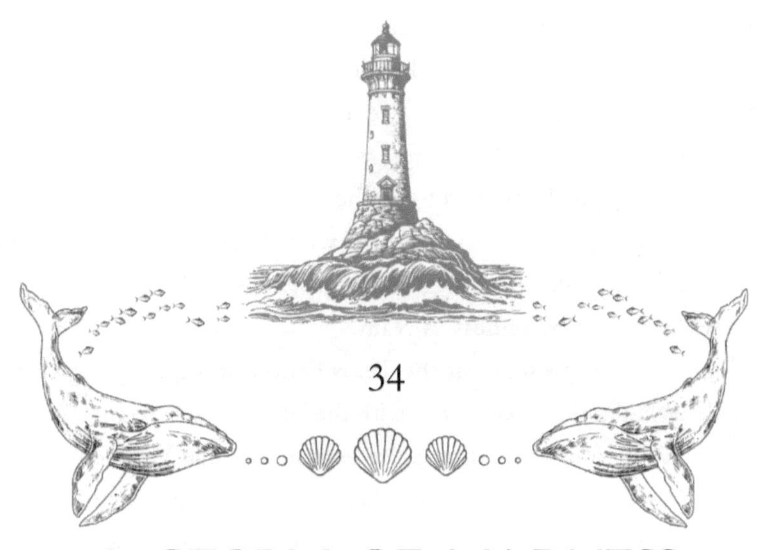

34

A STORM OF MADNESS

Jac

Tenby, Wales
October 1996

"I THOUGHT YOU SAID THAT THE portal couldn't be accessed by mere request." Jac glanced at Orsin as he cut a broccoli stalk and placed it in a basket before moving onto the next plant. Merri crouched in the adjacent row, plucking fresh carrots from the earth and putting them in a basket of her own.

"I did, but that doesn't mean we stop trying. A whale isn't coming to *shore* to bring us back." Orsin crossed his arms, the bag hanging off his shoulder swinging with the movement. "We can still trust Esias and *act* at the same time."

It was now late October, almost November, and the weather was beginning to nip noses and whisper words of winter. After Jac's revelation a few weeks ago, his dreams had declined in frequency, and Orsin had stopped by the Telor Pendu no less than three times a week. The old man always came to see if time was "on their side"—something he never ceased to stop saying.

And today just happened to be the third time that week.

Jac exchanged a knowing glance with Merri, watching her bite back a hidden smile. They were both growing to like Orsin, but the man was almost as relentless as Nain.

His constant presence at the Telor Pendu prompted Jac to place a small basket in the tower room with the label "Orsin Counter" taped to the font, where they'd drop a prediction on when he'd arrive next. It had started out as a funny joke, but eventually it turned into something else. Since the end of September, Merri's writing had improved significantly to the point where she'd started writing *to* Jac instead of merely writing the day of the week. He wouldn't deny that each time he saw Merri's lavender sticky note resting in the bottom, it pulled a smile from him. He'd always be sure to leave a green note in return.

"How are you today?" she'd written.

"Grateful for another day in Tenby. I don't know if I'm ready for what's next," Jac responded. *"How are you?"*

"I think the same," she answered. *"I will miss it here."*

Jac had contemplated asking her deeper questions—of more memories of their past together or how she'd gotten legs if she was a sea maiden, but all of that felt too personal for a sticky note. Maybe in time he'd learn the truth, but he wanted to get his memories back first. Maybe he would already know the answers if only he could remember them…

Jac fixed his mind back on the present, avoiding looking at the old man towering before him. "We've already gone out on Barti's boat twice this week." He'd told Orsin of his connections with the fishmonger when they were trying to figure out a plan…but now it seemed like it was the *only* plan. *We're already pushing our luck running around with the Madman of Tenby as it is.* Though Jac no longer believed Orsin was crazy, that didn't mean everyone else thought the same. They didn't know what transpired in red ink and muted memories in the form of dreams.

He finished with the broccoli before moving on to the winter squash, cutting through the prickly vines with a lopper.

"What is one more?" Orsin planted his feet firmly on the ground, his posture immovable. For an old man, he sure didn't act like it.

"Quit haggling them, will you?" Nain called from the front door of the lighthouse. When Jac glanced her way, he nearly snorted, seeing as her scowl didn't meet her eyes. Her hands remained fisted by her hips like she was afraid they'd fly away. *She's in good spirits today.* "There's no need to rush off."

"You call waiting a whole month 'rushing off'?" Orsin hollered back. "And why have you got His Royal Highness working outside like this anyway? Does royalty mean nothing to you?"

"He's a prince, not an invalid!" Nain yelled and slammed the door behind her.

All of them laughed. Jac wouldn't have wanted it any other way. He was more Jac Hughes than Olivander Daws. He didn't know life otherwise, so it was a comfort still to have some normalcy when it came to his grandmother. Even if it meant harvesting the last of the vegetables.

"Back to my point," Orsin continued. "I think that Barti fella's finally getting used to me by now. Why wouldn't he? The seagulls sure are."

"Only because you keep feeding them Nain's baps. You know she bakes those for *people*, not flying rats, right?"

"You're *what?*"

They all turned to see Nain's face quickly disappear from the kitchen window.

"That woman has ears everywhere, doesn't she?" Orsin whispered, and Merri laughed silently. He turned his gaze back to Jac. "Come on, then. The day's already half over, and there's to be a storm, Your Highness."

Jac lifted his chin. "How do you know that?" He'd seen the sky earlier when he'd logged the conditions; he already knew what was coming. But not everyone was trained to read the weather like him.

"Did you glance at the sky this morning? It was a bloody pink, like the tender skin of a wound beginning to heal."

Jac snorted. "Very poetic. Can't we try again tomorrow when it's safer?"

"We could. But I have a good feeling about it this time. The sea will take us. Besides, it was a storm which prompted us to get swallowed in the first place, wasn't it?" Orsin winked and tugged his bag closer, his decision made.

Those weren't ordinary storms, though.

But for the twelfth time that month, Jac and Merri found themselves walking to Harbor Beach with the old man by their side.

"You sure picked an interesting day to go fishing. Tell me, what's gotten you so hooked all of a sudden?" Barti asked, his hands fixed on the wheel of the ship. "It's a good thing it's the off season for the *Gwylan Môr*, or else I wouldn't be able to swing this."

All four of them were aboard the schooner, its sails billowing roughly in the gusty wind. Choppy waves sprayed against the red-and-gray hull and splattered along the deck, drenching shoes and mingling with the strong smell of fish. They'd been on this boat so often that

Jac had grown as accustomed to it as the bathtub he still bedded in.

"I'm a practiced fisherman, and these two are eager to learn the trade," Orsin answered. It was the guise they'd all chosen in case Barti started asking questions. The old man said it wasn't too far from the truth, seeing as he'd fished often in Chaera.

And that wasn't the only secret he had.

"How are you able to afford all this?" Jac had asked him one day. Barti had said he'd do it for free the first couple of times, but after the fourth, Orsin felt it best to start compensating him.

"Didn't I tell you? I'm a published author. Written a few books here and there under the name Gerard Platt."

"Wait." Jac did a double take. "*You* wrote *Tales of a Lost World?*" His mind flashed back to Orsin's home with all the watercolor paintings, and it slowly came together. The man was an artist *and* a writer.

"We are one in the same." He chuckled. "If you haven't noticed, my *real* name isn't accepted around here."

And that had been the end of that.

"Well, I don't see why you all couldn't have picked a better day," Barti prattled on. "Normally, I wouldn't take you out on the brink of a storm, but that's when the fish tend to bite best. So, you're all crazy, but…I guess you're in luck, too." Barti steered the ship past a red buoy bobbing in the water, but not before Jac had seen his gaze cast in Orsin's direction. His eyes were slitted whenever he looked at the old man. Jac wasn't certain how the fishmonger felt about the Madman of Tenby being on his ship, but he could venture a guess.

Even if he didn't like him, Barti trusted Jac. And that seemed to be enough. Plus, it helped that Orsin *had* proven himself sane the past twelve or so encounters.

Still, people liked to talk.

The *Gwylan Môr* took them out to deeper waters, the sky overhead slowly growing darker the further the day wore on. Barti assured them they still had time, but they should be back to the docks no later than five o'clock if they wished to remain dry and not owe him thousands of pounds in new boat parts.

But Barti didn't know Orsin. The old man had a date with a storm, and he wasn't going to miss it.

At the onset of all this, Jac wasn't sure how going fishing would be enough to summon a portal-keeper, but Orsin kept saying that Esias would make a way if the time was right. At the first spotting of a tail fluke, that was their cue to jump into the ocean and get swallowed by the beast.

Only, the opportunity never came.

But perhaps tonight really would be different.

"Trust me, I have a plan," Orsin had said.

It didn't seem too different from their usual one. For this afternoon, they'd cast their fishing lines like always, using the rods Orsin had secured from a local bait and tackle shop a few weeks ago. They could have borrowed some from Barti, but in order for their ruse to appear legitimate, Orsin thought it best to look the part. They'd fish for a few hours, and then the hope was to ride out the storm as long as they could before heading back to shore. That way, the *Gwylan Môr* would have a greater chance of seeing a whale. When—*if*—one arrived, that would be everyone's cue to jump in.

The whole plan was risky. White humpbacks were rarer than a straight week of sun in Tenby.

And what of Barti? If a whale actually *did* come from the storm, would he get stranded all by himself in the middle of the ocean, unable to man the boat alone? Jac knew Barti was an experienced fisherman; the sea was his livelihood, but even so, it was poor taste to abandon him, wasn't it? Orsin must have thought of that, at least.

Jac told himself not to worry. Instead, he walked over to where

Merri stood, her fingers white-knuckling the ship's railing while her focus remained locked on the waves slapping against the hull.

"Still not used to boats, huh?" he asked. His smile faltered when he saw the look on her face.

She shook her head, her lips pressed into a straight line.

He stepped closer. "Are you afraid?"

She shook her head again.

If it wasn't fear, then what was it?

Her home is the sea, Jac. She misses it. How could he have forgotten?

He leaned on the railing and sighed. "You wish to be in the ocean instead of standing here, is that it?"

Merri nodded, seeming grateful not to have to explain. Knowing her, she was probably gripping the railing so hard to keep herself from jumping in.

He was still digesting the fact that she was a sea maiden, or used to be, rather. But his life was filled with oddities as of late. Merri's oceanic existence was the least startling of them all. Which was surprising.

"Well, whenever we return to Chaera, maybe there's a way for you to get your tail back. To go home again." Why did saying that make part of him ache inside? *Probably because if she gets her tail back, you may never see her again. And you'll miss her. Think about her often.* But weren't this prince and Merri friends? They had made it work before, hadn't they?

When did the term "friends" suddenly seem so insufficient?

"I guess this is a good place to stop," Barti shouted, his voice carrying over the wind. "Not too far from shore, but far enough that the catch is sure to be good. I'll drop anchor here."

"Here are your instruments," Orsin said.

Jac swallowed any remaining words and grabbed one of the fishing rods Orsin handed to him and Merri. The old man winked before walking away, which meant it was time to assume their positions.

"I think I'd be content if I never have to touch one of these again," Jac whispered to Merri, gesturing to the rod in his hand. Her quiet laugh tugged on his heart, but it was her smile which sent a jolt of joy through him. He felt he could do anything—maybe even become the prince of a foreign kingdom—if she would only continue to look at him like that. "There's really no telling how long we'll have to keep doing this." He shrugged, casting his line out anyway. At least Merri was beside him; that alone made it worth it, especially when she asked for his help. The past couple of weeks had been a learning curve for her. Apparently, she'd only fished by way of underwater traps or nets, which required little effort on her part. But Orsin had happily demonstrated the proper form, though that didn't mean she hadn't gotten hurt before. Jac had bandaged her bloody fingers pricked by one too many barbs, and he'd even come up behind her to reel in a large bass before it washed her out to sea.

But the woman never gave up. That was something Jac admired.

Merri cast her line back and let it fly overhead, only when the hook surged forward, it snagged the back of her jacket and sent her hood up over her head. A raspy scream escaped her windpipe, the rod clattering to the ship's deck as she fell forward on the railing, her feet already leaving the ground.

Jac didn't hesitate. He grabbed her around the waist and pulled her toward his chest, holding her securely, as if afraid she might still tumble into the sea. He could feel her heartbeat thumping wildly and it matched the one that pulsed in his own ears. *I almost lost her.*

"Everything tidy over there?" Barti asked from his position at the ship's bow. He'd just finished letting the anchor sink to the ocean floor.

"Yup. We're fine," Jac yelled over his shoulder. He stepped back and turned Merri around, his eyes not straying from her face. "Are you okay?"

She nodded, though she looked shaken. Tentative fingers reached toward her hood, revealing the culprit of her almost-demise. Her eyes widened. The fishhook cut clean through the fabric, just inches away from piercing the back of her skull.

But she's fine. It could have been a lot worse.

"You know, I wasn't planning on having a heart attack today." Jac chuckled away his remaining adrenaline, already working the pointed barb out of her garment. He could feel her watching him. But her blue doe eyes were no longer looking at the fish hook but up at him instead. His hands stilled beneath her gaze, only a breath away from her cheek. He couldn't help brushing one of his knuckles against her skin. "I'm glad you're not hurt, Merri." The corner of his mouth inched up into a wry grin. "Maybe this was just your attempt to finally swim in that sea of yours."

She turned crimson.

Jac resumed his task, and when the barb finally relented, he didn't step away. He lowered his voice and leaned in closer. "If rescuing you on this boat starts becoming a regular occurrence, I might take back my earlier statement of never wanting to fish again." *I don't mind playing the hero.* "Just some food for thought." He shrugged, but he couldn't keep the smile from spreading across his face, especially when hers mirrored his own.

Fishing resumed like normal, Orsin catching close to ten bass and cod combined, plus a smoothhound or two, while Jac and Merri collectively only scored about five, most of them flatfish or breams.

And still no sighting of a white whale.

Casting his line again, Jac blinked away a raindrop that fell in his eye. Another one splattered against his forehead and trickled down his chin. A gentle pattering soon followed as more droplets cascaded to earth, bouncing off of his jacket and the ship's deck. Then the sky relented like it had suddenly been granted permission to unleash its barrage of tears.

It's here. The storm's come.

Jac turned to where Orsin stood and was surprised to see him missing from his usual post. Jac scanned the deck but couldn't see much in the way of rigging and sea mists and rain getting in the way. But then the old man was there again, seeming to reappear out of nowhere. Their gazes locked, and Jac felt his stomach sink; the familiar gleam in the old man's eyes was replaced by something else Jac couldn't name. *What's gotten into him? We need to head back before this gets any worse.*

Jac walked over to Orsin and raised his voice above the wind. "I don't think a whale's coming. It's too dangerous staying out here any longer," he said, wondering why they hadn't already made for the shore.

"One will come." There was that look again. His piercing blue eyes were no longer the wise ones Jac had grown accustomed to. No. These were different.

"How can you be so sure?" Rain pelted against his face even harder, water spitting out of his mouth as he talked.

Orsin didn't answer; his gaze was stuck on the tumultuous ocean churning all around them.

Jac tugged on his arm. "What of Barti and the *Gwylan Môr?*" *What about the rest of us?* "We should turn back now and find another way to seek the whale when it's safer."

"He will be well enough," the old man said. "This ship runs a steady clip."

He's just gonna let Barti fend for himself. The man could get lost, maybe stranded, or worse. What if a whale never comes? He's sending all of us to our doom. Jac swallowed hard. *How bad are the typical storms off of Tenby's coast?*

He looked into Orsin's eyes again and finally understood. The man had cracked. Desperation was his only motivator now.

A thunderclap echoed somewhere in the distance, followed by a thin streak of lighting slicing through the gray horizon. The rain was falling even harder now, pelting against the sides of the boat and anything that wasn't seeking shelter. Jac saw Merri standing with her jacket draped over her head, huddling just over the hatch that led down to the cabin below.

Where was Barti?

"The blasted…! The anchor's jammed!" the fishmonger yelled, his words like a knife cutting through the storm. "Seek shelter immediately!"

Orsin ignored the man and stripped off his jacket, casting it aside before stepping onto the first rung of the railing.

Realization barreled into Jac like a wolfhound. *He's gonna jump. If I don't stop him, he's going to drown.*

"What are you doing, *wnco?*" Barti yelled at Orsin while still trying to fix the anchor.

Jac acted fast, adrenaline already pumping his blood to boiling.

Just as Orsin climbed the next rung, he was yanked backward, his back smacking against the slick wood of the schooner's deck. A groan left his mouth before he turned and pushed up to his elbows. He faced Jac, a wild look roaring beneath his gaze when he saw who had stopped him. "Your Highness?"

He stood again and ran to the railing once more, but Jac was quicker. He sprung at the man's ankles and tripped him, sending Orsin sprawling onto the wooden beams for a second time. His jaw thwacked hard, seeming to sap the strength out of the old man swifter than any words ever could. But then he rolled and tried getting up again, this time slower.

Jac didn't give him much of a chance and brought him down just as easily, but Orsin fought back this time, landing a punch clean to his eye. The contact smarted, and Jac blinked away the fuzzy stars for a few seconds. It was enough for Orsin to push him off and stagger to the railing once more.

But he never sought purchase. Jac lunged forward, and pretty soon the two of them were rolling on the ground, tumbling and slipping on the slick boards with every dip and swell of the deep. Jac wasn't trying to hurt the man, just stop him enough to keep him alive, but Orsin kept throwing punches and clawing at anything he could.

How can an old man be this strong?

"Tie the fool down!" Barti hollered. If he were a chimney stack, smoke would be coming out of his ears. Jac was convinced the fishmonger would never trust Orsin after this day. He didn't blame him.

"Get off of me! Let me go!" Orsin shouted, prostrate on the deck of the ship. Jac finally had the old man's arms pinned behind his back and was now tying them up with a rope Merri had secured from the hold. His ankles were next, which proved difficult with all his kicking. "I need to get back. Let me go!" His vehement shouts died on the wind with the last tightening of the slick ropes, the pelting rain drowning out his cries as it pooled around his sodden form.

Horror-stricken, Jac stood back and watched Orsin writhing in all his misery, his bonds making it impossible for him to get up. Merri watched from behind him, as if trying to hide herself from the sight. Another burst from Orsin had her gripping Jac's arm, her head pressed against his shoulder blade.

What on earth happened to him?

Eventually, the older man curled in on his side, and the shouting turned into wracking sobs. He cried out into the swirling chaos all around him, beaten and battered by the storm. His cheek lay pressed against the deck, mouth open like a sea bass that had lost its will to fight. His words were their own agony. "I'm sori, Gilda, my love." He sobbed even harder, eyes squeezed shut. "I'm sori, Fiona. Dane." A croak of defeat left his throat. "I'm sori your father won't be coming home."

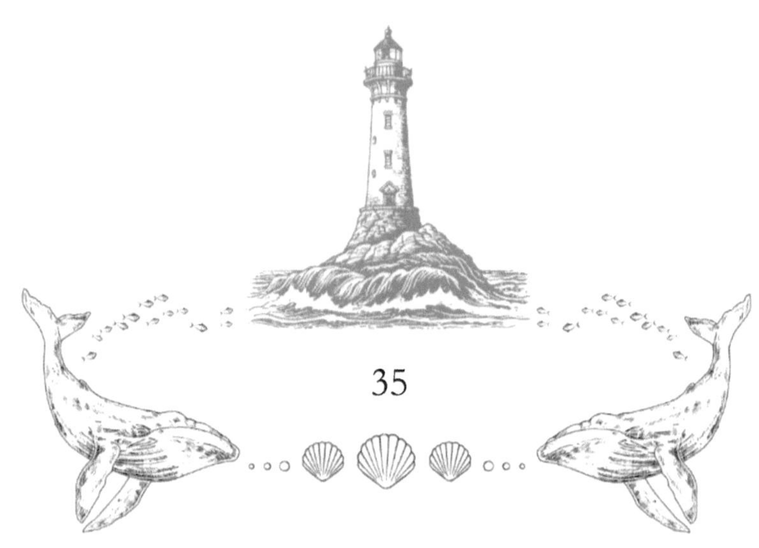

35

WALKS IN THE RAIN

Merri

Tenby, Wales
October 1996

MERRI HAD NEVER BEEN SO RELIEVED to touch land in all her life. Sure, she'd wanted to go ashore for various reasons, but now it was a matter of life or death.

Orsin broke, and we almost paid the price for it.

Rain continued to pelt them like rocks as they all exited the jostling *Gwylan Môr*, unsteady on their feet from the swells. Barti was yelling, stringing together sentences with words Merri had never heard before, though she had a feeling they didn't mean well since they were directed at Orsin.

"And you're to never come back, you understand?"

Jac waved a hand at Barti to placate him, apologizing with a singular look that bore no further words. The damage had been done. There would be no more fishing trips after this one.

Orsin was still tied up, though Jac removed his ankle bonds so he could at least walk the gangplank onto the beach. The quicker they could leave the fuming Barti, the better. Once they were a safe enough distance from the ocean, and curious bystanders, Jac removed the bonds around the old man's wrists. All three of them were shivering and soaking wet, standing beneath an awning—that's what Jac called it—of a local sweet shop.

"Do you need us to walk you home?" Jac asked, though it didn't sound like he wanted to.

"Na. Na." Orsin shook his head, his gaze glued somewhere on the sand. "I'll hail a cab." His voice was distant, as if his mind was elsewhere, trying to rectify what he'd just done.

Merri glimpsed the faraway expression in his eyes—so different from the desperation she'd seen clawing at them earlier. It had been etched into the deep crease of his brow, but now all that remained was a sad indent in his forehead.

Her chest constricted.

She remembered their last conversation on the rocks a few weeks ago. This man standing before her felt like a completely different version than the one who had given her advice. Than the one who had tried to comfort her and speak words of truth.

He's so broken. So lost.

She swallowed.

Like me.

"Are you sure?" Jac asked once more.

Orsin nodded, his silence something Merri wasn't used to coming from him.

"Okay. See you around." Jac grabbed Merri's hand and pulled her in the direction of the Telor Pendu. Holding hands was becoming as common as breathing lately, even though it still made her stomach flutter every time. They walked in silence for a few minutes, him not bothering to look back.

But Merri did. She couldn't help it. Orsin was now a sodden blob in the distance, walking behind them, though at a much slower pace. He was kicking pebbles in the rain. Whatever cab he said he'd hail, he never did. She had a feeling he never meant to.

"Is he still there?" Jac asked.

Merri nodded, her chest tight when she looked at him. Already, part of Jac's eye was swelling shut. Red and puffy and apt to turn a ghastly purple.

She knew people made mistakes; she was no exception. But she feared making more… The way Orsin just did now. But was it possible to falter and fall, only to be picked back up time and time again? Was it possible to receive forgiveness without limit if the heart was sincere in the asking?

Maybe it's possible. Esias says He's willing. Though His grace wasn't something to misuse either.

"Come on, let's get away from this rain." Jac increased his pace and started running with her hand in his, but not before Merri stole one last glance at the mournful man behind them.

Please, Esias, she prayed. *Be near.*

36

TO BE FORGIVEN

Jac

Tenby, Wales
November 1996

JAC'S EYE HAD TURNED A HORRID PLUM and puce since Orsin hit him several days ago. He thought about checking in on the older man, but even Nain said it was best to wait. She'd known Orsin long and well enough to learn he did best with some time and distance. But Jac wasn't sure how much time or distance could fix things. Not when Barti was spreading news around that the Madman of Tenby was truly mad, after all. Unbeknownst to Jac, the fishmonger had a storm camera affixed to the top mast of his ship, and he'd captured the whole ordeal and submitted it to the local news.

Jac had expected more from him.

Now all of Tenby could replay the events of a youth tackling an old man to the ground. It didn't matter that he was doing it to save a life. Jac had encountered enough folks in town to know that while some deemed him a hero, the majority waggled their fingers in his face, saying he could have used more tact. Though they all agreed upon one thing: Orsin was crazy.

Jac was only too glad they lived on the outskirts of town and didn't own a television.

It had been a foolish plan from the beginning. They could have ended up dead if Barti hadn't found the issue with the anchor Orsin had secretly jammed. It was a miracle they had made it home alive and in one piece. Still, Jac cringed whenever he replayed what happened.

He shook his head and tugged his jacket closer to his neck as he kicked the loose gravel of the Telor Pendu's walkway. He lifted his chin toward the cloudy November sky and sighed. "What's the purpose of all of this?" *Of me being a prince from a foreign land. Forgetting my memories. Falling for a girl I should already know. Befriending a man who's lost his mind. And now getting lambasted by my whole town.* "I'm just a lighthouse keeper."

He could feel another headache coming on at the base of his skull.

Someone touched his elbow, and he jumped, releasing a shaky breath when he saw who it was; it was only Merri. His racing thoughts stilled beneath her gentle smile, calming him in more ways than he thought possible. He hadn't heard her come outside. She was always a welcome sight in the midst of the spinning torrent that was his mind.

She held out a plate for him. One of her lavender notes was stuck to the top of the cling film, flapping in the gentle breeze.

Jac pulled off the sticky note and grinned when he saw the words. "'To cure your misery,'" he read aloud and pulled off the clear layer of stretchy plastic to better see what was beneath. His eyes grew wide. "A cannoli?" His mouth watered just at the sight. "I didn't know Nain knew how to make these."

Merri fished out a notepad and took a few seconds to write something down. When finished, she handed it to him.

"I told her you like Italian food. She taught me how to make them."

The space inside his chest warmed. "You're amazing, Merri." He didn't waste another minute. Grabbing the cannoli, he took a generous bite, feeling the flaky exterior give way to a sweet cream filling. It was the perfect texture. Otherworldly. "This isn't fair, you know. You being so good at everything."

Merri smiled and that familiar blush crept up her neck. She seemed happy lately. Here. With him. And that was all he could have ever hoped for. She reached toward his eye and fingered the tender flesh around the socket. It looked worse than it felt, but it was still a little tight. "It's getting better," he said, answering the unspoken question in her eyes. She nodded, and he offered her the other half of the pastry before knocking his shoulder gently into hers. "Come on, let's go back insi—"

"A moment of your time."

A familiar voice stopped Jac in his tracks, causing the hairs on the back of his neck to rise. He didn't have to turn around to know who it was, but he did anyway. Orsin stood at the end of the lighthouse path, his hands crushing a tweed cap and looking more like a tentative child than a wise old man.

He opened his mouth and closed it in the same breath, as if he didn't know what to say. "Lovely weather this morning," he finally said, his tone hesitant, though still just as deep.

Jac nodded. "It's turning out to be a mild autumn." Merri stood rigidly by his side. One glance at her revealed that she was surprised to see him. Orsin had broken all their trust in a matter of moments, and it would take something significant to repair it any time soon. If he came any closer, Jac would do whatever he could to diffuse any danger, madness or not.

Thankfully, Orsin stayed where he was, though everything but his feet were moving. Eyes doing their own dance, fingers still twisting his hat, shoulders pulling back only to sag again. He looked like he wanted to say something more but didn't know how. He cleared his throat. "About that night—"

"Don't worry about it," Jac interrupted. Recounting all the details made him recoil, and he didn't feel like reliving that right now. "It's in the past."

Orsin shook his head. "Nothing that still haunts someone is ever in the past. It can only be put to rest by making what's wrong into something that's right."

Jac remained silent, willing Orsin to continue.

"I was wrong, Jac." Hearing his old name again suddenly felt more serious. "I never should have used you all like I did. Barti's right to hate me, to plaster my face all over Tenby for the madman I proved myself to be. Yes, I saw the news." He ground his teeth. "I lost control of myself. I snapped. I thought this would finally be the time I would get to see my family after so many years. After accepting my fate for so long—*thirty* years' long—it felt like Esias had opened a pathway to the impossible again. It was like finally tasting water after an unrelenting drought." He shook his head again. "But I went about it all wrong."

Jac listened to Orsin's apology in silence, measuring the weight of his words against his actions. The man had made a grave error, and Jac had a shiner to prove it. But matters could have been worse. No one died. It was only their reputations which suffered the most.

"I never should have fought you. I—I..." The old man's throat grew hoarse. "I'm grievously sori, Your Highness. If we ever return to Chaera, I plan to step down from my position as Keeper of Prophecies. You're free to explain the reasons to your father, though it might be best if he hears it from me." Orsin sighed dejectedly. "I understand this is all very confusing for you, considering your forgotten memories. And you have no reason to trust a word I say. Not anymore, anyway."

Then he looked at Merri and sighed, his shoulders and eyes betraying even more guilt.

"A lot of good I did spewing half-lived truths of trusting Esias and then paving my own way. My life story must seem a sham." He shook his head before meeting her eyes again. "I was earnest that night on the rocks with you, Merri; our Maker has done a lot to change this old, calloused, and battered heart. But one taste of long-forgotten hope, albeit a good thing, made me hunger for more. Made me act like a fool and put those who trusted me in harm's way. How I acted was wrong, and I have lived enough life to know I never should have let my emotions control me the way they did." Orsin's eyes were like pools of liquid glass, ready to overflow should a lone drop get added to them. "But what guts me the most is if I made you question Esias' role in your own story and His power to redeem." His eyes now vacillated between Jac and Merri's faces, his own earnest and sincere. "I am truly sori for the ways I hurt you both. And I hope, in time, you will come to forgive me."

When he finished his speech, a weighty silence charged the space between them. What could Jac say to a man so broken and repentant? It was almost impossible to hold anything against him now, but what else would it take to make the man crack a second time? Desperation drove people to dark places, so what happened if he didn't resist its tug again?

That's not for me to hold against him. I wouldn't want someone recounting my mistakes in anticipation of making more.

Merri moved from Jac's side and, within a matter of moments, walked over to Orsin and embraced him. Her action was the lone drop which turned the old man's glassy eyes into rivers. "I am sori." He hugged her tight, her kindness making him sob quietly into her gooseberry hair. "So sori."

In that moment, Jac felt like the two understood one another better than he ever could.

And he did what needed to be done.

Walking over to Orsin, he stopped when he was close enough to pat the man on his shoulder. "I forgive you," he said. Jac's shoulders lightened almost instantly, and he knew he truly meant what he said.

Orsin looked up, his eyes red-rimmed and wet. "You both have shown me more kindness than I deserve."

"What's going on out here? Some sort of cuddle huddle?" Nain's voice carried over to them from the doorway.

Orsin chuckled as he stood to his full height. "I wouldn't mind if it was. I came to apologize."

"Nonsense." Nain swatted her hand through the air like she would swat at a fly. "We all lose ourselves sometimes. No need to make this so serious." Then she looked at Jac. "Didn't I tell you the man wasn't crazy? He's not, as you clearly can tell."

"Can always count on you, Nain, for the inflation of my ego." Orsin placed his tweed cap, now wrinkled, on his head and looked leagues lighter than when he'd first arrived.

"Well, don't just stand there; come in!" She waved for everyone to go inside.

Orsin shook his head. "Not now. I've yet to make my peace with Barti. And I have a feeling he won't be taking too kindly to me showing up on his doorstep."

Jac snorted. "That's an understatement. But good luck anyway."

Merri smiled at Orsin and gave him one last hug before he left.

He waved goodbye and faced the road once more, but not before Jac heard him singing.

37

STICKY NOTE SERENADE

Jac

MORNING TURNED INTO EVENING AGAIN and again and again, and before Jac knew it, another week had passed. Aside from all the recent revelations concerning his life, everything was returning back to normal. Even the talk of the town had died down enough for Jac to deliver bread again. But just in case, Nain had instructed him to go to specific people who "won't put their opinions where they're not supposed to." Which included Orsin's house, but the man hadn't been home. In fact, Jac hadn't seen him since the morning he stopped by the Telor Pendu to apologize.

He'd just gotten back from his errand and leaned his bike against the lighthouse. A lightness in his chest kept his footsteps quick. He was about to see Merri. Funny how being away for any amount of time had him wondering when he could see her next. Her presence at the Telor Pendu was so commonplace now that he had difficulty remembering what life was like before she arrived.

He opened the front door and stepped inside the kitchen, expecting to find her at the counter with his grandmother since that's where she usually was most afternoons, but Nain was alone, knitting in a chair at the table.

"Is Merri here?"

Nain nodded. "She just went to the outhouse but a moment ago."

"I'll wait for her upstairs, then." He moved to the stairwell and climbed the first couple of steps.

"Why haven't you told her how you feel?"

Her words made him stop short. He turned, the tips of his ears growing warm. "What?"

Nain shook her head. "Don't play coy with me, Jac. I see the way you look at her. The way she looks at *you*."

"It's complicated."

"Why?" Nain pushed away the knitting from her lap and leaned forward. "Just because you're this prince from a land only God knows about?"

He stifled a groan. She raised a brow.

"Why does it have to be so complicated, Jac?"

"She knows I care for her," he said, descending to the ground floor. "But I can't promise anything if I'm only a shell of who I once was." He wouldn't hurt her like that. Couldn't. And he hoped more than anything that she understood.

"A *shell*?" Nain raised her voice even higher. "*Cariad*, you're more whole than the lot of Tenby! Memories are important, ie, but even the best ones fade with time, softening around the edges until what's left is only how you felt. And how do you feel when you're with Merri now?"

Complete. Understood. Seen. The list could go on. He shook his head. "Feelings aren't enough to base a relationship off of, Nain. Not when she remembers who I was before and I only see what's in front of me now. She deserves someone who can love her fully, not by halves."

Nain stood up and quietly walked over to him. She reached up a hand and caressed one of his cheeks, looking him tenderly in the eyes. "You don't think I know that better than most, Jac? I loved Alun with my whole being, even when the feelings strayed or if I couldn't recall our earlier days. It was a relationship built on *choosing*, not dependent on our qualifications to love." Her voice was the gentlest Jac had ever heard from her, though her words seemed to grip his throat. "And you, fy machgen, do *not* love by halves. And that won't change whether you remember who you once were or remain as you are now. Both versions of you are equal to the choosing. And I believe Merri sees that."

He swallowed, feeling the warmth of Nain's hand leave his face, now replaced with the coolness of autumn. Her words still rang in his ears. *"I believe Merri sees that."* Maybe that was so, but until he could recall their past, he didn't think it was fair to plan their future.

Nain reclaimed her seat, but she didn't resume her knitting. Instead, she grabbed the teacup resting on the table in front of her and swirled the liquid inside, watching the dregs spin at the bottom. Then she sighed. "I would hate for you to miss out on a chance at love, Jac," she said, her voice still calm. "What if your memories never come back? What if you're putting too much hope into something that may never happen, and it robs you?" She met his gaze again. "I would hate to see your life be one filled with regret when you had every opportunity to choose otherwise."

Jac walked around the tower room as he waited for Merri, noticing the slight feminine touches she added to the space. A lavender blanket was now spread on his bed, a sketch of a milky whale and sea maiden was taped to the wall beside his ship, and the room smelled of honey and cinnamon from a candle burning on the table. But otherwise, most of it was the same.

The conversation he'd just had with Nain still lingered in his mind, and he couldn't shake the last part. Once he'd learned he was the prince from his dreams, he figured there was a way to remember it all. Or why else had his dreams been returning his memories? And when Orsin had mentioned it was because of a spell, then he had even higher hopes of breaking it. But one word from Nain had him second-guessing it all. *What if she's right? What if I never remember anything?*

His eyes caught on the "Orsin Counter" basket, and a grin slipped past his pensive frown. He peered closer. Instead of a single lavender note, there were three, all numbered in the order in which they should be read.

Jac unfolded the first. *"I hope Orsin is okay. We haven't seen him recently."*

He unfolded the second. *"How is your eye?"*

And the third. *"What happens now?"*

She could have written all these on one note, but he liked that she'd chosen three. It meant she'd thought of talking to him at least three separate times. He reached into his back pocket and drew out his pad of green sticky notes and a pen, aiming to answer her questions, when the sound of footsteps drew his attention to the door.

Merri smiled at him, once more in her lavender dress, but this time with an emerald-green sweater and white socks covering the bare parts of her skin exposed to the cold. Her cheeks were rosy, and he wondered if it was from the outdoors or something else.

"Helo," he said. "I was just about to answer your notes."

She nodded and walked into the room, taking a seat on the bed and watching him.

He smiled at her before writing his replies, choosing three of his own sticky notes to respond: 1) *"I'm sure he's hanging in there. How are you?"* and 2) *"It hardly hurts at all, thanks to all the ice you gave me,"* and, lastly, 3) *"I wish I knew. Wait out each day as it comes, I guess. Are you homesick?"*

There. He peeled off the papers and folded them before placing each in the basket for her to read later. He could have verbally responded, but it was an unspoken code that whatever came out of the basket was only discussed through the written word.

Which made some things easier to ask than others…

Nain's words came back to him again. *"I would hate to see your life be one filled with regret when you had every opportunity to choose otherwise."* He swallowed and scribbled something else on a fourth note before he thought better about it. He folded it up and stuck it toward the bottom of the basket, beneath the other ones he'd previously written. Then walked away as fast as he could.

"So." He stuffed his hands into his front pockets and joined her on the bed, sitting on its end while she sat near the top. "Would you like another grammar lesson today? You've already improved so much since you first started, so I'm not sure you even need it at this point," he said, shaking his head with a short chuckle. "You know, it's really uncanny how quickly you've taken to it. Is this a common trait of yours, learning skills so fast?"

Merri's blue eyes brightened, and she ducked her head as if embarrassed. She shrugged and picked at the fibers of the bedspread, but he could tell her cheeks were already turning pink.

"Come on, I've got to log the weather for today and could use your help."

She raised an eyebrow at him, giving him a pointed glare.

"Okay. Okay." He held up his hands in mock surrender. "I guess I could just use your company." He stood and held out his hand, heart thrilling when she took his offer. He helped her to her feet and led her up the spiral stair to the watch room.

38

THE DATE

Merri

Tenby, Wales
November 1996

"I'D LIKE TO TAKE YOU ON A DATE. How does Friday night sound?"

Merri reread those words over and over again, her heart soaring. Before going to bed that night, she'd remembered Jac's notes in the basket. Having read them in their proper order, she was most eager to read the one marked 4. It hadn't been a response; it had been its own question entirely, and now she was too excited to sleep.

Since coming to Tenby, she'd learned that the days of the week were different *here* than the ones in Chaera. Tomorrow was Thursday, or *Jorrven*. But Friday—*Draven*—felt closer now that it was nearing midnight.

She hastily wrote down her response. *"It sounds good."* Then she scribbled it out just as quickly. *No. It sounds more than good.* But she didn't want to sound too eager. Her emotions were still a jumble, and she was still grappling with so much loss, but maybe Jac wanted to change that. He'd mentioned it was a date, after all. But did she want his affection if he couldn't remember the past? *Yes. I'll always want Oli. No matter what form he comes in. Even if he remembers me as someone he never once loved before. He cares for me now, doesn't he?*

She'd overheard some of his conversation with Nain in the kitchen. But she'd only caught the tail end. *"I would hate for you to miss out on a chance at love, Jac."* Had his "chance at love" been about Merri?

Her head spun while her stomach did a dance. *Don't get too far ahead of yourself, Merriweather.*

She'd learned her lesson before, and she didn't want to make the same mistakes again.

Still, she'd fallen in love with his heart along the shores of Kerilow Bay long before Iun's, had recalled so much of his kindness and friendship…and that hadn't changed now that he went by a different name. He was still Oli to her. And he always would be. And it was hard not to get excited.

"I would love that." She wrote a new note and stuck it in the bottom of the basket before jumping into bed.

She'd wear her purple dress and green sweater again, and pull her hair back in a simple style. She needn't try *too* hard, but she wanted to look her best. Maybe Jac would even call her beautiful.

And for the first time in a long time, reality held more hope than any of her dreams.

"I hope you don't mind being on another boat, especially so soon," Jac said, the oars in his hands slicing through the gentle ripples of the sea. He was in his characteristic jeans, but tonight he wore a tan corduroy jacket over a white t-shirt. He'd taken her into town, secured the small row boat from a local business along the harbor, and had packed another picnicked dinner. His thoughtfulness knew no bounds. "The first time I brought you to the ocean, we sat on the sand. This time, I actually wanted you to be able to touch the waves. The only thing I forgot to bring were the fishing rods." He tsked and Merri laughed.

This is perfect. She hadn't been sure about boats, but ever since Barti's, she'd grown to love them. And being out here, alone with Jac… Well, it was even better.

She dropped one of her hands into the water, letting her fingers dip into the coolness of the sea. It was hard not to jump in, but for now, feeling the rise and fall of the tide was enough. The sun was beginning its return journey home, painting the sky in reams of pinks, oranges, and blues along the way. She'd never seen a more perfect sunset, a wonder as magnificent as the stars, to be sure.

"Merri." Jac cleared his throat across from her and she watched as he fished something out of the bag by his feet. He leaned toward her and held out a little purple box for her to take. "I got this for you."

Another gift? Her eyebrows asked the question.

He grinned. "Don't thank me just yet. Open it, and you'll see."

Merri's insides fluttered as she lifted the lid. *What could Jac possibly give me now?* Her hand stilled when she saw what was underneath. The most beautiful pen in the most perfect shade of purple stared up at her, shimmering and shining like her long-forgotten tail. She lifted her head to meet Jac's gaze, willing him to read her every emotion.

"I know it's not much, but it made me think of you when I saw it. You have the power to write your thoughts now, so you deserve a good pen that will hold up to the task. It's also waterproof, so you can take it with you in the ocean, if you choose."

Merri's chest swelled like the sea; this was her Oli, one of the most thoughtful men she'd ever known. Being Jac hadn't changed that one bit. Everything in her wanted to bridge the gap between them and embrace him, but Jac's words made her pause.

"There's also one more thing." This time, he pulled something white out of his pocket, and when Merri's gaze made the short trek from the paper in his hand to his eyes, she froze. He was looking at her with such intensity and longing, it stole her breath. "I, uh—" He cleared his throat. "I wrote you something."

Her insides quaked with anticipation. *Steady. It's just another note.* But her organ built on love had a hard time reasoning with her mind. *Why does he look so…serious?*

"I'd like to read it if you don't mind."

Merri nodded, her hands gripping the pen box like a lifeline.

He cleared his throat, shifted in his seat. "Dear Merri." A glance at her, a swallow. "Ever since you came to our small town of Tenby, life hasn't been the same. You've made the days seem shorter, the sun appear duller, and you've claimed more hearts than you should."

Merri's heart felt like it was bouncing around in her stomach.

"Your presence has been a beautiful disruption in my mundane life," Jac read on, his gaze looking up from the paper every so often. "Before you, I was simply a lighthouse keeper, but now, I'm a teacher, a better friend, and apparently, some prince from a foreign kingdom." He shook his head. "By all rights, none of this makes sense, but if I were to wait for the events in my life to be something I understood, something I *remembered*, then I might be waiting a long time."

Jac paused, and Merri couldn't take her eyes off of him. *Is he saying what I think he's saying?* His gaze latched onto hers like a beacon, and he didn't need the paper to utter the following words. "Merri, I've become enchanted by you. And I"—his fingers slackened on the parchment—"want you to know that I—" Suddenly, the letter was wrenched from his grasp by the wind, the special moment cracking as if someone had just shattered an earthen glass.

'I want you to know' what? *What is it, Oli?* Merri wanted to scream.

Jac was too stunned to continue, watching his confession swirling in the space above them. He tried reaching for it, but the wind kept taking it higher.

I need to get that paper. Before it falls into the ocean and disappears forever. But there wasn't much time. It was nowhere near their boat and was aiming fast for the sea.

"Merri, what are you doing?"

She was saving hearts, that's what she was doing. Only death would stop her from retrieving that letter. Grabbing one of the oars, she redirected their boat in its direction. Jac caught on and soon took over, bringing their small vessel to where the letter had just met the waves.

"This really isn't necessary, Merri. I can just tell you what I wrote."

She shook her head. *No.* Words were precious little things. They needed rescuing, protecting. Maybe it was because she couldn't speak, but the idea of losing a note, one of the only ways she could ever communicate…it sent a lonesome ache to her gut. Besides, if this was a love letter, she wanted to keep it and treasure it forever.

I'm getting that letter.

Jac rowed on and Merri leaned as far as she could over the bow. They were getting closer. Little by little. Hope surged in her fingertips as it brushed against the parchment, but it wasn't enough. The paper was absorbing the sea, growing heavier with the words beginning to bleed. It started to sink.

No. Merri leaned some more.

"Be careful!" Jac warned. "You told me you couldn't swim, remember?"

She leaned a bit farther, her fingers barely brushing the corner that still remained afloat.

"Merri, watch out—"

The boat tipped a little too far, and she fell overboard, the ocean cocooning her body in cold and bubbles and salt. Water funneled into her nose as she tried taking a breath, but the deep had other plans. Coughs wrecked her lungs before she slipped under.

"Merri!"

The one-time sea maiden couldn't move, her useless legs kicking frantically beneath her. Nothing had changed; she was still a leaden stone, an anchor. Fear clogged her senses and pulsed through every vein in her body. Her lungs begged for mercy.

Jac was going to tell me something, and now I'll never be able to hear it. She watched the remnants of his letter float away until it dissolved into the darkness. Sorrow etched another scar on her heart. *That's the end of that.*

If only the surface didn't feel so far away.

Suddenly, a splash broke through the water above her, and she saw Jac's body plunging downward. It took him a few seconds to open his eyes, and once he did, he pushed his way through the water to get to her. With one arm snagged around her waist, he used the other to propel them forward in the direction of the sun.

Praise Esias. She gasped desperately for air, a burst of coughs squeezing the water from her lungs. Now that she was no longer drowning, she shivered uncontrollably, and was completely and utterly embarrassed.

"Don't let go, okay?" Jac held her close, using his legs and one of his arms to tread water.

I wouldn't dream of it.

He turned his head to the left and then the right before spinning the both of them around in a circle. Merri thought she heard him utter a curse under his breath. *What's wrong?*

"I can't find the boat."

What? She scanned the ocean herself, but being only a head above sea level proved futile. Every dip and swell of the tide only made seeing the horizon even harder. *He's right. The boat's gone.*

Her dinner fought to climb her throat. She never should have fallen out of the boat. Jac wouldn't have tried to rescue her. They wouldn't have lost their vessel. *It's all my fault.* She swallowed a bitter note. *And now the gift he gave me is lost, too.*

What have I done?

"We need to swim back to shore," Jac said, his voice close to her ear. What he didn't say was, *I can't hold us both forever.* If they didn't move, they'd drown, and it would be Merri's fault. But the problem was…she hadn't learned how to swim without a tail. "I'll carry you as far as I'm able," Jac reassured her. "If I grow tired…well, we'll cross that bridge when we get there."

Merri held onto Jac, lightly gripping his shoulders while he used his whole body to lead them to safety. *What a date this turned out to be.*

A distant voice, almost like a hum, echoed in her ears.

"Another has arrived before you, who is no longer a few paces behind."

She turned her head and saw nothing.

"I promised I would come back for you, child." The voice drew nearer still.

She recognized to whom it belonged now. Her spirits rose. *Eldarwielle?*

"You look refreshed," he said.

Suddenly, a spray of air and water shot through the surface beside them, and Merri could feel the tightening of Jac's shoulders beneath her. "Woah!" he cried, tugging her closer as if on instinct. "Is that…?"

She nodded, seeing the pearlescent back. *It's a whale. My very best friend.*

"It is time, Merriweather. We must be off."

Already? It felt like she'd just arrived here. Had finally been filled after running on empty for so long. And they were to leave *now*?

She'd miss Nain, helping her in the kitchen and listening to her bicker with Jac. She'd miss the Telor Pendu and the way it wasn't only a beacon of hope for ships, but the way it had been *her* beacon, too. She'd miss the quaint town of Tenby and all its colorful shops. She'd even miss Orsin. She caught her breath. *Wait.* They couldn't leave without him, could they? He'd been an integral piece to this whole ordeal, and he needed to see his family.

"This time, maybe you want to open your eyes." Eldarwielle ceased swimming beside them and dove.

"Where's he going?" Jac asked, searching the water. Then it was as if a light dawned. "This is it, isn't it?" he asked her. "The portal?"

Merri nodded, clinging to him as if afraid he wouldn't be swallowed, too. He seemed to feel the same way, for he wrapped an arm around her waist and took a deep breath, the anticipation building behind his eyes.

And then all was darkness.

"Open your eyes, dear one. Look at the stars."

Merri cracked open tightly sealed lids to see nothing. *What stars?* Everything was dark, a blackness so rich and unfathomable, it was hard not to get lost. *And where's Jac?* She felt around for him on all fours, the ground beneath her a strange mixture of softness, warmth, and moisture. When suddenly, her head smacked into something hard.

A muffled grunt followed. "Seems like we both had the same idea." Jac laughed, reaching out to find her hand. The other gently cupped her face. "Is your head okay?"

She nodded so he could feel her movements; otherwise, her silence in this darkened place would reveal nothing.

"It's blacker than pitch. You sure we're inside a portal? I thought Orsin mentioned—"

Suddenly, the blackened host above them burst into brilliant twinkling lights of whites, yellows, and celestial purples and pinks. Merri had never seen such an awe-inspiring canvas before, though she wouldn't tell Eldarwielle that she still preferred Jac's Orion.

"Stars," Jac finished, mouth agape. Merri turned to find his profile lit up by the beaming heavens. He looked striking in any lighting.

It's beautiful, Eldarwielle.

"Hold fast. Our journey's almost finished," he hummed. *"Prepare to fly."*

Jac squeezed Merri's hand even tighter as the two of them cast their gazes upward, both not knowing what fate awaited them on the other side.

39

BACK HOME

Jac

Kerilow Bay, Chaera
Sol 1198

STARS GAVE WAY TO SPINNING. Twisting, pulling, and…soaring? Jac couldn't tell what was up from down when his body landed with a thud and skidded to a scraping halt. He lifted his head and felt the strain in his neck, taking in the view around him. He was lying on some sort of beach and sand was sticking to every inch of his wet and exposed skin. Lifting his gaze, a wall of mountains and hills towered like a monstrous backdrop. He squinted. Was that a castle? Something white-stoned gleamed in the sun with blue flags snapping from its pinnacles. Since when did it become morning? And why did it feel like the middle of summer all over again?

The portal. The white whale.

Where's Merri?

He turned toward the ocean and saw her body splain like his across the sand, but closer to shore. He pulled himself to his feet and rushed over to her.

"Merri?" He brushed the hair off her face.

She didn't stir.

"Wake up, Merri. Come on." He placed his hands on her shoulders and started rubbing her arms. His stomach curdled. *I thought these portals were safe.* Hadn't he just been launched out of the ocean? "Merri?" *Wake up…*

Like the sun breaking through the dawn, her eyelids fluttered open. And then she smiled.

Jac released a sigh of relief. "Are you hurt at all?"

She shook her head.

"Good." He held out a hand and helped her to her feet. The two brushed any remaining sand off their clothes and scanned the beach around them. He had no idea where they were. *Is this Chaera?* "That was some ride, huh?"

Merri nodded, and with a hand over her head to block the sun, she squinted and looked farther down the shore. She remained that way for a time, and then without warning, she started running.

"Wait. Where are you going?" Jac didn't waste another moment and ran after her, soon overtaking her slower pace when he saw what she was heading toward. Someone was on the shore, and he wasn't moving.

What's up with this place? He'd never seen so many bodies carelessly thrown about a beach before. He bent closer to the man and rolled him over, taken aback to see a familiar face. He'd even brought his bag, which was currently smooshed beneath him. "Orsin?"

Merri knelt beside him and started feeling for a pulse near the collar of his plaid shirt. But it wasn't necessary. His eyes cracked open, and mumbled words followed next.

"I'm almost home, Gilda. Only a little…little bit longer now. Just…hold on, dear one."

"He's delusional." Jac wasn't sure how long Orsin had been out here, or even *how* he'd gotten here to begin with, but he saw something that made his blood turn cold. Red stained Merri's fingers, a look of horror on her face as she removed her hand from Orsin's neck.

A quick inspection revealed a wound at the base of his skull from a small rock, and though the damage looked far worse than it was, he would recover. But they needed to wake him up first.

"Orsin." Jac grabbed one of his shoulders and gently shook him. He wasn't responding. "Orsin." He shook him harder.

Water splashed across the old man's face, and he suddenly started to cough. He rolled to his side and heaved the liquid out of his lungs, blinking away the moisture from his eyes. When he spotted his rescuers, his exhaustion gave way to surprise. "What in the depths was that for?"

Merri hid half of a large oyster shell still dripping with water behind her back and side-eyed Jac with a suppressed smile.

He stifled a laugh. "We thought you needed help."

"I was sleeping, not dead." The old man grunted and pushed to a seated position. He wobbled a little but righted himself and sighed deeply. "See? Right as rain." Then his face broke into a broad grin behind his bushy beard. "It's good to see you both again."

"How'd you get here?" Jac asked.

"I would imagine the same way as you," Orsin said.

"The portal?"

He nodded. "A couple of days ago…well, to be honest, I can't recall how long ago now, but I was looking out my window back in Tenby and noticed one of the buoys moving. Not bobbing like usual, mind you, but getting tugged along, almost as if it were trying to signal someone. So I had a hunch. I swam to it, and before I knew it, I wound up on this shore." Orsin rubbed the back of his head and winced when his hand found the recent wound. "Though typically, the landing is a little gentler than this. At least, it differs every time. Some exit you in the water while others blow you straight into the air."

Jac remembered getting flung himself, though his landing hadn't been as hard nor had he sustained injury.

"Where are we?" Jac asked, glancing around the beach once more. It looked a lot like his dreams. "Is this Chaera?"

Both Orsin and Merri nodded.

Jac turned around and scanned the mountainous terrain behind him. His eyes climbed the rocky and green hills and paused when they saw the limestone castle from earlier, perched on the edge of a tall cliff. He sucked in a breath and puffed it out through his cheeks. *I guess that's my home.* Goosebumps pricked his skin at the thought. He'd hoped that he'd recall *something* once he got here, but if anything, his memories seemed even further away than ever. It was strange standing in a place he should know without having any recollection of it at all. Would that ever change?

He glanced at Merri, and his soul ached. *I really hope so.* He'd been so close to telling her how he felt, but now…nothing felt normal.

"All that's left is to find that wicked sea witch Darya." Orsin stood with shaky legs. Merri helped steady him. "Then we can end her curses and set things to rights."

Darya. Jac hadn't heard her name before. "How are we supposed to find someone who lives in the sea?" Wouldn't that require, well, going into it?

Orsin nodded. "I was hoping our Merri would help us with that."

"Merri?" Just because she was a sea maiden didn't mean she knew where the witch lived, right? He raised his eyebrows. "Why would she know where she lives?" Merri placed a steadying hand on his arm and looked at him intently, her cheeks a little pinker than before. Jac got the message. "You've been to her before?"

She nodded. His stomach dropped. What need had she to visit a sea witch?

"Well, lead the way, little lady." Orsin gestured for her to start moving. "We don't want to waste another moment."

Merri didn't move. She shook her head and pointed to the sky.

"What is it? Are you afraid it'll rain?" Orsin asked. "There isn't a cloud in the heavens."

She shook her head again and used her hands to form a circle with her fingers. Then she pointed overhead once more.

"Sori, little lady. I wish I were more skilled at reading minds as I am with words." Orsin looked at Jac. "You're going to have to help me, Your Highness."

He nodded. If only they had a way for her to write something down. *Wait a second.* "Orsin, do you have any spare paper?"

The old man raised an eyebrow and then looked down. "Ah. This bag's become so much a part of me that I almost forget it's there." He lifted a flap and pulled out a book of cream paper and handed it to Jac. "Now as for a pen...well, mine has the last of my Winderplume. I had to conserve it these past few years, but I could spare a drop of ink if—"

"Don't worry about that. I came prepared." Jac reached into his pocket but dropped his hand when he saw Merri already writing something in the sand with a piece of driftwood. *Or that works, too.* He studied her letters, and it didn't take her long to finish.

"'We can only find her by nightfall,'" Jac read aloud. He furrowed his brow. "By nightfall? Wouldn't that make things harder?"

Orsin stroked his bearded chin. "This reminds me... I heard of this rumor once. Now that I think of it, maybe this was largely why your father's men had been unsuccessful in finding her. He always sent scouts under daylight."

"So, I guess that means we have to wait." Jac rubbed the base of his neck and sighed. He had no idea what was happening, and he had to keep his mind from dipping into insanity every time he thought about it too hard. Sometimes it was just easier to go along with things, trusting that his brain would catch up eventually.

"That does not stop us from searching now." Jac snapped his gaze in the old man's direction as Orsin tugged the strap of his bag tighter and began a wobbly plod down the shore. Nothing stopped him.

Merri grabbed Jac's arm and glanced between him and the retreating Orsin. From their vantage point, blood was caked into his salt-and-pepper hair, and though he appeared fine, there was no promise of him lasting long without being attended to. Especially if they waited until dusk.

"He needs to see a doctor," Jac said. "Is there one nearby?"

Merri pursed her lips in thought. Something seemed to pass over her that he couldn't read, but she soon made up her mind and grabbed his hand, drawing him in Orsin's direction.

"Do you know of a place?" he asked.

She nodded. With some heavy-handed coaxing and many head nods from Merri, the two men found themselves escorted to a nearby village only a few minutes away.

It didn't take them long to reach the winding path that led into the center of the small fishing town. Docks lined the shores this side of Kerilow Bay, with nets and wooden tackle boxes filled to overflowing with what looked like cod and sea bass. The nearby houses were dressed nothing like the pastel ones in Tenby and could best be described as a type of wattle and daub from the Stone Age but with cedar shingles instead of clay. It was well kept and quaint and smelled distinctly of the sea. They passed through the small center with various vendor stalls lined up along the main road and tapestries draped above them to keep the sunlight from beating down too intensely.

Jac's stomach rumbled when he detected something sweet cutting through the seaside smells, his taste buds already missing Nain's baking. *Will I ever see her again?* He hadn't had a chance to say goodbye. But something curious grabbed his attention. Each stall he passed had a paper tacked somewhere on its front. When he finally passed his tenth one—a baker who looked to be selling rolls and pastries—he couldn't help but stop to read the gray-inked words:

Bring our wives and daughters back home to Chaera. Heed the call of the masses before an inevitable uprising. The citadel be hanged.

"Sir?" He addressed the man at the stand. Merri and Orsin stood beside him. "What's the meaning of all these signs? Every stall seems to have one."

The vendor lifted his eyebrows, studying their clothing. "Not from around here, eh? The citadel sent all the maidens in Chaera away until next Maunt. For no reason. And no one will answer our questions."

The citadel has the power to do that?

"Are you saying there isn't a maiden left here? In all the kingdoms?" Orsin chimed in.

The vendor nodded. "That's right. All between the ages of fifteen and twenty-three. Gone. For a full year, if not more. Who's to say they'll ever come home if we don't do something first." He studied Merri more carefully and leaned in closer to speak. "You look to be of that age, young lass," he whispered. "Your presence here will be like gnats to a flame; you would do well to keep hidden, lest the citadel take you."

She nodded, and Jac's pulse thrummed in his ears while he

digested what he'd just heard. *Lest the citadel take you.* He looked at Merri. *Over my dead body.*

"What happened to this place I called home?" Orsin mumbled under his breath. He looked up at the vendor and tipped his head. "Thank you for your time, and the warning, but we must keep to our course." They turned to continue their way through town, Merri now sandwiched between them, but not before the vendor stayed their retreat.

"Wait," he said, reaching into a bin resting on a tree stump behind his booth. "Take these. Wherever you're from, we could use some help spreading the word. These pamphlets are already circulating Chaera, but they'd do better outside our country. Maybe some of our loved ones have been sent to your home." The vendor handed Orsin a stack of papers. "*Pleisan*—please."

The old man nodded. "Of course. We'll see what we can do." He made to walk away but paused and reached into his bag. When he withdrew his fist, he flicked a bright blue coin toward the man, who caught it with eager hands, and grabbed a roll from his stand. "We shall be off now."

After another parting, Merri was once more between them as Orsin quartered the bread. All was silent, aside from their chewing, until they left the center behind and made for another part of town.

"That was—"

"Odd? It most certainly was," Orsin filled in, cutting Jac off.

"What was that you gave him for the bread?"

"Lumara. Eobreth's currency. Light-filled tokens where the color indicates its worth."

This really is nothing like Wales.

"What do you think's going on?" Jac indicated the papers Orsin still carried.

The old man shook his head, stuffing the remaining flyers inside his bag. "I can't say, but I have a feeling we're about to find out."

"Merri?" A woman stood at the entrance of her home, eyes wide and fearful. "Wha-what in Chaera are you doing here? Is my Luci with you?" She looked over Merri's shoulder, frowning when she only saw Jac and Orsin standing behind her. She wrung the life out of the poor dish towel in her grasp.

"Ma, who's at the door?" A young man, looking around Jac's age, came to stand by his shorter mother. His eyes grew round when they saw who she was talking to. "Bay's Depths! Merri?" Confusion coated his words. "How are you back so soon? And why are you dressed like that?"

Who are these people?

"She can't speak to us, Iun. And she hasn't brought Luci with her either." The woman stifled a short sob and covered her mouth with her hands.

"It's all right, Ma. Luci will come home soon. Why don't you go back inside and I'll see to our visitors?" the man named Iun said.

His mother didn't argue, simply nodding and continuing to twist the towel in her hands, her eyes now red-rimmed and dotted with unshed tears.

When she disappeared inside, Iun stepped out onto the small porch and closed the door behind him. He walked forward and grabbed Merri by her wrist. "What's this all about? It's the end of Sol. You only left about three months ago. Why are you here?" He wasn't necessarily unkind in his tone, but there was something about it that Jac didn't like. And he especially didn't like the way he was touching her. "And why isn't Luci with you?"

Jac cleared his throat. "Alright. You don't know me"—*or at least,*

I don't think you do—"but my name's Jac Hughes, and we've come here for some help. Our friend, Orsin, is hurt and could use some aid."

"Or not, if it's too much trouble," the old man interjected.

"Why isn't Luci here?" Iun's grip on Merri's arm hadn't budged as he ignored the two men standing behind her. "Our family has lost so much. I thought you both were sticking together. Why isn't she with you?" His tone sounded desperate, pained. Accusing.

Merri winced.

That's it.

"You will let go of her now." Jac stepped forward and blocked Merri from Iun's unwarranted aggression, causing him to loosen his hold. "Can't you see you're hurting her?"

Iun's eyes darkened, his anguish amplified. "Who are you to speak of pain? Don't let her legs deceive you; she's one of *them*. A *sea maiden*." He said the words like they were a curse. "I should've known her coming ashore would only lead to something bad. Because of her, my sister is gone." He glanced back at Merri. "You had me fooled for a while, you know. Seemed so sweet. So kind. But now I know it's all been a ruse. Just to leave my sister behind while you come waltzing back to our doorstep. Why isn't Luci with you?"

What is the lunatic talking about?

Iun reached for her again, but he didn't get far. Jac grabbed him by the wrist and turned his arm inward. Without so much as a blink, he shoved Iun against the side of the house, pressing his elbow near the base of his spine. Jac was seeing red. "I don't care one spit about her being a sea maiden. Nor your baseless claims. Touch her again and you die."

Die? Where had that come from? He knew he'd do anything to protect Merri, but he hadn't realized his reflexes were this keen. This dangerous. He could feel Iun's sharp intake of breath as his Adam's apple bobbed along the shingles of his house. But Jac wasn't done.

"Merri trusted you. Your family. She thought this place was one she could come to and be safe. But you've just proved her wrong."

"Get off me," Iun seethed.

"Happily." With one final shove, Jac backed away and gathered Merri into his arms. Then they left, Orsin following quietly behind. If Jac had his way, he'd never have to see the likes of that lowlife Iun again.

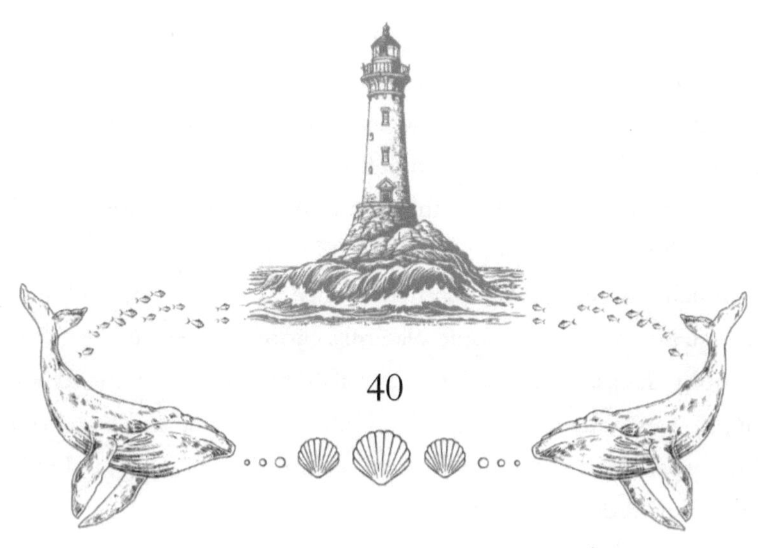

40

FOLLOWING THE TRAIL

Merri

"YOU KNOW, I NEVER MUCH LIKED DAALL," Orsin said, his beard moving along with his words. "Aside from fish, that coastal town's been wary of what comes from the sea since the beginning…"

The three of them sat around a small campfire on the outskirts of town, Orsin prattling on while the sun began its descent and invited a chill in its place. Merri hadn't been to this spot before, but she liked the seclusion. After their encounter with the Hatch family, she would be content to never walk Daall's streets again.

She watched as Jac tended to the flames. The warmth snaking around her middle had little to do with the crackling fire. *He defended me. He held me close like something to protect.* It was only after they'd started to make camp that he finally let go. She bit her lip. *Iun never loved me.* She thought the confirmation would hurt worse than it did, but oddly enough, it was only her wrist which stung. Her heart was intact; if possible, it felt more whole than before.

"Suspicious of sea folk, they were. And most wouldn't use the Winderplume. Hardly purchased any from the weekly market. Seems not much has changed during my absence." Orsin sighed. "I'll never understand why some people blatantly choose to ignore a gift freely given by Esias. But maybe I am too old to comprehend such things…especially now." His head pulled to the side and he let out a sharp groan. "Are you quite finished yet, little lady? I told you, I'm not dying. This really isn't necessary."

Merri stifled a laugh and pulled the strip of cotton material into a taut knot at the base of his skull so it wouldn't budge. They hadn't found a healer, so she'd taken up the task of tending to Orsin herself.

"You should be thanking Merri. She just saved you from passing out from further blood loss," Jac said over his shoulder, and her eyes strayed to the torn hem of his shirt.

Orsin huffed, but he didn't complain any longer. "I guess I should be thanking you *both*. Not that this warranted the casualty of a good garment." He shooed Merri's worrying hands away. "Stop fussing, lass. I'm already feeling leagues better, thanks to you."

Merri reclaimed her seat on a fallen log, and when Jac had finished adding another to the fire, he joined her. He sat near enough that his shoulder was almost brushing against her own. All was silent as they stared at the burgeoning flames, the summer sun melting into the horizon beyond.

That's what didn't make sense. She was still trying to wrap her mind around something Iun had said. *How is it only Sol?* She'd been gone for almost three months in Tenby. Had been stuck inside Eldarwielle's portal for a while before then. They'd left Wales in autumn, but it was still summer in Chaera. Was this what Orsin meant by time working differently between worlds? That he'd aged almost twice as fast while on Earth? Merri hadn't thought it was possible until now…

Jac cleared his throat beside her. "So, what are we planning on doing when we find this sea witch?" He leaned forward with elbows on knees and hands peeling the bark off of a lone stick. "She's not going to undo her charms by mere request, is she?" He threw a piece into the fire.

Merri watched it burst into flame.

Orsin chuckled. "Oh, dear me, no. It doesn't work like that, I'm afraid. Mere requests end in mere consequences. No, she works best with bargains."

Jac lifted a brow. "We're to bargain with the she-devil, then?"

"Something like that." Orsin pulled two green-wrapped sticks from out of his bag and tossed one of them in their direction.

Jac snatched it out of the air in a snap, lifting a brow when he saw what it was. "A Peperami?" He shrugged and started peeling away the packaging, his shoulder and thigh now pressed against Merri's so there was barely any space between them. She didn't mind the extra warmth—or having him so close—one bit. "I haven't had one of these in years." He held out the strange food item for her to take a bite first. It wasn't for taste, merely for substance, but the gesture was kind.

"The perfect travel snack, in my humble opinion." Orsin raised his Peperami in a faux salute. "Power-packed pork for the task ahead. They don't exist here, so cherish it while you can." He bit into his own, a knowing smile behind his beard when he looked at them. *Is the man smirking?* "I only brought two, but figured you both could share one considering you're already looking pretty cozy over there. Hope you don't mind."

Merri felt her cheeks redden. *We aren't that cozy, are we? Should I move?*

"One's fine. Glad you were thinking ahead." Jac ate his portion of the Peperami and didn't so much as blink twice in Orsin's direction; it seemed the old man's words didn't faze him in the slightest. Jac hadn't budged an inch from her side, and that made her blush even harder.

Merri fixed her gaze on the sky and stifled a sudden yawn. She watched the gathering dusk in the waning of the ever-dropping sun as it approached the horizon. They'd been out here for hours now, and pretty soon they would be heading to Darya's cave. Nerves twisted her stomach. The idea was terrifying, and though her cavern would take some time to get to, seeing that wicked sea witch again was inevitable.

Too soon. It's too soon since I last went to her, and I don't know if I can face her again. I don't want to.

Orsin had mentioned they needed to strike a bargain. Merri had made one and regretted the deal almost instantly, but not the good that had still happened because of it. But there wasn't a bargain they could strike in order to end the sea witch's charms. The witch was too cunning. Her ways too dark and knowing. She'd see through them and know their motives without ever having to hear a word at all.

A bargain won't be enough.

A shiver ran down Merri's spine. She didn't know what the solution was, but she wished more than anything that they could remain here by the fire and share each other's company a while longer, even into the encroaching night and beyond. *Is that too much to ask?*

"Merri?" Something warm pressed against her fingers, snapping her eyes downward. It was Jac, his hand resting on hers. He leaned in close, his voice a mere whisper. "You look worried."

I am. More than you know.

"I promise you, whatever happens when we find this Darya person, I won't let her hurt you."

Her gaze found his, and she could feel blooms of liquid begin to gather on her waterline. *How, Oli? How can you promise something you have no idea of?* Though his words had settled the knot in her middle that had been writhing and coiling like some unforgiving snake. *Maybe I can face her again with them by my side.* She glanced at Orsin, who was nodding off to sleep, slouched forward with his arms crossed over his chest. *I won't be alone this time.*

She nodded and yawned again, the firelight a mesmerizing dance of relaxation and comfort.

Jac interlaced her fingers with his own and squeezed. "Why don't you try getting some sleep? It's getting late, and who knows how long it'll be before we can rest again."

Merri didn't protest. Her body was already following after Orsin's, her eyelids heavy and her spiraling thoughts too exhausting to sort out. *I'll worry about Darya later. Not now.* She rested her head on Jac's shoulder, and all she remembered before falling asleep was his steady, safe presence beside her and the warmth of his hand still in hers.

❦

"Are you sure this is the way?" Orsin asked, his gait only a step or so behind Merri and Jac's. He was keeping pace pretty well despite his climbing years. Both men carried torches, the flickering heads of fire giving them confidence in where their feet trod.

Merri nodded. She couldn't say why or even how, but she knew where that sea witch lived. It was rumored that once someone visited her lair, the path to it was brandished into their memory like a strip of white in a skein of dark thread. It didn't matter if the path was different now that she was human; it still showed clearly for what it was, but only activated in the hues of night. Hence what made finding her cavern for the first time so difficult and finding it a second rather easy.

Still, she'd hoped never to go there again.

Merri saw the path clearly in her mind's eye and led Jac and Orsin over varied terrain: grass, rocks, sand, and dirt, all the while their torchlight flickered strange shadows all around. They'd gone through groves of trees, walked past another village, and were now close to the water's edge once more. This part of Kerilow Bay wasn't one she'd familiarized herself with, though. It was hidden and almost unreachable by foot, nigh unrecognizable from the spot where she had grown to love the prince.

Merri paused, standing on the shore in a copse of overgrown brush and trees. Jac and Orsin were on her right, finalizing last-minute plans for when they saw Darya. By the light of the moon, various-sized stepping stones jutting out from the sea and leading toward a large rock sticking out of the water like a giant eel's head became visible. The light in her mind sparked brilliantly until it faded into nothing, and Merri knew without a doubt that she'd found it.

She pointed in its direction. *In there. Darya's cavern lies just ahead.*

"This is where the sea witch dwells?" Orsin asked, his eyes locked on the ominous rock.

Merri nodded.

"I'll lead the way, then." Jac lifted his torch higher and stepped foot on the first stone. Merri came next, and Orsin took the rear.

Together, the three picked their way carefully over the slippery rocks. Water splashed Merri's ankles, stinging them with cold. It would have been refreshing if she were still a sea maiden. But all she felt now was a chill creeping into her bones.

Jac had just covered the distance from the last rock to the lip of the cave's entrance when Merri crossed to meet him. She landed awkwardly, her foot barely making it on the landing's edge. She was falling backward, arms flailing…then an arm shot around her back and pulled her forward. Her heartbeat pounded against Jac's chest.

"I've got you," he assured. "That gap was a little bigger than I anticipated. I should have told you to jump so I could catch you." After making sure she was okay, he reached an arm out for Orsin to grab. The old man graciously took it and joined the two of them on the cave's ledge.

"What now?" Jac asked, his green eyes a deep, shadowed emerald by the light of the flickering torches.

"Well, I suppose we should go inside." Orsin shuffled around them and scanned the towering rock. "There is bound to be an entrance somewhere."

Merri nodded, already knowing where it was. *It's around back, facing the bay. Only those who pass by in boats can see the entrance. And most never come this way for fear of crashing along the rocks.* Though she had only ever swam through the hidden entrance from the water below.

Orsin led the charge around the towering rock, Jac taking the rear with Merri walking between the two men once more. She wished she felt safer, but knowing Darya dwelled on the other side had her wishing she could disappear. *What will she do when she sees me again?* Merri's stomach almost revolted. *What if she hurts Orsin and Jac? And I'm the one who led them to her.*

She now learned a new fear.

"Not a single light within." Orsin held his torch over a dark hole carved into the rock. All was pitch black, a darkness that rivaled a starless night, beyond the glow of the fire's reach. Sweeping his torch lower revealed a set of natural-looking stairs made smooth as if sanded by the sea. "Let's go." The old man started to descend, but Jac grabbed him by the shoulder.

"Are you sure our plan will work?" he asked.

Merri bit her lip beside him, hugging her arms tightly around her middle. *There has to be another way.*

Orsin looked at both of them carefully. "I have waited too long to sit idly by and let fear dictate my actions. This sea witch will succumb one way or another, mark my words." He held up his bag and nodded. "A prophecy tells no lies, and yours *will* come to pass, Your Highness. No grip of darkness, however strong it be, can stop the will of Esias." The old man disappeared inside the rock, and Jac and Merri had no other choice but to follow.

If Orsin was as confident as his words, then maybe Merri had no cause to fear, after all.

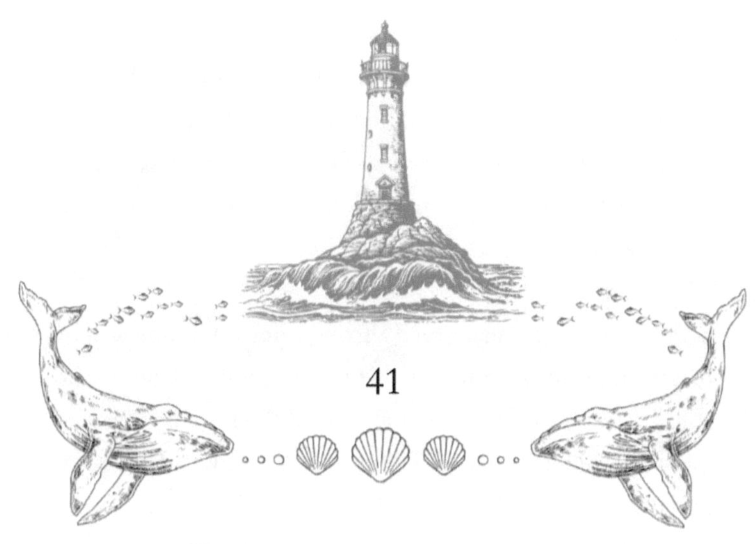

41

ΦΑRYA'S CAVERN

Merri

"IT'S ONLY A POOL," JAC SAID, running his torch over the still water. Not so much as a ripple puckered atop the ominous basin. "I wonder how deep it goes."

Deep enough. Merri knew what lurked below the surface, and it was only a matter of time until *she* came. The anticipation was dreadful. Merri had never been on this side of the cavern before, but she could tell it was designed to keep unwanted passersby out. If no one knew to look for a sea witch, they'd only see a pool and turn away. But she knew better.

"Have any idea how we're to call this sea witch, little lady?" Orsin asked her, his gaze flitting about the high walls of the rock cavern. She did the same.

There wasn't much around the circular enclosure aside from some strange-looking orbs lying around the lip of the pool. *How do the human folk get Darya to come to them?* Merri picked up an orb, wanting to study it closer under Jac's torch, when suddenly it glowed green beneath her fingers. It began slowly at first, and then it pulsed as if readying a signal. *What is—?*

Ouch! A sudden pulse zapped through her fingertips and into her palm, causing her to drop the orb. It landed with a clanging thud and rolled until it was swallowed by the deep of the pool by her feet. *What just happened?* That orb had felt like it was filled with some sort of electric light, the kind she'd seen back in the Telor Pendu or in the shops in town.

Jac held the torch closer and took her hand. "That thing burned you."

Her skin throbbed, but that's not what held her attention. All was forgotten when she looked once more at the pool. The orb had disappeared into the water, but now the whole basin emanated a glowing, green light. And bubbles were rising to the surface, popping once they released into the open air.

Orsin stared at the basin. "Looks like that worked."

The orbs are a summons. Merri couldn't help thinking back to when she and Olivander had devised a similar idea with the coral. There wasn't much else one could do when they lived below the sea. But now her heart was in her throat; she wasn't the one coming for Oli along the shore of Kerilow Bay. *No.* Darya, the wicked sea witch who had given her legs and stolen her tongue, was rising from the deep.

An eerie cackle rent the air, splintering the ominous silence. And then words, beautiful and terrifying, rang out from the murk. "Now to what do I owe this pleasure?" the sea witch asked, her presence still unseen.

Merri grabbed Jac's hand and remained as still as a rock. If she didn't remind herself to breathe, she would surely pass out.

"We have come to bargain," Orsin said. "Show yourself, and talk will be had."

More laughter. "My, my, my." Chills crept up Merri's spine. Darya's voice seemed to come from everywhere all at once, the gliding cadence reverberating in her ears as if the room was filled to the brim with cacophonous chatter. "Plucky, are we." And then the water started bubbling even more, rippling in larger waves. A figure of a striking woman rose through the surf on a familiar coral-wrought throne, and she was grinning, two pointed canines giving her a feral beauty. "I like that," she said, her voice now singular and centralized, no longer sounding in every direction. It was no less jarring.

There was Darya in the flesh, the alluring sea-maiden-turned-witch, her midnight hair as dry and perfectly coiffed as if she hadn't just risen from the depths. Her turquoise irises were rimmed in electric green, giving her an otherworldly feel, and her skin had never seen a blemish, the pearlescent tone rivaling the perfection of porcelain. Half in the water, half out, her tail remained lurking below.

She was beautiful. It was horrifying. And her gaze was locked on Merri's.

"You have returned. I didn't think you would come so soon." A slow smile pulled the edges of her perfect lips into a knowing grin. "And who is this you brought with you?" Her gaze flicked to Jac. "The commoner you fell in love with? Tell me"—she fixed her eyes on Merri once more—"was it worth losing your tail to go to him? Or is that why you are here, regretting your decision? Oh, that's right." The sea witch snickered. "You cannot speak without your tongue."

Merri's mortification resurfaced. She pulled her hand out of Jac's to wrap her arms around her middle. She was a worn flask filled to the brim with regret. *You did this to me, Darya. You ruined me.* She could feel

Jac's questioning gaze on her, and one glance confirmed it. She wondered what he thought of her now. *Pathetic.*

Orsin stepped forward and cleared his throat. "You are mistaken, Darya. This is Windkeep's heir, Prince Olivander Daws. He is no commoner."

The sea witch's eyes lit up in understanding, studying his worn and haggard appearance. "Ah, the old keeper's returned. You look well." Then she faced Jac. "Along with the prince." She edged nearer, moving off her throne to get a closer look at him. She glided across the water and appeared only inches from his face now. Jac didn't move. "The prince of prophecy. The one who lost his memory. Quite a pair you both make, hm? You"—she gestured to Merri—"cursed by love, doomed never to speak. And you"—she looked at Jac again—"cursed by memories doomed always to forget. You should be dead." Her gaze then flicked to Orsin's. "As should you."

"Well, we're not." Jac hadn't budged an inch from Merri's side. Though he no longer held her hand, he remained a pillar, true to his word.

"Interesting. Those storms should have killed you both. How did you escape them?"

"The portal-keepers," Orsin answered.

"Ha!" Darya tsked. "Those useless whales. I should have known Esias would try to undermine my work. Quite foolish of me to think He would stay His intervening hand. No matter; I will make sure that doesn't happen next time."

Next time? Merri trembled. *What's she planning on doing to the whales? To Eldarwielle?*

"This brings me back to my original question: To what do I owe this pleasure? For surely everyone who seeks me out must be in want of *something.*" Darya reached one of her pointed fingernails and trailed it along Jac's jaw. He flinched.

"We came here to bargain," he said through gritted teeth. "Not to be toyed with."

Darya barked a laugh. "You humans are cute. Adorable, truly." She removed her hand and crossed her arms over her chest. "What is it you would like to bargain for?"

"We wish to know who sought you out. Who sent me away and then took the prince's memories," Orsin said.

The sea witch's eyes glimmered. "Why?" She glided over to the old man. "So you can have your sweet revenge?" She licked her lips as if she was tasting the bitterness of the word and reveling in it.

"We simply need to know."

"No." Darya glided back to the center of the pool.

"No?" Orsin countered.

"He has yet to uphold his end of the bargain, so I cannot let you intervene until I get my way. It would…ruin things for me. For my daughter."

"What did he promise you that you don't already have?" Jac asked, and Merri was only too glad he did because she wanted to know the same thing.

"The prince speaks wisely." Orsin tilted his head. "It's hard to think someone like you would rely so heavily on someone else. I've heard much about you, Darya, but none have said you were weak."

Her wicked canines gleamed in the green light of the pool below. "What else have you heard?"

"It is right to assume that if one avoids a question, they are too afraid to answer it," Orsin said.

She pursed her lips, her voice rising. "Fine, you want to play this game? Let's play." She leaned forward. "I asked him to bring me something of great value, though most would simply cast it aside. As for my daughter…well, she is waiting for a once-in-a-lifetime opportunity, especially for one at only twenty-three. So young, so full of life. Soon to have something mighty in her grasp."

Merri glanced at Orsin and Jac, the two of them looking confused but more at ease than she felt. She was on tenterhooks, experiencing every tremor of her nerves down to her toes. Darya was speaking in riddles, and she was enjoying watching them squirm.

"Does that satisfy you, bargainers?" Darya taunted, her midnight tresses draped around her like an ethereal cloak.

Orsin cleared his throat. "Is your daughter a..." He glanced at Darya's lower half, submerged in the murky deep. One couldn't tell much from the lighting, but Merri knew she boasted no ordinary tail. "A sea maiden like yourself?"

"Ha," she cackled. "You humans think too small." A shake of the head. "No, my dear Kelde lives in Rune and is walking the land as we speak. Much like you." She winked at Merri, whose blood turned cold inside her veins. "Though she did not lose her tongue in the exchange."

"*You* cut out Merri's tongue?" Jac balled his hands into fists and stepped forward, but it was Orsin who pulled him back before he charged the sea witch.

"Steady, son," he whispered to Jac, his hand on his shoulder. "I still have a few more questions." He looked at Darya. "When was the last time you saw your daughter?"

Her laughter turned into confusion. "Back at the beginning of Maunt. Why?"

"That's over three month's time," Orsin countered. "That seems a long time for one who lives so close."

The sea witch shrugged. "It's of little consequence. Ours is a unique relationship. Why does this interest you, pathetic human?"

He lifted his chin, a smugness there that wasn't before. "You don't know, do you?"

Her eyes narrowed. "Know *what?*" she snapped, a new edge to her voice.

Orsin unclasped the flap of his bag and pulled out a ream of paper. He held the stack out in front of him for Darya to read. "Ages fifteen to twenty-three," he added.

The merriment in her eyes shifted instantly as they roved the flyer. "Lies!" Green wreaths of smoke plumed out of her ears as she snatched the papers from his grasp. "Where did you get these?"

"In Daall," Orsin stated matter-of-factly. "They were posted everywhere. There will be an uprising to bring the maidens back home, I've no doubt. But it seems you didn't even know your daughter was missing in the first place. She's not around to claim her reward."

"I don't believe you. The citadel… You are trying to trick me." Darya threw the papers, watching them twirl and spin until they cascaded to the unforgiving water, their fates sealed. The cavern started swelling with more green pulses of light as her figure rose higher from out of the water. "I am *not* to be trifled with."

She's going to kill us.

Green flames blazed in the palms of Darya's fists when suddenly, her gaze snapped toward the entrance of the cave. "Someone is here." The fire extinguished.

Another has come to bargain with the sea witch. Their dark deeds have become our salvation.

"Quick, cast your torches into the pool. Flee to the shadows. Now!" she barked the command, watching the three of them race to the outer rim of her cavern. "Not a word."

The green and orange hues diffused into utter blackness, and all Merri could see were dots flickering every time she blinked. Her pulse echoed in her temples, only made steady by the pressure of Jac's shoulder brushing against her own. She dared not move now.

Who in Kerilow Bay is coming?

A faint glow steadily grew brighter as the new arrival came nearer.

The torch preceded the body, but even in the dim light, Merri could tell the newcomer was a man. She'd never seen him before, and his wardrobe failed to give away any details of where he hailed from.

She watched as the man approached the pool, grabbed an orb, and flicked it into the water before it even had a chance to turn green.

He's been here before.

"Darya, you best not waste my time," the man shouted into the murky pit.

The pool emanated green, and in a flash, the sea witch had risen on her underwater throne once again. "You are late."

"What? No hello?"

"It is nearly Sollun, and I told you to come by the end of Verd."

"Well, I am here now, aren't I? The least you could do is greet your best client."

Darya scoffed. "Rainhold, we meet again. A pleasure." She rolled her eyes. "Now, did you bring it? I was starting to think you had forgotten."

Rainhold? Like the province?

"Geia. Cease your griping." He took something out of his pocket and tossed it to the sea witch, a brow lifting when his gaze lingered on her tail, half-coiled out of the water. "That was yellow last time I was here. I see you've changed some while I was gone."

Yellow? Darya…a Tidallyn?

"I could say the same about you." Darya caught it in a flash, eyes narrowed. Merri thought she'd seen the faint traces of something purple as it flew through the air. She squinted to try and see better. "The turnings have made you bold, Rainhold. *Careless* with that tongue of yours. What hindered your coming at the appointed time?"

He shrugged. "I had some unexpected loose ends to tie."

A sudden chill nipped the base of Merri's spine. *Loose ends? Who is this Rainhold? And what did he just give her?*

The witch looked at the vial in her hands and smiled, canines gleaming as she tied it around her neck. "At least it's full."

"A bargain's a bargain." Rainhold grimaced when he eyed her tail once more, then took a few steps back.

"All magic comes with a price, as you know. And this was happily bought."

He swallowed. "Right. Well, you have your dust. I'd best—"

"Speaking of bargains…something new has recently been brought to my attention. And it had me wondering," she began.

"About what, exactly?" Rainhold fidgeted, his eyes moving to the entrance, though he remained where he was standing.

"Why the citadel has sent all the maidens away from Chaera. And amongst them, my daughter."

Rainhold blanched in the flickering torchlight, his mouth agape like some swimming trout. "Who—who told you?"

Darya seethed, her eyes lighting up like emerald flames. "*You* did. You just confirmed it, you lying dog!" The sea witch lifted her hand above the water and up came one of Orsin's papers, cutting through the surface, perfectly dry. She sent it flying toward his face. "Care to tell me why my daughter is no longer here for you to fulfill your end of the bargain?"

Rainhold grabbed the paper and scanned it over, his hands shaking. "I, uh," he stuttered.

"We had a deal!" Darya screamed.

"A deal indeed." Orsin stepped out from the shadows and looked at Rainhold in a fuller light. "Do my eyes deceive me…Reve?"

Orsin, don't! Darya told us to stay put, and now you'll only invoke her ire.

The man named Rainhold turned around, his brow drawn together. He studied Orsin carefully. "Who are—" But even the years couldn't hide Orsin's true character because Rainhold's eyes widened, as if he'd just seen an apparition. "No. Impossible. You're supposed to be dead!" He backed away from the old man.

"Impossible has a way of becoming possible when you have the right connections," Orsin said.

"I guess I'm not supposed to be here either. Right?" Merri heard Jac before he pulled away from her and stepped into the ring of light.

"Prince Olivander." Reve swallowed, looking more like a child caught playing unfairly in a game than a grown man making deals in the dark. He snapped his attention back to Darya. "This is all your doing! You promised me you would uphold your end of the bargain. That you would get rid of them. What of the prophecy?"

Prophecy? Olivander's prophecy?

"You mean this?" The sea witch snapped, and up from the depths flew a scroll, soaring and twirling until it landed in her hands. "The ink never changed," she spat, throwing it on the ground. "Or did you forget the laws of your precious dust?"

Orsin bent to retrieve it and had the scroll unrolled in a flash. He scanned the contents and shook his head. "No. No, no, no. This is all wrong. *This* is not the prince's prophecy. The ink is black."

"For perfidy, correct?" Darya chimed in. "I should have known you had an ulterior motive built into those words when you wrote them."

"Reve, what is the meaning of this?" Orsin asked. "*You* inscribed this? Why?"

"I don't answer to the likes of you," the fraudulent keeper snapped. He had a wild glow in his eyes that made him look even more deranged amid the flickering shadows.

Merri pressed her back further into the wall of rock behind her. She wished more than anything that Jac was still by her side.

"You answer to the throne of Windkeep." Orsin held steady. "Why would you do this?"

"You want the truth? Is that what everyone wants?" Reve seethed.

Darya lit her hand with flames. A warning. "Speak."

Reve looked around frantically and then bolted. But he didn't get very far. Jac pinned the man down as green bars of pulsing light barred the exit.

"You will speak, worm." Darya's hands burned greener than before.

Reve fought Jac's hold, but he was no match for the youth. Finally, he gave up, his form lying prostrate on the floor as he spilled his confession. "The Winderplume never should have gone to Windkeep. It belongs in my homeland. In Rainhold."

"Who are you to speak of Rainhold as your homeland?" Orsin's tone commanded authority. Merri was having a hard time figuring out who was in charge: Darya or the old man.

"The king," Reve said. "Everard Jerathen Stoll Fleet."

Everyone went silent. *Two royals in the same room. As different from each other as the land is to the sea.*

Orsin spoke first. "*Our* king trusted you. Your presence has been in Windkeep for years… How did no one know it was you?"

Reve snarled. "It was all a ruse. A pinch of Winderplume really can do wonders for the imagination; I cast an illusion charm so no one knew it was me while my body double remained back in Rainhold. He was me in every sense unless it came to my wife; I slipped in and out of my home province to sire my sons. All you lot use it for is *small* magic—scrubbing pots and magicking weapons." He spat on the ground. "But even that was not the greatest feat. People really are predictable. You get on their good side, and they will believe anything you do. It wasn't hard; only took a little time because of that unforeseen prophecy. Though it appears all my work has been for naught now."

"What *work* do you speak of?" Orsin prodded.

Reve barked a laugh. "Ridding the kingdom of that sickly king for good. It was only too convenient that the queen had a weak heart."

Rainhold's king killed Oli's parents. Merri slumped against the stone. One look at Jac's wide eyes revealed his confliction: to know this truth and yet not feel the weight of it.

"Murderous treason!" Orsin grabbed Reve by the back of his hair, crouching down to the man's level. "You should be behind bars. Or worse, hanged for your crimes."

"There will be time enough for that soon," Darya said. "This lowlife still needs to answer for his treachery. Speak on, slug."

"I sent you away," Reve said to Orsin. "Sent the prince away, too. Had Darya cast a memory enchantment on him that would span the entire realm. Gave him a false identity should he survive. Used Alyward and Shad like a baited hook. But it was not enough."

"That blasted memory charm seems to be the only thing that *did* work, you scoundrel." Orsin thrust Reve's head against the floor till he heard the sound of scraping flesh. "Not to mention the lives you took."

"You still have yet to answer the question about my daughter. Why has she been sent away?" Darya leered.

Reve grimaced. "I snuck into Orsin's chambers and copied my own version of the prince's prophecy, altering anything I could except for time, for even magic has little control over it. Stole a few others while I was there just to make my role as keeper believable; only had to smear out the dates for them to pass as true. That part was easy, though. Matteo appointed me as the new keeper in Orsin's absence, but because the old git never died, none of my writing ever turned accordingly. I even double-checked that cursed poem in *The Old Archives*, penned my purpose countless times just to watch the ink turn from gray to black, but never crimson."

"That's because you're a bloody charlatan," Orsin growled.

Reve ignored him. "The prophecy's words were the last pieces to the puzzle, and they needed to fall just right. I coaxed Alyward into sending the maidens away from Chaera, using the same tactic with Suntower's so-called king, Shad Sulmaane." His words were mocking, calculating, dripping with their own poison. "Rainhold needed no persuading, which goes without explaining. My son is to follow in my footsteps, after all."

"Get on with it, parasite." Darya gritted her teeth and, if it were possible, fisted her hands even tighter.

"I did it for one purpose and one purpose only." Reve tilted his head up to stare Darya directly in the eyes and smirked. "I never intended for Zaker to marry Kelde; my son is as good as betrothed to another, not to mention your daughter reeks of that slime pit you call the sea. With her gone, I would return to my province and see Zaker wed to a worthier woman, though I hadn't anticipated the delay. I would have left earlier if only I realized how difficult the Winderplume would be to transport. But I eventually found a way. After I handed over the prince's cast-offs, I aimed to leave at first light tomorrow with the rest of the dust. Still do, mind you."

That's why the dust looked familiar. She has Oli's Winderplume.

"Belligerent fool! My daughter is supposed to be *queen*!" Darya's flames snapped and coiled, burning brighter than before. "Don't you know you can't go back on a bargain?"

Reve scoffed. "The bargain was forfeit when the old keeper and prince arrived on your doorstep. Don't you see? What's done is done."

Darya's flames climbed her arms now, burning a blazing green inferno. "Hypocrite! I upheld my end. What came of it was none of my concern."

Thunder cracked overhead, and lightning poured from the rocky ceiling, charring the stone where it zapped. Darya grasped the vial around her neck and shattered the glass with her hand, causing the purple grains to turn an electrifying green-black. They swirled around her torso and fused to her body, disappearing into her skin. Suddenly, Darya began to change, as if the dust was the catalyst, and a wretched howl came from her throat. Her once-pearlescent skin was peeling, revealing a layer of slimy green underneath. Her once-turquoise eyes were now yellow and rimmed with horrifying lime, and her body was becoming less and less human as her arms disappeared, melding into her sides.

Merri's stomach twisted in a giant knot. Revolted. She shot up a hand, covering her mouth to stop the bile from climbing her throat. Had she ever known such fear? *Darya's turning into a monster. A monster to match her tail.*

"Now you will pay." The words boiled out of the sea witch's mouth, all of her teeth now sharp and pointed, ready for the kill. "Oh, how you will pay."

Then she lunged.

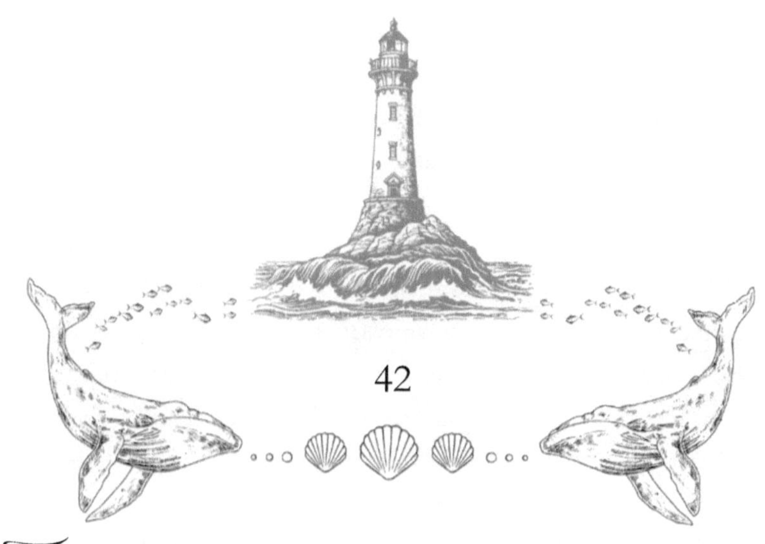

42

THE BATTLE IN KERILOW BAY

Jac

Kerilow Bay, Chaera
Sol 1198

JAC DOVE OUT OF THE WAY of the sea witch's monstrous mouth and rolled across the floor, leaving Reve to his own doom. The man whipped out a concealed dagger and held it up before him, a glinting shield. Little good that did. He screamed as the metal clanged against the calcified bone of Darya's teeth, slicing her gums, and was dislodged from his grasp. Droplets of green venom and blood smeared in her canines. Gone was the unnatural beauty of the sea witch. She was now the embodiment of an electric eel.

"I will tear you limb from limb, Rainhold," Darya growled. "And then I will come back for the rest of you." In a flash, she yanked Reve's terrified body off the ground and dove beneath the now-churning pool.

Jac watched in muted horror as the writhing waves gentled into stillness. He held his breath. It didn't take long for plumes of crimson to float to the surface of the water.

Reve's dead. Just like that.

Darya will return.

Merri. He pushed up from the ground and found her along the wall, her wide eyes never straying from the water. "Focus on me, Merri. On me." Jac blocked her gaze with his torso, his hands on the sides of her face. *No one should have to see that.* "We have to get out of here." A hard thudding reverberated in his chest. *We can't die here. Not like this.*

"The exit's still barred," Orsin said from the ground. He'd just gotten to his feet and was shuffling to the doorway.

"If we stay here, we die," Jac said, leading Merri to the exit, where pulsing green cords like prison bars stood guard. "There has to be a way out." He barely touched one of the bars before he found himself shot backward to the ground, the skin on his fingertip now singed red. "Great," he said, pushing himself up. "She's made this place our tomb. And the only way out is if we fry ourselves to death before she does the job herself."

Orsin shook his head. "But your prophecy! This can't be the end—"

A low grumble resounded from the pool, the still waters beginning to bubble once more.

She's coming.

Jac scanned the floor and found Reve's dagger. He grasped the knife and hid it behind his back while placing himself in front of Merri. He'd do whatever he could to protect her with what little skill he had; he'd promised.

Another moan issued from the swell, and within seconds, water splattered over the lip of the pool and rippled out in waves that drenched the walls and their legs up to their thighs. Darya was looming once more in all her hideous glory, Reve's shirt hanging from one of her pointed teeth. Blood stains rimmed her mouth.

"Esias, help us," Orsin breathed.

"I am afraid your god can't hear you now." The eel cackled. "Now, who to take first." She swiveled her giant head over their small group and grinned. Her smile stretched unnaturally wide, her eyes terrifying dots of madness. "You will do."

The beast lunged. Jac's stomach hardened. *No.*

Darya arched her head upward and snaked to the right with teeth ready to claim her prize, but Jac was faster. *You won't take her. Not Merri.* He plunged the dagger along the eel's neck up to its hilt and let go before his arm ripped from its socket. The contact wrenched a cry from the beast as she kept going in her course, resuming her looming position from the basin once more. "Taking the path of Rainhold, are we?" she spat. "Fool!"

It had been effective, but now Jac was weaponless and desperate, little left in the way of fighting. He was surprised he was still standing with how badly his limbs were shaking. He'd thank his adrenaline later.

"Let us try this again, shall we?"

Jac stood his ground, prepared to barricade Merri from the witch's bloodlust, only…she changed tactics. In a snap, Darya plucked his body from the rocks and tossed him aside as if he weighed nothing. His back smacked hard against the wall, and he tumbled to the ground. He lifted his head just in time to see Darya's tail grab Merri around her middle. Their gazes met, and all Jac could see was pure terror in those blue eyes he'd learned to love.

No. No, no, no.

"Try to keep up, princey boy." Then the eel disappeared beneath the waves, taking Merri with her.

"No!" Jac screamed. He rushed to the edge of the pool, readying to jump in, sea witch be cursed.

Orsin grabbed him by the shoulder. "Wait, son."

"*Wait?*" Jac snapped. "Any moment longer and she'll have Merri through her teeth."

"Windkeep needs their king. You go in there, and you may die."

"If I don't go in there, Merri *will* die. And I'll die in this cave all the same."

Orsin nodded slowly. "Then go." Jac turned to the pool again, but the old man hadn't loosened his grip. "There's word that Darya has a secret armory from her past conquests. Merely rumors, but you know how those go. Do with this what you will, Your Highness. You might not remember how to wield a sword, but your muscles will." And before Jac had a chance to jump, Orsin pushed him in.

The water was cool, but he hardly felt it as his lungs sought purchase beneath his ribs. *Relax, Jac. You'll lose your breath too fast.* He steadied himself, his body familiar with the feeling of waves and water pushing around him from all those late night swims in Tenby. *Focus on finding Merri.*

He swam downward, his eyes adjusting to the stinging feeling of brine. It was murky and dark beneath the surface but, thankfully, not too deep. The pool was actually pretty shallow. Green pulsed along the walls and lit up the space, revealing it for what it was: a witch's brewing chamber. A cauldron sat on rocks in the center of the space, vials of various shades lined the shelves, and there—a wall of weapons gleamed a welcome invitation as Orsin had suggested.

But where's Merri and that blasted witch?

Another turn revealed nothing, merely blackness. *There must be an exit. They couldn't have vanished.*

Then Jac saw it. A trail of dismemberment leading away from the cave and down through some winding tunnel. *Please let it be Reve.*

Time was running out. If he remained down here and longer, lack of oxygen would claim him before Darya had her way. But he had to keep going, and he hoped beyond all else that Merri was still alive. Only Orsin's parting words made him pause. *"You might not remember how to wield a sword, but your muscles will."* Jac was taking a chance, but it was one worth trying. For Merri.

He ripped one of the weapons from off the wall. The hilt was metal, but it was wrapped in something that felt like rubber, the grip odd to the touch. But he didn't have time to grab another; it would have to do.

Jac swam with everything he had left in him and left the cavern. Darya wouldn't know what was coming.

He didn't know how much longer he could hold his breath for, but that didn't matter. The tunnel was long and dark with the green light fading behind, but if Merri lay on the other side, her body as mangled as Reve's, he'd never forgive himself for it.

Where is she?

Jac pushed himself forward. His lungs screamed, and the weight of the sword made his progress lopsided and sloppy. But he couldn't give up. Not yet.

Come on, Merri. Where are you? God, let her be alive. Please.

There, just ahead, light seemed to blur into the deep, a shaft of muted yellows and silvers piercing through the water.

The moon. I'm outside.

He raced to the surface. Relief like no other flooded his lungs once his head burst through the waves, the cool night air startling as much as it was welcome. But where was Merri?

Kicking his feet, he spun around, getting his bearings. He gasped for air. Fog rolled across the water in sporadic coils, marking it difficult to see. Darya's cave was there, from what he could tell, and he assumed he was in deeper water now considering how far he was from shore. But still no sign of Merri.

Then a whisper, a voice, cut through the air, and he turned to find the electric eel weaving in and out of the vaporous plumes of fog, looking more wraithlike than creature. Merri was secured in her tail, head tilted back to stare into the face of the hideous beast which kept her bound. *She's alive.*

Darya's voice had lost its alluring quality and was now a full-blown monster. "I am not one for playing with my meals, but I wanted a change of scenery. Having you die out here, in your once-beloved home…" Darya growled. "Well, that just makes this all the sweeter."

Jac saw Merri's eyes close, as if she were accepting her end. And it broke him. *No.*

"Let her go." Jac swam in their direction, pounding through the choppy waters to get to Merri. He'd strung the sword through his belt loop and now used both arms, wishing he'd thought of it sooner. "You will not harm her."

Darya leered, her brazen eyes flicking to him. A wicked grin split her features. "Ah, princey boy's come at last. How fitting, seeing as you were next on my repast." She brought Merri closer to her mouth.

"Release her!" Jac swam nearer and pulled out his sword, stabbing the weapon into any part of the beast he could find. It was enough. Darya hissed as the metal sunk into her slimy hide, and green blood seeped into the surrounding waters.

"Fool!" she seethed.

Jac thrust his sword again, the water slowing the blow, but his blade sought purchase a second time, and now, Merri fell. He started swimming toward her.

Darya screamed, her blood spilling out faster than before. "Fine," she roared. "I can start with you. It makes no difference to me!" She plunged beneath the waves, sending giant ripples of water surging overhead. But Jac didn't stop. He didn't care. He just needed to reach Merri and get her somewhere safe.

"I've got you," he whispered, grabbing the trembling girl around the waist and pulling her onto his back. "We have to head to shore." He felt Merri nodding against him. He started to swim, but he knew freedom was too good to be true. Darya was beneath them, and it was only a matter of time until she blasted through the water and snatched him up like fish bait.

A pressure on his foot, and he realized it was now. Jac and Merri were launched into the air, twirling and twisting, now separated as if shooting stars trying to enter the stratosphere. Darya snapped her jaws and caught Jac by his shirt, and he watched as Merri and his sword tumbled like sacks to the waves below. *Merri.* His heart cracked watching her smack the water and disappear. *She can't swim. She's going to drown.*

Darya's tail coiled around Jac's middle, and she released him from her jaws, if only to stare at her meal before devouring it whole. He was eye-level with the beast, her exhale of breath a mixture of misery and death, causing bile to rise in his throat.

"You don't have to do this," Jac said. Was he really trying to reason with a monster? He'd seen the way she'd ended Reve. She'd even cut out Merri's tongue. Darya wasn't above doing anything evil just to get her way. She *was* evil itself.

"Oh, really?" The eel breathed heavily, her teeth barred in a horrific grimace. "I am sure whatever you have to say will sway my mind, peasant." She spat on his face. "So, please, humor me."

Her saliva burned on his skin, but he tried not to think about it. He just needed to buy himself some time. Enough for him to escape and rescue Merri. She still hadn't come up for air.

"You got Reve. He's the one who betrayed you. Why do you want us?" Jac gritted through his teeth as her tail squeezed him tighter. He needed to get to Merri before the ocean claimed her first. *Let me go*, he willed Darya. *Please.*

"Why? Now that you found me, you will seek me out later for the kill. I know how it works. Wonder how I got those swords? It was from those who came to regret our bargains, thinking they could take me down and seek recompense." She spat again. "But Darya always gets her way. And your precious citadel won't find me here."

"But you took my memories. No one's supposed to know who I am." *If they did, they would have recognized me in town.* "At least spare Merri. She's done you no wrong."

"You are so naive. This is what *love* does to people; it makes them weak. She is already dead, princey boy. Drowned like the land-rat she is. And you're wasting my time up here."

Despair dredged up Jac's last meal and he fought to hold it down. *No. I don't believe it. Not yet.*

"As for *you*," she growled, squeezing him even tighter, lungs screaming for air. "What would stop you from claiming what was once yours? That leach of a keeper holds more sway than mere words. If he vouches for you, the whole citadel will come blazing across my doorstep. Not like I can't stop them. Let them come!" Darya seemed to get lost in her tirade, her eyes manic and wide. "Let them come!" She laughed even harder, and Jac felt his insides shake. "Let all of them—"

Waves crashed from somewhere below them, and Darya swayed, as if suddenly losing her balance, toppling from her looming position in the sea. A searing screech and she fell, loosening her hold on Jac. It was enough. Jac squirmed free. He and the electric eel plunged into the depths, and the pressured quiet of the ocean flooded to his ears. *I need to find Merri.* Jac didn't waste a second. He kicked his feet and broke through the surface, blinking and spitting the water from his mouth. Turning in a circle, he expected to see Darya already towering over him. Yet he was alone. *What happened? Where is she?* He spun around again. *There.* Something in the distance was drawing nearer. He squinted, his arms and legs treading to keep him afloat, all the while bracing himself for impact. *But wait. That's not...* Gliding above the waves was sunshine itself. *Merri. She's alive.* Relief flooded every part of him. *My heart, she's alive!* But how is she flying above the sea?

A low, sonorous cry echoed from the deep. But it wasn't from the eel. The reverberating notes held a promise of hope, a tune of peace, a battle cry of rescue. It all clicked into place. *She's riding a whale!*

Merri came speeding toward him on the back of the white creature, bent on all fours with one hand on the whale's hump and the other outstretched. Jac took the hint. He grabbed ahold of her hand and pulled himself up onto the back of the swimming mammal, feeling the tug as momentum carried them both along. As soon as he was securely beside her, she pointed down, and there, beneath her knee, was the familiar sight of his sword.

She nearly drowned, and she thinks all I care about is this sword? He pulled her into his arms and held her close. "I thought I lost you, Mer. Don't do that to me again." He kissed the top of her head, almost afraid to let go, all the while the choppy waters of the sea lapped over them with every dip and ascent of the whale they rode.

This was the craziest experience of his life, but he knew it was far from over.

A piercing roar rent the sea, and within seconds, the towering form of Darya resumed her imposing stance once again. A bruise now showed on the lower abdomen of her eel-like form, indicating where she'd been hit. He now understood. *The whale must have breached against her body pretty hard in order to leave that mark.* Darya may have speed on her side, but the whale had strength and size on his. Jac didn't think humpbacks were that aggressive. Maybe a lot of them weren't. But he was glad he'd been wrong about this one.

Darya lifted her head and barked into the sky, vibrations of electricity snaking out from her maw and lighting the expanse above them in eerie bursts amidst the fog. "Mangy fish!" Her eyes blazed fire toward the whale. Her entire body lit up in electric waves to match the crackling heavens. Then, as if the clouds overhead became charged, they shot the lightning back down to earth, the streaks of illumination zig-zagging and piercing the water with fiery eruptions.

The whale didn't hesitate. It submerged beneath the surface, taking Merri and Jac with it. And just in time. Jac felt the horizontal spread of the electric current graze the tops of his hair, just milliseconds away from frying his whole body. And deeper still they went. Jac held tightly to Merri's waist with one hand while the other secured the sword. They couldn't stay down here forever, and whenever they reached the surface again, he'd be ready.

When his lungs felt like they would hold no longer, fresh oxygen forced Jac's mouth open to suck in a deep breath. The whale had brought them up again, but this time on Darya's other side.

The monster barred her canines and leered, her eyes calculating. "You think you can hide from me forever now that you have your *pet?*" she spat, swaying in the plumes of fog, her body pulsating with electricity. Lightning still flashed overhead, but thankfully it stayed amongst the clouds. "You think you can still bargain with a creature like me?"

Jac stood up, Merri's hand now in his own. "The bargain's off!" he yelled, though he had little hope of it changing anything. He'd come to the realization early on, but it was finally starting to take root. He'd have to kill the eel if they ever were to escape these waters alive. And it was up to him to do so with what little skill he had.

"Oh?" Darya cackled. Her eyes fixed on the object in his hand.

When it moved, her eyes tracked it. "And what do you plan on doing with that? Skewering my hide?"

"Something like that."

"Then make haste, princey boy. I shall revel when your damaged sea-wench watches you bleed out in my waters."

He tightened his grip on the sword's hilt. "Her name is Merri."

Darya lunged, and the fight began.

Gone was her taunting and laughing hysterics. She was all teeth, with muscles rippling through her electric, serpentine body. Where she lacked arms, her tail did her bidding, and all that feared darkness was embodied in her lime-rimmed eyes.

Jac parried and dodged, all the while fighting toward the back of the whale while Merri remained closer to its head. *Anything to keep her safe. Please.*

Waves sloshed over Jac, making him slip and fall every now and again, but the humpback was smooth. Quick. Affected little by Darya's electric charge with his blubbery hide. He circled back and came again, always before Darya could launch another attack.

Lightning hung in the sky, and any time it zapped toward the waters, the whale dove deeper, taking Jac and Merri with it. They clung to the mammal's flippers on either of its sides, before scrambling atop the creature when it resurfaced.

This was the routine of battle. And neither side had made strides enough to indicate who was winning.

Darya lunged again, this time snaking left before changing tactics. She dove beneath the whale and came up on the other side, taking Jac by surprise. But he was quick, too. He swung his arm outward and used the momentum to parry the attack. Fortunate—her teeth met the weapon and not flesh, the ringing of calcified bone against metal cutting through the air in sparks. The contact sent a shockwave up the weapon, but it stopped once it reached Jac's hand, dying out completely. *The sword.* The rubber hilt was the perfect match against electricity. Though he was unused to the strain, his muscles would hold. Orsin had been right. Whatever Prince Olivander learned in the way of fighting, it was proving useful now.

Darya reared her head and came again, wielding her mighty dome like a hammer. Jac held his sword up, like an inverted nail ready to be driven into its mark, but the monster countered. Her tail sliced through the water and swiped him underfoot, sending Jac sprawling on his back and groaning as an electric shock twitched through his limbs. The sea witch slammed her skull into his stomach, and more electricity coursed through him. He felt the wind flee his lungs. His body began to slip. His grip faltered on his sword.

The eel brought her head back for a second blow, but Jac knew better. *She can't touch me again. If she does, I'll die.* He rolled to the side as her head crashed onto the whale's hind, a low moan from the beast a signal it didn't appreciate being struck. Jac pushed himself up, his lungs still screaming for purchase as he brought his sword into an uppercut, slicing the underside of the eel's chin. A pool of green blood coated the water.

Death was knocking, and it was only a matter of who would answer the door.

"Snake!" Darya yelled, lunging for Jac and puncturing his shoulder through with one of her venomous fangs. A cry ripped from his windpipe. Piercing was the wound, but his sword blocked any further attack, pushing her back before she could claim any more of him. He felt the burning instantly, the sudden chill spreading into his blood. *Ignore it.* He ground his teeth and took his stance again as Darya swayed overhead, horrific eyes now slits of pure fury. "This is the end."

Her tail crept through the water like an assassin honing in on its target. It locked around Jac's waist like an electric band and dragged him under, shock waves pulsing through his body. Twitching.

Writhing. Cold entered his mouth as his lungs, still desperate for air, now filled with water. He was choking. Choking and dying from the shock. She was drowning him. He couldn't die like this. Not when he still held his sword.

Jac, electricity rendering him nearly useless, took the hilt with both hands and thrust his arms back before pressing the double-edged blade deep into the soft tissue of the slimy sea serpent. The electric current faltered, giving him a moment's reprieve. Then he twisted the metal, his mouth slatted into a thin line as waves of green blood pooled into the waters around him.

The eel convulsed beneath him, a piercing cry in the aerospace above, only muted by the waves. Just as suddenly, he was flung out of the water, flying through the air past Darya's head and into the open sea beyond. He watched as the eel screamed in agonizing fury, horrified at her tail now laying limp and useless. Jac hit the water with a terrific smack and only came up enough to see Darya wrench the mutilated piece of flesh off with her teeth, the nub now cauterized by her own electric current.

She did not just do that.

His body was reeling from electricity, his movements slow and docile. He stroked his arms forward only to find himself sinking. Spent. He turned on his back and floated instead, looking up at the waifs of fog and lightning striking overhead. It was hard to fight the urge to sleep or the temptation to slip beneath the waves. His shoulder was throbbing from Darya's fang, and he knew the only thing keeping him alive was adrenaline. But even that was waning now. *Is this what being close to death feels like?*

Pressure came up beneath him, and before he knew it, the whale had found him once again. Merri was by his side in a flash, dragging him farther up the back of the creature. Jac nearly cracked when he saw the look of fear in her widened eyes when she touched his shoulder, scanned over his bruised and battered body. *How bad is it?*

He looked up at her and cupped one of her cheeks, wiping away a stray tear. "I'm okay." *Am I?*

Darya screamed and thrust her maw into the sky, more lightning piercing the clouds.

It's not over.

"Now you have done it, princey boy!" she screamed. "I will peel your hide from your bones and eat you nice and slow." She lurched once more and disappeared beneath the waves.

Crippling fear struck him. *She's beneath us. It's better to keep an enemy close. So you can see them.*

Bubbles and ripples surrounded their whale-mount, and Jac knew in any moment the eel would launch another one of her vicious attacks. He just wasn't sure he'd be able to fight back.

Movement on his left. No, his right. All around him. He pulled himself up and braced for impact, whatever awaited them beneath the churning waters. Low, somber cries issued from the deep instead. Jac looked closer. *There. And there. Another.* A pod of whales surrounded them—most of them gray-blue humpbacks with some white like their mount, but he could see blue and baleen interspersed—flanking them on all sides three rows wide. *Where did they all come from?*

"There's so many," Jac breathed. *At least fifteen.*

Merri squeezed his hand and smiled, though it didn't reach her eyes. *She's still afraid. While Darya lives, there is still no time for celebration.*

As if on cue, the electric eel burst through the waves some distance on their right. When she saw the whales, she screamed, plumes of green fire jetting out of her mouth. She disappeared and came up somewhere on their left, screaming once again. *She can't get to us. The whales are boxing her out.* She came up again, but this time, some distance in front of them. She swayed her body, eyes livid at the oncoming army of whales. She reeled and barked at them, hungry for power. The pod moved as one and posed as a barricade, stifling Darya's advance. They hit against her sides, knocking her left and right; it was enough to buy Jac some more time, catch his breath, and plan his next move. But it didn't hold. Darya cackled and swerved. Their ranks were infiltrated by the slimy and slippery serpent dodging between them like a car through traffic cones. Within seconds, she was on top of them, looming higher than ever. "You are mine!" She lunged, bloodlust written in every feature on her malevolent face.

This is it. This is the kill blow.

"Watch out!" Jac pushed Merri off the humpback and sprinted. It didn't matter that he was about to fall over. He raced toward the whale's tail and hoped—*prayed*—his idea would work. *Please read my mind. Somehow. And save Merri.* There wasn't a spare moment to lose. The whales had come to help, but this battle was up to him and his sword. And there would be no other way to end this.

"Look how he runs!" Darya spat behind him. "Coward!"

Please, Jac pleaded.

He was nearing the end of his runway, the sea still covering half of the whale, when...he started going higher. Slowly, slowly, the beast's tail was lifting, and Jac was now feet above sea level. *It's working. Keep going.* He ran on, arms outstretched to maintain balance as the tail decreased in width. And then he was there. *Now.*

In a flash, the fluke snapped forward and sprung Jac backward through the air in Darya's direction. For the briefest of moments, he had the higher ground. And that's all the advantage he needed. He gripped the hilt of his sword with both hands and spun around, letting his body fall like a deadweight toward the eel's head. She looked up for a split second only to see her fate sealed. Eyes wide, yellow and lime-rimmed dots of fear.

"Fool—"

Crack.

Jac's blade sought purchase and drove deep into the eel's skull. He held on as she writhed, a dirge of wrath in her scream while plumes of green and lightning struck the sky in one last attempt to take her prize. She was fading fast.

And so was Jac.

Darya fell, bringing him down with her into the smashing waves below. And there was Merri, now safely on the whale's back…

What was left of the eel's tail whipped out and grabbed her around the waist in a flash. Hope snuffed from Jac's chest like a passing vapor.

"If I go, she comes, too," the sea witch spat her last words. And for the second time, Jac watched in horror as Merri slipped into the depths. Gone.

No. Get her. Rescue her. He willed one of the whales or his battered body to allow it. *Do something!*

But his waning strength was giving out. He was slipping. Vision muddling to black hues as the sky overhead began to clear. Dawn was coming, sleep coming swifter.

Darya was dying. He'd done it.

But it felt like he'd lost everything.

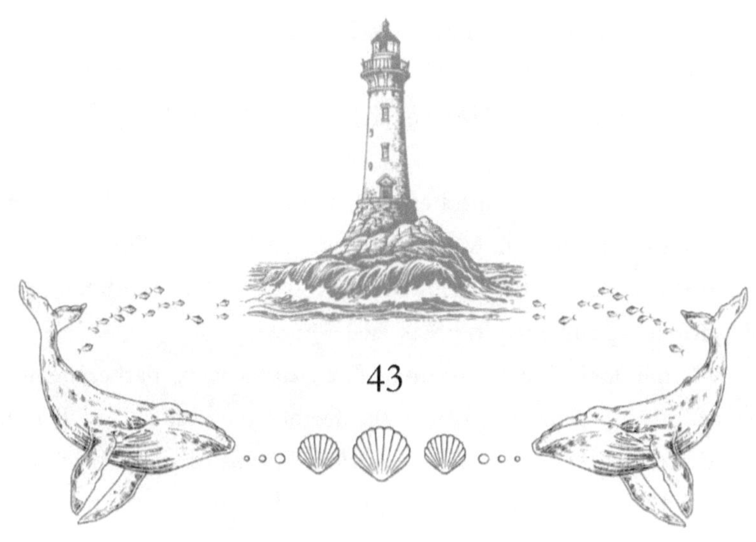

43

WHOLE IN PART

Merri

Kerilow Bay, Chaera
Sol 1198

MERRI FELL THROUGH THE COOL WATERS of the bay once again. She'd lost count how many times now. But after Jac had pushed her, she'd scrambled back onto Eldarwielle once Darya had swam past. Jac had a plan, and she trusted him.

He'd slayed the sea monster.

Though she hadn't anticipated Darya's final move.

Down, down, down she plunged through the depths, the eel's tail still firm around her middle. It lacked the pointed end she was used to and was merely a nub now, but that didn't matter. She was trapped and couldn't breathe.

Let me go. She tried wiggling free. *I will not die this way when Jac has already won. He needs me. He's fading, too.*

Still, the deeper Darya took her.

Her lungs screamed. Her feet kicked. But there—had she scooted up an inch?

Darya was slipping, and her tail was loosening its hold. It wasn't much, but it was enough. Merri wriggled, gripping the slimy flesh and pushing herself upward. Not much progress at first, but with her lungs vying for air, she needed to break free. Quickly.

Another inch. Then another. The waters were darkening into deeper hues of blues and blacks the farther they sank. But then an electric current below her. An explosion. Sparks of green-black dust shot out before changing colors, pure in their shades from Darya's many conquests, the most prominent being lavender. *Oli.* The colors surged into the waters and spread around Merri, kissing her skin before dissipating altogether. Where they returned to, she did not know, but the Winderplume was at peace.

Darya was no more.

Stinging pricked Merri's toes and shot up her legs, burning and throbbing and melding and twisting. She wanted to vomit. Dig her nails into something to divert the pain. It was the feeling of being tossed in a fire, refined and burned like dross into something new. Something whole.

She kicked with her legs, only…they weren't there.

Merri looked down, and beneath her purple dress showed the promise of a fin. *My tail!* She was desperate to see her lavender scales once more in all their shimmering glory, her leafy top, too. Oxygen filled her lungs despite being underwater, and a smile spread wide on her face. *It's back! I'm back!*

With one final thrust of her tail, she swam free of Darya's loosened grip and her dress from Tenby—she'd miss the latter—and rushed to the surface, her mission now paramount. *Find Jac. Rescue him.*

Bring him back to shore.

Adrenaline speeding her along, Merri covered the distance of their battlefield and didn't see any signs of him. But maybe her dearest friend would know.

"E—" The word never came. She tried calling him again, but nothing worked. *No.* Darya's spell had broken. Her tail was back. She could breathe again beneath the waves. But her tongue…the empty space inside her mouth was telling enough. *How can something that was cut out grow back? I am not a starfish.* She stuffed down her disappointment and swam to find the humpback. There were more pressing things at hand.

Eldarwielle? She called to him with her thoughts, swimming until she found her beloved friend. His pace had slowed since the battle, and the pod around him had dispersed. Still, a few smaller whales lingered nearby.

"Merriweather, you have returned." A smile. *"And with your fin."*

She nodded. *Have you seen Jac? Is he alive?* Please.

A low hum met her ears. *"He is well. A boat came only moments ago and brought him to shore."*

Relief. Her shoulders dropped. *I need to go to him.* She wanted to make sure he was okay. He'd saved her. All of them. And now Darya's enchantments were broken. *Will he remember me now?* The thought sent a zing of nerves through her middle.

"Steady, young one. You have only just arrived. He will be fine with a few more moments of your time being spent here."

Merri nodded, though everything inside her protested.

"I hope you know I would have been by your side had I thought you were in danger just now." His tone was deep and sincere. *"It was only a matter of time until you got your tail back, and I thought you would want to experience that joy alone."*

She warmed at his comforting words.

"Though I had hoped I would be one of the first you wanted to see once you got it back." His tone was light now, teasing. Was that his attempt at humor?

Merri stilled, feeling a touch of remorse. Had she learned nothing at all? She'd left Eldarwielle behind to spend time with Iun on shore. Little good that turned out to be. And now she wanted to leave him again to go see Jac. *To see Oli.* But this time was different. Iun hadn't been close to death.

I'm sorry, Eldarwielle. I-I… How was she to vocalize all that she was feeling? There was so much to say. So much she still couldn't.

"Child, you did well."

What? Merri looked into one of his eyes, watching as the luminous humpback swam his gentle path, her following along beside him. She shook her head. *No. I messed up. I didn't trust Esias as I should have. I failed Him. I—*

"What Darya wrought for evil intent, even if sought out by your own doing, Esias can use for good. Has used it in spades. There is purpose in the shadowy places, Merriweather. Darkness has no mastery over the light. And your course, albeit foolish at the time, was filled with it."

Merri was stunned. How could something so foolish actually be used for good? But hadn't she hoped for that this whole time? That somehow, Esias would deem her worthy even after her failings? *But I still can't speak. My tongue…it can never grow back. How is that good?*

"Some of us still bear the scars of our mistakes even after we have been forgiven. But that does not mean we are no less redeemed." Eldarwielle hummed. *"Scars tell their own tales. They make us recall what we often forget. And that is also a grace."*

She nodded, some of her disappointment abating in the tide. She'd have to bear this scar for the rest of her life, but if it served as a reminder to keep her gaze where it should be, then so be it. It was more grace than she deserved.

Merri lifted her chin toward the surface and sighed, eager to see what became of her Jac. He wasn't doing well when she'd last seen him, and she was itching to make sure he was okay. To see his face, see his green eyes, hear his voice…

"*Merriweather,*" Eldarwielle whistled. She returned her gaze back to her friend. He hummed and seemed to resume his somber quality once again. "*What will you do now that you have found your prince?*"

What do you mean?

"*You have loved him your whole life. And now that he shares your heart, what will you do?*"

He doesn't—he's never told me that.

A rumbling click echoed through the waves. Was he laughing? "*One does not need mere words when it is written in his actions. His eyes. I may be bound to the sea and know little in the ways of humans, but his affections are as sturdy as the tide.*" He hummed again. "*So what will you do when he proclaims his love? To what lengths will you go to claim it as your own?*"

Merri's heart rate sped. Was this a warning? A test? Her past decision led her to regrettable ends. There was no going back on what she'd done. But how to move forward? How to make a decision when she desired what was so out of reach?

She'd have to stay. Remain in Kerilow Bay while he ruled in the citadel. There was no other way around it. She'd choose Oli no matter where it placed them—together, the sea, or in a different world like Tenby. He was worth the distance. And if on the off chance that he wanted a sea maiden as a wife, she'd serve the kingdom as best she could from where she was.

I'd remain here. As I am. Whether he has me or not. She thought the words boldly until they found a place inside her heart to root. A truth she would learn to believe, to live. *This is how Esias made me. I'd do well to remember it.*

Eldarwielle hummed, this time a higher note that pierced the waters and reverberated around them. *"A fast learner, are we, Merriweather?"*

I'm a Dorsaleene, don't forget.

The whale laughed again. *"Go to him, child. You have chosen well. I shall see you when you return."*

Thank you. Merri raced toward the surface and stopped before her head crested the waves. She turned, watching her friend slip away, gliding in and out of the sunbeams refracting through the water. Her dearest friend. She retraced her path and wrapped her arms around the side of Eldarwielle's head, holding tight. Tears swam to her eyes, unbidden, but she didn't care. She let them fall and meld with the brine.

Thank you, Eldarwielle. Sincerity coated every thought, and she hoped he could hear the depth of her gratitude. *Thank you for never giving up on me.*

She let him go and swam away.

There was a boy on shore who she was already missing more than her own voice.

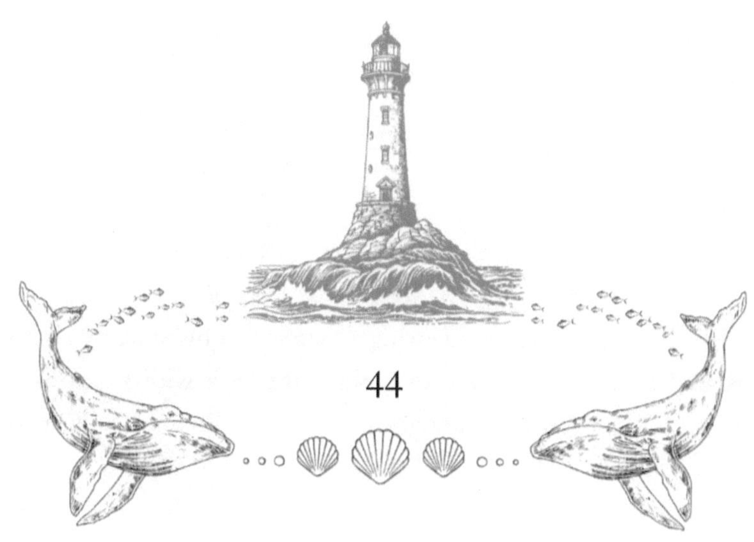

PRINCE OLIVANDER

Olivander

Kerilow Bay, Chaera
Sol 1198

A LIGHT DAWNED BEHIND HIS EYES, clarity flooding into his mind at the speed of light. Burning, searing, etching. Eager to take a permanent hold after being forgotten for so long. Oh, the pain. It was blinding. His head wanted to explode.

Olivander grabbed his throbbing pate, gritting his teeth so as not to scream as his memories became his own. *My parents are dead. I left Merri behind; I loved her and never told her. Keeper Reve betrayed us all; he framed Alyward and murdered my parents. He sent the maidens away. And all along, I was livid with the wrong man.*

A groan slipped past his lips, but he bit it back and fought the agony that pierced his chest. *So much loss. So much.* He tugged on his hair and felt moisture trickle down his cheeks. To know these truths once more was almost unbearable. *I was the cause. I let it all happen. Mum, Da! I could have saved them.*

His head spun, and another wave of bile threatened to push up his throat.

Nain. He'd left her behind, too. *The lighthouse without a keeper. And she's too old to tend to it. I was like family to her. She to me.*

It was as if he was experiencing a merging of his soul, two halves separated for too long, only to be brought back with the force of electricity. *No.* He'd had enough to last him a lifetime. Still, it was shocking to his mind.

How long will this accursed pain last? It was too much… Too intense.

And then peace.

Stillness.

A sudden reprieve amidst the torrent. A pinch like fire blazing all over his body. Olivander snapped his eyes open and had to shield them from the light above. *Where am I?* He breathed heavily and felt his surroundings, gripping grains of sand in his fingers. The light above him was the sun.

That's right. Memories came flooding back. *Darya.* His shoulders rose and fell, every movement their own pain. Ragged breaths racked his chest. He was so warm. Too warm.

Merri. He tried pushing himself up only to fall again. His eyes were too heavy to keep open. *Where is she?*

"Should we move him to the citadel?" a voice asked nearby.

"We have done all we can for now. He needs rest. Let the sun work out the poison for the time being. Keep him close to the water."

"What happened? He looks like he has seen some things. And what in Kerilow Bay are you both wearing?"

"Nevermind that. It's only his wounds. He will be well enough soon." Voices carried on, but in Olivander's delirium, he couldn't make out who they were. Though one sounded a lot like Orsin's. "Let him sleep."

Sleep. He wanted nothing more than to walk the earth and find his Heart, but his mind was already swimming in a fuzzy pool of black.

Merri… Be safe.

A pressure was on his hand, something weaving through his fingers.

Please.

"He is stirring again."

Olivander cracked open his eyelids to see several men in uniforms staring down at him, their appearances more silhouette than anything with the backdrop of the blazing sun. He turned his head and noticed an old man beside a boat pulled onto the sand along the shore. Someone stood next to him.

Then the pressure on his hand again. Another turn of his head. A sea maiden with a lavender fin was holding it.

Wait. Royal guards from the citadel. Orsin back from the cave. Windkeep's healer. Merri, holding my hand in her own. She has her tail back! His two worlds were blending together again, and it was akin to drowning. He opened his mouth to speak, but all he tasted was salt.

"Your Highness, it's good to see you awake," one of the guards said.

"You've been missing for a little over three months now. No one knew where you went," said another.

Orsin stepped away from his boat and drew nearer, his footsteps crunching the shells on the sandy shoreline. "The prince will recover, gents. Your purposes would serve better elsewhere. Like getting Lord Alyward's attention. He should've already been summoned by now."

The guards dipped their heads in silent acquiescence. They left their post and traced the path back toward the citadel.

Olivander's head spun, but there was one thing he focused on that set his nerves at ease. *Merri's alive.*

"How are you feeling?" The healer crouched down and touched his shoulder, the flesh biting underneath. "The coltsfoot should be doing its job, and the sun the rest. You should be thanking Esias that it's a warm start to these summer months, Your Highness. Easier this way, hmm. But we should move you inside soon to finish sweating it out."

Sweating it out? "For—" Olivander's voice croaked. "For what, exactly?"

"You were poisoned, Your Highness. By that wretched sea witch." The healer placed a few drops of something that tasted like tree bark in his mouth. Olivander grimaced. "The citadel's been trying to find her for years, and you managed to defeat her in less than a day. If this was your aim these past few months, I wished you would have taken some reinforcements with you. A prince has no business risking his life in such a way as you have just done now."

"My apologies," Olivander said, glancing away from the healer and to the woman on his left. *Merri.* She was still holding his hand, and he wanted nothing more than to share some quiet moments with her. Apologize. Tell her the truth.

The healer laughed and stood to his feet. "You will be right as rain in no time, Your Highness. Though I'm no advisor, I highly encourage you to keep to the citadel while you heal. You would regress otherwise. You will be crowned king within the week, I am certain."

King. He'd disappeared before the official ceremony. His country must think him a fool, a coward, appearing to have run away from his duties before claiming his royal seat. *I can't control what they think. I can only control what I do now.*

"He is all yours, Keeper. Good to have you back," the healer said. He dipped his head toward Merri. "Lady." Then he left, following in the path of the retreating guards.

Olivander turned to face Merri when the old man cleared his throat. "I won't keep you"—he eyed the two of them—"but I only ask for a moment more of your time."

The prince didn't mind. He still had so many questions, and aside from the remaining guards standing by, it was nice having just the three of them after Darya almost killed them all.

"How did you escape her cave?" Olivander's curiosity had him asking the first question.

The old man smiled. "Thought you'd be curious. The bars began to flicker, and then they simply went out. I assumed it meant Darya's power was waning. I found a boat by the cave's entrance; figured it was Reve's—the traitor did *something* useful, after all. Serves him right, the old git." He shook his head. "I rowed out to sea and saw the last of the battle, you flying through the air like a featherweight. You delivered the final blow. And then you fell, the little lady here going down with the witch." He looked at Merri with remorse-filled eyes. "I'm sori I didn't go back for you, Merri. The prince was fading fast, and already I could see guards lining the shore. They were searching for him, no doubt. When Darya died, her enchantments died with her, alerting the citadel that their prince was missing." He hesitated. "Still, it doesn't mean the decision was easy. I—"

Merri shook her head, her smile one of forgiveness and sincerity. It was evident she held no ill feelings toward the man, and everything turned out okay in the end. The way it was supposed to. Olivander was only too glad. He didn't want to know a life without Merri in it.

"How did you know I could wield a sword like that?" Olivander was grateful his muscles had remembered even when his mind was elsewhere. But even still, Orsin had been sent away before he knew of the prince's training.

"It had always been your father's goal to train his offspring to protect Windkeep and its people. I knew his purposes wouldn't have faltered should death or tragedy fill his shoes." Orsin's voice grew surprisingly hoarse. "Speaking of which…I hadn't realized, Your Highness. The guards told me about your parents."

Olivander swallowed. Nodded. "Thank you. I'm forever in your debt, Orsin."

The keeper tipped his head, a silent understanding passing between them. "Think nothing of it. Just doing my duty." Though Olivander knew it was more than that. They'd formed a friendship back in Tenby, one that would always hold more weight than mere acquaintance. The three of them knew a life outside of Chaera that no one else did. And Orsin and Merri were the only ones living who had known him when he remembered nothing of his past. There was something both strangely isolating and comforting in the thought, and yet it was more than he'd hoped for. To have anyone remember him at all.

"And to you…" Olivander turned to Merri, his eyes searching her face. "You saved me, riding in on that whale like you did."

Merri reddened, but she didn't let go of his hand. He squeezed it in return.

Orsin cleared his throat, pulling his attention away from Merri and back to him. "There's something I wanted you to hear, Your Highness. Before a carriage comes to take you home." The old man lifted the satchel off his shoulder and placed it on the sand. He crouched down and opened the bag, leafing through some rustling papers to finally pull out a rolled-up scroll. "*This* is the prophecy from your naming day. The one I wrote down and which Reve falsified to suit his dark deeds." He cleared his throat and began.

"A prince of Chaera
In the province of Wind
The Keepers of Plume
And peace within.
Born of water
A maiden shall come
Cloaked in fire
That rivals the sun.
The prince, take heart
Whose reign draws near,
She seeks to aid
In his eighteenth year.
Her, as his memories
And him, as her voice,
Will kill Chaera's Darkness
And all shall rejoice!

It has been writ from the beginning, from Esias Himself. Everything has happened as it should, as is the way with prophecies," Orsin said. "I kept Reve's for comparison's sake. That way, I can review the differences in the citadel before I take my leave."

"Take your leave?" Olivander lifted his head off the sand. "You aren't going anywhere, old man."

Orsin's eyes brightened as he laughed. "Well, in that case, I guess I will get cozy in your home."

"As you should. You've earned it."

Orsin nodded. "Thank you, Your Highness." He bowed, about to step away, but paused. "Concerning the prophecies, would you like to see them both now?"

Olivander shook his head, "Later is fine." He was still ruminating on the words Orsin had spoken. *"In his eighteenth year."* All along, the prophecy had predicted he would become king at an early age; whether that meant his father was to die or simply step down beforehand, it didn't make it any easier of a reality. He thought back to the prophecy's middle, the maiden born of water coming, cloaked in a fire that rivaled that of the sun. She'd been his place of refuge then, she'd been his means of remembrance in Tenby, and she was a vibrant flash of hope in his future.

I can never thank her enough for all that she's done for me.

"Merri, I—"

"Ah, Alyward, so good of you to come," Orsin said.

Olivander turned to see the two men lock arms and then embrace, the gesture one of friendship and too many years gone by.

"Lysander, can it be? After all these years? I thought you were dead! We all did." Lord Alyward sluiced off his countless questions, as he was wont to do.

"Geia, in the flesh and blood."

The regent looked at him fuller before his gaze flitted to Olivander. His brows rose high as he took in their strange appearance. A question was posed on the edge of his tongue, but whatever it was, he swallowed it back and chose a different course. "But what of Reve? How is this possible?" He didn't have to expound; if Reve was the Keeper of Prophecies, then Orsin shouldn't—*couldn't*—be alive.

"The numbskull's a traitor to the crown, Alyward, which is why Windkeep needs its old keeper back. Esias has a purpose for me yet." Orsin winked at Olivander. "It's a long story, one told best over a drought of something warm, which we'll do in a bit. But first, how is my Gilda and the kids? Are they well?"

Lord Alyward nodded, though he now appeared more troubled than before. "As ever. Gilda's been helping Head Cook in the kitchens, and Fiona is married with two children now. Dane works in the stables and has promise to be one of the best farriers this side of

Chaera, I guarantee."

Orsin nodded, his eyes glossy and voice thick. "Good. Good to hear it."

"And you." Lord Alyward brought his gaze once more to the sand, where Olivander still lay on his back, one hand shielding his face from the sun and the other still gripping Merri's. "What in the Bay's Depths do you think you were doing, charging death like a bull? You may be ranked highest above all in this land, but by the depths, you sure do not act like it. What would your father think, having you go off and fight that blasted sea witch all on your own? What about your kingdom? Your duty *here*? What ab—"

"Easy." Orsin's hand came down on Lord Alyward's shoulder. His one word snapped the regent's mouth shut.

"Nice to see you, too, Alyward." Olivander grinned up at him. He was too tired to fight with spite. He'd done that enough. Though his father's advisor was a nuisance, he meant well, even if he valued safety above respectable conversation.

Lord Alyward nodded. "Very well, then. Thank Esias you are still with us. You will be coming back to the citadel post haste to rest and prepare for your coronation. This is an order, Your Highness."

The smile fell from Olivander's face. Didn't he have a say in the matter?

What about Merri? She was the one he'd wanted to talk with most and hadn't yet gotten the chance. He was just to leave her all alone again?

"Guards." Lord Alyward called a few men over, and they began preparations to move the prince. Try as he might, his body was still reeling from electricity and poison, so walking wasn't an option. He grunted as they heaved him onto some sort of stretcher. He grimaced when his shoulder hit against the side of a wooden pole.

"What about Merri?" He looked at the sea maiden sitting alone along the shore. Heart take him, he couldn't just leave her behind.

"You can visit her when you recover. Now, you must focus on regaining your strength to resume your duties as king. It is sorely needed." He sniffed the air above Olivander and cringed. "And a good soak, too. We will have Jasper ready your bath."

Ready my bath. So different from showering in the cold water of Tenby's outhouse.

The guards lifted Olivander into the air and began walking toward a carriage. Orsin and Lord Alyward followed. He was going home.

Another glance at the ocean revealed Merri, a lone figure on the edge of the sea. "I'll be back," he called to her. "I promise." Though he wasn't sure how good his promise would sound to someone he'd broken his promise to years ago. *Please believe me.*

The guards lifted him into one of the two carriages waiting along the road nearest the beach. *Carriages. Lord Alyward's decree.*

Something needed to be done about that.

Olivander cleared his throat and focused on the one thing in his control. After all that transpired, the regent wouldn't dare to fight him on this now. "I believe it's time to gather the maidens home, Alyward. They needn't remain away any longer."

His eyes widened. "But the prophecy!"

"'Twas a sham," Orsin added. "Come, we have much to discuss."

The regent and keeper went to their own carriage while Olivander remained flat on his back in his. The door shut, and he soon felt the movement of the horses pull forward, traveling the short road back to his kingdom.

There was so much that lay ahead. Preparations to be made. Memories to recollect.

Bay's Depths. But all Olivander could think about was who he left behind in the sea and the purple fin disappearing in the water. He was afraid he'd never see her again.

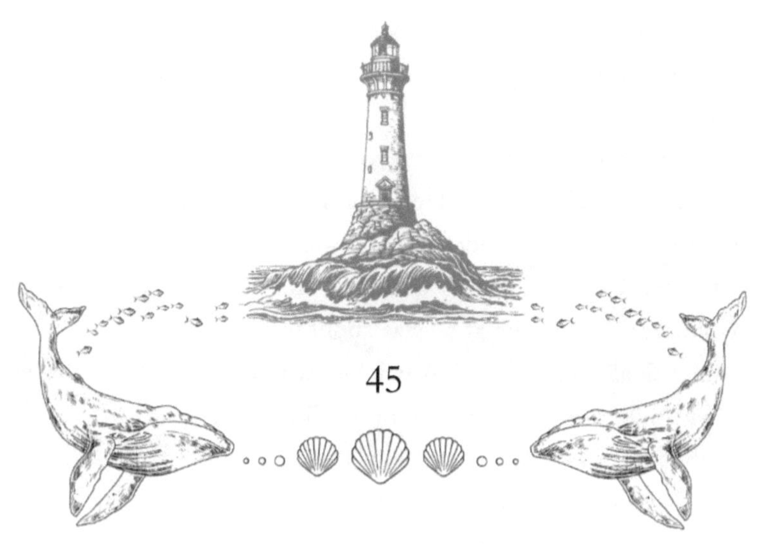

45

IT'S ALWAYS BEEN YOU

Olivander

Kerilow Bay, Chaera
Sollun 1198

Weeks went by with Sol turning into Sollun, and Olivander was now up on his feet again. Thanks to the Winderplume, his body no longer reeled from the effects of electricity and his shoulder had healed. It was merely sporting a long, white scar—matching the one on his hand—which served as reminders for everything he'd been through. The maidens had all returned home to their families, Orsin was reinstated as keeper, the Winderplume was restocked for foreign distribution, and everything was more or less resuming as normal. Aside from a fragile relationship with Rainhold that would take months, maybe even years, to repair.

Olivander walked toward the kitchens, aiming to find a basket, when he ran into someone most welcome.

"Gogden maurn, Your Majesty," Orsin said to him. "Where are you off to this morning?"

Oh, yes, and he'd also been crowned king.

"Taking a walk," he said. He was hoping to sneak out of the citadel without Lord Alyward noticing. If he was unsuccessful, the man was sure to send a host of guards with him, and they weren't needed at a time like this. Not for what he was about to do.

"Is it finally time, then?" A twinkle gleamed in the old man's eye.

Olivander nodded. "I just hope she'll take me."

"She will," another voice said, and this time, when Olivander looked over his shoulder, it was Jasper standing there, a knowing smile on his face. "A queen's always good for keeping a king sane. Good to know we won't have to see you lose your wits anytime soon, Vander."

The king laughed, clapping his manservant on the shoulder. "You wouldn't have a choice regardless, Jasper. You'd have to deal with me either way."

Jasper shook his head and Orsin chuckled.

"What are you both doing down here anyway?" Olivander asked.

"Seeing my wife, of course," the keeper answered. It had been a shock to the Locke family to see Orsin return home, especially older than expected, but so great was their joy to be united once again.

"And I am getting a new cloth to scrub that chamber of yours clean. That place gathers dust faster than any other, I assure you. Must be because of all that sunlight from your aversion to curtains." Jasper winked good-naturedly.

Olivander smiled. "Glad to hear it. I'll see you both then." He dipped his head and disappeared inside the kitchen, patting his pocket. He couldn't get to the bay fast enough.

Olivander spread a quilt on the sand and secured it with large rocks on each of the four corners. Then he took out the simple fare— a Wind Cake and some of Cook's infamous candied yams—and placed them on the blanket. He stood back, assessing his job, and nodded. "That'll do." *I hope.*

He walked toward the back of the little rock alcove and paused, an earth-shattering realization piercing him clean through. *No.* The coral still wasn't there. He'd forgotten about that, had planned this whole surprise around this possibility, and now he had no way of summoning Merri.

Bay's Depths. You're a fool, Oli. A downright fo—

Something orange tumbled by his feet and came to a stop only a few inches away from him. *The coral.* He picked it up and turned, a drumming in his chest when he saw Merri leaning on her rock in the water, her lower half submerged in the waves. A nervous smile pulled at her lips. Her hair was different today, pinned into a low bun, with dots of pearls along the sides above her ears. She looked radiant. Perfect.

"You came." He stepped into the water. "And I didn't even throw anything in the water."

She nodded, her gaze going to the waves.

"Were you waiting all this time?"

Merri looked up, eyes revealing the truth.

"I'm sorry to make you wait so long. I promised I'd return."

She nodded again.

"But you were afraid I'd forget." Not a question, but something that needed to be said. "Rightly so." He stepped into the surf, his dark trousers already drenched through to the calves. "I hurt you all those years ago. I left you behind and didn't even tell you why." He stopped when he was mere inches from her, his hands gently cupping her shoulders. "I was a fool then, Merri. Still am, to be honest. But I shouldn't have let my parents' deaths nor my duties as a royal come between us. The grief was real, but that didn't mean I needed to push you away. I could have let you in. Let you grieve with me. I was a fool to think you wouldn't understand. I'm so sorry. I hate that I've given you a reason to distrust me."

Memories of their time in Tenby flashed before him. Of her hesitancy in accepting his help. Of her distance whenever he drew near. Of her questioning and nervous glances, which thankfully gave way to trust earned. But he felt he didn't deserve it. Not then. Not now.

Bay's Depths. He hoped now.

"Merri, I—" He stepped nearer, an urgency he couldn't hold back, as he brought his hands to her neck. He cupped her chin ever so gently and looked into her beautiful doe eyes. "I love you." His breaths shortened, the truth spilling out. "I think you've held my heart for as long as I've known you. Since that first day we met. Do you remember it?"

She nodded, eyes glimmering with tears on their lower lids. He hoped they were the happy kind. *Please be happy*. She smiled, and the world seemed well again.

"That's right." A short snort escaped him. "You have a better memory than me. You're a Dorsaleene, after all." *That explains why she learned how to read and write so quickly.*

She laughed, bringing her arms around his waist from her seated position. Hesitantly at first, and then confidently as if she'd determined it was okay.

"Remember that night in Tenby? The night we shared our first kiss?" he asked, his thumbs now by her cheeks. "And how I said I wouldn't kiss you again until I got my memories back?"

She nodded, her blue eyes round and never straying from his face.

Desperate. Hope-filled. Full of longing.

"Well, I remember. I remember it all. The game we used to play; Seek, we called it. The meals we shared along the shore. Your whale-friend, Eldarwielle; he was the one who saved us, wasn't he? Our friendship, always waxing and never waning like the moon—constant. The gifts we gave each other. The way you encouraged me, saying I'd make a great king. Turns out I was a lousy friend for a time, but I hope to change that. I'd do *anything* to change that." He swallowed. "How I've always thought you were a goddess from the sea, with the most brilliant smile I've ever seen. And your voice—I remember every inflection, every rise and dip and intonation as if I'd heard you speak for the first time only yesterday. That'll never change even if you never speak again. Merri, I—"

She pressed her lips to his, strong and fervent, and his hands cradled her face close. His thumbs brushed against her cheeks, feeling moisture gathering on her skin. *Is she crying? Bay's Depths, please no.*

He pulled back, wiping the tears from her eyes. "I'm so sorry I've hurt you, Mer."

She shook her head and pointed to her heart. She was smiling. The biggest he'd ever seen. Then she mouthed the words he'd been longing to hear, and it had the power to turn the rain into sun.

"You love me?" *Me? A fool?* She nodded, more tears slipping from her eyes. "Since when?"

She pointed to him and smiled. *The same.* "Since the beginning?"

She nodded again.

Olivander laughed. He had never felt so light. They'd both loved each other from the start, and it only took them ten years to admit it.

"I love you so much, Mer." He wrapped her in a giant hug and kissed her again, this time soft and slow. His lips explored hers, two vessels connected through years, time, and memories, and that wasn't changing. His heart was hers. It had always been hers.

What an unexpected joy to know her heart had been his, too.

But what now?

He was eighteen, a king, and ruling the land alone. But he wanted to change that. More than anything, he did. Would Merri take him, a man upon the shore? There was little he could do about bringing her to the citadel or visiting her home, but if there was anything he'd learned over the course of his young life, it was that she was worth it. It would require little sacrifice on his part. Only, would she have him if they had to remain apart?

He pulled away and looked into her eyes. "Merri." He loved saying her name. "My beautiful sea maiden." He brushed a piece of gooseberry hair behind her ear. "We've known each other for over ten years now. We've just confessed our love. Is it too forward of me to ask you to spend the rest of your life with me? As my wife?"

If it was possible, Merri's blue eyes were now pools of liquid joy. She smiled and shook her head, her hands now held in his own.

Olivander's grin spread wide as he dropped to one knee in the water, now soaked up to his waist. They were at eye-level when he pulled an object out of his pocket and held it up to his bride. "I believe this is yours."

Her eyes widened. It was the purple pen he'd given her back on their first date in Tenby. When she'd tumbled overboard, he'd grabbed it before jumping in to rescue her. Merri took hold of the treasure, seeming relieved to have it once again.

"Okay, now for the real gift." Olivander removed a small bag from his pocket and tipped it over into his hand. A ring with an opal stone affixed in the middle, surrounded by a host of small diamonds, stared back at him. It had been his mother's. He held it up to her between his pointer finger and thumb. "Merri, will you marry me? I think we've already established the love part, but I don't want to know a future without you in it. Will you take me as your husband? A man who ardently adores you and sometimes forgets important things? Even if it means we have to remain apart, one in the citadel, the other in the sea?"

The sea maiden bit her lip as if in thought, her eyes glistening in the morning sun. And then she stood, her small frame now a few heads taller than Olivander's kneeling form. And that's when he saw them. Poking out beneath the hem of a lavender dress once lost to the sea.

She has her legs back! He hadn't noticed until now with his eyes never straying from her face. "Since when?" he uttered in wonder. "I saw you with your tail."

Merri's smile grew wide as more tears fell. She mouthed the word "Esias," and he understood instantly. He'd granted her this gift because of Olivander. Because of Merri. Because a prince and a sea maiden had fallen in love and didn't want to know a life apart, especially after everything they'd endured.

"I can't believe it!" Olivander hadn't known such joy. He pulled her closer and hugged her tight against his chest, as if he was afraid to let her go. Her arms did the same to him. "Does this mean…will you come to live in the citadel as my bride, Merri?" He whispered the words in her hair, words that felt almost too good to be true.

He pulled back enough to see her nod, a radiant smile lighting up every feature of her beautiful face. And he grinned like a fool; he couldn't help it.

"Good. I was afraid you might say no."

Her mouth fell open in mock surprise, and he laughed before kissing her again, this time spinning her in circles in the water. The picnic spread behind them was completely ignored as the waves broke all around them, crashing against their waists.

So much had happened standing on the edge of this sea.

First love. Heartbreak. Lost memories. A journey to Tenby,

Wales. A battle. And now full arms and fuller hearts, with a woman he could call his own.

He didn't know what the future held, but Esias had held Olivander the whole time, even when he'd been forgotten by many, including himself. He had to trust that whatever came next, He would do the same.

Once forgotten and now whole.

He liked the sound of that.

He ventured a guess that Merri did, too.

EPILOGUE

Windkeep, Chaera
Ondin 1198

14 Lunen

Dearest Jac,

Do you like it when I call you that? I think of it fondly whenever I remember our time in Tenby. Your name there was like a whispered reprieve. Different, but it became a new familiar. To me, you are many things. Olivander. Jac. My king. My husband. I love them all equally because they are all you.

Anyway, you asked how I am feeling. I am well, better now that I am writing to you. I actually sat and talked with my father today and one of my sisters, Jade, if you recall. She is the second youngest of the four. Still off chasing suitors even though she is four years my senior. I hope *she settles down soon, or else finds a new hobby. I can't keep track of all the men she brings around, both sea gents and human.*

And of the sea? The waters are perfect today, seeing as it is early autumn. Why don't you come for a swim and feel it yourself? That way you will have a more accurate answer. Don't forget, I am still a sea maiden, and the temperature doesn't affect me like it does you.

How is everything back in the citadel? Only two days and two nights until I am with you and walking your halls again. Is it silly of me to admit that sometimes I count the hours? I don't care one coddle shell. I miss you.

Your ever-adoring wife,
Eirin Mair

14 Lunen

My beloved Eirin Mair,

It is only fair I call you your Tenby name if you call me mine. Besides, you can't blame me for it if you signed off your last letter with that epithet. To me, you are also many things, but some are far too precious to inscribe in gray ink. I will save them for a whisper in your ear once you are back in my arms.

As for your father and sisters, I trust all are in good health. But maybe I should be asking how you are after hearing Jade's running list of suitors. Seems taxing. Though I am sure she has her share of stories. What is family without a little drama?

Don't tempt me, Merri. You know as well as I that it doesn't take much for me to abandon my throne and see my queen of the seas. Can you believe almost three months have passed since we wedded? I feel as if it has been longer, and yet time has a funny way of always seeming too short. If it weren't for Alyward's insistence I weigh in on foreign policy, not to mention I am still smoothing things over from Reve's treason—Shad Sulmaane has many grievances concerning his daughters—I would come see you. But as it stands, I will have to take your word for it. The water is perfect for you in all seasons.

Life in Windkeep is much the same since you last left it. Orsin is still guarding the Winderplume. He keeps stressing how important it is to keep a closer eye on the magicked dust ever since Reve's near-treason. Well, full treason, but you get the idea. Can't say I blame him, now knowing Darya's story. He is almost done rewriting "Tales of a Lost World: Sea, Land & Sky" as well. Too unfortunate about Tenby's black ink, though. It is an arduous task for the old man, but a pertinent one nonetheless, lest he be charged with treason. It will be worth it in the end; I have been wanting to brush up on the rest of Esias' keepers. Orsin says he is changing some of the wording, as it is now written for Tallidoore, a realm of folklore and magic, and he wants to offer the book as gifts to Suntower and Rainhold when completed. Chin up, darling, you will no longer be labeled as "fictional."

If you are silly, then I am a fool. I have been counting down the minutes. Could you ask that Eldarwielle of yours again to extend your weekly stay one day more? Four on land hardly seems enough. Though, if I am being honest, even seven days wouldn't be either. I can't get enough of you, Eirin Mair.

I miss you, too.

Ever Yours,
Jac

⊛ 🐚 ⊛

15 Maren

My dearest husband,

I have asked Eldarwielle about extending my stay and he said, in these exact words, "That is not my call to make. I am merely the messenger." He trusts Esias has given me this gift of land and sea for a purpose, one of them being queen, which I don't deny and should not take lightly. So for now, it is three days with a fin and four days with legs. It is more than I have ever hoped for, so why does it not seem enough? My answer is the same as yours; even seven days a week is too short a time when I am with you.

Orsin is a determined and honest man; I am only too glad he came back with us. On that same note, I love my Winderplume; not many down here have some, nor have they seen it. They ask for green dust of their own each time I visit, but they have little understanding its color is because of your eyes. How shall I answer them, then? As a friend or as their queen?

I have been thinking about Tenby again. I miss the Telor Pendu. What of your Nain? I hope she is well. I don't like thinking of her all alone with no word from you. Is there a way to reach her? Maybe I am thinking too much about this. If so, please tell me.

I have a request, if it is not too much. I am running out of paper, and the parchment I have left has fallen in the ocean, save for this letter. In your next response, could you send Jasper along with some more? Preferably in a waterproof bag like the Keeper's? Esias bless that man for agreeing to share our correspondence. He must really care about you. As he should.

In other news, Iun Hatch visited just this morning with his sister Luci. He apologized for the way he treated me when you met him. I still don't trust him, but it was kind of him to make amends. We all are in need of forgiveness.

Only two more sleeps until my side of the bed is no longer cold. Your arms are my favorite place to be.

Your impatient wife,
Merri

15 Maren

My queen of the bay,

Enclosed in this letter is the paper you asked for. A waterproof bag will be sent separately by way of Orsin. He plans to have something specially crafted for you, a gift worthy of a queen.

I am glad to hear your Winderplume suits you, my love. Our magicked dust has chosen one another much like our hearts. As to your question, answer them as both: friend and queen. One is neither different from the other. If the peoples of the bay would like some dust, they need only ask. It is a gift to be given, not withheld. Just give me the word, and I will send one of our vendors over. I know it is not customary for your kind to pay with Lumara, but perhaps we can do a trade. Maybe I can even make the exchange myself; it's the perfect excuse to see you.

My thoughts have lingered on Tenby, too. I have been meaning to ask… There is another request I would like you to pose to Eldarwielle, if you can. Orsin said the portal-keepers aren't genies who grant mere wishes, and I respect that. But could you ask him if it is possible to form a connection to North Beach? If such a thing exists. I would love for the chance to visit Nain again, or even have the opportunity to bring her here. After all we have been through, I would hate for her to think she is forgotten. No one deserves that.

I must admit, the last part of your letter had me gripping the edges of the paper. Iun has hurt you in ways that deserve the stocks. If I had my course, he would be three countries over. And yet my wife extends grace, reminding me to do the same. If he ever troubles you again, I can send another guard down to the bay. The one stationed there might not be enough if he let Iun through. I can never exercise too much caution when it comes to protecting my bride.

I love you, Merri.
I am waiting just as impatiently for your return.

Your enamored husband,
Olivander

16 Tharien

Dear Oli,

My people would gladly receive some Winderplume, thank you. Maybe we can make the exchange together as king and queen once I return to land. We don't have Lumara, but we have fish and pearls to trade, if that is to your liking.

I spoke with Eldarwielle, and he didn't push back like I feared he would. Instead, he smiled and mentioned something about a Deepkey. I don't know what that is, nor do I have his answer yet, but I believe he will give me one before I return to the citadel. It would be wonderful to go back and see Nain again. I miss it there. Besides, I have a certain tote bag and jar of sand I would like back in my possession.

I miss you. One more night stands between us, and I find myself wishing the sky would simply fold in half and make the time shorter. Why is it the longer I am away, the harder this gets? Maybe it is because I have something exciting to share with you. Something that will forever change our lives for the better. But I want to see your eyes light up when I do.

I am getting antsy. Can it already be tomorrow? At dawn, I will be running back home.

Keep the light on for me, would you?

Your expectant wife,
Mer

16 Tharien

Dear Heart,

Your note brings me joy. We will do just as you have requested. And I will expect to hear Eldarwielle's reply upon your return if he gives you an answer.

403

These three days of your absence have felt harder than the rest. I agree; it is not getting easier. And I could venture a guess as to what you will tell me, but I won't spoil the surprise. I want to see your smile when I read your words. Though maybe this has to do with you feeling sick the past couple of weeks? I won't conjecture.

Has my wife forgotten who she is? No, you will not be running back home; I will pick you up in our carriage, and we will take the long way back. Just you and me.

It has been too long since I have kissed you.

Counting the seconds,
Oli

BONUS CHAPTER

Merri

Kerilow Bay, Chaera
Verd 1199

"DO YOU SEE HIM?" Olivander asked, rowing their fishing boat, *The Golden Sand*, into deeper water, plumes of purple and green dust in every oar stroke propelling them forward.

Merri sat across from him, her gaze already on the sea. The spring sunlight reflected off Kerilow Bay in rippling and glistening waves, warm and inviting as always despite the chilly breeze. But still no sight of the whale.

She shook her head. *Eldarwielle, where are you?* It had been a few months since she'd last visited him, nearly six since she'd last donned her tail.

He said he'd be here the first of Verd around noontide. He wouldn't forget, would he?

A spray of water shot into the air behind them, misting over the surface and floating until it kissed their necks with cold.

"Looks like he just arrived."

Merri smiled, brushing her fingers through the lapping waves and onto the whale's milky back as he approached. *Good to see you again, old friend. It's been a while.*

He hummed, low and deep. *"Near ancient, more like. But I will happily take old. How is Windkeep's king and queen faring today? Your little one?"*

Merri rubbed her middle, feeling the pronounced bump beneath her lavender dress; this little life was the reason for her temporary separation from the bay. Which meant more time with Oli—a gift she hadn't expected. *We are well. Only three more months now.*

"Are you sure you are fit to travel? The Deepkey is set. Can this not wait?"

Merri was grateful Eldarwielle had granted them an open gateway to Tenby, but she shook her head. *No. We've waited long enough as it is. It's time to let Nain know she has a great-grandchild on the way before they're born.*

Eldarwielle made a clicking sound. *"She has been lonely. It will be good for you both to see her."*

"Greetings, Master of the Deep. Keeper of Realms. Defender of the Tides," Olivander said, brushing his hand along the back of the whale as he swam alongside their boat. He looked up at Merri, whose brow was raised high over one eye. "What? Too many epithets?"

She laughed and shook her head.

"Are you ready?" Eldarwielle bellowed, the sound rippling through the sea.

Merri looked at her husband, and he seemed to understand. He gave a nod. It was time.

Take us away, Eldarwielle.

"Hold steady. Do not leave your craft."

Merri and Olivander gripped the sides of their small boat as

Eldarwielle disappeared beneath them.

"I always hate it when he does that." Her husband shifted in his seat, and Merri couldn't help but giggle. The sea wasn't *that* scary when one was accustomed to living in the deep.

In a moment, Eldarwielle's mouth slowly came up and around them, encasing their vessel in darkness.

Olivander found his wife's hand and squeezed, probably more for his sake than hers, but she appreciated the reassuring gesture all the same. Darkness wasn't her friend, but she was learning that when one carried the light inside them, fear was merely a passing thought.

Stars burst forth overhead, the familiar sight stealing her breath. *I've missed these.*

"They've grown brighter," Olivander breathed.

She didn't tear her gaze from the sight. *They have.*

In a matter of moments, darkness and stars spun, giving way to sunlight. Waning, but sunlight all the same.

Their vessel crashed into water, rocking back and forth until it righted itself, steadying amid the choppy waves. It was cool, but not the cold of winter, and Merri was wondering what time of year it was now.

She cast her gaze toward the horizon and felt something inside her swell at seeing the coastline. *The Telor Pendu.* Its rotating light struck the waters like it always had, the sight as familiar as one's reflection in the mirror. She could only imagine how Olivander must feel, being back to the place he'd called home after he'd lost all he'd ever known.

"We're here," he said, interlocking his fingers with hers. "There she is." His gaze was on the lighthouse, and Merri thought she heard a trace of sorrow in his voice.

"Enjoy your stay. I will be waiting whenever you see it fit to return. Though do not tarry too long; you do not want your wee one to rush their time."

Thank you, Eldarwielle. Merri bid him goodbye while Olivander grabbed the oars.

It didn't take them long to reach shore and haul their small boat onto the rocky beach near the lighthouse. Plants were green and flowers were blooming, so it couldn't be the latter half of the year, could it? Olivander secured the oars inside the vessel and tied the boat to a nearby post, pausing when he was finished. He stared up at the towering form of the Telor Pendu.

Merri stood by him in silence, unsure what to do.

"I've missed it here," he said. "I didn't think it was possible to love two places at once, but here I am. Missing the life of a lighthouse keeper while I'm standing in the regalia of a king." He chuckled, a wry half-smile pulling the corner of his lip higher than the other. "I hope she understands."

Merri wrapped one of her arms around his waist and pulled his over her shoulder. *She will. She loves you, Oli. That won't change now.*

"Are you ready?" he asked.

She nodded as he led her up the rocky coast and toward the front door of the lighthouse. They didn't even make it to the path lined with eirin Mairs when a voice stopped them both in their tracks.

"Fancy travelers being lost in such *gwenny* attire." Nain's voice. "It's spring now, not Nos Galen Gaeaf."

Merri looked up and saw her face poking out of the kitchen window, the glass raised just enough for her voice to creep out.

"Nain." Olivander's one word had her eyes wide and her form running from the window.

"Jac?" The door smacked open and rattled on its hinges. "Merri?"

"It's good to see you again," he said.

"Good?" She threw her hands in the air. "Are you trying to shock this old woman to death or something? Showing up here at the start of April, looking like some little things in costumes for that bloody festival?" She assessed them, taking in their medieval-looking garments. "No, no. It's not good. It's *great*."

Nain practically leapt off the steps and embraced him, tears already welling in her eyes. He hugged her back, and Merri choked back tears of her own.

"And you, annwyl. Don't think you're getting out of one of Nain's hugs. Come here." She latched onto Merri and pulled her into a warm embrace. She'd never felt more loved by an elder than by this woman. Nain was all things loving and brazen and good.

"Come in, come in." She dragged them both inside and pulled out chairs, her rheumatism not seeming to bother her in the slightest. "Now." She messed about the kitchen and was putting things on plates. "Tell me what I did to earn such a gift as your presence on my doorstep." Finished with her task, she set the plates of bara brith and rolls on the table and took a seat of her own, waiting.

Olivander reached for the bread and didn't waste any time making quick work of it. "Wow, I've missed these."

Merri grabbed one, too, and nodded in thanks.

"We wanted to come back and see how you fared. It's been a few months."

"How I *fared?*" Nain snorted. "Seems you're taking your new role pretty seriously. And no, fy machgen, it's been a few months plus a year. It's 1998."

Olivander's eyes widened. "That long already? Well, how are you, then? Who's taken over my tasks since I've gone? The light's still working, so I assume you've been getting help."

"What, these old bones can't climb the stairs anymore? Is that what you're saying?" Nain's laugh turned into a slow smile. "You're right. Been getting some help from those in town until I find a permanent replacement. Barti was here earlier this morning."

Barti. Merri remembered the fishmonger; their last parting hadn't been the best.

"Interesting choice of help," Olivander commented.

Nain shooed his remark away. "Anyone is worthy of being helpful as long as they've got the willingness for it. I don't rightly agree with his rumor spreading, but I'll happily receive his aid if he's wanting to give it. Besides, Alban's coming tomorrow…"

"Alban? Isn't he the love poet?"

Nain guffawed. "Not even close. He's a cobbler."

"Could have sworn he was a poet with all those sonnets I've heard him reading off to you. Doesn't he know anything other than Shakespeare?"

Nain looked at Merri. "He's a bit overprotective, isn't he?"

Merri giggled. *He is. And I adore it.*

"Nothing is going on between us, Jac. And nothing ever will. It'll take someone pretty special to fill Alun's shoes."

Olivander nodded, his mouth now full of bara brith. Merri hadn't seen him eat like this since their time in Tenby. It was endearing.

"So, what are you *really* doing here, Jac? Why now, after all this time?" Nain prodded, spreading butter over one of her rolls.

He swallowed and shrugged. "I missed you. We both did. Simple as that. And…" He looked at Merri, grabbing her hand beneath the table. "We're pretty certain our child will miss you, too, whenever they have to say goodbye again."

Nain's eyes grew round as she dropped her knife, the metal clattering against the wooden grains of the table. "Child? *Child?*"

Merri moved aside her cloak to reveal the small bump underneath. She smiled.

Nain threw her arms in the air and screamed, jumping up to hug Merri and then Olivander in turn. Her eyes were now leaking tears. "Can this day get any better? Praise God for this little miracle. When did you get married? Find out? How much longer?"

"We married in the summer. And we have about three months

left, give or take. You know how the first time usually goes. We found out at the beginning of autumn…though I can't recall what that time of year would be for you."

Merri's mind was still trying to wrap around the portal's time difference. But according to Orsin, it appeared time moved faster in Tenby than it did in Chaera. Which made Eldarwielle's parting words make a lot more sense. Before their return home, Olivander had been in Wales for over five months, she even less so. And all the while, only a little over three had passed back in Windkeep.

"Praise be," Nain said, grabbing Merri's hand and pulling her from her thoughts. "My sweet granddaughter, my *wyres*. I'm going to be a great-nain. How long are you both able to stay? Can I get you anything more, annwyl?"

Merri shook her head and looked at her husband, waiting for him to answer. She knew he wished to stay longer, but the citadel and Lord Alyward said otherwise.

"Only for a day, unfortunately. I'm needed back at the citadel. A king's work never sleeps."

"King?" Nain sat up straighter. "I thought you were a prince." Realization seemed to dawn behind her eyes, and remorse filled the space between them. "Oh, I'm so sori, fy machgen. I had no idea."

He nodded. "Thank you." Another bite of the roll, and he resumed talking. "We actually had a question for you."

"Oh?" She looked at Merri, who was smiling at the older woman.

He nodded again. "How would you feel about coming with us? It doesn't have to be tomorrow when we leave, but we'd love to show you Chaera. You're as welcome there as any, and you'll always have a place to stay should you say—"

"Ie!" Nain perked up. "I'll go."

Olivander leaned forward and Merri's spirits soared. "Really? Just like that?"

"Have you ever known your nain to back down from something new, Jac? No." She shook her head. "Just like that." She snapped her fingers and walked toward her bedroom.

"Where are you going?" Olivander asked.

She smiled over her shoulder before disappearing inside. "Well, to pack, of course."

GLOSSARY AND LORE

LANGUAGES:

FICTIONAL TONGUES:
Common Englasi – English; the universal language of Tallidoore
Old Chaeran – the language of Chaera many turnings ago

OLD CHAERAN TERMS & SLANG:
Dawnling – a child between ages zero-twelve
Haelen [hEY-len] – 'hello'
Geia [gEE-uh] – 'yes'
Gogden maurn [gOG-den mARn] – 'good morning'
Midfoot – a child between ages thirteen-seventeen
Ne [nAY] – 'no'
Panci eoullym [pAN-see ee-YOU-lim] – 'thank you'
Pleisan [plEA-suhn] – 'please'
Tha lun skeul ealni wef cnaw fryth [thAH luhn skEWl ee-AHl-nee wEHf nah frith] – 'this land shall always know peace'
Wylecuman [why-LEY-cume-en] – 'welcome'
Wyndsmeoca [wind-smee-yOH-ka] – 'Winderplume'

WELSH TERMS & SLANG:
Aberffraw Biscuits – 'Welsh shortbread'
Alright – 'hi' or 'hello'

Annwyl – 'dear'
Bae Caerfyrddin – 'Carmarthen Bay'
Baps – 'bread rolls'
Bara brith – 'traditional Welsh tea bread/fruit loaf'
Beibl Sanctaidd – 'Holy Bible'
Cariad – 'love'
Clustog Fair – 'Mary's Pillow' - a pink perennial flower
Crempogs – 'pancakes'
Croeso nôl – 'welcome back'
Cwtiar – 'coot'
Cymru – 'Wales'
Daps – 'sneakers'
Diolch – 'thank you'
Eirin Mair – 'gooseberry'
Fy machgen – 'my boy'
Geneth – 'lass' or 'lady'
Gwenny – 'old-fashioned' or 'out of date'
Gwylan Môr – 'The Seagull'
Helo – 'hello'
Hwyl – 'goodbye'
Ie – 'yes'
Lesgyrn – 'good heavens'
Ling di long – 'aimless stroll'
Na – 'no'
Nos Galen Gaeaf – 'Halloween'
S'mae – 'hi' or 'hello'
Sori – 'sorry'
Tatws Pum Munud – 'Five Minute Potatoes' - a stew where everything is
thinly sliced, so as to lie flat
Telor Pendu – 'black cap' and is the lighthouse, home to Nain and Jac
There's lovely – means 'great' or 'fantastic'
Tidy – slang for 'great' or 'very good'
Wnco – 'old man'
Wyres – 'granddaughter'
Ystafell ymolchi – 'outhouse/bathroom'

LOCATIONS:

PLACES MENTIONED:
Chaera/Chaerans [kAH-rah; kAH-runs] – home of the main characters
Croastan/Croastans [cROE-stin; cROE-stins] – country northwest of Chaera
Daall [dAHl] – fishing town in Windkeep
Eobreth [AE-oh-breath] – main continent in Tallidoore; home of Chaera
Geshal/Geshalans [gESH-uhl; gESH-uhl-ins] – country northeast of Chaera

Hollms / Hollmsish [hOHlms/hOHlms-ish] – country west of Chaera
Igriadran [ig-rEE-ah-dran] – another realm
Jabor [jah-bORe] – continent in Tallidoore
Letun [lEE-tun] – continent in Tallidoore
Lisethoorn [lEE-seht-hoorn] – farming village in Hollms
Mosoa [muh-zOH-ah] – continent in Tallidoore
Oclein / Ocleins [OH-kleen; OH-klee-ins] – country east of Chaera
Rune [rOOn] – woodland coastal village in Windkeep
Tallidoore [tAL-ih-dore] – realm of folklore and magic; home of Chaera,
surrounding countries, and other continents beyond

LORE:

DAYS OF THE WEEK:
Sonen [sOH-nen] – Sunday
Lunen [lOO-nen]– Monday
Maren [mAR-en] – Tuesday
Tharien [thAIR-ee-en] – Wednesday
Jorrven [jOR-ven] – Thursday
Draven [drAY-ven] – Friday
Zephren [zEHf-ren] – Saturday

ESIAS' GIFT:
Winderplume - magicked dust given to the Chaeran people to revive the land;
aids in healing and other small tasks

FICTIONAL BOOKS MENTIONED:
The Old Archives, Vol. 1, by Anonymous
Tales of a Lost World: Sea, Land & Sky, by Gerard Platt
The Ancient Script - Tallidoore's Bible, translated from all the old languages
into Common Englasi

IVORY KEEPER & GIFT:
Humpback Whales - Keepers of Realms; portal-keepers
Deepkey - an open portal connection between worlds

MONTHS:
Ledir [le-dEEr] – January
Frar [frAHr] – February
Maunt [mAUNT] – March
Verd [vURd] – April
Kipp [Kip] – May
Sol [Soul] – June

Sollun [Soul-luhn] – July
Attol [a-tOLE] – August
Medir [meh-dEEr] – September
Ondin [On-dihn] – October
Nosh [nOSH] – November
Ekorm [EH-korm] – December

SEA MAIDENS:
Dorsaleenes [dORE-sah-leens] – purple, pink & gray tails; known for good memories & quick learning
Finnilows [fIN-ee-lows] – green & blue tails; known for growing plants & befriending animals
Tidallyns [tIE-dah-lins] – yellow, orange & red tails; known for strategy & tinkering, which is another way of saying they make and fix things

PEOPLES:

CHARACTERS:
Olivander Soryn Daws – Crown prince of Windkeep
Matteo Armadeus Soryn Daws –Late king of Windkeep; Olivander's father
Firan Lou Gossard Daws – Late queen of Windkeep; Olivander's mother
Jasper Clyffton – Olivander's manservant
Lord Alyward – Regent of Windkeep
Keeper Reve – Keeper of Prophecies in Windkeep
Merriweather Lea-Finna Caspiana Dorsaleene – Sea maiden
Eldarwielle – Ivory whale; Keeper of Realms (portal-keeper)
Orsin L. (Lysander) Locke – "The Madman of Tenby"
Gilda Locke – Cook's helper & wife of Orsin
Fiona & Dane Locke – Children of Orsin & Gilda
Matilde Lamson – Head Cook in Windkeep
Gabeheart Lamson – Cook's son
Horace Teague – Butler in Windkeep
Gibbs Gable & Galahad – Windkeep's falconer and his hawk
Arth & Iylan Hatch – Husband & wife who live in Daall with their four kids
Iun, Pitar, Luci, & Calla Hatch – Children of Arth & Iylan
Llana & Len Bateson – Owners of Batesons Farm in Lisethoorn, Hollms
Jac Elis Hughes – Lighthouse keeper of the Telor Pendu
Nain Hughes – Lives in the Telor Pendu; adopted Jac
Bronny Vaughan – Librarian; Jac's friend
Barti & Elaine Morgan – Fishmonger in Tenby & his wife
Darya Lyn-Nami Adrielle Tidallyn – Sea witch who lives in Kerilow Bay
Kelde Rin-Echo Adrielle Finnilow – Sea witch's daughter
Everard Jerathan Stoll Fleet – King of Rainhold

HOW THE PORTAL TIME DIFFERENCE WORKS

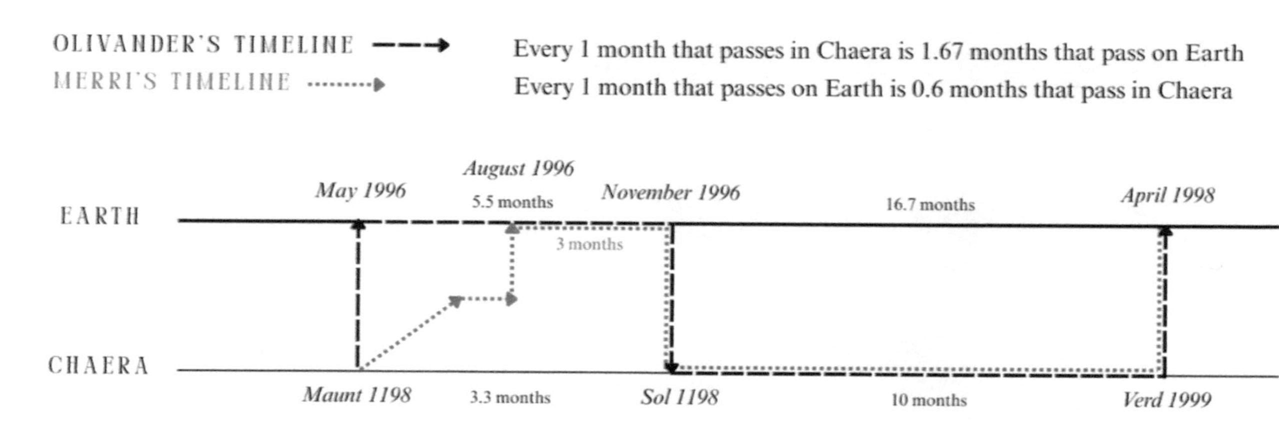

ACKNOWLEDGEMENTS

This is my seventh publication and arguably my favorite for a variety of different reasons. After what felt like months of being in a postpartum creative drought, *On the Edge of the Forgotten Sea* was born from countless walks with my newborn daughter and a desire to reclaim what was once lost. I don't think I've ever had as much fun writing a story as I did with this one. And there are many people to thank.

Firstly, my family. For my mom and dad and their constant support. Never a day goes by where they don't tell me how proud they are of me. For my brothers and their encouragement. A special thank you to Nick for doing the math and helping me figure out the portal time difference; without him, my head would still be swimming. For my relatives both near and distant, who always ask about my writing progress: thank you. I love all of you.

For my husband, who hears probably way more about my stories than he bargained for, but who is always patient and willing to lend a listening ear. Thank you for all your help and encouragement in all my endeavors. I love you endlessly.

For my sweet Goosie girl, who made me a mom. Truly, there is no greater gift than getting to love you and watch you grow. I hope that one day you get to read The Chronicles of Chaera, and the books that came before. I've been writing with you in mind all along.

For my beta readers, Sara Thren, Maggie McGrath, Anna Christine, Danielle Million, Danielle Bullen, Tara Koch, and Bekki Beilby, who all took the time to read this story in its lack-luster form and offer incredible advice to make it what it is now. Thank you all so very much.

For my dear friend and editor, Caitlin Miller, who pored over every detail of this story so diligently and with the utmost care…I don't know what I'd do without you. Thank you!

For the wonderful Micaiah Keough, thank you for proofreading this manuscript and catching all those last-minute typos that always seem to stick around. Grateful for you!

For Bethany Giinthir, who painted the loveliest ivory whale for the case laminate version of this book. It turned out beautifully! And for A.C. Sanders, who illustrated the cover of my dreams. I am still in awe whenever I see the masterpiece you created.

For Ann Brennan and her painting of Eldarwielle (offered as a preorder incentive in the form of a sticker) and Ellie Tran and her drawing of Merri and Olivander (offered as a preorder incentive in the form of an art print). You are both so talented.

For my endorsers, Joanna Ruth Meyer, Hannah Lindsey, Amanda Dykes, Becky Dean, and Chelsea Bobulski, thank you for taking the time to read my words before publication. You are all some of the loveliest humans whom I've had the pleasure of getting to know over these past couple of years. So grateful for you all.

For my friends to whom this book is dedicated to…Sarah and

Jordan, you girls are the sweetest and dearest. So blessed the Lord gave me you.

For my Lord and Savior Jesus Christ, to whom receives the utmost praise and glory for any acclaim I could ever achieve. He gave me this story seemingly out of nowhere (a true gift), and my aim is to honor Him with all my pursuits. My prayer is that readers come away with a deeper grasp of His love and sovereignty; His plans are always better than our own.

And lastly, for you, my readers. Thank you for taking a chance on this story. For flipping through these pages and spending a while in Chaera, Tenby, and Kerilow Bay. I hope you come back for more adventures; they're only just beginning!

Alissa J. Zavalianos grew up in New Hampshire and currently lives there with her wonderful husband, sweet daughter, and mischievous cat, Moo. As a child, she always had a love for nature, books, and fairy tales, and as she grew older, that love bloomed all the more. Alissa loves Jesus and is inspired by birds, mountains, castles, Tolkien, Lewis, and the way a cold breath of wind feels on her bare toes.

Feel free to follow Alissa on her website
https://alissazav.wixsite.com/website and on
Instagram @authoralissajzavalianos.